continued . . .

"Andrews blends action-packed fantasy with myth and legend, keeping readers enthralled. *Magic Strikes* introduces fascinating characters, provides a plethora of paranormal skirmishes, and teases fans with romantic chemistry." —*Darque Reviews*

"Ilona Andrews's best novel to date, cranking up the action, danger, and magic . . . Gritty, sword-clashing action and flawless characterizations will bewitch fans, old and new alike." —*Sacramento Book Review*

"Doses of humor serve to lighten the suspense and taut action of this vividly drawn, kick-butt series." —*Monsters and Critics*

"From the first page to the last, *Magic Strikes* was a riveting, heart-pounding ride. Story lines advance, truths are admitted, intriguing characters are introduced, and the romance between Kate and Curran develops a sweetness that is simply delightful." —*Dear Author*

"An engrossing, superbly written urban fantasy series." —*Lurv a la Mode*

"Write faster . . . I absolutely love the relationship between Curran and Kate—I laugh out loud with the witty sarcasm and one-liners, and the sexual tension building between the couples drives me to my knees, knowing I'll have to wait for another book." —*SFRevu*

MAGIC BURNS

"Fans of Carrie Vaughn and Patricia Briggs will appreciate this fast-paced, action-packed urban fantasy full of magic, vampires, werebeasties, and things that go bump in the night." —*Monsters and Critics*

"With all her problems, secrets, and prowess both martial and magical, Kate is a great kick-ass heroine, a tough girl with a heart, and her adventures . . . are definitely worth checking out." —*Locus*

"[*Magic Burns*] hooked me completely. With a fascinating, compelling plot, a witty, intelligent heroine, a demonic villain, and clever, wry humor throughout, this story has it all." —*Fresh Fiction*

MAGIC BITES

MAGIC
SLAYS

ILONA ANDREWS

ACE BOOKS, NEW YORK

THE BERKLEY PUBLISHING GROUP
Published by the Penguin Group
Penguin Group (USA) Inc.
375 Hudson Street, New York, New York 10014, USA
Penguin Group (Canada), 90 Eglinton Avenue East, Suite 700, Toronto, Ontario M4P 2Y3, Canada
(a division of Pearson Penguin Canada Inc.)
Penguin Books Ltd., 80 Strand, London WC2R 0RL, England
Penguin Group Ireland, 25 St. Stephen's Green, Dublin 2, Ireland (a division of Penguin Books Ltd.)
Penguin Group (Australia), 250 Camberwell Road, Camberwell, Victoria 3124, Australia
(a division of Pearson Australia Group Pty. Ltd.)
Penguin Books India Pvt. Ltd., 11 Community Centre, Panchsheel Park, New Delhi—110 017, India
Penguin Group (NZ), 67 Apollo Drive, Rosedale, Auckland 0632, New Zealand
(a division of Pearson New Zealand Ltd.)
Penguin Books (South Africa) (Pty.) Ltd., 24 Sturdee Avenue, Rosebank, Johannesburg 2196,
South Africa

Penguin Books Ltd., Registered Offices: 80 Strand, London WC2R 0RL, England

MAGIC SLAYS

An Ace Book / published by arrangement with Ilona Andrews, Inc.

PRINTING HISTORY
Ace mass-market edition / June 2011

ISBN: 978-0-441-02042-3

ACE
Ace Books are published by The Berkley Publishing Group,
a division of Penguin Group (USA) Inc.,
375 Hudson Street, New York, New York 10014.
ACE and the "A" design are trademarks of Penguin Group (USA) Inc.

PRINTED IN THE UNITED STATES OF AMERICA

10 9 8 7 6 5 4 3 2 1

To Helen Kirk.
Thank you for reading our books.

ACKNOWLEDGMENTS

This book, like most books, took a lot more time and effort than first anticipated. Many people have helped us along the way. We'd like to thank the following people for their help, patience, and expertise:

Anne Sowards, our editor—thank you for having faith in us, despite all evidence to the contrary;

Nancy Yost, our agent, for unwavering support and vicious fighting on our behalf;

Michelle Kasper, the production editor, and Andromeda Macri, the assistant production editor—thank you for transforming our manuscript into a book and for not psychically destroying us with your great mind powers because we missed deadlines;

Judith Murello Lagerman, the art director; Annette Fiore DeFex, the cover designer; and Chad Michael Ward, the artist, for creating a spectacular cover;

Amy J. Schneider, the copy editor, for her mad copyediting skills;

thank you very much to Kat Sherbo, Anne's editorial assistant— the e-mails do not lie, we actually are crazy;

and thank you to Rosanne Romanello, the publicist, for always promoting our work.

We are also grateful to Skye and Aubrey, the best legal team the Pack ever had, for help with the shapeshifter real estate laws, and to Noa Rubenstein for assistance with interpretation of Roland's fable. As always, our thanks go to our intrepid beta readers for their generosity and great suggestions despite being repeatedly tortured with half-baked drafts. Thank you, Beatrix Kaser, Ying Chumnongsaksarp, Reece Notley, Hasna Saadani, Jeanine Rachau, Michael Finn, and Chrissy Peterson.

Thank you to Jeaniene Frost and Jill Myles. You are great friends.

Thank you to Peter Honingstock for saving us a great deal of frustration by always helping us find the right resource books in record time.

Finally, we would like to thank each other for not murdering ourselves along the way, and A&E programming—when we get really depressed about our skills in our chosen profession, you always show us something even more depressing.

PROLOGUE

———◆———

THE RINGING OF THE PHONE JERKED ME FROM MY sleep. I clawed my eyes open and rolled off my bed. For some reason, someone had moved the floor several feet lower than I had expected, and I fell and crashed with a thud.

Ow.

A blond head popped over the side of the bed, and a familiar male voice asked, "Are you okay down there?"

Curran. The Beast Lord was in my bed. No, wait a minute. I didn't have a bed, because my insane aunt had destroyed my apartment. I was mated to the Beast Lord, which meant I was in the Keep, in Curran's rooms, and in his bed. Our bed. Which was four feet high. Right.

"Kate?"

"I'm fine."

"Would you like me to install one of those child playground slides for you?"

I flipped him off and picked up the phone. "Yes?"

"Good morning, Consort," a female voice said.

Consort? That was new. Usually the shapeshifters called me Alpha or Lady, and occasionally Mate. Being called Mate ranked somewhere between drinking sour milk and getting a root canal on my list of Things I Hated, so most people had learned to avoid that one.

"I have Assistant Principal Parker on the line. He says it's urgent."

Julie. "I'll take it."

Julie was my ward. Nine months ago she "hired" me to find her missing mother. We found her mother's body instead, being eaten by Celtic sea demons who had decided to pop up in the middle of Atlanta and resurrect a wannabe god. It didn't go well for the demons. It didn't go well for Julie either, and I took her in, the way Greg, my now deceased guardian, had taken me in years ago, when my father passed away.

People around me died, usually in horrible and bloody ways, so I'd sent Julie to the best boarding school I could find. Trouble was, Julie hated the school with the fiery passion of a thousand suns. She'd run away three times in the past six months. The last time Assistant Principal Parker called, a girl in the school's locker room had accused Julie of being a whore during the two years she'd spent on the street. My kid took exception to that and decided to communicate that by applying a chair to the offending party's head. I'd told her to go for the gut next time— it left less evidence.

If Parker was calling, Julie was in trouble again, and since he was calling at six o'clock in the morning, that trouble had a capital *T* attached to it. Julie rarely did anything halfway.

Around me the room lay steeped in gloom. We were on the top floor of the Keep. To my left a window offered a view of the Pack land: an endless dark sky, still untouched by dawn, and below it dark woods rolling into the night. In the distance the half-ruined city stained the horizon. The magic was in full swing—we were lucky it hadn't taken out the phone lines—and the distant industrial-strength feylanterns glowed like tiny blue stars among the crumbling buildings. A ward shielded the window, and when the moonlight hit it just right, the entire scene shimmered with pale silver, as if hidden behind a translucent gauzy curtain.

The female voice came back online. "Consort?"

"Yes?"

"He put me on hold."

"So he calls because it's urgent and puts you on hold?"

"Yes."

Jackass.

"Should I hang up?" she asked.

"No, it's okay. I'll hold."

The world's pulse skipped a beat. The ward guarding the window vanished. Something buzzed in the wall and the electric floor lamp on the left blinked and snapped into life, illuminating the night table with a warm yellow glow. I reached over and turned it off.

In the distance, the blue feylantern stars winked out of existence. For a breath, the city was dark. A bright flash sparked with white among the ruins, blossoming into an explosion of light and fire. A moment later a thunderclap rolled through the night. Probably a transformer exploding after the magic wave receded. A weak red glow illuminated the horizon. You'd think it was the sunrise, but the last time I'd checked, the sun rose in the east, not the southwest. I squinted at the red light. Yep, Atlanta was burning. Again.

Magic had drained from the world and technology had once again gained the upper hand. People called it the post-Shift resonance. Magic came and went as it pleased, flooding the world like a tsunami, dragging bizarre monsters into our reality, stalling engines, jamming guns, eating tall buildings, and vanishing again without warning. Nobody knew when it would assault us or how long each wave would last. Eventually magic would win this war, but for now technology was putting up a hell of a fight, and we were stuck in the middle of the chaos, struggling to rebuild a half-ruined world according to new rules.

The phone clicked and Parker's baritone filled my ear. "Good morning, Ms. Daniels. I'm calling to inform you that Julie has left our premises."

Not again.

Curran's arms closed around me and he hugged me to him. I leaned back against him. "How?"

"She mailed herself."

"I'm sorry?"

Parker cleared his throat. "As you know, all of our students are required to perform two hours of school service a day. Julie worked in the mail room. We viewed it as the best location, because she was under near-constant supervision and had no opportunities to leave the building. Apparently, she obtained a large crate, falsified a shipping label, and mailed herself inside it."

Curran chuckled into my ear.

I turned and bumped my head against his chest a few times. It was the nearest hard surface.

"We found the crate near the ley line."

Well, at least she was smart enough to get out of the crate before it was pushed into the magic current. With my luck, she'd end up getting shipped to Cape Horn.

"She'll come back here," I said. "I'll bring her back in a couple of days."

Parker pronounced the words very carefully. "That won't be necessary."

"What do you mean, not necessary?"

He sighed. "Ms. Daniels, we are educators. We're not prison guards. In the past school year Julie has run away three times. She's a very intelligent child, very inventive, and it's painfully obvious that she doesn't want to be here. Nothing short of shackling her to the wall will keep her on our premises, and I'm not convinced that even that would work. I spoke to her after her previous caper, and it's my opinion that she will continue to run away. She doesn't want to be a part of this school. Keeping her here against her will requires a significant expenditure of our resources, and we can't afford to be held liable for any injuries Julie may incur in these escape attempts. We're refunding the remainder of her tuition. I'm very sorry."

If I could reach through the phone, I'd strangle him. On second thought, if I had that type of psychic power, I might pluck Julie from wherever she was instead and drop her in the middle of the room. She would be begging to go back to that bloody school by the time I was done.

Parker cleared his throat again. "I have a list of alternative educational institutions I can recommend to you . . ."

"That won't be necessary." I hung up. I had a list of alternative educational institutions already. I had put it together after Julie's first escape. She shot all of them down.

A wide grin split Curran's face.

"It's not funny."

"It's very funny. Besides, it's better this way."

I swiped my jeans off the chair and pulled them on. "They kicked my kid out of their school. How the hell is that better?"

"Where are you going?"

"I'm going to find Julie and I'll ground her ass until she forgets what the sun looks like, and then I'll go over to that school and pull their legs out."

Curran laughed.

"It's not funny."

"It's also not their fault. They tried to help her and cut her a lot of slack. She hates that damn school. You shouldn't have put her there in the first place."

"Well, thank you, Your Furriness, for this critique of my parenting decisions."

"It's not a critique, it's a statement of fact. Do you know where your kid is right now? No, you don't. You know where she isn't: she isn't at the school and she isn't here."

Pot, meet kettle. "As I recall, you didn't know where your chief of security and his entire crew were for almost a week." I pulled on my turtleneck.

"I knew exactly where they were. They were with you. I could've fixed that situation, but some wannabe pit fighter stuck her nose into my mess and made a mistake into a disaster."

I picked up my sword. "No, I saved the day. You just don't want to admit it."

Curran leaned forward. "Kate."

The sound of my name in his voice stopped me in midturn. I don't know how the hell he did it, but whenever he said my name, it cut through all other distractions and made me pause, as if he'd clenched me to him and kissed me.

Curran rubbed my shoulders. "Put the sword down for a second."

Fine. I put Slayer back on the night table and crossed my arms.

"Humor me. What's the harm in keeping Julie here? With us? She has a room already. She has a friend—Doolittle's grandniece really likes her."

"Maddie."

"Yes, Maddie. There are fifteen hundred shapeshifters in the Pack. One more screwed-up kid isn't going to break anything."

"It's not about that."

"Then what is it?"

"People around me die, Curran. They drop like flies. I've gone through life leaving a trail of dead bodies behind me. My mother is dead, my stepfather is dead, my guardian is dead, my aunt is dead—because I killed her, and when my real father finds me, he'll move heaven and earth to make me dead. I don't want Julie to live stumbling from one violent clash to another, always worried that people she cares about won't survive. You and I will never have normal, but if she stayed in that school, she could have."

Curran shrugged. "The only people who can have normal are the ones unaffected by all the fucked-up shit that happens around them. Julie doesn't want normal. She probably can't deal with it. She'll get out of that school and run right into the fire to prove to herself she can take the heat. It will happen one way or another. Keeping her away just ensures she won't be prepared when she's on her own."

I leaned back against the night table. "I just want her to be safe. I don't want anything bad to happen to her."

Curran pulled me close. "We can keep her safe here. She can go to one of our schools, or we can take her to somewhere in the city. She is yours, but now that we're mated, she's also mine, which makes her the ward of the Beast Lord and his mate. Trust me, nobody wants to piss the two of us off. Besides, we have three hundred shapeshifters in the Keep at any moment, and each one of them will kill anything that threatens her. Can't get safer than that."

He had a point. I couldn't have Julie staying with me before, when I lived in a shabby apartment with failing heat. It got attacked every time I found a lead on one of my cases. I'd worked for the Order of Knights of Merciful Aid back then, and it demanded every ounce of my time. Julie would have been on her own for most of the day, without me to take care of her and make sure she ate and stayed safe. Things were different now. Now Julie could stay here, in the Keep full of homicidal maniacs who grew teeth the size of switchblades and erupted into a violent frenzy when threatened.

Somehow that thought failed to make me feel better.

"You will have to train her one way or another," Curran said. "If you want her to hold her own."

He was right. I knew he was right, but I still didn't like it. "We're about a hundred miles from Macon?"

He nodded. "Give or take."

"She'll be staying away from the ley line and she's carrying wolfsbane."

"Why?" Curran frowned.

"Because the last time she took off, Derek picked her up at a ley point and brought her here in a Pack Jeep. He even stopped to get her some fried chicken and ice cream. She had a great time, so I told her that if she pulled this stunt again, she wouldn't get anywhere near the Keep. I would either come myself or send somebody who would find her and take her straight back to the school. No going to the Keep, no getting attention from me and Derek, no gossiping with Maddie, no passing go or collecting two hundred dollars. She wants to avoid being caught, so she's walking home."

Curran grinned. "She's determined, I'll give her that."

"Could you send a tracker out there to watch over her but keep out of sight?"

"What are you thinking?"

"Let her walk. A hundred miles over rugged terrain, it will take her a couple of days." When I was a kid, Voron, my stepfather, would drive me into the woods and drop me off with nothing but a canteen and a knife. Julie wasn't me. But she was a smart kid, good on the street. I had no doubt she could make it to the Keep on her own. Still, better safe than sorry.

"Two birds with one stone: it's a good punishment for running away and when she gets here and we let her stay, she'll feel like she earned it."

"I'll send some wolves out. They'll find her and they'll keep her safe."

I kissed his lips and picked up my sword. "Thank you. And tell them not to spoil her with fried chicken if they have to pick her up."

Curran shook his head. "I can't promise that. I'm not a complete bastard."

CHAPTER 1

———◆———

MY OFFICE OCCUPIED A SMALL, STURDY BUILDING ON Jeremiah Street, in the northeast part of town. Jeremiah Street used to be called North Arcadia Street, until one day a Southern preacher walked out in the middle of the intersection of North Arcadia and Ponce de Leon and started screaming about hellfire and damnation. He called himself the second Jeremiah and demanded that the passersby repent and cease their idol worship. When the crowd ignored him, he unleashed a meteor shower that leveled two city blocks. By the time a Paranormal Activity Division sniper shot him with a crossbow, the street was a smoking ruin. Since they had to rebuild it from the ground up, they renamed the street after the man who'd demolished it. There was a lesson in there somewhere, but right now I didn't feel like looking for it.

Once technically part of Decatur and now just part of the huge sprawling mess that was Atlanta, Jeremiah Street wasn't as busy as Ponce de Leon, but tinker shops and a large auto repair yard sent a lot of traffic past my place. I left my Jeep idling in the street, got out, unlocked the chain that secured my parking lot, and drove in.

My office must've been a house at one point. The side door

from the parking lot led into a small but functional kitchen, which in turn led to the large main room, where my desk waited for me. At the back wall wooden stairs offered access to the loft on the second floor complete with a cot. Several smaller rooms branched from the main room. I used them to store my herbal supply and equipment, both of which currently excelled at collecting dust.

I deposited my bag onto my desk and checked my answering machine. A big red zero looked back at me from the digital display. No messages. Shocking.

I walked to the windows and pulled up the shades. Morning light flooded the room, sectioned by the thick metal bars securing the glass. I unlocked the door on the off chance any prospective clients happened by. It was a huge door, thick and reinforced with steel. I had a feeling that if someone fired a cannon at it, the cannon ball would just bounce off and roll down the street.

I went back to the kitchen, flipped the coffeemaker on, came back to my desk, and landed in my chair. A stack of bills lay in front of me. I gave it an evil eye, but it refused to squeal and take off for the hills.

I sighed, pulled a throwing knife out, and opened the cheap brown envelopes. Electric bill. Water bill. Charged-air bill for the feylanterns. Trash collector bill with a threatening notice to do irreparable harm to my person unless I paid the bill. An envelope from the trash collector with the check for the bill returned. The trash company insisted on misspelling my name as Donovan, despite repeated corrections, and when I sent them the payment, they failed to find my account. Even though I put the account number on the damn check.

We'd gone through this song and dance twice now. I had a feeling that if I walked into their office and carved my name in the wall with my sword, they'd still manage to get it wrong.

I leaned back. Being in the office put me into a sour mood. I'd never had my own business before. I'd worked for a Mercenary Guild, which handled magic hazmat, took the money, and asked no questions. Then I'd worked for the Order of Knights of Merciful Aid, which delivered that violent aid on their terms only. The Order and I had parted ways, and now I owned Cutting Edge Investigations. The business officially opened its doors a month ago. I had a solid street reputation and decent connections. I took out an ad in a newspaper, I put the word out on the street, and so far nobody had hired me to do a damn thing.

It drove me nuts. I'd had to rely on the Pack to finance the business, and they had fronted my utility bills for a year. They gave me the loan not because I was an efficient and skilled fighter and not because I at one point had Friend of the Pack status. They gave it to me because I was mated to Curran, which made me the female alpha of the Pack. So far Cutting Edge was turning out to be one of those pet businesses rich men gave to their wives to keep them busy. I wanted it to succeed, God damn it. I wanted to be profitable and stand on my own two feet. If things kept going this way, I would be forced to run up and down the street screaming, "We kill things for money." Maybe someone would take pity and throw some change at me.

The phone rang. I stared at it. You never know. It could be a trick.

The phone rang again. I picked it up. "Cutting Edge."

"Kate." A dry voice vibrated with urgency.

Long time no kill. "Hello, Ghastek." And what would Atlanta's premier Master of the Dead want with me?

When a victim of the Immortuus pathogen died, his mind and ego died with him, leaving a shell of the body, superstrong, superfast, lethal, and ruled only by bloodlust. Masters of the Dead grabbed hold of that empty shell and drove the vampire like a remote-controlled car. They dictated the vampire's every twitch, saw through its eyes, heard through its ears, and spoke through its mouth. In the hands of an exceptional navigator, a vampire was the stuff of human nightmares. Ghastek, like ninety percent of vampire navigators, worked for the People, a cringeworthy hybrid of a cult, corporation, and research facility. I hated the People with a passion and I hated Roland, the man who led them, even more.

Unfortunately, beggars couldn't be choosers. If Ghastek was calling, it was because he wanted a favor, which would mean he'd owe me. Having the best Master of the Dead in the city in my debt would come in handy in my line of work. "What can I do for you?"

"A loose vampire is heading your way."

Bloody hell. Without a navigator, an insatiable hunger drove the bloodsuckers to slaughter. A loose vampire would massacre anything it came across. It could kill a dozen people in half a minute.

"What do you need?"

"I'm less than twelve miles behind her. I need you to delay her, until I come into range."

"From which direction?"

"Northwest. And Kate, try not to damage her. She's expensive . . ."

I dropped the phone and dashed outside, bursting into almost painfully cold air. People filled the street—laborers, shoppers, random passersby hurrying home. Food to be slaughtered. I sucked in a lungful of cold and screamed, "Vampire! Loose vampire! Run!"

For a fraction of a second nothing happened, and then people scattered like fish before a shark. In a breath I was alone.

The parking lot chain I'd unlocked this morning lay coiled next to the building, the padlock hanging open. Perfect.

Two seconds to the parking lot.

A second to yank the padlock off the ground.

Three more seconds to drag the chain to an old tree.

Too slow. I looped the chain around the trunk and worked the other end into a slipknot with the padlock.

I needed blood to bait the vamp. Lots and lots of blood.

A team of oxen turned the corner. I ran at them, drawing a throwing knife. The driver, an older Latino man, stared at me. His hand reached for a rifle lying on the seat next to him.

"Get off! Loose vampire!"

He scrambled out of the cart. I sliced a long shallow gash down the ox's shoulder and ran my hands along the cut. Hot crimson drenched my fingers.

The ox bellowed, eyes mad with pain, and charged off, pulling the other animal with it, the cart thundering behind them.

I grabbed the chain loop.

An emaciated shape leaped off the rooftop. Ropes of muscle knotted its frame under skin so tight that every ligament and vein stood out beneath it. The vampire landed on the pavement on all fours, skidded, its long sickle claws scraping the asphalt with a screech, and whirled. Ruby eyes glared at me from a horrible face. Massive jaws gaped open, showing sharp fangs, bone-white against the black mouth.

I waved my hands, sending bloody droplets through the air.

The vampire charged.

It all but flew above the ground with preternatural speed, straight at me, pulled by the intoxicating scent of blood.

I waited, my heartbeat impossibly loud in my ears. I'd have only one shot at this.

The vampire leaped, covering the few feet between us. It flew, limbs out, claws raised for the kill.

I thrust the chain loop up and over its head.

Its body hit me. The impact knocked me off my feet. I crashed to the ground and rolled upright. The vamp lunged at me. The chain snapped taut on its throat, yanking the undead off the pavement. The bloodsucker fell and sprung up, twisting and jerking on the end of the chain like a feral cat caught in a loop of a dog-catcher's pole.

I took several steps back and took in a lungful of air.

The vampire flipped and lunged in my direction. The tree shook and groaned. It dug at the chain noose around its neck, gouging the undead flesh with its claws. Blood spurted from under the chain. Either it would snap the tree or the chain would slice its throat.

The bloodsucker threw itself at me again, snapping the chain taut, and fell to the ground, its leap aborted. It picked itself up and sat. Intelligence flooded into its burning red eyes. The huge jaws unhinged and Ghastek's voice came forth.

"A chain?"

"You're welcome." About time he decided to make an appearance. "I cut an ox to get the vamp fixed on me. You need to compensate the owner." The ox was its owner's livelihood. No reason for him to get hurt because the People couldn't keep their undead on a proper leash.

"Of course."

You bet your ass, of course. An ox cost about a grand. A vampire, especially one as old as this one, went for about thirty times that.

The vampire squatted in the snow. "How did you manage to get a chain on her?"

"I have mad skills." I wanted to sag against something, but

showing weakness of any sort in front of Ghastek wasn't a good idea. I might as well taunt a rabid wolf with a pork roast. My face was hot, my hands were cold. My mouth tasted bitter. The adrenaline rush was wearing off.

"What the hell happened?" I asked.

"One of Rowena's journeymen fainted," Ghastek said. "The woman is pregnant. It happens. Needless to say, she's now barred from navigation."

The journeymen, Masters of the Dead in training, were perfectly aware that if their control over the undead slipped, the vampire would turn the city into a slaughterhouse. They had nerves like fighter pilots pre-Shift. They didn't faint. There was more to it, but Ghastek's tone made it clear that getting any more information out of him would take a team of lawyers and a medieval torture device.

Just as well. The less I interacted with the People, the better. "Did it kill anybody?"

"There were no casualties."

My pulse finally slowed down.

Several blocks away to my right, a Humvee swung into the street at breakneck speed. Armored like a tank, it carried an M240B, a medium machine gun, mounted on the roof. A PAD First Response Unit. The PAD, part of Atlanta's Finest, dealt specifically with magic-related issues. The First Response Unit was their version of SWAT. They shot first and sorted through the bloody remains later.

"Cavalry," I said.

The vampire grimaced, mimicking Ghastek's expression. "Of course. The jocks got all dressed up to kill a vampire and now they won't get to shoot the big gun. Kate, would you mind stepping closer? Otherwise they might shoot her anyway."

You've got to be kidding me. I moved to body-shield the vampire. "You owe me."

"Indeed." The bloodsucker rose next to me, waving its front limbs. "There is no need for concern. The matter is under control."

A black SUV turned the corner into the street from the left. The two vehicles came to a screeching stop in front of me and the vampire. The Humvee disgorged four cops in blue Paranormal Activity Division armor.

The tallest of the four cops leveled a shotgun at the vamp and snarled, "What the hell do you think you're doing? You could've killed half of the city!"

The SUV's door opened and Ghastek stepped out. Thin and somber, he wore a perfectly pressed gray suit with a barely visible pinstripe. Three members of the People emerged from the SUV behind him, a man and two women: a thin brunette and a red-haired woman who looked barely old enough to wear a suit. All three were meticulously groomed and would've looked at home in a high-pressure boardroom.

"There is no need to exaggerate." Ghastek strode to the vampire. "No lives were lost."

"No thanks to you." The tall cop showed no signs of lowering the shotgun.

"She's completely safe now," Ghastek said. "Allow me to demonstrate." The vampire rose from its haunches and curtsied.

The PAD collectively turned purple with rage.

I backpedaled toward my office, before they decided to remember I was there and drag me into this mess.

"See? I have complete control of the unde—" Ghastek's eyes rolled back into his head. His mouth went slack. For a long second he remained upright, his body completely still, and then his legs gave. He swayed once and crashed into the dirty snow.

The vampire's eyes flared bright murderous red. It opened its mouth, revealing twin sickles of ivory fangs.

The PAD opened fire.

CHAPTER 2

THE GUNS ROARED.

The first bullet sliced into the vampire's chest, punched through dry muscle, and bit Ghastek's journeyman in the shoulder. He spun from the impact, and the steady stream of rounds from the M240B punctured the vampire and cut across the journeyman's spine, nearly severing him in two. Blood sprayed.

The women hit the ground.

The bullets chipped the pavement. Half a foot to the right and Ghastek's head would've exploded like a watermelon under a sledgehammer. I dived under gunfire, grabbed Ghastek's legs, and pulled him out of the line of fire, backing up to my office.

The women crawled toward me across the pavement.

The vamp twisted around, shuddering under the barrage of bullets, leaped onto the fallen man, and tore into his back, flinging blood and flesh into the air.

I dragged Ghastek's body over the doorstep and dropped him. Behind me, a woman screamed. I ran back, jumping over the dark-haired woman as she pulled herself through my doorway. In the street, the redheaded girl hugged the ground, clenching her thigh, her eyes huge as saucers. Blood stained the snow with painfully bright scarlet. Shot in the leg.

She was too far out in the street. I had to get her out of here before the vamp keyed on her or the PAD shot her again.

I dropped to the ground, crawled to her, grabbed her arm, and pulled with everything I had. She screamed, but slid a foot toward me across the pockmarked asphalt flooded with melting snow. I backed up and pulled again. Another scream, another foot to the door.

Breathe, pull, slide.
Breathe, pull, slide.
Door.

I pushed her inside, slammed the door shut, and barred it. It was a good door, metal, reinforced, with a four-inch bar. It would hold. It had to.

A wide red stain spread on the floor from the wounded woman's leg. I knelt down and sliced her pant leg open. Blood spurted out of bullet-shredded muscle. The leg was ripped wide open. Bone shards glared at me, bathed in wet redness. Femoral artery cut, great saphenous vein cut, everything cut. Femur shattered.

Shit.

We would need a tourniquet.

"You! Put pressure here!"

The dark-haired girl stared at me with shocked glassy eyes. No intelligent life there. Every second counted.

I grabbed the redhead's hand and put it over her femoral artery. "Hold or you'll bleed out."

She moaned but pressed down.

I ran to the storeroom to get the medical supplies.

Tourniquets were last resort devices. Mine was the C-A-T, military issue, but no matter how good it was, if you kept one on too long, you risked major nerve damage, loss of a limb, and death. And once it went on, it stayed on. Taking it off outside an emergency room would get you killed in a hurry.

I needed paramedics, but calling them would do nothing. Standard operating procedure said, when faced with a loose vampire, seal off the area. The ambulance wouldn't come unless the cops gave the paramedics the all-clear. It was just me, the tourniquet, and a girl who would likely bleed her life out.

I knelt by the woman and pulled the C-A-T out of the bag.

"No!" The girl tried to push away from me. "No, I'll lose my leg!"

"You're bleeding to death."

"No, it's not that bad! It doesn't hurt!"

I gripped her shoulders and propped her up. She saw the shredded mess of her thigh. "Oh God."

"What's your name?"

She sobbed.

"Your name?"

"Emily."

"Emily, your leg has almost been amputated. If I put the tourniquet on it now, it will stop the bleeding and you might survive. If I don't put it on, you'll bleed to death in minutes."

She clutched at me, crying into my shoulder. "I'll be a cripple."

"You'll be alive. And with magic, your chances of keeping your leg are pretty good. You know, medmages heal all sorts of wounds. But we've got to keep you alive until the magic wave hits. Yes?"

She just cried, big tears rolling down her face.

"Yes, Emily?"

"Yes."

"Good."

I slipped the band under her leg, threaded it through the buckle, pulled it tight, and wound the windlass until the bleeding stopped.

Four minutes later the gunfire finally died. Ghastek was still out. His pulse was steady, his breathing even. Emily lay still, whimpering in pain, her leg cinched by the wide tourniquet cuff. Her friend hugged herself, rocking back and forth and mumbling over and over, "They shot at us, they shot at us."

Peachy.

That was the problem with the People: most of them saw action only through the vampire's eyes while they sat in a safe, well-armored room within the Casino, sipping coffee and indulging in an occasional sugary snack. Getting shot at while riding a vampire's mind and dodging actual bullets were two different animals.

A loud bang resonated through the door. A male voice barked. "Atlanta Paranormal Squad. Open the door."

The dark-haired girl froze. Her voice fell to a horrified whisper. "Don't open it."

"Don't worry. I got it under control." Sort of.

I slid a narrow panel aside, revealing a two-inch-by-four-inch peephole. A shadow shifted to my left—the officer had pressed against the wall so I couldn't shoot him through the opening.

"Did you get the vamp?"

"We got it. Open the door."

"Why?"

There was a small pause. "Open. The. Door."

"No." They were hot from killing the vampire and still trigger-happy. There was no telling what they would do if I let them in.

"What do you mean, 'no'?"

He seemed genuinely puzzled.

"Why do you need me to open the door?"

"So we can apprehend the sonovabitch who dropped a loose vampire in the middle of the city."

Great. "You just killed one member of the People in the cross fire, wounded another, and you want me to let you have the rest of the witnesses. I don't know you well enough to do that."

The PAD generally stuck to the straight and narrow, but there were certain things one didn't do: you didn't turn over a cop's killer to his partner and you didn't surrender a necromancer to the First Response Unit. They were all volunteer, and sanity was an optional requirement. If I gave Ghastek and his people to them, there was a good chance they would never make it to the hospital. The official term was "died of their injuries en route."

The male voice huffed. "How about this: open the door or we'll break it down."

"You need a warrant for that."

"I don't need a warrant if I think you're in immediate danger. Say, Charlie, do you think she's in danger?"

"Oh, I think she's in a lot of danger," Charlie said.

"And would it be our duty as law enforcement officers to rescue her from said danger?"

"It would be a crime not to."

One person dead, one painting the floor with her blood. I guess it was time for jokes.

"You heard Charlie. Open the door or we'll open it for you."

I leaned a touch farther from the peephole. If they tried to break in, I could probably take them, but I could also kiss any sort of future cooperation from the PAD good-bye.

"Stop." A familiar female voice rang outside the door. It couldn't be.

"Ma'am, step back," the cop barked. "You're interfering with a police matter."

"I'm a knight of the Order. My name is Andrea Nash; here is my ID."

Andrea was my best friend. I hadn't seen her for two months, ever since my aunt trashed half of Atlanta. After the final fight with Erra, Andrea had disappeared. About two weeks later I got a letter that said, *"Kate, I'm sorry about everything. I have to go away for a while, please don't look for me. Don't worry about Grendel, I'll take good care of him. Thank you for being my friend."* Five minutes later I was on my way to the city to look for her, His Grumpiness the Beast Lord in tow. We found nothing. No sign of Andrea or my attack poodle, who had ended up in her care after the chaos of my aunt's demolition derby. Then I'd pestered Jim, the Pack Security Chief and my Mercenary Guild buddy, until he put one of his units on combing the city for her. They came back empty-handed. Andrea Nash had vanished into thin air.

Apparently she was still alive. If I got out of this siege, I'd punch her in the face.

The cop's voice gained a new edge. Knights of the Order didn't screw around. "That's nice, Miss Nash. Step back or we'll place you under arrest and you can call the Order from the station and have them bail you out."

"Look up above the door. You see a metal paw bolted to the wood?"

"And?"

"This business is the property of the Pack. If you break the door down, you'll have to appear before a judge and explain why you invaded these premises without a warrant, arrested guests of the Pack, and caused damage to Pack property."

"We can do that," the cop said.

"No, you can't—because I'll testify that you had no reasonable cause to enter said building. Unless you're planning on killing me, in which case, start praying now, because I'll put a bullet through the head of every man in your squad before you get off a single shot."

"I wouldn't call that bluff," I said. "I've seen her shoot. She's being modest."

"Whose side are you on anyway?" the cop growled.

"I'm on the side of serving and protecting," Andrea said. "Your squad killed a civilian in the cross fire."

"It was a justifiable kill," the cop said. "I'm not going to debate it with you."

Andrea's voice vibrated with steel. "One man is already dead. And judging by the blood trail on the pavement, somebody in that building is wounded. Someone either crawled or was dragged to that office and is probably bleeding out inside it. You now have a choice. You can either get the paramedics in there or you can let another civilian die of their injuries, break into an office owned by the Pack, assault the Beast Lord's wife, and shoot a knight of the Order. You can do it either way, but I promise that if you somehow survive, twenty years from now, when you're old and broken, you'll look back at this moment and wish you had taken two seconds and thought about what you were doing, because this is the point where it all went very wrong."

Wow. "What she said."

There was a long pause. They were thinking it over.

"Look, I worked with you guys before," I called. "Call Detective Michael Gray. He'll vouch for me. If you get paramedics here, I'll open the door. No fuss, no damage, everybody is happy, nobody gets hauled to court. We're going to need an ambulance pretty soon, too. I've got one of the girls in a tourniquet and if we don't hurry this along, she'll bleed to death."

"Tell you what," the cop said. "Open the door, let us take the wounded girl out, and then we'll call Gray."

Like I was born yesterday. "The moment I open the door, you'll rush me. I'll wait until the paramedics get here."

"Fine. I'll make the call, but you're playing with her life. She dies—it's on you, and I'll personally book you."

I slid the metal guard shut and went back to the women. The dark-haired woman stared at me with haunted eyes. "You're going to let them have us?"

"If it's a choice between your friend's life and your freedom, yes. For now, we'll wait. My best friend is on the other side, and she won't let them do anything stupid." I looked at the dark-haired woman. "When Ghastek fainted, why didn't either of you grab the vampire's mind?"

"I tried. It wasn't there."

"What do you mean, not there?" Vampire minds didn't just blink out of existence.

The dark-haired woman shook her head. "It wasn't there."

"She's right," Emily said. "I tried, too. It's like I couldn't navigate anymore." She shivered on the floor. "I'm cold."

I went into the storage room, pulled a spare cloak from the hook, and covered her with it.

Emily's lips had turned blue. "Am I going to die?"

"Not if I can help it."

CHAPTER 3

———————

MINUTES DRIPPED BY, COLD AND SLOW. FIVE. SIX. Eight.

A loud knock echoed through the door. "Kate?" Andrea's voice called.

"Yeah?"

"I have paramedics with me. Let me in."

I unbarred the door and swung it open. Four paramedics sprinted into the room. Andrea followed them. She was short and blue-eyed, and for some reason the tips of her short blond hair were frosted with neon blue. The barrel of a rifle protruded over the shoulder of her jacket. Knowing her, she probably had two SIG-Sauers under that jacket, a combat knife, and enough bullets to take on the Golden Horde.

Normally Andrea's face wore a nice easygoing expression that made random strangers want to pour their hearts out to her. One look at her now, and they would cross to the other side of the street. Tension locked her face into a rigid, strained mask, and she moved like a soldier in enemy territory, expecting a bullet between the shoulder blades at any moment and ready to fire back in a split second.

Behind her two cops in PAD uniforms waited at the door,

giving me their best versions of a cop scowl. Strangely, I felt no urge to quiver in terror.

Andrea stepped closer and kept her voice low. "I leave you alone for eight weeks and you get into a pissing match with the PAD."

"That's just how I roll," I told her.

Emily screamed.

"Excuse me." I went over to where the paramedics had lifted her onto the stretcher. She reached out and gripped my hand.

"It will be okay," I told her. "You're going to the hospital. They'll take care of you."

Emily didn't say anything. She just clutched my hand and didn't let go until they loaded her into the ambulance. A stretcher with Ghastek followed into the second vehicle, and then the dark-haired woman came out, wrapped in a blanket, led by two paramedics. The ambulance doors closed and the two emergency vehicles took off wailing like banshees.

When I came back into the office, it was empty, except for Andrea and a puddle of blood on the floor. "Where are the cops?"

She shrugged. "They cleared out."

We looked at each other. She'd saved my bacon. That didn't change the fact that she'd disappeared for two months. And now something was wrong.

"What the hell?" Andrea glared at me. "How in the world did you end up with three navigators in your office with the PAD outside? They were ready to storm your office. Are you nuts?"

"What the hell back at you. Where have you been? Did you forget how to use the phone?"

Andrea crossed her arms. "I wrote you a letter!"

"You wrote me a note that made my hair stand on end."

The phone rang. Now what? I marched to my desk and picked it up. "Yes?"

Curran's voice filled the phone. "Are you okay?"

It was completely absurd, but hearing him instantly made me feel better. "Yeah."

"Do you need help?"

His voice was perfectly even. The Beast Lord was a hair away from charging to my aid.

"No, I'm good." For some reason my insides clumped into a painful knot. I could've been shot and I would have never seen him again. That was a new and unwelcome feeling. Great. Now I had anxiety. Maybe if I slapped myself real hard, I'd snap out of it.

I forced the words out. They sounded strained. "Who snitched?"

"We have people monitoring police radio frequencies. They gave Jim a heads-up in case our security had to storm the PAD offices and bust you out of there. I found out when I saw Jim walking down the hallway snickering to himself."

I made a mental note to punch Jim in the arm the next time I saw him. "Thought it was funny, did he?"

"I didn't think it was funny."

I bet. "People were about to die and I could save them. There was a girl . . . Anyway, I'm not hurt. I'll be home for dinner."

"As you wish," he said.

My heart made a little jump. *I love you, too.*

The tension in his voice eased. "You sure you don't need your Prince Charming to come and save you?"

The knot in my stomach evaporated. My Prince Charming, huh. "Sure, do you have one handy?"

"Oh, I think I could scrounge one up somewhere. As often as I have to rescue you . . ."

"I'm going to kick you in the head when I get home. Repeatedly."

"You could try. You probably need the exercise since you sit on your butt in the office all day."

"You know what, don't talk to me."

"Whatever you want, *baby*."

Now he was just jerking my chain. I growled at the phone.

"Hey, before you hang up—I sent Jackson and Martina down to track Julie. We should know something tonight."

"Thanks."

I hung up. *Rescue me.* Bastard. I wouldn't just kick him, I would kick him so hard he'd feel it.

"Nothing changed, I see." Andrea grinned. The smile looked a bit brittle around the edges. "Still enjoying your honeymoon? It's all rainbows, and sugar hearts, and chocolate kisses?"

I crossed my arms. "Where is my dog?"

"In my truck, eating the upholstery."

We both looked at the blood. If we let Grendel in, he'd try to lick it.

I went to the back room and got rags, peroxide, and a bucket. Andrea set her rifle aside and pulled up her sleeves.

We knelt and began to mop up the stain.

"God, that's a shitload of blood." Andrea grimaced. "Do you think the girl will survive?"

"I don't know. She took several shots from an M240B. Her leg is all tore up to hell." I squeezed the blood from the rag into the bucket.

"How did it happen?" she asked.

I wanted to grab her and shake her until she told me where she had been these past months. But at least she was here and she was talking. I would get the story out of her sooner or later.

"Ghastek called. Said they had a loose vamp and it was heading my way. I went out there and chained it up. I had it wrapped around the tree, then Ghastek got close enough to grab it. His guys and the PAD's First Response showed up with the big gun. They had some words, and then Ghastek fainted."

Andrea paused, her hands on a bloody rag. "What do you mean, fainted?"

"Took a dive. Kissed the pavement. Swooned like a Southern belle after her first kiss. Had a dreadful case of the vapors."

"That's weird."

"His eyes rolled up and he went down, like someone knocked him out." I dumped some clean water on the floorboards. "Then the vamp's eyes ignited red and the PAD opened fire. Ghastek had three people with him. The man was cut down in the first second or two and the bloodsucker went for him."

"And then?"

"And then I got the four of us in here and barred the door, and the rest you know."

Andrea sighed. "It's not good to deny the PAD access. They don't like that."

"Tell me something I don't know." Like where she'd been these past two months. Maybe she'd joined a nunnery. Or the French Foreign Legion.

"You could've called the Casino. They would've unleashed a horde of lawyers." Andrea poured peroxide onto the wet wood.

I straightened. "The First Response Unit is all trigger-happy jocks. They were still swimming on the high of taking out a bloodsucker. I listened to them pound bullets into the pavement for nearly five minutes. It was overkill. The only way their day could have gotten better would be if they could kill another vampire. Or perhaps several. If I called the Casino, no matter what I said, the People would send a vamp out. That's their default response. The PAD would shoot it, and the People would retaliate. It would spiral out of control, and I wanted everybody calm so I could keep Emily breathing."

"Did Ghastek say why they had a loose vamp running around?"

I grimaced. "Something about a pregnant girl fainting."

Andrea wrinkled her nose in a telltale shapeshifter sneer. "I smell bullshit."

She was right. Two navigators, both fainted while piloting the same vampire? Ghastek fainting? That just didn't happen.

I got a dry rag and wiped up the peroxide. The stain didn't look too bad now. Still, once blood stained something, it stayed there forever, even if you could no longer see it. My office was christened in Emily's blood. Yay.

I dumped the rag into the bucket and looked at Andrea. "My day didn't go well."

"I see that."

"The PAD probably wants to shut me down, the People will find some way to blame me for the slaughter of the vampire and expect restitution, and Curran found out that I risked my life to save a Master of the Dead, which means I'll have a lot of explaining to do at dinner, because Curran believes I'm made of glass. If I had been shot and the Pack found out that the Beast Lord's mate and sugar woogums had been injured as a result of the People's fuckup, they would have collective apoplexy and storm the Casino."

"Aha," Andrea said. "I'm going to ignore that you just referred to yourself as 'sugar woogums.' Is there a point to this story?"

"The point is, I have no patience left. You will tell me where you went when you vanished. Now."

Andrea raised her chin, as if daring me to take a swing. "Or?"

Or what exactly? "Or I will punch you right in the face."

Andrea froze. For a second I thought she would bolt for the door. She sighed instead. "Can I at least get some coffee first?"

WE SAT IN THE KITCHEN AT THE OLD, SCARRED TABLE, and I poured two-hour-old burned coffee into our mugs.

Andrea looked into her cup. "I was on the north side of the gap when your aunt appeared for her final showdown. I was still pissed off about . . . things and it messed with my head. So I picked out a nice spot for myself on a pile of debris right on the lip of the gap and set up my rifle. It seemed like a good idea at the time. When your aunt made her grand entrance, I tried to shoot her in the eye. Except she moved and I missed. And then she started blasting fire all over. That's where the lack of clear head bit me in the ass—I had no exit strategy. She barbecued me like a rack of ribs. By the time they peeled me from that debris, I had third-degree burns over forty percent of my body. The pain was too much. I passed out. Apparently I changed into my other self in the hospital bed."

Shit. Lyc-V, the shapeshifter virus, stole pieces of the host's DNA and dragged them over to its next victim. Most of the time animal DNA transferred over from animals to human hosts, resulting in a wereanimal: a human who took on beast shape. Once in a while the process happened in reverse, and some unfortunate animal ended up as an animal-were. Most of them were pathetic creatures, confused, mentally shortchanged, and unable to comprehend the rules of human society. Laws meant nothing to them, and that made them unpredictable and dangerous. Regular shapeshifters murdered them on sight.

However, every rule had an exception, and Andrea's father, a hyenawere, had been one. Andrea remembered very little of her father. She once said he had the mental capacity of a five-year-old. That didn't prevent him from mating with Andrea's mother, who was a werehyena, or bouda, as they preferred to be called. His blood made Andrea beastkin, and she went to great lengths to hide it. She joined the Order as a human, subjected herself to torturous methods to pass all the necessary tests, graduated from the Academy, and excelled at being a knight. She was on the fast track climbing the Order's chain of command when a case went sour and got her transferred to Atlanta.

The head of Atlanta's Order chapter, Knight-protector Ted Moynohan, knew that something was wrong with Andrea, but he couldn't prove it, so he kept her on support duty. Ted didn't play nice with shapeshifters. In fact, he didn't even consider them human. That was one of the reasons I left. Despite it all, Andrea remained fanatically loyal to the Order. For her, the Order meant honor and duty and a sense of serving a higher cause. Shifting in the hospital bed had blown her closet door wide open.

Andrea kept her gaze firmly in her cup. Her face had a strained blank look, her jaw set, as if she were dragging a heavy boulder up a mountain and she was determined to make it to the top.

"The thing with your aunt didn't go well. Ted had called in reinforcements from everywhere. Twelve knights died, among them two masters-at-arms, one diviner, and a master-at-craft. Seven others were severely injured. The Order conducted a hearing. Since my cover had been blown anyway, I thought it would be a good time to make a case that someone like me could be of use to the Order."

Now things made sense. This was her crusade. I should've seen it coming. We'd talked just before I quit the Order, and Andrea had argued against my quitting. She wanted me to stay and fight with her to change the Order for the better from within. I told her that even if I tried to change the Order, I couldn't. I wasn't a knight. My opinion carried no weight. But Andrea was a knight, a decorated veteran. She saw it as her chance to make her mark.

Andrea took a small sip of her coffee and coughed. "Damn, Kate, I know you're pissed but did you have to put motor oil into my drink?"

"That was the lousiest joke I've ever heard you make. Stop stalling. What happened?"

She glanced up and I almost did a double take. Her eyes were hollow and bitter.

"I had one of the best Order advocates in the South. He thought there was a chance we could make a difference. There are others like me in the Order. The not-quite-pure human. I wanted to make their lives better. He advised me to separate myself from the shapeshifters, so I wrote you that letter. I was going to bring Grendel back too, but we had to leave in a hurry, so I just took him with me and went to Wolf Trap."

Wolf Trap, Virginia. The Order's national headquarters. Everyone knowing Andrea was a beastkin. It must've been pure hell.

Andrea rubbed the rim of her cup, as if trying to remove some dirt only she could see. If she rubbed it any harder, she'd make a hole in it.

"We spent a month preparing twenty-four-seven, gathering documents, pulling all of my records. My advocate spoke for three hours at the hearing and made a very passionate, logical argument in my favor. We had charts, we had statistics, we had my service decorations on display. We had everything."

A cold feeling sprouted in the pit of my stomach, telling me exactly how this would end. "And?"

Andrea squared her shoulders and opened her mouth.

Nothing came out. She clamped it shut.

I waited.

Her face paled. She sat rigid, the mouth of her line tense. A faint reddish glow tinted her eyes—the hint of hyena sneaking through under pressure.

Andrea unclenched her teeth. Her voice came out completely flat, sifted through the sieve of her will until every last hint of emotion had been scrubbed from it.

"They awarded me Master-at-Arms and retired me due to being mentally unfit for duty. The official diagnosis is posttraumatic stress disorder. The decision is final and I can't dispute it. I can't even accuse them of discrimination, because my final orders don't address the fact that I'm beastkin. They simply refused to acknowledge it, as if it weren't an issue."

Those fuckers. They didn't just throw her out like a piece of garbage, they sent a message with her. *If you're not human, it doesn't matter how good you are. We don't want your ass.*

"So." Andrea took a deep breath and pushed the words out. "I failed."

For Andrea the Order was more than simply a job. It was her life. She'd spent her childhood in a pack of shapeshifters who reviled her because her father was an animal and her mother was too weak to protect her. Every bone in Andrea's body had been broken before she was ten years old. Andrea rejected all things shapeshifter. She locked that part of herself deep inside and dedicated her existence to becoming completely human, to stepping between the weak and the strong, and she was damn good at it. Now the Order had made her into a pariah. It was a monumental betrayal.

"Everything is gone." Andrea forced a smile. Her face looked like it would shatter any second. "My job, my identity. If the cops had looked closer at my ID, they'd see it said RETIRED on it. People I thought were my friends won't talk to me, like I'm a leper. When I came back to Atlanta, I called down to the chapter looking for Shane. He'd taken over the armory when I left. A couple of those weapons are my personal property. I want them back."

Shane was a typical knight: no family to tie him down, top physical condition, competent, by the book. He and I didn't get along, because he never could quite figure out where I fit into the Order's hierarchy. But he and Andrea had hit it off. They were colleagues. Buddies even.

"How is he?" I asked.

Outrage sparked in Andrea's eyes. "He wouldn't talk to me. I know he was there, because Maxine took the call and you know how her voice gets all distant when she is talking in someone's head at the same time? It was like that. She must've asked him if he wanted to talk to me and then she took a message. Shane hasn't called me back either."

"Shane is an asshole. I was riding back from a job once—it was raining so hard I could barely see—and he was jogging with his rucksack on. I asked him why. He told me that it was his day off and he was trying to take twenty seconds off his time so he could score an even three hundred on the PE scale. He has no brain of his own—he opens his mouth and the Order's Code comes out."

In a real fight the extra twenty seconds wouldn't help him. I could kill him in one. Shane lacked the predatory instinct that turned a well-trained man into a killer. He treated each fight as a tournament match, where someone was totaling his points. And despite his obvious zeal, the Order recognized it, too. All knights started out as knight-defenders. The Order gave you ten years to distinguish yourself, and if you failed, at the end of your dime you became a master-defender, a rank-and-file knight. Shane clearly aimed higher than that, but he was nine years into his tenure with the Order, and Ted showed no signs of promoting him.

Andrea crossed her arms. "Shane is not the point. I don't

give a damn about Shane. He's just the straw that broke the camel's back. Anyway. After the hearing me and Grendel holed up in my place for a couple of weeks licking my wounds, but I can't hide in my hole forever. And talking to the fur-face only gets you so far. Also, he eats things that are bad for him, like rugs and bathroom fixtures. He chewed a hole in my kitchen floor. In a completely flat surface."

"It doesn't surprise me."

Just her and the freakishly large smelly poodle hiding in her apartment together. No friends, no visitors, nothing, just sitting there in her own misery, too proud to unload it on anybody else. It was something I would've done. Except now when I went home, someone was there waiting for me and he would turn the city inside out if I was more than a couple of hours late. But Andrea had nobody. Not even Raphael—she very carefully didn't mention his name.

"I've got a dog-training book," Andrea said. "It says Grendel needs mental stimulation, so I tried to train him, but I think he might be retarded. I figured you would want to see your dog eventually, so here we are. He's probably eaten my dashboard by now."

If she was lucky. If not, he would've also puked on the floor and then peed on it for a good measure. I leaned back. "So what now?"

Andrea shrugged her shoulders in a jerky, forced movement. Her voice was still a matter-of-fact monotone. "I don't know. The Order offered me a pension. I told them to shove it up their asses. Don't get me wrong, I've earned it, but I don't want it."

I wouldn't have taken it either.

"I've got some money put away, so I don't have to look for work right this second. Maybe I'll take up fishing. I suppose eventually I'll have to find something, probably in law enforcement. Just not now. They'll do background checks and I don't want to deal with it."

"Would you like to work here with me?"

Andrea stared at me.

"We have no clients and the pay is shit."

She kept staring. I couldn't even tell if she heard me.

"Even if business were booming, I still couldn't afford to pay you what you're worth." No reaction. "But if you don't mind sitting in the office drinking motor oil coffee and bullshitting with me . . ."

Andrea put her hands over her face.

Ah crap. *What do I do now? Do I say something, do I not say anything?*

I kept talking, keeping my voice as light as I could manage. "I have an extra desk. If the PAD comes to shut us down, I might need sniper support, and I can't shoot a cow from ten feet. We can turn our desks over and lob grenades at them when they storm the door . . ."

Andrea's shoulders shook slightly.

She was crying. Fuck me. I sat there, not sure what to do with myself.

Andrea kept trembling, eerily quiet.

I got off my ass and came back with a handkerchief. Andrea took the hanky and pressed it to her face.

Pity would only make it worse. She wanted to keep her pride—it was all she had left and I had to help her preserve it. I pretended to drink my coffee and stare at my mug. Andrea pretended not to be crying, while trying to mop up her tears.

For a few minutes we sat like this, awkward and grimly determined to act like nothing was happening. If I glared at this mug a moment longer, it would burst into flames from the sheer tension.

Andrea blew her nose. Her voice came out slightly hoarse. "Do you even have anything to shoot the PAD with?"

"I have an armory upstairs. The Pack gave me some guns and ammo. It's in boxes to the left."

Andrea paused. "In cardboard boxes?"

"Yeah."

Andrea groaned.

"Hey, guns aren't my thing. If they had brought me swords, that would be different. That's where you come—"

Andrea got up and hugged me. It was a split-second hug, and then she was off, going upstairs, handkerchief in hand.

This best friend thing was seriously kicking my ass.

Upstairs something clanged.

Okay. I had to get on with the program. I took her keys from the table and went to get Grendel out of her truck before he demolished it.

CHAPTER 4

———◆———

HALF AN HOUR LATER I SAT AT MY DESK, THINKING up a proper amount of money to bill Ghastek for the capture of the vampire. The vamp was now deceased, but it didn't change the fact that I had caught it. The huge shaggy monstrosity that was Grendel sprawled at my feet. When I first found him, his fur had solidified into foul-smelling dreadlocks and the groomer ended up shaving the whole mess off. Now his fur had partially grown out and it looked like a karakul coat I once saw on one of the Guild's upper-class clients: short, curly, and glossy black. He even smelled halfway decent.

Grendel raised his head and licked my hand. I opened the top drawer, took out an oatmeal cookie, and offered it to him. He took it very carefully out of my hand and sucked it in without chewing, as if he hadn't been fed in a thousand years.

Over at the second desk, Andrea rummaged through a giant cardboard box she had dragged down from upstairs.

"There is a loup cage in one of the rooms," she said.

It was the biggest loup cage I'd ever seen too, eight feet wide, eight feet long, seven feet tall. They had to bring it into the office in pieces and assemble it in the room. The steel-and-silver-alloy bars were as thick as my wrist. All Pack offices came equipped with a loup cage. The shapeshifters knew better than anyone how quickly they could snap. But since I was technically a human, Jim kept trying to find some diplomatic name for it. He thought calling it a loup cage would scare off my clients.

"It's not a loup cage, you know," I told her. "It's a holding cell. Or safe room. Or secure room. I don't think Jim ever settled on a term he could live with."

"Aha. It's a loup cage." Andrea cleared her throat. "I touched it with my finger and it hurt. Is that in case of marital problems?"

"Did the Order return your sense of humor as part of the severance package?"

"Oh, burn. Burn!" Andrea hesitated. "Kate . . . Are you happy? With Curran, I mean."

"When I can get out of my own way."

She glanced at me. "And the rest of the time?"

"The rest of the time I'm in a state of silent panic. I'm afraid it will end. I'll lose him. Lose Julie. Lose everyone."

"I've done that," Andrea said. "Lost everyone. It's a bitch."

No kidding.

Andrea lifted a black firearm, holding it as if it were covered with slime. "This is a Witness 45. It has a molding flaw on the grip right here, see? If you fire it, it will blister your hand."

She picked up another gun. "This is a Raven 25. They haven't made them since the early nineties. I didn't even know they were still around. It's a cheap junk gun. They used to call them Saturday Night Specials. You can't put twenty rounds through it without it jamming, and the way this one looks, I wouldn't even risk loading it. It might blow up in my hand. And this? This is a Hi-Point, otherwise known as a Beemiller."

"Is that supposed to tell me something?"

She stared at me. "It's like the crappiest gun out there. Normal guns cost upward of half a grand. This costs like a hundred bucks. The slide is made out of zinc with aluminum."

I looked at her.

"Look, I can bend it with my hand."

I'd also seen her bend a steel rod with her hand, but now didn't seem the best time to mention it.

Andrea put the Hi-Point on the desk. "Where did you get these again?"

"They're surplus guns from the Pack. Confiscated, from what I understand."

"Confiscated during violent altercations?"

"Yes."

Andrea sagged into her chair. Her blue-tipped hair drooped in defeat. "Kate, if someone used a gun against the shapeshifters and now the shapeshifters have said gun, it wasn't a very good gun, was it?"

"I'm not arguing with you. I didn't have a choice. That's what was here when I moved in."

Andrea extracted a fierce-looking silver handgun from the box. Her eyes widened. She looked at it for a moment and tapped it on the corner of her desk. The gun responded with a dry pop.

She looked at me with an expression of abject despair. "It's plastic."

I spread my arms at her.

Andrea tossed the plastic gun to Grendel. "Here, chew on this."

The poodle sniffed it.

A careful knock echoed through the door.

Grendel surged to his feet and snarled, bouncing up and down.

It was probably the PAD come to shut me down. *Knock, knock, let us in, we brought a court order and a howitzer . . .* "Come in!"

The door swung open and a redheaded woman carrying a manila envelope stepped into my office. Tall, lean, and long-limbed, she moved like a fencer, light but sure-footed. You had a feeling that if lightning struck her, she'd lean out of the way and stab it through before it hit the ground. She wore khaki pants, a turtleneck, and a light leather vest. A leather glove hid her left hand. The long rapier on her sword belt and tall boots completed the outfit. I'd seen her before. Her name was Rene and the last time we'd met, she was running security for the Midnight Games, an illegal gladiatorial arena featuring things that went bump in the night.

Behind her two men brought up the rear. Both wore tactical vests and carried enough weapons to take on a small army and win. The man on the right was young, blond, and walked with a light spring in his step that telegraphed a seasoned martial artist. The man on the left was leaner, older, and darker, with a distinct military air and a small scar on his neck. The scar had ragged edges. Something had clawed his neck at some point, but he had lived to fight another day.

Rene's dark gray eyes regarded me.

"I'm sorry, milady," I said. "Athos, Porthos, and Aramis just left."

"They said something about riding to England with d'Artagnan to retrieve some diamonds," Andrea added.

"You two think you're really funny," Rene said.

"We have our moments," I said. "Down, Grendel."

The dog showed Rene his teeth, just in case she decided to try something funny, and lay down to gnaw on his gun.

Rene looked at Grendel. "What in the world is that?"

"That's our mutant attack poodle," I told her.

"Is he chewing on a gun?"

"It's not a real gun," Andrea said.

Rene sighed. "Of course not. That would be irresponsible of you, wouldn't it?"

The older man on Rene's left leaned to her. "This might be a bad idea."

She waved him off.

The blond man on Rene's right squinted at Andrea's desk. "Is that a Hi-Point?"

Andrea turned beet red.

I leaned forward. "What can we do for the Midnight Games?"

"The Red Guard no longer works with the Midnight Games." Rene carefully folded her long frame into my client chair. The two guys behind her remained standing. "In the aftermath of recent events, we had to answer a lot of questions and we chose to disengage from the venue."

Translation: you ruined our fun and screwed me out of a job. "I thought you were an independent hire."

She shook her head. "No, I'm Red Guard. Have been for the last twelve years."

Twelve years in the Red Guard was nothing to sneeze at. "In that case, what can we do for the Guard?"

"We would like to hire you."

Come again? "In what capacity?"

Rene folded her hands on her knee. "We've misplaced an item and we need it retrieved."

"Do you know where the item is?"

She grimaced at me. "If we knew who had it, we wouldn't need to hire you, would we?"

"So the item wasn't misplaced, it was stolen."

"Yes."

Right. "Anything you say in this office is confidential, but not privileged, meaning it stays between us unless we're hit with a subpoena. It would save all of us a lot of time if you just lay it out, so we can decide if we'll take the job or not."

Rene opened the envelope and shook the contents into her hand. A photograph slid into her palm. She placed it on the desk.

A man who looked to be in his early fifties stared back at me. Curly brown hair, going gray; a pleasant enough face, neither handsome nor ugly. Deep lines around the mouth. Sad eyes. He looked like he'd been gutted by life and managed to pull himself together, but some part of him hadn't quite made it.

"Adam Kamen," Rene said. "Thirty-eight years old. Brilliant engineer, genius applied-magic theorist. We were hired to guard him while he worked on a valuable project. Adam was financed by three separate investors."

"How well?" I asked.

"Well enough to pay for an elite guard unit."

That was some serious cash. Elite Red Guard units didn't come cheap.

"We put Adam into a safe house in the middle of nowhere. The property was protected by two defensive wards: an inner-perimeter spell that shielded the house and the workshop and a wider, outer-perimeter spell that protected a quarter-acre area with the house in its center. The house was watched by a crew of twelve people: four per eight-hour shift. I cherry-picked every one of the guards. All of them had passed background checks and showed long records of distinguished service."

Rene leaned back. "Last night Adam and the prototype vanished. His absence and the mutilated body of one of the guards was discovered this morning during a shift change."

Okay. "Mutilated how?"

The line of Rene's mouth hardened. "You would have to see for yourself. I want you to find Adam and retrieve the device."

Figured.

"Which of those two is top priority?

"Obviously my employers would prefer to recover both. The official line says the device has priority; personally, I want Adam saved."

Once a bodyguard, always a bodyguard. Rene had been hired to guard Kamen, and she took her job personally.

Rene braided her long fingers on her knee. "Right now only four people besides the guards and those of us in this room are aware of this issue. Three of those four are Adam's investors, and the fourth is my direct superior. It's essential that no information is leaked. The damage to the Red Guard's reputation would be catastrophic."

Lovely. We would have to look for him without making any noise. My investigative technique mostly consisted of going through the list of interested parties and making as much noise as possible, until the culprit lost his patience and tried to shut me up.

Rene focused on me. "Being subtle is very important in this case."

"We can do subtle," I assured her.

"It's our middle name," Andrea added.

For some odd reason Rene didn't look convinced.

I took out a pad of paper and a pen. "What was the nature of the device?"

Rene shook her head. "We weren't privy to that information. To my knowledge, it was never successfully tested."

Okay. "I need the inventor's full name, address, family, and known associates."

"His name is Adam Kamen. We know that he is thirty-eight, a widower. His wife had diabetes and was undergoing dialysis for kidney failure. Eventually, the disease killed her. Adam was severely traumatized by her death. His work is connected to that event, but I can't tell you how. He spoke without an accent, he didn't seem religious, and he expressed no strong political views."

"How long have you had him?" Andrea wrote a note on her own pad.

"Ninety-six days. He had no visitors while in our custody. Beyond that, we know nothing: no address, no known relatives, no information about enemies or friends." Rene picked up another piece of paper. "This is the latest image of the device in question."

On the picture a metal cylinder stood level with a worktable, approximately three feet tall and probably a foot in diameter. Odd patterns covered the gray metal, some pale, almost white, some with a familiar yellow sheen of gold, others a dozen shades of silver and blue. They twisted and overlapped one another, some so elaborate it must've taken hours of work and jewelers' tools to create them.

I glanced at Rene. "The main cylinder is iron?"

"Iridium. The squiggles on it are gold, platinum, cobalt, and lead. He has half of the periodic table in that thing."

Hmm, all metals, all rare, all expensive, and all took enchantment extremely well, except for lead. Lead was magically inert: magic bounced off it like dry peas from a wall. Why build a magic device and add lead to it? "Any idea at all what it was supposed to do?"

Rene shook her head.

"Do you have any thoughts as to who might have wanted to steal him or his device?" Andrea asked.

"No."

I tapped the paper. "Can you give me the names of the three investors?"

"No."

Andrea frowned. " 'No' as in you don't know who they are, or 'no' as in you won't tell us?"

"Both."

I tapped the paper with my pen. "Rene, you want us to find you-don't-know-who and to retrieve his you-don't-know-what for you-won't-tell-me-whom?"

Rene shrugged. "You will have full access to his workshop, the safe house, and the body. You can interview the guards and you will have our full cooperation. I'll give you a code and advise the master sergeant that you'll be coming. The investors' identities are confidential by contract—if they want to approach you, they can, but we can't force them to do it, so my hands are tied there. As to Adam, we were hired to guard his body and his work, not interview him about his family history."

"I heard background checks are a standard requirement for the Red Guard." I tapped my paper with my pencil.

"They are."

"So why didn't you do them?"

"Because the client gave us a truckload of money." Rene smiled, a controlled sharp baring of teeth. Some unsettling emotion flickered in her eyes and vanished. "We aren't investigators. We're bodyguards. We need a professional to resolve this situation. Hiring the Mercenary Guild is out of the question: they don't know how to be discreet. Hiring the Order isn't an option either: I don't want their fingers in our pie, because they'll try to claim ownership of the whole thing. That leaves us with a private firm. I know you, I've seen you work, and I know you will do it cheaper than anybody else in town, because you have no choice. You opened up shop a month ago and you have no clients. You need a significant case to put your name back on the map, or you'll go out of business. If you succeed in assisting us, the Red Guard will publicly endorse you."

Rene nodded to the guy on her left. He set a small duffel bag on the table. Rene pulled it open. Five stacks of bills looked back at me.

"Ten grand now and ten grand plus expenses when Adam and/or the device are returned to us. Twenty grand if Mr. Kamen is alive and free of life-threatening injuries."

Twenty grand and an endorsement from the best bodyguard outfit in the city or sitting on my ass, drinking motor oil coffee. *Let me think . . .*

Rene watched me. There it was again, an odd flicker of distress in her eyes. This time I was ready for it and I caught it—fear. The woman who used to run security for Midnight Games was scared out of her wits, and she was trying her best to hide it.

I glanced at the two men behind her. "Can we speak in private?"

Rene waved her hand, and the twin walking arsenals departed.

I leaned forward. "There are several experienced PI firms in the city that would be happy to take care of this for twenty grand. The Pinkertons, John Bishop, Annamarie and her White Magnolia, any of them would take that paycheck and say thank you. But you came here."

Rene crossed her arms on her chest. "Are you trying to talk me out of hiring you? A peculiar business strategy."

"No, I'm stating a fact. We both know that my reputation is now shit, because Ted Moynohan told anyone who would listen that I was the stray rock in the gears of his great plan."

On the right Andrea's jawline hardened—she'd clenched her teeth.

"Moynohan says a lot of things," Rene said. "He's damaged goods, and nobody likes excuses."

"I have no formal investigative training and my résumé is short. My point is, if I had lost a valuable object and my career were riding on retrieving it, I wouldn't hire me. I might hire Andrea, because she has both experience and formal training. She can tell you the height of the attacker from the trigonometry of the blood spatter, while I'm fuzzy on what trigonometry is. Hiring us because of Andrea would make sense, but you had no idea she worked here until you walked through the door. The only time you've seen me do my thing was in the Pit." Where I killed things with much bloodshed.

Rene gave me a flat look. "Go on."

"You didn't come here looking for a detective. You came here looking for a hired killer. So why don't you level with me. Why do you need me?"

A strained silence hung between us. A second passed. Another.

"I don't know what Adam was building," Rene said, her voice barely above a whisper. "I know that when I told my direct supervisor that Adam and the device were missing, he called his family and told his wife to pack the children, throw the bare essentials into the car, leave for North Carolina, and not come back until he called them."

"He told his family to get out of town?" Andrea blinked.

Rene nodded. "My brother is bedridden. He can't be moved. I can't take him out of the city. I'm stuck in Atlanta." She leaned forward, her face grim. "You care about your friends, Daniels. Enough to jump on a sword for them. You have a lot to lose and if you get worried enough, you'll strong-arm the Pack into helping you, which is a lot more manpower than I can muster. Find Adam and find his device for me. Before the thief turns it on and does something we both will regret."

• • •

THE DOOR SHUT BEHIND RENE. ANDREA ROSE AND moved to the narrow window, watching her and her goons cross the parking lot to their vehicle. "I've been hired for two hours and we already have a client and a job from hell."

I took five thousand dollars out of the bag. Andrea moved away from the window, and I handed the duffel with the rest of the money to her.

"What for?"

"Gun budget."

Andrea ran her thumb, riffing through the stack of twenty-dollar bills. "Cool. We need ammo."

"Did she look scared to you?" I asked.

Andrea grimaced. "She is a cold bitch and she masks it well, but I spent my entire childhood reading faces so I'd know where the next punch was coming from. And I'm a predator. I lock onto fear, because it signals prey. She's really rattled. We're probably going to regret this."

"Maybe we should take the other offer. Oh wait. We don't have another offer."

"You are so witty, Miss Daniels. Or is it Mrs. Curran?"

I gave her my hard stare. She barked a short laugh.

I set my bag on my desk and unzipped it to check the contents. Dead bodies had the annoying tendency to decay. The sooner we got to the scene, the better.

Andrea checked her guns. "So Ted told everyone you ruined his parade?"

"Pretty much."

"One day I'll kill him, you know."

I glanced at her. She was deadly serious. Killing Ted would unleash a storm of catastrophic proportions. He was the head of the Atlanta chapter of the Order. Every knight in the country would hunt us down to their last breath. Of course, Andrea knew all that.

"I'm over it." I swiped my backpack off the desk. "Ready to go?"

"I was born ready. Where is this workshop anyway?"

I checked the directions Rene had given me. "Sibley Forest."

Andrea swore.

CHAPTER 5

———◆———

I OWNED TWO CARS: AN OLD BEAT-UP SUBARU NAMED Betsi that ran during tech and a horrid nightmare of a truck called Karmelion. Karmelion took twenty minutes of intense chanting to warm up and made more noise than a gaggle of drunk teenage boys in a bar on a Saturday night, but it ran during magic.

Unfortunately the Beast Lord had condemned both vehicles as unsafe and instead I now leased a Pack Jeep I called Hector. Equipped with dual engines, Hector worked during magic or tech. He didn't go very fast, especially during magic, but so far he hadn't stalled on me either. As long as our high-speed chases stayed under forty-five miles an hour, we would be all set.

Andrea eyed Hector. "Where is Betsi?"

"She's back at the Keep. His Furriness made me lease Hector from the Pack instead. Betsi didn't meet with his exacting standards." I climbed into the driver's seat.

Andrea popped the passenger door open and Grendel bounded into the space behind it, where there once was a rear seat and now was space where I stored equipment. "Oh yeah?"

"Yeah. I believe the exact words he used were 'a deathtrap with four wheels.' We had a glorious fight about it."

She grinned and patted Hector's dashboard. "You lost."

"No, I chose to gracefully accept the Pack's generous offer."

"Aha. Keep telling yourself that."

Careful, thin ice. "A third party explained to me in detail that when you're running a business, people judge how successful you are based on your appearance. If you're driving a shabby vehicle, they think you need money and your business is struggling."

"That sounds like Raphael," Andrea said.

And she nailed it. "Yep."

She clamped her mouth shut. I started the engine and maneuvered Hector out of the parking lot.

One . . . two . . . three . . .

"So who is he hooked up with now?"

Three seconds. That was all she lasted. "Nobody that I know of."

She stared straight through the windshield. "I find that hard to believe."

Given that Raphael was a bouda and they viewed sex as a fun recreational activity that should be practiced vigorously and often, normally I would've agreed with her. But Raphael was a special case. He hounded Andrea for months until she finally gave him a chance. For a few blissful weeks they were in love and happy, but then Andrea had to pick between the Order and the Pack and it all fell apart.

"He hasn't been with anybody since you had that fight," I told her.

She snorted. "I'm sure some cute piece of ass will catch his attention sooner or later."

"He's too busy moping."

Andrea glanced at me. "Moping?"

"Pining." I made a wide curve around a large pothole filled with odd-looking blue goo. "If he starts singing sad Irish ballads, we'll have to stage an intervention."

"Oh please." Andrea turned to her passenger window.

"He withdrew from the bouda clan."

"What?"

"Not officially, of course." I shrugged. "But he stopped doing whatever it is that the bouda alpha male does." In the bouda clan, as in nature, females were dominant. Aunt B ran that clan with steel claws, and Raphael, being her son, served as the head of the males. "He killed Tara."

Andrea's blue eyes went big. "The third female?"

"Yeah. Aunt B mentioned it in passing the last time we spoke. He was in the bouda clan house for some sort of business-related thing and Tara came up and grabbed his balls. Apparently she wanted to check if they were still there. He punched her in the face. She shifted into a warrior form and went for his throat. From what Aunt B said, he didn't just kill her, he ripped her to pieces. He hasn't been to the clan house since."

"Holy shit."

"Yeah, that's pretty much what I said." It was one of those idiotic things that could've been resolved in a split second. Tara had no right to touch Raphael, and once she did, he had every right to punch her. She should've left it at that, and now she was dead because she didn't. Bouda males voluntarily took the beta role, but in a fight they were vicious, and Raphael was the best of their lot. I wouldn't fight him unless he left me no choice. I could take him, but he'd tear me up before I finished him.

"I keep thinking about the People thing," Andrea said. "I think something went very wrong in the Casino."

And we'd changed the subject. Andrea one, Kate the matchmaker zero. "How do you figure?"

"Two navigators fainted, both while piloting the same vampire."

And one of these navigators was Ghastek, who could pilot a vampire through an obstacle course studded with rotating saw blades and pits of molten lava while carrying a full glass of water and not spilling a drop. If I had to take a wild guess, I'd say the People had stumbled onto something, some sort of magic that was too much for them, and it had somehow tainted the vampire. But getting to the bottom of this mystery would be impossible. And besides, nobody had hired us to resolve the People's navigation issues.

"Of course, it could be a coincidence." Andrea shrugged. "We don't know anything about the woman who fainted, except that she was supposedly pregnant. We don't know what relationship she and Ghastek had prior to this mess. Maybe they went to breakfast together and ordered a bad omelet."

"That would be a hell of an omelet."

"I don't know, have you eaten at the Grease Trap lately? Their omelets are gray."

Technically the place was called the Greek Wrap, but nobody called it by its real name. The Grease Trap served breakfast 24/7, offered token wraps that had nothing to do with Greek cuisine, and openly admitted to having rat meat on the menu. It was the kind of place you went when your earthly troubles became too much for you and you were looking for a creative way to commit suicide.

"Why the hell would anyone be eating at the Grease Trap? I've seen flies die from buzzing by that place."

Andrea crossed her arms. "Oh, I don't know, probably because your career just ended and you are depressed and don't feel like breathing, let alone going out, but your body still needs food and that's the closest place to your apartment and they don't mind if you bring a giant dog with you."

"What, you couldn't find a Dumpster that was closer?"

Andrea glared at me. "What are you implying?"

"The Dumpster would have better food in it."

"Well, excuse me, Miss Fine Dining."

"Ghastek wouldn't be caught dead at the Grease Trap."

Andrea waved her arms. "It was just an example."

I glanced into the rearview mirror at Grendel. "What kind of brave canine companion lets his human eat at the Grease Trap? You are so fired."

Grendel waved his tail. Whatever horrors happened in his canine life, Grendel always bounced back with easy enthusiasm whenever some food made an appearance. A treat, a blanket in a nice warm house, an occasional pat on the head, and Grendel would be as happy as he could be.

If only people were so easy.

"Could you take a vampire away from its navigator?" Andrea asked.

I paused, thinking about it. "I could."

I could do a hell of a lot more than that. In the raw-power department, I blew even Ghastek off the scale. I could walk into the Casino right now and empty their stables, and all of the Masters of the Dead combined wouldn't be able to wrest control of their undead away from me. I wouldn't be able to do anything with my vampire horde except make it run around in a herd, but it would be a very impressive herd. Nobody except Andrea and Julie knew I could even pilot the undead, and if I had any hope of hiding, I had to keep it that way.

Of course, after the death of my aunt, hiding was a moot point.

"If I did that, the vamp would be under my control. It wouldn't be loose. I'd asked the journeymen and both of them said they couldn't get a lock on the vamp's mind. As if they had lost their ability to navigate. I have no idea how to make a vampire's mind disappear."

Andrea frowned. "Can Roland do it?"

"I don't know." Considering that my biological father had brought the vampires into being, nothing was out of the realm of possibility.

"Don't take this the wrong way, but why isn't he here?"

I glanced at Andrea. "Who, Roland?"

"Yes. It's been two months since someone killed his near-immortal sister. You'd think he'd send someone in to investigate by now."

"He's five thousand years old. To him two months is more like a couple of minutes." I grimaced. "Erra attacked the Guild, the Order, the Pack, the civilian businesses, the Temple, basically anything she ran across, which constitutes an act of terrorism of federal proportions. Right now nothing officially ties Erra to Roland. If he claimed responsibility for her behavior, the United States would feel compelled to do something about it. I have a feeling he doesn't want a full-blown conflict, not yet. He'll send someone down once the city cools off a bit, but when is anybody's guess. It might be tomorrow, although I doubt it, or it might be in a year. Hugh's absence bothers me more."

Hugh d'Ambray was my stepfather's successor and Roland's Warlord. Hugh had also developed an unhealthy interest in me after witnessing me break one of Roland's indestructible swords.

"I can solve that mystery for you," Andrea said. "I asked some very careful questions while in Virginia. Hugh is in South America."

"Why?"

"Nobody knows. He was seen leaving Miami with some of his Order of Iron Dogs goons in early January. The ship was bound for Argentina."

What the hell did Hugh want in Argentina?

"Any luck on the blood armor?" Andrea asked.

"No." My father possessed the ability to mold his own blood. He fashioned it into impenetrable armor and devastating weapons. I'd been able to control my blood a couple of times, but every time I'd done so, I was near death. "I've been practicing."

"And?"

"And nothing. I can feel the magic. I know it's there. It wants to be used. But I can't reach it. It's like there is a wall between me and the blood. If I'm really pissed off, I can make it spike into needles, but they only last a second or two."

"That sucks."

Control over blood was Roland's greatest power. Either I mastered it, or I needed to start working on my own gravestone. Except I hadn't the foggiest idea of how to go about learning the power, and nobody could teach me. Roland could do it; my aunt had done it; I had to learn to do it. There was some sort of trick to it, some secret that I didn't know.

"Hugh will come back eventually," Andrea said.

"When he does, I'll deal with it," I told her.

Hugh d'Ambray, preceptor of the Order of Iron Dogs, trained by Voron, enhanced by my father's magic.

Killing him without blood armor and blood weapons of my own would be a bitch.

We turned onto Johnson Ferry Road. After the Chattahoochee River decided to swell into a deep-water magic monster paradise, the bridge at Johnson Ferry became the fastest way to the west bank. Except today: carts and vehicles clogged the road. Donkeys brayed, horses whipped themselves with their tails, and a variety of odd vehicles belched, sneezed, and rattled, polluting the air with noise and gasoline fumes.

"What the hell?"

"Maybe the bridge is out." Andrea released her seat belt and slipped out. "I'll check."

She took off, breaking into an easy jog. I drummed my fingers on the steering wheel. If the bridge was out, we were screwed. The closest crossing was at the old Interstate 285, five miles away, and given that I 285 and most of the area directly surrounding it lay in ruins and required mountain-climbing equipment to conquer, it would take us at least half an hour to get there. Add another hour to wait for the ferry to carry us across the river and the morning was down the drain.

The cars roared; the beasts of burden neighed and snorted. Nobody moved an inch. I shifted the car into park and turned off the engine. Gas was expensive.

The driver of the cart in front of me leaned to the left, and I saw Andrea sprinting along the shoulder. She dashed to the car and jerked the door open. "Get your sword!"

I didn't have to get my sword—it was on my back. I pulled the keys out of the ignition, jumped out, and slapped the door shut, aborting Grendel's desperate lunge for freedom. "What's going on?"

"The Bridge Troll is out! It's rampaging on the road!"

"What happened?" Three years ago the Bridge Troll had wandered out of Sibley and onto the Johnson Ferry Bridge in an attempt to prove that the Universe indeed possessed a sense of humor. It'd proved really hard to kill and the mages had lured it under the bridge and put it under a sleep spell. The troll required magic to wake up, so during the tech he hibernated on his own, and during the magic waves the spell kept him in dreamland. The city had built a concrete bunker around him and he'd been impersonating Sleeping Beauty for years now. Unless the wards around the bunker failed somehow, he should've stayed sleeping.

Andrea took off down the shoulder. "The sleeping spell collapsed. He woke up, lay around for a while, and then decided to bash the bunker down and hulk out on the bridge. Come on, we've got to save the public."

And get paid. I chased her. "Reward?"

"A grand if we take him down before he finishes off the truck he's working on."

A shiny green truck hood shot out from behind the cars like a missile and crashed into a cart ten feet to the left of us. A dull guttural roar followed.

I put some effort into it and we sprinted along the line of cars to the bridge.

CHAPTER 6

———◆———

SIBLEY FOREST HAD STARTED OUT AS AN UPSCALE subdivision, tucked away into the bend of a small wooded area hugging Sope Creek before it emptied into the Chattahoochee River. In its heyday, the subdivision boasted around three hundred homes set among lush greenery and sporting price tags of half a million and up. It was a safe, pleasant, affluent neighborhood until the Shift, when the first magic wave kicked the world in the face.

As Downtown crumbled, Sibley Forest fell prey to the magic as well. It started with the river. About five years after the Shift, the Chattahoochee gained strength, eating at its banks and causing floods. Sope Creek quickly followed suit. The small tame forest bordering the subdivision held out for another year or two, and then magic bloomed deep in the heart of Sibley and caused a riot.

Trees claimed the manicured lawns, growing at an alarming rate, taking bites out of the subdivision. At first the homeowners' association cut the new growth down, and then they burned it, but the woods kept advancing, stretching to the sky practically overnight, until they swallowed the subdivision and Sibley became a true forest.

The trees continued their assault, trying to fight their way north, to join forces with the Chattahoochee National Forest. Animals came from deep within the woods, padding on soft paws and flashing big teeth. Odd things crawled out from the darkness beneath the tree roots and prowled the night looking for meat.

Finally the association gave up. Most of the owners fled. The remaining few spent small fortunes on wards, fences, and ammo. Now having an address in Sibley Forest meant you had money, you liked privacy, and you didn't mind weird shit on your lawn. Sometimes literally.

We turned down Twig Street. Ahead the forest rose like a massive wall tinted with pale green. Here and there flowers bloomed. The buds in the rest of Atlanta were barely waking up.

"Are you seeing this?"

Andrea bared her teeth. "I'm seeing it. I hate this place. It smells wrong and strange shit jumps out of the bushes and tries to gnaw your legs off."

The only thing I could smell was the troll blood staining our shoes. Folklore said two things about trolls: they turned to stone at dawn and they regenerated. The troll definitely hadn't gotten the petrifying memo, but regeneration he performed with huge success. We'd ended up herding the beast back into the ruined bunker and then keeping him there until the PAD arrived. But now we were a grand richer.

The road passed an enormous oak. Huge, its bark scarred, the massive tree towered over the street, and the Jeep careened and swayed as it rolled over the waves in the pavement made by its roots. The branches facing us shivered with narrow green leaves, still sticky from being rolled up in their buds, while the branches facing the forest were sheathed with bright green and clusters of long yellow threads, the oak flowers, busily sending pollen into the air.

A wooden sign sat by the oak roots. Letters cut the sign, sliced into the wood in sharp strokes.

**SIBLEY
LIONS & TIGERS & BEARS
OH MY.**

We rolled on, down the road. Brush rose on both sides of what once was a curvy subdivision street. In the weak light of the overcast afternoon, the woods looked surprisingly ethereal, as if ready to float away. Tall trees touched with green moss vied for space. Small clumps of flowers bloomed in bright patches here and there: yellow dandelions, purple henbits, tiny white blossoms in a nest of green—they looked like hairy bitter cress, but I wasn't sure. My knowledge of herbs mostly broke down into two categories: those I could use for medicinal or magic purposes and those I could eat in a pinch.

A wide island of forsythia bushes flowered on the left in a froth of vivid yellow, as if dipped into whipped sunshine. On the right, a nameless vine dripped from the branches, threatening to spill delicate lavender flowers. Downright idyllic. You half expected Pooh Bear to waddle out through the brush. Of course, knowing Sibley, Pooh would open a mouth full of deepwater teeth and try to take a chunk out of our tires.

Andrea flipped open Rene's manila folder. "It says here the dead guard's name is Laurent de Harven, thirty-two years old, hair brown, eyes gray, four-year stint in the Army, MSDU unit, six years as a cop down in sunny Orlando, Florida, and four years with the Red Guard. Promoted once, to the rank of Specialist. Expert swordsman, prefers tactical blades. Krav Maga, black belt, Dan five." Andrea whistled. "Tough guy to kill."

"What else have we got?"

"Let's see, Guard in Charge: Shohan Henderson, Marines eight years, Guard eleven years, expert in a list of weapons a mile long. We can also look forward to meeting Debra Abrams, the shift supervisor; Mason Vaughn; and Rigoberto 'Rig' Devara."

Andrea kept reading the notes. After fifteen minutes, it was clear that the four guards and their master sergeant could fend off an angry mob, would throw themselves into a bullet's path in the blink of an eye, and had records so stellar, they had to lock their résumés in a drawer at night, so the golden light streaming from the pages wouldn't keep them awake.

Directions said two rights, one left, then straight. The first two turns were easy enough; the left was a tight squeeze between two pines. Beyond the turn, tall bamboo hugged the road, forming a dense green tunnel. I steered the Jeep through it.

"Are you sure you know where you're going?" Andrea frowned.

"Would you like me to pull over and ask that bamboo for directions?"

"I don't know, do you think it will answer?"

We peered at the bamboo.

"I think it looks suspicious," Andrea said.

"Maybe there is a heffalump hiding in it."

Andrea stared at me.

"You know, heffalump? From Pooh Bear?"

"Where do you even get this shit?"

The bamboo ended abruptly, spitting us into a gravel drive-way leading up to a large modified A-frame. Wrapped in a railed porch with the roof extending all the way over the porch steps, the house looked like it had grown from the forest: stone foundation, dark cedar walls, brown roof. Shrubs hugged the porch steps. No unnatural colors, no ornaments or carvings.

"Look at all that window space. Built pre-Shift," Andrea murmured.

I nodded. I could see eight windows from where we sat; most were as tall as me and none had bars. Modern houses looked like bunkers. Any window larger than a bread box was barred.

I drove midway up the driveway and stopped with the engine idling. Good guards didn't prance around the perimeter making themselves into easy targets. They hid.

"A sniper in the attic," Andrea said.

It took me a second, and then I saw a dark shape, obscured by the gloom under the gable—a black outline of a rifle barrel stretching from the attic window.

I stepped out of the Jeep and leaned on the bumper. Andrea joined me.

"Pine, nine o'clock," I said.

Andrea glanced to where a man in a camo suit did his best to blend with the foliage. "Bushes at two." She inhaled deeply. "Also, someone is behind the Jeep."

"That makes three. The fourth is coming up at us from the left," I said.

"Should we go meet him?" Andrea arched an eyebrow.

"I think that's poison ivy over there. I vote we sit here and wait until they ask us for the code."

The bushes on the left parted and an older black man stepped out. His graying hair was cropped into a severe high-and-tight. Henderson, looking exactly like the picture in the file Andrea had shown me. Judging by the hard lines of his face and the flat look in his eyes, he'd left the Marines, but the Corps hadn't quite left him. The Red Guard shield patch on Henderson's shoulder had two red stripes—he'd been promoted twice as a sergeant, which made him Master Sergeant. Rene oversaw this job, but she probably oversaw others, too. Henderson quarterbacked only one job at a time, and while he had it, he owned it. His guys had screwed up and lost the body they were guarding. He looked like somebody had pissed in his sandbox, and he was none too pleased that we'd come to dig in the mess.

I nodded at him. "Afternoon, Master Sergeant."

"Names?"

"Daniels and Nash," Andrea said.

The master sergeant checked a small piece of paper. "Code?"

"Thirty-seven twenty-eight," I said.

"Name is Henderson. Don't let the 'master sergeant' muddle your thinking. I work for my living. You're clear to proceed. Park at the top of the driveway."

We got back into the Jeep and I pulled up to the house. Henderson trotted behind us and up to the doors.

I stepped out of the vehicle. "Where is de Harven's body?"

"In the workshop."

We followed Henderson behind the house.

The workshop occupied a wooden shed large enough to contain a small apartment. The garage-sized wooden gate stood ajar.

Henderson halted. "In there."

I stepped inside.

Counters ran along the wall, filled with tools and metal junk. Plastic bins filled with screws rose in towers next to boxes of lug nuts, bolts, and assorted metal trash that would've been more at home in a metal jungle lining the bottom of the Honeycomb Gap. On the left counter, delicate glass tools of unknown purpose vied for space with a jeweler's loupe and tiny pliers. On the right, metalworking tools were spread out: angle grinders of assorted sizes for cutting metal, shears, hammers, saws, a large lathe with a metal cylinder still fixed on it. A delicate pattern of glyphs decorated the left end of the cylinder—someone, probably Kamen, had begun to apply the complex metallic lattice but hadn't finished.

A nude male body hung from the rafters in the middle of the shop, suspended by a thick chain, likely attached to a hook that bit into the corpse's back. His head drooped to the side. Long

dark hair spilled from his scalp down onto his chest, framing
a face frozen by death into a contorted mask. Light gray eyes
bulged from their sockets. The man's mouth gaped open, the
bloodless lips baring his teeth. Panic and surprise rolled into
one. *Hello, Laurent.*

I dropped my backpack and pulled a Polaroid camera from it.
Magic had a way of screwing up digital cameras. Sometimes it
wiped the memory cards clean, sometimes you would get noise,
and occasionally the pictures came out perfect. I wasn't willing
to play Russian roulette with my evidence. The Polaroid was
hideously expensive, but the pictures were instant.

Andrea raised her eyebrows. "Look at you, all high-speed."

"Yeah, you'd think I was a detective or something."

Andrea held her hand out. "You'll jinx it."

I put the camera into her hand and crouched, trying to get a
look at the floor under the body.

"No drip?" Andrea asked.

"Nope. You smell anything? Decomp, blood . . ."

She wrinkled her nose. "Cayenne pepper. The place reeks of
it. It drowns out everything else."

Odd.

I dropped to all fours and bent lower. A faint line of rusty
powder crossed the floorboards. I leaned over, trying to get a better look. The line ran into the counter on the right and touched the
wall on the left. A telltale spatter stain marked the wall boards.

I pointed at it. "Urine."

Andrea craned her neck and raised the camera. "Such glam-
orous jobs we have. Taking pictures of pee stains."

I turned my head. An identical stain marked the other wall,
exactly across from the first one. "That's why we do it. For the
glamour."

"A shaman?" Andrea asked.

"Possibly."

All living things generated magic, and humans were no exception. The magic was in the blood, in the saliva, in tears, and in
urine. Body liquids could be used in any number of ways. I sealed
wards with my blood. Roland made weapons and armor out of
his. But urine usually pointed to a more primal magic. Shamans,
witches, and some neo-pagan cult practitioners all used urine.
People who considered themselves close to nature. It tied in with

animals marking their territory and a number of other primal things.

The cayenne line looked like some sort of ward to me, and the presence of urine confirmed it. Someone had marked a boundary on the floor and sealed it with their body fluid, probably to contain something. What was anybody's guess at this point. With the magic down I sensed nothing, not a drop of power.

I stepped over the cayenne line and padded forward, pulling Slayer from the back sheath and staying to the right to give Andrea a clear shot.

The camera clicked. A moment and the Polaroid slid from it with a faint whirr. "One more . . ." Andrea murmured.

"All that glassware and the delicate instruments on the counters and nothing is broken. You'd think with all his training Laurent would've put up a fight."

"Maybe he knew his attacker and didn't view him as a threat until it was too late."

That would make Adam Kamen or another guard the prime suspect. A bodyguard wouldn't expect to be assaulted by a man he guarded or his own buddies. Everybody else would've been met with violence.

Laurent's corpse showed no wounds except for a long black scar that cut his body from his chest down to his groin: a vertical line that split into three at the navel, like an upside-down imprint of a crow foot or like some perverse peace symbol torn out of its circle. Unusual cut. Looked almost like a rune.

The camera clicked, flashing, once, twice . . .

The magic hit, rolling over us like an invisible tsunami. Andrea raised the camera and pushed the button. No flash. Not even a click. She glanced at the camera in disgust. "Damn it."

The black scar shivered.

I took a step back.

A faint shudder ran through the body. The black line trembled, its edges rising, and boiled into movement. *Oh shit.*

"Kate!"

"I see it."

The body swayed. The chains creaked, louder and louder. Power swelled, straining within the corpse.

I backed away to the ward.

The corpse's stomach bulged, the black line swelling.

I stepped over the cayenne pepper line. Magic sparked on my skin.

The black scar burst.

Tiny bodies shot at us and fell harmlessly on the other side of the line, drenching the floor in a dark torrent. Not a single speck of black made it over to us.

Behind us, Henderson exhaled. "What the hell is that?"

"Ants," I said.

The black flood swirled, twisting, slower and slower. One by one the small bodies stopped moving. A moment and the floor was completely still.

Dead ants. A five-gallon bucket full of them strewn all over the floor.

The body rocked back and forth. All of the man's flesh had vanished. His skeleton was stripped bare and the skin hung on the bone frame like a deflated balloon.

"Ooookay," Andrea said. "That's one of the freakiest things I've ever seen."

WHEN FACED WITH THE FREAKIEST THING YOU'VE ever seen, the best strategy is to divide and conquer. Andrea decided to m-scan the scene, while I took the enviable task of interviewing Henderson. He didn't look pleased.

I maneuvered him to a steel patio table sitting between the house and the workshop. We sat in the hard metal chairs. From here both of us could watch the workshop and the driveway, where Andrea prepared to swipe the m-scanner out of the Jeep and Grendel prepared to escape the moment she swung open the door.

The portable m-scanner resembled a sewing machine covered in clockwork vomit. It detected residual magic and spat the result out as a graph of colors: green for shapeshifter, purple for undead, blue for human. It was neither precise nor infallible, and reading an m-scan was more art than science, but it was still the best diagnostic tool we had. It also weighed close to eighty pounds.

Andrea opened the Jeep door and thrust her hand in. Grendel lunged and collided with her palm. The impact knocked him back. Andrea grabbed the m-scanner, yanked it out of the

Jeep, and shut the door in Grendel's furry face. The attack poodle lunged at the window and let out a long despondent howl. Andrea turned and headed to the workshop, carrying the eighty-pound scanner with a light spring in her step, as if it were a picnic basket. Shapeshifter strength came in handy. Too bad the cost of Lyc-V infection was so high.

Henderson watched Andrea walk across the yard. "A shapeshifter?"

"Yes." *You got a problem with that?*

"Good." Henderson nodded. "We could use her nose."

I took out my notepad and my pen. "How many people are assigned to this detail?" Rene had said twelve, but it never hurt to check.

"Twelve, including me."

"Three shifts of four guards, eight hours each?"

"Yes. Day, night, and graveyard."

I wrote it down. "Which shift do you work?"

"I alternate between evening and graveyard. I worked the evening shift yesterday, fourteen hundred to twenty-two hundred."

Figured. Most trouble happened after dark, and Henderson struck me as the type of man who wanted to meet trouble head on and punch it in the teeth. And the one time it did show up, he'd guessed wrong and missed it.

"When was the body discovered?"

"Oh six hundred at shift change." Henderson crossed his arms. The good master sergeant plainly didn't like the way my questions were going. Strange. Rene had already given me most of this information, so why did talking about it twist his panties in a bunch?

"Could you walk me through how the body was found?"

"Each shift has a shift sergeant. At five fifty-five a.m., day shift sergeant Julio Rivera and graveyard shift sergeant Debra Abrams made a routine check on the subject in the workshop."

"Why the workshop? Why not the house?"

If Henderson's face could harden any more, it would crack. "Because the man was last seen entering the workshop."

If I still had my Order ID, this entire conversation would've gone a lot smoother. The ID commanded instant respect, especially from a former soldier like Henderson. His world broke into two camps, pro and amateur, and right now he pegged me for a hired gun of the second category. Rene had ordered him to cooperate and he was a company man, so he answered my questions, but he didn't exactly recognize my right to ask them.

"Did Adam often work through the night?" I asked.

"Night, day, morning, whenever it struck him. Sometimes he'd work all day, sleep for two hours, and go back to work, and sometimes he'd do nothing for two days."

Aha. "When was the last time he was seen?"

Muscles played along the master sergeant's jaw. "Three hours past midnight."

I closed the notebook. "If I had an erratic subject who wandered to and fro between the workshop and the house whenever the inspiration struck him, I'd have my guys checking on him every hour. Just to make sure he didn't break perimeter and blunder off into Sibley in a creative daze. And I don't even have two stripes on my sleeve."

Henderson hit me with a hard stare. It was a heavy stare, but it had nothing on looking into Curran's golden irises when he was pissed off.

I held his gaze. "My job isn't to pass judgment. My job is to find Adam Kamen and his device. That's all. Whatever happened here is between you and your chain of command, but I need to know what it was so I can move on. If you make it hard for me, I'll go through you."

He leaned forward an inch. "Think you can?"

"Try me."

Henderson was a large man, and he was used to people backing down when he pushed. He was a guard and a soldier, but he wasn't a killer. Oh, he would shoot back if someone shot at him first, and he might stab you if it came to it, because it was his job, but he wouldn't slice a man's throat and step over his twitching body while the hot blood spurted on the ground. I would. And it wouldn't bother me much. In fact, I'd been out of action for over two months now. I missed it, missed the edge and the fight.

We stared at each other.

I would kill you in an instant with no hesitation.

A slow recognition rolled over Henderson's face. "So it's like that," he said.

That's right.

Henderson narrowed his eyes. "Why would Rene bring your kind in?"

"What kind is that?"

"You're not a soldier, and you're not a PI."

"I used to be an agent of the Order." I nodded at the workshop. "And she is a retired master-at-arms knight. Rene brought us in because it's not our first rodeo. What happened to your shift, Master Sergeant? This is the last time I'm asking."

Henderson drew himself upright. He wanted to send me packing. I saw it in his face. He thought about it, but he must've glimpsed something he didn't like in my eyes, because he unhinged his jaw. "The graveyard shift fell asleep."

"All four guards?"

Henderson nodded. "Except de Harven."

"At their posts?"

Henderson nodded again.

Crap. "How long?"

"Approximately from zero four until the shift change."

Two hours. More than enough time to kidnap a man. Or to slice his throat, bury him in the forest, and steal his magic project. How the hell did de Harven fit into it? Did he surprise the thieves? Of course, Adam Kamen could've killed his über-bodyguard and bolted with the goods. Because he was secretly a ninja, adept at mortal combat and vanishing into thin air. Yes, that was it. Case solved.

Trained Red Guardsmen didn't just fall asleep on their own for two hours in the middle of their shift. Magic or drugs had to be involved. Even so, three of the guards passed out while de Harven went into the workshop. And why wasn't he impersonating Sleeping Beauty? "Where are the guards now?"

"Both graveyard and day shifts are waiting by the house. I figured you'd want to talk to them." Henderson paused. "There is more. We've searched the area."

"Found something?"

"We found something, alright." Henderson rose and strode farther behind the house. I followed. A large Humvee waited, parked under an oak. The canvas top was pulled back, exposing the rear bed containing two rucksacks and a plastic bin. Henderson set the bin on the ground and opened it with careful precision, as if he expected a pissed-off copperhead inside.

A simple rectangle of pale cotton lay inside the bin, displaying an assortment of herbs. Green poppy heads, hops cones, silver stems of lavender with purple petals, catnip, valerian, and a thick pale root, curved almost like a man in a fetal position, his legs bent at the knees. Mandragora. Rare, expensive, and powerful.

Traces of fine brown powder dusted the fabric. I touched it, licked my fingertip, and the familiar peppery taste nipped at my tongue. Kava kava root, ground to dust. There was enough herbal power here to put a small army to sleep.

I'd seen this before. The herbs had been combined with several pounds of dried kava kava powder, bound in cloth, treated with some heavy-duty magic, and then sealed. At the right moment the owner of this magic bundle tossed it on the ground, breaking the seal, and the pressurized magic exploded, spreading kava kava dust through the air. Instant knockout for anyone with lungs in a quarter-mile radius. They called it a sleep bomb.

The sleep bombs were invented shortly after the very first magic wave as a means of crowd control to peacefully subdue the panicked population during the Three-Month Riots. Back then magic was a new and untried force, and there was some question as to whether the sleep bombs would work. Unfortunately it was soon discovered that when the cops dropped the sleep bombs into the crowd, they worked so well that some of the rioters never woke up. The bombs were outlawed now.

Making a sleep bomb required a crapload of magic power, expertise, and some serious money. The best mandragora came from Europe, and kava kava had to be imported from Hawaii, Fiji, or Samoa. That cost a solid chunk of change. Adam had investors with deep pockets. Perhaps one of them had decided not to share the candy with the rest of the class. Sleep-bomb the guards, kidnap Adam, grab the device, keep all profits for yourself. Good plan.

I needed to get a list of those investors.

I glanced at the guts of the sleep bomb spread out on the cloth. All those herbs packed a magic wallop even when sealed. "Rene said this place was warded."

Henderson nodded. "Twice. The inner ward starts at the top of the driveway and protects the house and the workshop. The outer starts at the bottom of the driveway and circles the property."

"Are we inside the inner ward right now?"

"Yes."

"What's the threshold?" The defensive spells varied by intensity. Some let nothing through; some let specific magic through.

"If you're magic and not keyed to it, you can't pass," Henderson said. "It's a level-four ward."

The level-IV ward would keep out pretty much anything. "So a shapeshifter wouldn't be able to pass through it, correct?"

"Correct," Henderson confirmed.

"We just watched Andrea walk to the car and back. The magic is up. Where is the ward?"

We stared at the driveway.

Henderson pulled a chain from around his neck. A small piece of quartz hung from the metal next to his dog tags. He marched to the driveway and held out his hand. The stone dangled from the chain. Henderson stared at it for a long moment, swore, and turned down the driveway. I followed. At the foot of the gravel road Henderson waved the crystal again. It remained dull.

Henderson looked at me. Wards were persistent spells and they didn't just go missing. It was possible to break a ward—I'd done it a few times—but wards began to regenerate almost immediately. They absorbed magic from the environment. If the wards had been broken, they should've started rebuilding themselves as soon as the new magic wave came. We were standing right at the ward boundary and I felt nothing. It was as if the defensive spells had never been there in the first place. That just didn't happen.

Besides, having your ward shattered felt like a cannon fired inside your skull. Sleep bomb or not, if someone had burst the wards, the guards would've awakened.

"The wards are gone," I said. Kate Daniels, Master of the Obvious.

"Looks that way," Henderson said.

"Were the wards present last night?"

"Yes," Henderson said.

"Sleep bombs emit magic even when sealed. You can't carry one through a level-four ward, so it must've been brought in during tech. Did Adam have any visitors?"

"No."

Muscles played along Henderson's jaw. I didn't need to spell it out. The person who had dropped five grand worth of rare herbs onto the inventor's lawn was wearing a Red Guard patch on his sleeve. And since everybody else was off in dreamland, that left Laurent de Harven as the most likely culprit. The Red Guard had a mole in it, and since Rene had handpicked people for this assignment, the buck stopped with her. She would have steam coming out of her ears.

That still didn't explain what had happened to the wards.

Andrea emerged from the shed, carrying an m-scanner printout in her hand.

"We have a problem," I told her.

"More than one." She handed me the paper. A wide strip of cornflower blue sliced across the paper, interrupted by a sharp narrow spike of such pale blue, it seemed almost silver. *Human divine.* That was an unmistakable magic profile, one of the first everyone learned when studying m-scans. De Harven had been sacrificed.

HENDERSON PACED BACK AND FORTH AT THE TOP OF the driveway. The three remaining guards from the graveyard shift stood in front of him at parade rest. Judging by Henderson's face, he was unleashing an ass-chewing of colossal proportions. Both Debra and Mason Vaughn, a stocky redhead, looked pissed off and embarrassed. Rig Devara did his best to pretend to be pissed off and embarrassed. Mostly he looked bored. According to the file, he was the most junior of his shift. Usually shit rolled down the hill, but by the time it got to him, there would be nothing left.

Andrea and I watched from the porch. Henderson had a lot of frustration to vent. He wouldn't be coherent anytime soon.

"We have a dead body and the weather is warming up," I said. "We have to figure out what to do with de Harven or he'll go ripe."

"What do you mean, what to do with him? We'll just call it in to Maxine and . . . oh, fuck it." Andrea grimaced.

Yeah. The telepathic Order secretary, who conveniently took care of minor details like dead bodies, was no longer available. Welcome to the real world. If we called it in to the cops, they would quarantine the body. Neither one of us was law enforcement, and getting access to the corpse would be next to impossible. We might as well load our evidence into a rocket and send it to the moon.

I started toward the house. "If the phone is working, I'm going to call Teddy Jo."

"You're calling Thanatos? The guy with the flaming sword?"

"He is Thanatos only part of the time. The rest of the time he's Teddy Jo, who isn't that bad of a guy. He bought a mortuary freezer a few months ago for a job he had to do. It's sitting in his shed." I knew this because the last time I stopped by Teddy's place, he bellyached for an hour about how much the damn thing had cost him. "I'm going to make him an offer and see if I can take it off his hands. I think he might have a body bag or two to throw in with the freezer."

Andrea sighed. "I'll start processing the house."

The phone did work and Teddy Jo answered on the second ring. I had once read that every day offered a new lesson. The lesson for today, among other things, seemed to be that bargaining with the Greek angel of death should be avoided by any means, because it cost you an arm and a leg.

"Seven thousand," Teddy Jo's gruff voice announced over the phone.

"Four."

"Six five."

"Four."

"Kate, the thing cost me five grand. I've got to make a profit."

"First, it's used."

"Now look here," Teddy Jo growled. "It's not a Cadillac. It's a body freezer. The value doesn't drop because you drive it off the lot."

"I don't know what sort of bodies you stuck in there, Teddy. You might have put a leucrocuta in there. Those things stink."

"It's not like the dead gonna care. They can't smell shit, and they themselves ain't gonna get to smelling any better."

He had a point, but I didn't have to admit it. "Four five."

"How's the business going, Kate?"

Where was he heading with this? "Business is going fine."

"The way I heard it, you ain't doing shit. So the fact that you're calling me about a body freezer says to me that you suddenly have a body in dire need of freezing. That means you finally landed a client. Now then, about four minutes after death, the body cells experience oxygen deprivation, which raises the level of carbon dioxide in the blood, simultaneously decreasing the pH, making the body environment more acidic. At this point the enzymes begin to cannibalize the cells, causing them to rupture, releasing nutrients. This is called autolysis or self-digestion, and the more enzymes and water organs contain, the faster they degrade. Organs like the liver and brain go first. Before you know it, your body is putrefied, the skin sloughs off, and all of your evidence has degraded down to nothing. So you've got to ask yourself, is it worth it to keep arguing with me and risk losing the body and the client, or should you just give me my damn six thousand dollars?"

God damn it. "If you know that I haven't got any clients, then you probably know that I can't afford to pay you through the roof for the freezer."

Teddy Jo fell silent for a long second. "Five grand. My last offer. Take it or leave it, Kate."

"Three grand now, with two one-thousand-dollar payments within sixty days and delivery to my office."

"Business is so bad you've resorted to robbing honest folks now, is it?"

"Teddy, it's a damn body freezer. It's not doing you any good in your shed and people aren't lining up around the corner to take it off your hands."

"Fine. Screw it."

Finally. Something went my way today. "That was a nice bit with the autolysis. Been going to night school in your spare time?"

"I'm an angel of *death*. I don't need night school, woman. You should just give up on this detective shit and start killing people for a living. It's simple, honest work, and you ain't got the brains for anything else."

"Yeah, yeah. I love you too, Teddy."

I hung up. The down payment on the freezer would take a big bite out of my remaining five grand, and I had to keep money on hand to work the case. I could always ask the Pack to up my budget.

I'd rather eat dirt.

CHAPTER 7

———

IT TOOK US FOUR HOURS TO PROCESS THE SCENE. WE dusted the workshop for fingerprints and lifted enough partials to use up a whole roll of tape. Crawling on my hands and knees looking for evidence and taking samples of the urine stains did a number on me. My knee was a trouble magnet—first my aunt ripped it up, then the marathon of fights to the death that made me the Pack's alpha female had nearly done it in. I'd hobbled around with a cane for a month, a circumstance aggravated by the fact that I could only use said cane in my quarters, because doing it in plain view of the Pack telegraphed weakness. Now the knee had developed a steady annoying ache, and I had this absurd feeling that if only I could jam something sharp in there, the pain would go away.

We finished the workshop and walked the house. It was a spacious log cabin, all clean honey-colored wood and oversized windows. Adam led a simple life. I found enough clothes for a couple of weeks and a few dog-eared books, mostly engineering, physics, and magic theory. Andrea cataloged the groceries and reported lots of peanut butter and jam in the fridge. The Red Guardsmen's cabin came equipped with cooking utensils and an assortment of pots and pans hanging from the hooks in a wooden frame. The layer of dust on the pans told me they hadn't been touched in a while.

I found a picture of a young blond woman by Adam's bed. She was looking over the ocean, her face serious and tinted with resignation and sadness. Adam's wife. I bagged it and put it into our Jeep.

We took everyone's statements, made everyone sign everything, and drove back through Sibley's twisted roads onto Johnson Ferry. The traffic mess at the bridge had dissolved. An MSDU Humvee painted in blotches of slate gray and charcoal sat on the shoulder. Next to it a short, stocky man with dark brown hair packed an m-scanner into a van with PAD written on the side. The man's red hoodie read WIZARD AT LARGE.

I pulled over to the shoulder.

"Do you know him?" Andrea asked.

"Luther Dillon. He used to moonlight for the Guild a couple of years back. Hang on a second, I'll be right back."

I slipped out of the car and walked back along the shoulder, hands in plain view.

Luther saw me and sighed dramatically. "Stay away. At least three feet."

"Why?"

"The Order fired you for screwing up. Hence, you are besmirched. It might rub off on me."

If Andrea wanted to kill Ted, she would have to stand in line. "I didn't get fired, I quit. And considering that I wrapped up your troll for you, I expected a warmer reception."

Luther bowed and clapped. "Bravo! Bravissimo! Encore, encore! Was that kind of what you were hoping for?"

"That will do."

From where I stood, I could see the path leading down the slope and under the bridge to the troll's bunker. "How did it go?"

"He's sleeping like a baby." Luther shut the van's door and leaned against the vehicle. "Ate two hours out of yours truly's already-busy schedule, too."

"The least you can do since your wards failed."

Luther pushed from the car. "My wards don't fail. They're gone." He made a fist and snapped his fingers open. "Poof! No residue, no trace, nothing. Never seen anything like it. It's as if . . ."

"They had never been there," I finished. Déjà vu.

Luther focused on me like a pointer on a pheasant. "You know something."

When in trouble, stall. "Me?"

"You. Tell me."

"Can't." First, the wards around Adam's workshop. Then here. Crossing the bridge was the fastest way out of Sibley.

"Kate, stop screwing around. If someone is going around the city yanking wards out of the ground, I need to know about it."

"I can't, Luther. Client confidentiality."

"You want me to haul you in for questioning?" Luther said. "Because I'll do it. I'll do it right now. Watch me. I know people who will gently persuade you to be forthcoming."

I looked at him. "You really need to work on your threats. I can't tell if you're threatening me or inviting me for tea."

"The two aren't mutually exclusive. One cup of the tea at the station and you will tell me everything you know out of sheer self-preservation." He held his hand out and bent his fingers back and forth in the universal "bring it on" gesture. "Out with it. Or else."

Andrea stepped out of the Jeep and leaned against the bumper. Apparently she felt I needed backup. If we were lucky, Grendel wouldn't tear through plastic and devour de Harven's corpse in Hector's back.

"Luther, to haul someone in, you have to have probable cause, which you don't."

A faint scrape of a foot against dirt came from behind the van. I leaned to glance around Luther and saw a man walking up the path from the water. He wore black pants, black boots, a gray shirt, and a black tactical vest over it. Black aviator shades hid his eyes. Add dark blond hair cropped short and a clean-shaven jaw, and you had yourself a genuine Agent of Law Enforcement. Shane Andersen, knight of the Order.

Luther sighed.

"You think he's got 'government badass' tattooed on his chest?" I murmured.

A faint grimace skewed Luther's mouth. "And 'I'd tell you but I'd have to kill you' on his ass."

Luther wasn't hard to irritate, but there was some genuine hate there. "What did he do?"

Luther glanced at me. "He called me 'support.' I'm not support; I'm the damn primary on this case. Without me, they'd still be trying to mince the troll into a meat pie."

Shane hero-swaggered his way to the top of the path and stopped before us. "Hello, Kate."

"Hi."

He glanced at Luther. "Is she bothering you?"

"No."

"Mm-hm." Shane lowered his glasses on his nose and gave me his version of a severe stare.

I leaned a little toward Luther. "Is this the part where I faint in fear?"

Luther bit his lip. "He might also accept falling to your knees and holding your hands in humble supplication. Makes it easier for him to slap the cuffs on."

"Your presence here is a distraction," Shane said, obviously savoring every word. "You're keeping a PAD officer from his duties. Move along, Kate. There is nothing to see here."

Asshole. Let's see, two MSDU vehicles, cops down by the river. Too many witnesses. My brain served up a headline: BEAST LORD'S MATE PUNCHES KNIGHT OF THE ORDER IN MOUTH, KNOCKS OUT FOUR TEETH. Yeah, not today.

"Sorry, Luther, I've been told to move along." I shrugged. "Got to go. I'll call you if anything. Oh, and, Andersen, if you're still having trouble with that bug up your ass, let me know. I know a guy—he'll pull it right out."

I turned to the Jeep. Just in time, too—Andrea started walking toward me, focused on Shane like a bird of prey. Time to get the hell out of here.

"It's a shame about your being kicked out of the Order, Daniels," Shane called. "Losing your home like that, too. I always thought you were capable. I know people who could've helped. If you'd just come to me, I could've made things easier on you. Life is tough, but at least you wouldn't have to prostitute yourself to that creature."

"Dude." Luther exhaled.

Andrea picked up speed, her eyes furious. I had to get her out of here now. She was barely holding on to the edge of reason as it was. If she pulled her gun on him, she'd go to jail, and not even the Pack lawyers would get her out.

"Being in the Order doesn't make you untouchable, Shane."
I kept walking.

"Women sell themselves because they're starving, because
they've got kids to feed, because they are addicted," Shane said.
"I don't condone it, but I understand it. You sold yourself for
four walls on Jeremiah Street. Was it worth climbing into bed
with an animal every night?"

I ran into Andrea. She tried to push past me and I blocked
her. "No."

"Step aside."

"Not now, not here."

"Hello, Nash," Shane called. "You want me to box your guns
and send them to your apartment? Save you the shame of coming to the chapter?"

Andrea gripped my arm.

"Later," I told her. "Too many people now."

Andrea clenched her teeth.

"Later."

She turned on her heel and we went back to the Jeep. I slid
Hector back into the traffic.

"That bastard," Andrea squeezed out.

"He's a loudmouth who likes talking shit. There is no law
against being an asshole. Let him hide behind his shield for
now. That's all he can do."

Andrea squeezed her hand into a hard fist. "If I still had
my ID . . ."

"You would be the best of friends."

She glared at me.

"It's true," I told her.

She didn't answer.

The first ten years of her life, Andrea was the punching bag
of her bouda clan. She'd spent the last sixteen making sure she
would not feel powerless again. She had never walked the street
without the added weight of the Order's ID. She was used to
being a good guy, respected and even admired for what she did
and who she was. She was never pushed around by anyone with
a badge, because she carried one. But every choice had consequences, and now these consequences were hitting her right in
the face.

"We can't even do anything to that worm," she ground out.

"Not now."

She turned to me. "I don't think I can do this."

"You can," I told her. "You're a survivor."

"You don't know what it's like."

I laughed. It sounded cold. "You're right, I have no idea what it's like to take shit from people I could kill with my eyes closed."

Andrea exhaled. "Okay. Sorry. That was a stupid thing to say. I just . . . Argh."

"In the end, Shane doesn't matter," I said. "As long as you avoid him and don't give him an opportunity to hurt you, he's powerless to do anything except lather up some spit. However, if someone were to do something stupid, like shoot at him from some roof one night, we'd have real problems."

"I was a knight," Andrea said. "I'm not just going to start shooting every dickhead who mouths off to me."

"Just making sure."

"Besides, if I shot him, I'd do it so nobody could trace it back to me. I'd shoot him somewhere remote, his head would explode like a melon, and they would never find his body. He would just vanish."

This would be a long climb uphill, I just knew it.

FIFTEEN MINUTES LATER WE MADE IT TO THE OFFICE and met Teddy Jo, who was waiting with the freezer in the parking lot. I gave Teddy his down payment, we wrestled the freezer into the back room, and then I spent an hour chanting preservation spells and laying down wards just in case de Harven decided to rise in the middle of the night and have himself another ant party.

It was eight o'clock by the time I turned off the highway to the narrow dirt road leading to the Keep. I was tired and dirty, my leg hurt like a sonovabitch, and I hadn't eaten all day. You'd almost think I was back to working for the Order or something. Except I was working for myself.

I could relate to Andrea. My life had been much easier with the Order ID, too; I could bully people into answering my questions, I had access to criminal records, and if I did end up with a body full of ants, the Order would take care of it for me.

Still, I wouldn't trade my small office for anything in the world.

We had a lot of evidence, and none of it made much sense. De Harven had dropped the sleep bomb. That much we knew. The kava kava residue on his hands confirmed it, and we found a gas mask in the corner of the workshop.

He'd deployed the sleep bomb and gone into the workshop. Then something had happened that concluded with his death and Kamen and the device disappearing. Perhaps de Harven had tried to steal the device or harm Adam, and Adam had retaliated by killing him. Except Adam Kamen looked like he would have a hard time baiting a fishhook, while de Harven was a trained killer.

Suppose Adam did somehow best de Harven. Why take the time to sacrifice him? Besides, Adam's résumé had 'magical theorist' written all over it. Guys like him built complex devices. They wouldn't urinate on the walls, turn the flesh of their attacker into ants, and then disappear into the night with a device weighing upward of three hundred pounds. Pulling off that kind of magic meant complete dedication to the deity to which the sacrifice had been offered. Devotion meant constant worship, and worship required ritual. The guards had never even seen Adam pray.

The cut on de Harven's stomach bothered me. An inverted crow's foot. It had to be a rune. There was no anatomical reason to cut the body that way, and runes were associated with neopagan cults and often employed in shamanistic rituals, which was consistent with the magic at the scene. Runes predated the Latin alphabet. Ancient Germanic and Nordic tribes used them for everything, from writing down their sagas and foretelling the future to bringing the dead back to life.

Runology wasn't my strongest suit, but this particular rune I knew very well. Algiz, one of the oldest runes, associated with sedge grass, and Thor, and Heimdall, and a number of other things depending on who you asked and which runic alphabet you used. Algiz had a universal meaning: protection. As a ward, it was completely reactive. It served as a warning or provided a defense, but in any case, Algiz wasn't going to do anything to you until you messed with it. It was the most responsible way for a runic magic user to protect his property, because Algiz would never attack first.

Why put it on a body? It didn't protect the body; it didn't warn anyone of anything. I'd been breaking my brain against it since I had seen it, and I'd come up with nothing. Zip, zilch, zero. And none of the gods from the Norse pantheon were strongly associated with ants.

Something was going on here, something bigger and uglier than it appeared. The fear in Rene's eyes bothered me. It started as a mild concern when I first saw it, getting worse and worse as the day progressed, and now it had matured into a full-blown anxiety. *You have a lot of friends, Kate. You have a lot to lose.*

Voron's voice surfaced from the depths of my memory. *"I told you so."*

I took a deep breath and tried to exhale my worry. Too late for warnings now. I was Curran's mate and the female alpha of the Pack. The welfare of fifteen hundred shapeshifters was now my responsibility. Whatever storm was brewing in Atlanta, I'd find it and fight it. If it was the price of being with Curran, then I would pay it.

He was worth it.

The Jeep rolled over the huge roots. The road needed clearing again—the thick trees crowded it, like soldiers trying to bar passage to intruders. Magic hated all things technology and gnawed its monuments down to nubs, turning concrete and mortar to dust. Skyscrapers, tall bridges, massive stadiums— the bigger they were, the quicker they fell. The same force that had turned the Georgia Dome to rubble also nourished the forests. Trees sprouted here and there, growing at record speed, as nature scrambled to reclaim the crumbling ruins that were once proud achievements of technological civilization. Underbrush spread, vines stretched, and before you knew it, a fifty-year-old forest rose where ten years ago were only thin saplings, roads, and gas stations. It made life difficult for most people, but the shapeshifters loved it.

The Pack's humble abode really deserved a better name. "Keep" didn't do it justice. It sat in the clearing among the new forest, northeast of the city, rising against the massive trees like a foreboding gray tower of doom. The tower went down for many levels underground. Not satisfied, the shapeshifters kept building on to the Keep, adding walls, new wings, and smaller towers, turning it into a full-fledged citadel of Pack supremacy. As I maneuvered the Pack Jeep to it, I couldn't help but note that the structure was beginning to resemble a castle. Maybe we needed a neon sign to brighten things up. **MONSTER LAIR, WIPE YOUR PAWS AND CHECK YOUR SILVER AT THE DOOR.**

I drove the Jeep through the massive gates, parked in the inner yard, went inside through a small door, and walked down the narrow claustrophobic hallway. The narrow passages were one of Curran's defensive measures. If you tried to storm the Keep and broke through the gate and the reinforced doors, you would have to fight through a hallway just like this one—three, four men at a time. A single shapeshifter could hold off an army here for hours.

The hallway led me to the stairway of a million steps. My leg screamed in protest. I sighed and started climbing. I just had to keep from limping. Limping showed weakness, and I didn't need any enterprising, career-motivated shapeshifters trying to challenge me for dominance right about now.

I had once mentioned my desire for an elevator, and His Majesty asked me if I would like a flock of doves to carry me up to my quarters so my feet wouldn't have to touch the ground. We were sparring at the time and I kicked him in the kidney in retaliation.

Eight o'clock equaled about two p.m. in shapeshifter terms. The Keep was full. People bobbed their heads at me as I passed. Most of them I didn't know. The Pack counted fifteen hundred shapeshifters. I was learning the names but it took time.

By the second flight of stairs, something started grinding in my knee. I had a choice: either I had it fixed now or it would fail me the next time I had a serious fight. My imagination painted a lovely picture of me lunging into battle and my leg snapping like a toothpick. Great.

I stopped on the third floor and not-limped my way to Doolittle's medical ward. The woman in the front room took one look at me and ran back to get the doctor. I landed in the chair and exhaled. Sitting was good.

The double doors opened and Doolittle emerged from the depths of the hospital, looking fussy. In his fifties, dark-skinned, his hair cut short, Doolittle radiated kind patience. Even if you were near death, the moment you looked into his eyes, you knew that he would take care of you and somehow everything was going to be all right. In the past year I had been near death quite a few times, and every time Doolittle had fixed me. He was hands down the best medmage I'd ever encountered.

He also carried on like a frazzled mother hen. That was why normally I avoided him at all costs.

Doolittle looked me over, probably searching for signs of bleeding and shards of broken bones poking through my skin. "What's the problem?"

"Nothing major. My knee is hurting a little."

Doolittle peered at me. "The very fact that you are here means that you're on the verge of fainting."

"It's really not that bad."

Doolittle's fingers probed my knee. Pain shot into my leg. I clenched my teeth.

"Heaven help me." The good doctor heaved a sigh. "What did you do?"

"Nothing."

Doolittle took my hand, turned it palm up, and sniffed my fingers. "Crawling around on all fours is very bad for you. Not to mention undignified."

I leaned toward him. "I've got a client."

"Congratulations. Now, I'm just a simple Southern doctor . . ."

Here we go. Behind Doolittle the nurse rolled her eyes.

". . . but it seems to me that it would be much more prudent to have a working leg. However, since you have no major bleeding, no concussion, and no broken bones, I shall count my blessings."

I clamped my mouth shut. Any discourse with Doolittle when he was in this mood would just result in an hour-long lecture.

The Pack medic whispered. His voice built to a low murmur, a measured chant spilling from his lips. The pain in my knee receded, dulled by medmagic. Doolittle straightened. "I'll mix you a solution and send it up to your quarters. Will you be needing a stretcher?"

"I'll make it on my own power." I pushed to my feet. "Thank you."

"You're welcome."

I left the hospital and continued my climb. The knee screamed but held. Eventually the stairs ended, bringing me to a narrow landing before a large reinforced door. During business hours, eleven a.m. to eight p.m., the door stood open. I walked through it and nodded to the guard behind the desk on the left.

"Hey, Seraphine."

Seraphine tore herself away from the bag of popcorn long enough to duck her head, sending her nest of braids into a shiver, and went back to her food. Being a wererat, she had the metabolism of a shrew. The rats ate constantly or they got the shakes.

Derek stepped out of the side office and nodded at me.

"Your nods keep getting deeper and deeper." Pretty soon it would be a bow, and we'd had words about that. The only things I disliked more than being bowed to was being called Mate.

He shrugged. "Maybe I'm just growing taller."

I surveyed him. Derek used to be embarrassingly pretty. Beautiful even. Then terrible things had happened, and now nobody would call him pretty, not even in weak light. No sane person would dare to even bring up the subject of his face. The boy wonder wasn't disfigured, although he thought he was and nobody could tell him different. His face had hardened and lost its perfect beauty. He looked dangerous and vicious, and his eyes, once brown and soft, were now almost black and had no give in them. If I met him in a dark alley, I'd think very hard about stepping aside. Luckily, he'd once played Robin to my Batman, and whatever happened, he was on my side.

We headed down the hallway. Derek took a deep breath, the way shapeshifters did when they sampled the air for scents. "I see Andrea is back."

"She is. And how is His Great Fussiness today?"

Derek's eyes sparked a bit. "His Majesty is in an ill humor. Rumors are flying that his mate almost got herself shot."

Derek worshipped the ground Curran walked on, but he was still a nineteen-year-old boy and occasionally he came out of his shell for a quip. His humor was dry and hidden deep. I was grateful it had survived at all.

"Where are my boudas?" Before I became a Beast Lady, Aunt B, the alpha of the boudas, and I struck a bargain. I'd help

Clan Bouda when they got in trouble—and they got in trouble
a lot—and in return Aunt B gave me two of her finest, Barabas
and Jezebel, who'd help me navigate the murky swamp of the
Pack politics. They referred to themselves as my advisors. In
reality they were my nannies.

"Barabas is asleep in the guardroom and Jezebel went
downstairs to get some food."

"Any messages for me?"

"The Temple called."

This ought to be interesting. I'd gone to the Temple trying
to restore a Jewish parchment to figure out my aunt's identity.
She took exception to that and the Temple had suffered some
damage. The rabbis had chased me off the Temple grounds,
but not before one of them healed my wounds. I hadn't handled
the entire situation very well, so when the storm was over, I'd
packed the parchment's fragment and sent it to the Temple as a
gift, with my apologies.

"Rabbi Peter sends his regards. He's very happy with the
parchment. It has some sort of historical value. You've been
forgiven and you may visit the Temple, provided you give them
twenty-four hours' notice."

To mobilize their forces, no doubt, and lay out an adequate
supply of paper and pens to counteract whatever trouble I
unleashed. Jewish mysticism was difficult to study, but it gave
its practitioners great rewards. When rabbis said that the pen
was mightier than the sword, they meant it.

Derek's lips curved into a slight smile. "Also, Ascanio Ferara got himself arrested again."

"Again?"

"Yes."

Ascanio was quickly turning into the bane of my existence.
A fifteen-year-old bouda, he was 125 pounds of batshit-crazy
hormones and had no sense to go with them. The kid had never
met a law he didn't want to break. The Pack was very much
aware that outsiders viewed them as monsters, and they made
a point of cracking down on any criminal activity with steel
claws. The same deal that brought me Barabas and Jezebel
compelled me to ask for lenience on Ascanio's behalf. Unfortunately, Ascanio seemed bound and determined to earn himself
some hard labor.

"What did he do now?"

"He was caught having group sex on the morgue steps."

I stopped and looked at him. "Define 'group.'"

"Two women."

It could have been worse.

"For a fifteen-year-old kid he's doing well for himself," Derek said, his face completely deadpan.

"Don't even go there."

Derek chuckled.

That was the problem with teenage werewolves—they had no appreciation for other people's pain.

He gave me a half bow, half nod, turned back to his office, and stopped. "Kate?"

"Yes?"

"You said once you didn't care for bodyguard detail. Why?"

Where was he going with this? "Two reasons. First, no matter how great you are, you account for only about fifty percent of the chance of success. The other fifty is riding on the body you're guarding. I've seen brilliant guards utterly fail, because the owner of that body couldn't follow a simple directive like 'Stand here and don't move.'"

"And second?"

"Bodyguarding is reactive by definition. You'll get some people who'll argue this point with you, but ultimately, you are in defense mode for most of the job. I don't have the mind-set for constant defense. I pick fights, I get aggressive, and I end up focusing on killing the target rather than keeping my client alive. I don't like to sit and wait. I can do it, because I was trained to do it, but it's not in my nature."

Derek gave me an odd look. "So you get bored."

"Yep. I guess that's it in a nutshell. Why do you ask?"

He shrugged. "No reason."

"Aha." We'd been down this road before, and then he got some molten metal poured on his face. "Don't get yourself into something you can't handle."

He grinned, a quick flash of teeth. "I won't."

"I mean it."

"Scout's honor."

"You're not that kind of scout."

The grin got wider. "You worry too much."

"If you get yourself killed, don't come crying to me."

Derek laughed and went back to the guard office.

He was up to something. If I slammed a lid on it now, he would never forgive me for treating him like a child. If I didn't, he might get his face bashed in again. Either way, total fail.

Friends made life entirely too complicated.

I kept walking, not caring if I limped. Nobody would see me here.

On the right, Julie's black door came up. A dagger gleamed in the middle of it—Julie got the idea from the Order. A skull and crossbones drawn in fluorescent paint shone above the dagger. Under it assorted signs screamed warnings: DON'T COME IN, ENTER AT YOUR OWN RISK, DANGER, MY ROOM NOT YOURS, ABANDON ALL HOPE YE WHO ENTER HERE, CAUTION, STAY OUT, KNOCK BEFORE ENTERING.

Staying in that school might have been the right thing for her, but I missed her. She was happy in the Keep. And she had Maddie for a friend, which was great because Maddie was sensible. Normally Julie and sensible couldn't fit into the same building. She had gotten her wish—she was coming home. Except it would be on my terms and she didn't have to like it.

I HAD PEELED OFF THE LAST SHRED OF CLOTHES FROM my body when Curran walked through the door of our rooms. Some men were handsome. Some were powerful. Curran was . . . dangerous. Muscular and athletic, he moved with an easy, confident grace, perfectly balanced, and you knew just by watching him that he was strong and fast. He could stalk like a hungry tiger, moving across the floor in absolute silence. I'd spent a lifetime listening for faint noises of danger and he would sneak up on me just to see me jump, because he thought it was funny. But his physical power alone didn't make him special— many men were strong and fast and could walk quietly.

It wasn't his body that set Curran apart. It was his eyes. When you looked into them, you saw chained violence baring teeth and claws back at you, and your instinct told you that if he ever let himself off that chain, you would not survive. He was terrifying on some deep, primordial level, and he wielded that fear like a weapon, using it to inspire panic or confidence. He walked into each room as if he owned it. I used to think it was arrogance—and it was; His Overbearance had a rather high opinion of himself—but egotism accounted for only a fraction of it. Curran radiated a supreme confidence. He would handle any problem he encountered efficiently and decisively, and if you stood in his way, he didn't have even the slightest hint of doubt that he could kick your ass. People sensed it and rallied behind him. He could walk into a room of hysterical strangers, and in seconds they would calm down and look to him for leadership.

He was dangerous. And difficult. And he was all mine.

Sometimes in the morning, when he worked in the gym one floor below, I'd stand by the gym's glass wall for a few minutes before I came in to spar. I'd watch him lift dumbbells or do dips with the weights attached to his belt, powerful muscles bulging and relaxing with controlled exertion, while the bars creaked under his weight and sweat slicked his short blond hair and skin until it glowed. Watching him never failed to send a slow insistent heat through me. He wasn't working out now. He was standing there in sweatpants and a blue T-shirt, carrying some sort of bottle, and I was ready to jump his bones. I could picture him above me in the bed.

At least it didn't show on my face. I had to have some dignity left.

I'd missed him so much, it almost hurt. It started the moment I left the Keep and nagged at me all day. Every day I had to fight with myself to keep from making up bullshit reasons to call the Keep so I could hear his voice. My only saving grace was that Curran wasn't handling this whole mating thing any better. Yesterday he'd called me at the office claiming that he couldn't find his socks. We talked for two hours.

I've faced many things in my life. But this emotion scared the living daylights out of me. I had no idea how to handle it.

Curran smiled at me. "I was told you got in and went to see Doolittle."

The Keep had no secrets.

"So I stopped there to check on your diagnosis." Curran lifted the bottle. "You're supposed to take a hot bath with this in it. And I have to watch you very closely from a very short distance to make sure your knee doesn't fall off."

Aha. I'm sure Doolittle said it just like that, especially the watching from the very short distance part. "Would you like to sit in my nasty medicated bath with me?" And why did that just come out of my mouth?

Curran's eyes sparked. "Yes, I would."

I arched my eyebrow. "Are you trustworthy enough to be let into the tub?"

He grinned. "Let?"

"Let."

"I own this tub." Curran leaned toward me. "I don't know if you heard, but I kind of run this place. Not only am I totally trustworthy, but my behavior is beyond contestation."

I lost it and went into the bathroom, laughing under my breath.

Being the Beast Lord's main squeeze had its perks, one of which was the enormous bathtub and a walk-in shower with water that was always hot, no matter if magic or tech had the upper hand. Most things in Curran's quarters were oversized. His bathtub was the deepest I'd ever seen, his sofa could seat eight, and his criminally soft bed, custom made to be extra wide to accommodate his beast form, rose four feet off the floor. At heart, Curran was a cat. He liked soft things, high places, and enough room to stretch out.

I took a quick shower to wash off most of the blood and dirt and climbed into the tub. Sinking into near-boiling hot water smelling of herbs and vinegar hurt for a split second, and then the burn inside my knee eased.

Curran came back from the kitchen, carrying two beers. He set them on the tub's edge and stripped, peeling the clothes off his muscular torso. I watched the fabric slide off Curran's back. All mine.

Oh boy.

He stepped into the tub and sat across from me, presenting me with a view of the world's best male chest up close.

Seducing him in the tub smelling of vinegar was out of the question. There had to be boundaries.

Curran leaned over to hand me a beer. I reached for it and then his arm was around me. His face was too close. He laid a trap and I totally fell for it. He dipped his head and kissed me.

On the other hand, we could do it in the tub. Why not?

Curran's gray eyes looked into mine. "Pupils don't seem to be dilated. You aren't high, you aren't drunk. What the hell possessed you to run out of a nice safe office into a gunfight?"

And he just shot his chance for sex into outer space. "I told you, there was a girl. The PAD opened fire and cut her leg almost completely off. She might have been twenty, tops. She almost bled to death in my office."

"It was her choice. If she wanted to stay safe, she could've joined the Girl Scouts. She isn't out selling cookies, she's piloting diseased corpses for a living."

I took my beer out of his hand and drank. "So you would've stood by and let the PAD kill four people?"

Curran leaned back, sprawling against the tub wall. "Four of the People. Not only that, but I can take a shot from an M24. You can't."

"When you offered me this business, did you think I would stay in the office all day baking cookies?"

"Nobody ever died of being shot by a cookie."

He had me there. I groped about my brain for a snappy comeback. "There is always a first time."

Oh, now that was a brilliant response. No doubt he'd collapse at my feet in awe at my intellectual magnificence.

"If anybody could manage being shot by a cookie, it would be you." Curran shrugged. "We agreed you wouldn't take chances."

"We agreed you would let me do my job as I see fit."

He drank his beer. "And I'm holding up my end of that agreement. I didn't drop everything and charge over there to shield you from bullets, shove guns up the PAD's asses, and slap the People around until they could come up with a good reason for this clusterfuck. I knew you could handle it."

"Then why are you chewing me out?"

Little wicked lights sparked in his eyes. "Despite showing superhuman restraint, I was still worried about you. I was emotionally compromised."

"Really? You don't say. Emotionally compromised?"

"Aunt B used that phrase today to explain to me why I shouldn't punish a fifteen-year-old idiot for having a threesome in front of the morgue."

Aunt B had jumped the gun. Should've let me handle it first.

Curran pondered his beer. "Never would've thought to use that to describe the kid's problem."

"Well, how would you describe it?"

"Young, dumb, and full of cum."

That pretty much summed it up. "You missed your calling. You should've been a poet."

Curran drained half of his beer and moved over to sit by me. "Don't take stupid risks. That's all I ask. You're important to me. I wish you were that important to you."

Trying to distract Curran was like trying to turn a train: difficult and ultimately futile. "If I kiss you, will you let it go?"

"Depends."

"Never mind. The offer is withdrawn." I leaned my head on his biceps. It was warm in the lion's embrace, as long as you didn't mind the huge claws. "I've got a client."

"Congratulations." Curran raised his beer. We clinked our bottles and drank.

"Who is it?"

"Remember the chick in charge of security at the Midnight Games?"

He nodded. "Tall, reddish hair, green rapier."

"She works for the Red Guard."

I brought him up to speed on everything, including Teddy Jo's freezer.

"Sounds like the Red Guard wants you to save their ass, and if it blows up in their faces, they'll blame you for it."

I leaned back. "I have to start rebuilding my reputation at some point. This would go a long way toward fixing it."

A fierce gold light backlit Curran's eyes. Suddenly he looked predatory. If I weren't one hundred percent sure he loved me, I would've gotten the hell out of that tub. Instead I leaned over and stroked the light stubble on his jaw.

"Picturing killing Ted Moynohan in your head again?"

"Mrm."

"Not worth it."

He slid his hand along my arm and I almost shivered. His voice was like velvet, hiding a hoarse growl just beneath the surface. "You thought about it."

I drank my beer. "I did." Actually right now I would've

liked to punch Shane even more. It would be good for me. Therapeutic even. "Still not worth it."

"If you need more money, all you have to do is dial accounting," Curran said.

"The budget we set up is fair. I'd like to stick to it. Anyway, I told you mine, will you tell me yours? What's bugging you?"

Curran's fingers trailed along my arm, up to my shoulder, and over to my side. Mmm.

"A render went off the reservation," he said.

Renders were specialized warriors. All Pack members were trained to fight as soon as they could walk, but rank-and-file shapeshifters had other jobs: they were bakers, tailors, teachers. Warriors had no other job. In battle, they specialized according to their beast. Bears functioned as tanks—they took a lot of damage before they went down and cleared paths when they charged. Wolves and jackals were jacks of all trades, while cats and boudas were renders. Drop a render in the middle of a fight and thirty seconds later they would be panting in a ring of corpses.

"What sort of render?"

"A female lynx. Name's Leslie Wren."

My memory served up a fit woman with honey-brown hair and a sprinkling of freckles on her nose, followed by a six-foot-tall, muscled shapeshifter in a warrior form. I knew Leslie Wren. A few months ago, when we battled a demonic horde during the flare, she fought beside me. She had killed dozens and enjoyed the hell out of it. But I had seen her again, and recently, too . . . "What happened?"

Curran grimaced. "She failed to report in. We cleared her house—all her weapons are gone. Boyfriend is shocked; he thinks she must be in trouble."

"What do you think?"

Curran's frown deepened. "Jim's people tracked her scent down to the Honeycomb. They got a hundred feet in and hit wolfsbane."

The Honeycomb was a screwed-up place, full of wild magic and riddled with paths that went nowhere. It changed all the time, like some mutated cancerous growth, and it stank to high heaven. Add wolfsbane to it, which guaranteed an instant severe allergy attack for the weretrackers, and you had a clean getaway.

"No other scent trails with her?"

Curran shook his head. So nobody had held a gun to her head. She went into the Honeycomb on her own and used wolfsbane, because she didn't want to be found. Leslie Wren had gone rogue. Shapeshifters went rogue for any number of reasons. Best-case scenario, she had a problem with someone in the Pack, couldn't resolve it, and decided to cut and run. Worst-case scenario, she went loup. A regular shapeshifter going loup meant a killing spree. A render going loup meant a massacre.

"I have to go hunting tomorrow," Curran said.

Hunting Leslie Wren before anyone got hurt. I finally remembered where I'd seen her last—she let Julie and Maddie come with her to hunt a deer in the woods near the Keep. It made perfect sense for Curran to go. A render would wipe the floor with an average shapeshifter. Curran would be able to take her down with minimal damage. I understood it, but I didn't like it.

"Need help?" I asked.

"No. Is your knee still hurting?"

"No, why?"

"Just wondering if you need any distraction from the pain." Mmm. "What sort of distraction did you have in mind?"

Curran leaned down, his eyes dark and full of golden sparks. His lips closed on mine. The shock of his tongue against mine was electrifying. I slid my arms around his neck, molding myself against him. My nipples pressed against his chest. The hard muscle of his back bunched under my fingers, and I kissed him, his lips, the corner of his mouth, the sensitive point under his jaw, tasting his sweat and the sharp touch of stubble on my lips. He made a quiet masculine noise, halfway between a deep growling rumble and a purr.

Oh my God.

His hands slid over my back and down, caressing, shifting me closer, until I felt the hard length of his erection press against me. Oh yes.

"We should move out of the tub." I nipped his lower lip.

He kissed my neck. "Why?"

"Because I want you to be on top and I don't have gills."

Curran rose, lifting me out of the water, and carried me to the living room.

WE LAY ON THE COUCH, TANGLED IN A BLANKET. "SO what are you going to do about Ascanio?" I asked him.

Curran sighed. "Most young guys have somebody to imitate: their father, their alpha, me. When I was younger, I had my father and then Mahon. Ascanio has nobody. His father is dead, his alpha is female, and he can't relate to me. He obeys me and he acknowledges that I have the right to punish him, but he doesn't feel the need to be like me."

"You mean he doesn't instantly hero-worship you? Perish the thought."

He scowled at me. "I think I'll make mouthing off to the Beast Lord a punishable offense."

"Punishable by what?

"Oh, I'll think of something. Anyway, I decided to give him to Raphael."

Raphael was handsome, he earned a good living, women fell over themselves to line his path, and he was vicious in a fight. I could see how a young male bouda might think that nobody on Earth was cooler.

"I'll ask Raphael to mentor him," Curran said. "As a personal favor. Before he steps in, I'll make that spoiled brat's life pure hell, so when Raphael takes him off our hands, Ascanio will think he walks on water."

That made total sense, except Curran and Raphael weren't on good terms. In fact, Curran had once referred to Raphael as B's precious peacock. "You're going to ask Raphael for a favor?" I stopped and made a big show of staring into Curran's eyes. "Pupils aren't dilated. You aren't high or drunk . . ."

"He helped set up your business," Curran said. "And we have some things in common."

"Like what?"

"I know what he's going through. I've been there. Raphael is too much in his own head right now. The boy would be good for him. It will force him to think of something else."

I was pretty sure that nothing short of Andrea would get Raphael out of his head. "That would be great, except he is neck deep in his funk. Aunt B probably asked him already and he must've said no."

"I'm not Aunt B," Curran said.

"I noticed."

He stroked my shoulder. "Your tattoo faded. I can barely see it."

I turned my head, trying to get a look at the raven. The black lines of the design had faded to pale gray; the sword, and the words *Дар Ворона*, Raven's Gift, were almost gone.

"Doolittle says it's because of all the medmagic he's been subjecting me to over the last weeks. A lot of my scars faded, too. It's probably for the best. It was a cheesy tattoo anyway. Every time someone saw it, they'd ask what it said and why did I have Cyrillic letters on my shoulder . . ." I clamped my mouth shut.

"What?"

The Cyrillic alphabet was created by two Greek monks around AD 900. Before the Cyrillic alphabet, the Slavs used Glagolitic script, which took root in strokes-and-incisions writing—Slavic runes.

The inventor's last name was Kamen. Kamen meant "stone" in Russian. Usually Russian names ended on "-ov" or "-ev," but it was possible his family had changed their last name to make it easier for an English speaker.

I dialed the guardroom. Barabas picked up the phone, his slightly ironic tenor amused before I even had a chance to say anything. "Yes, Consort?"

"Why is everyone calling me Consort?"

"Jim designated you as Consort in official papers. You don't want to be called Mate, calling you Alpha is confusing, and 'Beast Lady' makes people laugh."

"Why is it necessary to attach a title to me at all?"

"Because you are attached to the Beast Lord."

Behind me Curran chuckled to himself. Apparently I amused everyone this evening. "I know it's late, but could you find a book for me? It's called *The Slavs: Study of Pagan Tradition* by Osvintsev."

Barabas sighed dramatically. "Kate, you make me despair. Let's try that again from the top, except this time pretend you are an alpha."

"I don't need a lecture. I just need the book."

"Much better. Little more growl in the voice?"

"Barabas!"

"And we're there. Congratulations! There is hope for you yet. I will look into the book."

I hung up the phone and glared at Curran. "What's so funny?"

"You."

"Laugh while you can. You have to sleep eventually, and then I'll take my revenge."

"You're such a violent woman. Always with the threats. You should look into some meditation techniques . . ."

I jumped on the couch and put the Beast Lord into an arm-lock.

CHAPTER 8

———◆———

THE TWO TRACKERS REPORTED IN EARLY THE NEXT morning. They had picked up Julie's scent, hit wolfsbane, lost her, and found her trail again at the crumbling Highway 23, except it was two hours old and mixed with horse scents. She was hitchhiking. Great. Awesome. At least she always carried a knife with her.

When I relayed this to Curran, he shrugged and said, "If she kills anybody, we'll make it go away."

Shapeshifter parenting motto—if your kid slits somebody's throat, always have a backup plan to make the body disappear.

I put on my clothes, grabbed my sword, kissed Curran good-bye, and headed to the lower floor. Barabas waited for me by the desk, slim, dapper, and wearing an ironic smile. The first thing you noticed about Barabas was his hair. Cut short on the sides and the back, it was about an inch and a half long on top of his head, and he brushed gel in it and rubbed gel in it until the entire inch and a half stood on end, like hackles on a pissed-off dog. It was also bright, fiery red. He looked like his head was on fire.

Technically, Barabas wasn't a bouda. His mother shifted into a hyena, but his father was a weremongoose from Clan

Nimble. As was customary in the interclan unions with the Pack, his parents had an option of belonging to either clan, and they chose the loving embrace of Aunt B and the protection of her razor-sharp claws. Faced with the same choice on his eighteenth birthday, Barabas chose to remain with Clan Bouda and pretty soon ran into some personal problems. When Aunt B gave him to me, it was for his benefit as much as mine.

"Good morning, Consort." Barabas handed me a package wrapped in shimmering red foil. A big red bow was set on top of the foil.

"Why the wrapping?"

"It's a gift. Why not make it special?"

"Thank you." I untied the bow. "This render Curran is supposed to hunt today. Leslie Wren. How good is she?"

"Pack's top twenty. I wouldn't fight her," Barabas said. "I know some alphas who wouldn't either."

Great. I unwrapped the paper, revealing an old edition of Osvintsev. "Where did you find it?"

"In the Keep library."

"The Keep has a library?"

"Both paper and digital."

I flipped through the pages. Runes, runes, runes . . . Runes. An inverted Algiz rune. The caption next to it said "Chernobog." The Black God.

Right. Of course, it wouldn't be Chernobog, God of Morning Dew on the Rose Petals, but a woman could always hope.

I riffed through the pages looking for the gods and goddesses. The Slavic pantheon broke into two opposing factions, benevolent and malevolent. I skipped the "good" faction.

The moment I turned the pages to the dark faction, an inverted Algiz rune stared at me. Next to it was a sketch of a man with a black mustache frosted with silver. His black armor bristled with spikes. His hand clenched a bloody spear. He stood on a heap of dismembered corpses covered in black ants while black crows circled over his head. Fury warped his face into an ugly grimace. The caption read:

Chernobog. The Black Serpent. Koshei. Lord of Darkness and Death. Ruler of Freezing Cold. Master of Destruction. God of Insanity. Embodiment of everything bad. Evil.

Barabas glanced over my shoulder. "This doesn't look good."

Understatement of the year. De Harven was sacrificed to Chernobog, probably by a volhv, a Slavic pagan priest. Volhvs had broad powers, like druids, but unlike the druids, who were very self-conscious about their human-sacrificing past, the volhvs had no aversion to violence. And Atlanta volhvs really didn't like me.

I tapped the book, thinking. The Slavic pagan community was self-regulating: light gods were counterbalanced by dark, and volhvs of both factions were equally respected. Sacrificing de Harven took a huge load of magic. A volhv packing that much magic would be well known and rooted in the community. I wouldn't get anywhere by talking with them. I had to find a Plan B.

The volhvs were all male. If you were female and practicing Slavic pagan magic, you were likely a witch, and the most powerful Slavic witch in the city was Evdokia. She was a part of the Witch Oracle and the last time we'd met, Evdokia told me she knew my stepfather. I had no idea if she would even talk to me, but it was worth a try.

The magic was still up, but I tried the phone anyway. Dial tone. I punched in Ksenia's number. Ksenia owned a small herbal shop on the north side. I'd stopped there a few times when my supplies had run low, and the last time I was there Ksenia boasted that Evdokia had bought some herbs from her. Maybe she could arrange for an audience.

OUTSIDE, THE MARCH WIND BIT AT ME WITH ICY fangs. Two people stood by my vehicle. The first was taller, his dark hair cropped short. He wore a dark gray hoodie and faded jeans. His posture was deceptively relaxed, but he watched me as I walked. Derek.

The second person was shorter, dressed in an inconspicuous ensemble of black jeans, black turtleneck, and a leather jacket, of all things. Black hair, angelic face, and devil eyes. Ascanio Ferara. The kid was so handsome, he almost looked unreal. Combine that with an agile face that went from innocence to remorse to admiration in a blink, and you had a pure chick magnet. Ascanio knew the effect he had, and he used every drop of it to his advantage.

"What are you doing here?"

Ascanio offered me a dazzling smile, broadcasting "I could never do anything wrong" with all his might. "Obeying the Beast Lord, Consort."

"Elaborate."

"I've been assigned to bodyguard you."

You've got to be kidding me.

Derek snorted.

Ascanio pretended not to hear it. "The Beast Lord spoke to me this morning. I'm responsible for your well-being, and if you get injured, I'll answer to him personally."

Oh, that bastard. Found the kid an impossible job, did he?

Derek laughed quietly.

Ascanio finally deemed it necessary to acknowledge Derek's existence. "Is something funny?"

"I don't even know you, and I feel sorry for you."

Ascanio turned a shade paler. "Are you saying I'm not capable of protecting the Consort, wolf?"

Derek let out a derisive chortle. "You got arrested by two human cops while getting your freak on at a morgue. You're not capable of protecting yourself, let alone her."

"They were female cops," Ascanio said. "And I had a fun time. When was the last time you got laid? Let me know if you need some pointers."

Derek bared his teeth.

I hit him with my hard stare. "I'll be right back. Stay here. Don't touch each other."

"You don't have to worry about me," Ascanio said. "I can't speak for the wolf, but I prefer women."

"Zip it."

I turned around, marched back into the Keep, picked up the first phone I saw, and punched 0011 into it. The phone rang once and Curran's voice answered. "Yes?"

"What is wrong with you?"

"Many, many things."

"I'm not taking him with me. He's a kid."

"He is a fifteen-year-old male bouda. He maxes out his bench press at three sixty and his alpha tells me he has a decent half-form."

"Curran!"

"I love it when you say my name. It sounds so sexy."

"I'm investigating people who sacrifice trained killers to dark gods."

"Perfect. It will keep him occupied."

Aaargh. "No."

"He needs an outlet for all that energy, and you could use him."

"In what capacity?"

"Bait."

Why me, why? "I hate you."

"If you don't take him, the ball is back in my court and I have to give him hard labor. The last time I sentenced him to the Keep building, he was bench-pressing rocks to bulk up 'for the girls.' He has a brain, and hard labor accomplishes nothing in his case. This way he can waste his energy trying to bodyguard you and might accidentally learn something in the process. It might be what not to do, but that's also useful. When Raphael comes to liberate him, he'll be kissing his boots."

"Curran, I'm not running a nursery here. This shit is going to turn hairy. You know it and I know it. The kid might get hurt."

"I have to bloody him sometime, Kate. He came to the Pack late. Most kids his age have already had their first fight with real consequences. He hasn't. B has a soft spot for him, because he is male and he had a rough childhood. She won't take him in hand, and even if she did, there are seventeen males in the bouda clan right now, all of whom are under the age of ten or over twenty. He has no peers and he's isolated."

"So put him with other kids his age."

"No. He can't be challenged, because he's a minor, but adolescents fight for dominance among themselves. He doesn't get the pecking order, and he thinks it's all a big game. He'll run his mouth, and they will beat him, which will accomplish one of two things: either they will break his spirit or he'll snap and kill somebody, and then neither B, nor you, nor anybody else in this Pack can protect him. He needs to learn how to be a Pack male."

"And you think that I can teach him that?"

"You—no. But Derek can."

Ah. Now it all became clear. He'd arranged this whole thing, like moving chess pieces on a board. I unclenched my teeth. "I'm really pissed off at you right now. You could've told me all this last night and asked me to take him. Instead you manipulated me into a corner. I don't like feeling manipulated, Curran. I don't appreciate being put into this position, and in case you've forgotten, I'm not one of your flunkies. I don't need to be managed and led by the hand."

His voice dropped into a measured patient tone that made me want to rip his head off. "You're blowing this out of proportion. You're trying to make a fight out of nothing."

I hung up.

The phone rang. I picked it up.

"Kate," he snarled.

"Guess what? I don't have to listen to you." I hung up again and marched outside. Derek and Ascanio stood on opposite sides of the vehicle. I pointed at Ascanio. "Into the car. Now."

Ascanio climbed into the Jeep. I turned to Derek. "What are you doing here?"

"I quit."

"Quit what?"

He smiled. "My job."

What in the name of all that was holy . . . "Why?"

Derek shrugged. "Just felt like it."

Like pulling teeth. I tried to speak slowly and form coherent sentences. "What precipitated you quitting your job?"

He looked up at the night sky above us. "Curran and I had a conversation."

I wondered if kicking him in the head would make the whole explanation pop out of his mouth in one chunk. "What did he say?"

"He said that I was doing a good job. He asked what would be the highest a bodyguard could go in the Pack. And I said, protecting the Beast Lord and his mate."

"Aha."

"He nodded and asked how old I was."

Curran knew perfectly well how old he was. "You said, 'Nineteen,' and?"

"He said, 'Okay, what's next?'"

Now it made sense. Derek was wasted on bodyguard duty, and Curran knew it. Derek had talent and a will to make something out of it. He couldn't climb any higher up the bodyguard ladder, and he was comfortable where he was. Apparently my sugar woogums decided it was time to make him uncomfortable. That still didn't explain what the boy wonder was doing here.

"So what *is* next?"

Derek looked at me, his dark eyes luminescent with telltale shapeshifter glow. "I said, 'Next I fight Jim for his job.'"

I felt an urge to hit my head against something hard. "Brilliant move, boy wonder. What did Curran say?"

"He said, 'In about thirty years, maybe.'"

"Put fighting Jim out of your mind. You're not there yet."

Derek rolled his eyes. "Yes, His Majesty explained to me in detail how if Jim sneezes in my direction, I'd have a weeklong stay in the hospital."

"Jim is deadly. It's not an exaggeration, it's a fact. Also, he's been at this game for a lot longer than you. No fighting Jim. Yes?"

"Yes," Derek agreed.

Maybe he had some sense after all.

"So . . ." Derek shifted from foot to foot. "Can I have a job?"

I closed my eyes and counted from ten backward.

"Kate?"

"The last two times you and I crossed paths, you got your leg ripped up and had molten metal poured on your face."

"The metal was my fault, not yours." All humor fled from his eyes. A wolf looked at me, a vicious wolf with a scarred face. "I've worked for Jim for three years as a 'face.' I went in undercover, I obtained information, and I brought it back, safe. After that, I ran Curran's personal security for six months. I know the security protocols, I know procedures, and I've proven I can effectively use resources at my disposal. If you hire me, I would be a valuable asset."

"Very nice. How many times did you rehearse this speech?"

"I'm serious, Kate. I can be useful to you. Besides, you need somebody to ride shotgun. You gave Grendel to Andrea, so you don't have a wingman. I can vomit better than a shaved poodle, I promise. And honestly, you could use a driver."

"What are you implying?"

"I'm not implying, I'm saying it. You're the opposite of Dali. She drives like a maniac, you drive like an old lady . . ."

Bloody hell. I closed my eyes. I couldn't tell him no and he knew it.

"Are you okay?"

"I need you to go to the garage and get another Jeep, because mine only seats two. Then I need you to follow me in that Jeep. And if I hear as much as a whisper about my driving abilities, I'll fire you on the spot."

"Thanks, Kate." He grinned and took off running.

Curran got rid of Ascanio and saddled me with not one, but two bodyguards. God help anyone who dared to look at me funny. They would rip him to pieces, just to outdo each other.

NO MATTER HOW MANY TIMES I VISITED THE CASIno, it always took me by surprise. After the hard freezes of a freakishly cold winter, the early spring painted Atlanta in black, brown, and gray. Grim ruins thrust here and there, like dark husks stained with cold spring rain. Bleak houses glared at the streets with barred windows. Mud stained the streets, churned by the current of horses, mules, oxen, and an occasional camel. Wagons creaked, engines growled, drivers barked curses at each other, animals brayed . . . And then you turned the corner and ran into a castle straight out of the Arabian Nights. Pure white and almost delicate, it all but floated in the middle of a huge lot, flanked by elegant minarets and wrapped by a wall with a textured parapet. Long fountains stretched toward its ornate doors, and Hindu gods, cast in bronze and copper, posed frozen in time above the water.

For a moment it took your breath away. And then you saw the vampires, smeared in purple and lime-green sunblock, patrolling those snow-white walls and the reality came back real fast. There was something so alien and foreign about the undead crawling over all that beauty. I wanted to pluck them off like fleas from a white cat.

I parked in the far lot and shut off the engine. A moment later Derek pulled his vehicle next to mine, parked, and stepped out. "Are we going in?"

"We are."

"With him?" He nodded at Ascanio.

The kid bared his teeth. "What exactly do you mean by that?"

I turned to him. "Who is the primary enemy of the Pack?"

Ascanio hesitated. "The People?"

I nodded. "We have a very uneasy truce going. I have to go into the Casino to talk to Ghastek. He's a Master of the Dead. Because I'm the Consort, I can't go in there without a proper escort." Now I was calling myself the Consort. Kill me, somebody.

"If Kate goes in by herself, the People could claim that she did something to break the truce," Derek said. "Or something could happen to her. This way we'll act as witnesses."

"You have a choice: you can stay with the vehicles or you can come with us," I said. "But if you decide to come, you follow Derek and you keep your mouth shut. You don't flirt, you don't crack jokes, you give the People absolutely no excuse to take any kind of offense. One wrong word, and we're at war. Do I make myself clear?"

Ascanio nodded. "Yes, Consort."

"Good." I took a manila folder from the front seat of my Jeep and locked the car. "Put your badass faces on and follow me."

We crossed the parking lot, with me leading the way and Derek and Ascanio behind, stone-faced and emanating a willingness to kill, in case any stray People got out of line. Two solemn sentries with curved yatagan swords guarded the Casino doors. We walked right past them, across the floor filled with slot machines jerry-rigged to work during magic and card tables to the back, to a small service room. A young woman in the Casino uniform of black pants and dark purple vest looked up at me from behind the desk.

"Kate Daniels," I told her. "To see Ghastek."

She nodded. "Please have a seat."

I sat. The two boys remained standing, one on either side of my chair. The noise of the crowd floated through the door, a steady hum interrupted by periodic outbursts of laughter and shouts.

The side door opened and a blond man stepped out. "Good morning. I'm so sorry, but your escort will have to remain here."

"That's fine." I rose.

"Please follow me."

I followed him up the stairs and through the hallways, to a stairway. We went down, lower and lower, one floor, two, three. The air smelled of undead, a dry, revolting scent, laced with a tinge of foul magic.

We turned on the landing and another flight of stairs rolled down, ending in stone floor and a metal door. A vampire clung to the wall above it, like a steel-muscled gecko, its dull red eyes tracking our movement. Before the Shift, corporations installed cameras. Now the People installed vampires.

The blond man opened the door and led me into a narrow concrete tunnel, its ceiling punctuated by glowing warts of electric lights. The underbelly of the Casino was a maze of claustrophobic tunnels. Loose vampires weren't great with direction. In the event the locks on their cells malfunctioned, the personnel of the stables would evacuate, and the loose vampires would wander through the tunnels, confused and contained, until the navigators secured them one by one.

The tunnels ended, opening into a huge chamber filled with cells, set back to back in twin rows angling toward the center of the room like spokes of a wheel. The side walls and the backs of the cells were stone and concrete, but the fronts consisted of thick metal grates, designed to slide upward. The stench of undeath hit me full force and I almost gagged. Vampires filled the cells, chained to the walls, pacing behind the metal bars, crouching in corners, their mad eyes glowing with insane hunger.

We reached the empty center of the room and turned down another row of cells. In front of us, a glass-covered balcony protruded from the wall. The tinted glass panels looked opaque from this angle, but I'd been in Ghastek's office before. From the inside, the glass was crystal clear.

We walked through another door, up an access tunnel, and to a wooden door marked with Ghastek's symbol: an arrow tipped with a circle. My guide stepped aside. I knocked.

"Enter," Ghastek's voice called out.

Oh goody. I pushed the door and it swung open soundlessly under the pressure of my fingertips.

A large room greeted me, looking more like a living room

than the lair of a Master of the Dead. Shelves lined the back wall, filled to the bursting point with books of all colors and sizes. At the far wall a pair of medieval shackles hung on hooks, displayed like a priceless work of art. A crescent red sofa sat in the middle of the dark floor, facing the glass balcony that offered a floor-to-ceiling view of the stables. At the far end of the sofa sat Ghastek, dressed in tailored black trousers and a turtleneck. He was already thin, and the severe clothes made him seem almost gaunt. He was drinking a frothy espresso from a small brown cup. Two vampires sat on the floor by him, one on each side. The vampires clutched knitting needles, moving them with dizzying speed. A long swatch of knitted cloth, one blue, the other green, stretched from each of them.

Alrighty then. If this wasn't a heartwarming Norman Rockwell painting, I didn't know what was.

The needles clicked, chewing up the yarn. I could control several vampires at a time, but I couldn't make even one knit, even if the needles were as thick as its fingers and I were moving them in slow motion. Ghastek had two running at once. I fought a shiver. He could send one of those bloodsuckers forward and stab me in the eye, and I wasn't sure I'd be fast enough to stop it.

"Is this a bad time?" I asked. "I can come back if you and the twins are having a private moment."

Ghastek's gaze fastened on me. "Don't be crude, Kate. Would you like a drink?"

To drink was stupid; not to drink would be an insult. But then I doubted Ghastek would go through the trouble of poisoning me. It wasn't his style. "Water would be nice."

The left vampire dropped its needles and scuttled into another room.

I shrugged off my cloak, folded it over the sofa's armrest, and took a seat. "You can't blame me for thinking you might get kinky. You have shackles on the wall."

Ghastek's eyes lit up. "Ah. Those are interesting, aren't they? They're from Nordlingen in Germany, late sixteenth century."

"The Witch Trials?"

Ghastek nodded.

"Do you think you would have been burned at the stake in the sixteenth century?"

"No."

"Because you're not a woman?"

"Being a woman made little difference. Most witches burned in Iceland and Finland were men, for example. No, I wouldn't have been burned, because I'm not poor."

The undead returned and crouched by me, holding a glass of water with ice in its long claws. A narrow slice of lemon floated on the water. The vampire's mouth hung open, the narrow sickles of its fangs stark white against the darkness of its maw. Service with a smile.

I took the water and sipped. "Thank you. So why the cuffs then?"

The undead returned to its knitting.

"People view us and our vampires as abominations," Ghastek said. "They call the undead inhuman, not realizing the irony: only humans are capable of inhumanity. Four thousand years of technology, with magic shrinking to a mere trickle before the Shift, yet the world was just as evil then as it is now. It's not vampires or werewolves who committed the worst atrocities, but average people. They are the serial killers, the child rapists, the inquisitors, the witch hunters, the perpetrators of monstrous deeds. The shackles on my wall are the symbol of humanity's capacity for cruelty. I keep them to remind myself that I must fear those who fear me. Given your present affiliation, I would suggest you do the same."

That hit close to home. If my bloodline became known, people would be lining up around the block to either kill me or banish me as far as they could to keep themselves safe from Roland's wrath when he and I had our happy family reunion.

Ghastek took a sip of his espresso. "Strictly out of curiosity, what was the deciding factor in selecting the Beast Lord? You had options, and life with him must be regimented. He seems like the type to assert his dominance, and you always seemed like a person who dislikes being dominated."

"I love him."

Ghastek mulled it over for a second and nodded. "Ah. That explains it."

The vampires continued their crafting marathon. "Why knitting?"

"It's intricate. I could've had them thread beads or set up dominoes. It's an exercise."

Fainting had rattled him. He was trying to reassure himself that he still had it all under control. Maybe I could put in a request for a pair of handmade socks.

"How is Emily?"

Ghastek's stare gained an icy edge. "Her leg had to be amputated. She will have the best prosthetics we can provide. The city owes her a debt. I intend to pursue this matter with all the resources at my disposal."

Technically the law was on the PAD's side. When faced with a loose bloodsucker, they were obligated to do everything within their power to wipe it off the face of the planet, no matter the casualties. But the People wouldn't forget it. They held grudges forever, and then some.

I reached into my pocket. "I've brought you an invoice for the capture of the vampire."

Ghastek sighed. "Of course."

The vampire on the right scuttled over, took the paper from my hand, and delivered it to Ghastek. He scanned it. His eyes widened. He reached into his pocket, pulled out a leather wallet, extracted a dollar, and passed it to the vamp. The undead brought it to me and I placed it into the folder. "Paid in full. Would you like a receipt?"

"Please."

A receipt for a dollar. Why didn't that surprise me? I wrote out the receipt, leaned over, and handed it to him. "When you called me Wednesday morning, how did you do it?"

"I wasted a few valuable seconds at a pay phone."

That was what I thought. "I did some thinking."

"That is a very dangerous pastime," Ghastek said.

He'd made a joke. Surely the apocalypse wasn't far behind. "The vampire was loose. You had no way of knowing it would run toward my office. Loose vampires are attracted to blood. In the absence of blood they tend to blunder about aimlessly. However, vampires have scent glands near the base of their digits. They mark the ground as they run. The scent is very weak, but when a vampire follows the same route over and over, they create a tangible scent trail."

Ghastek nodded. "That's one of the reasons we prefer to run them along the rooftops."

"That and it makes killing people easier by leaping on your unsuspecting victims from above."

"Indeed."

"A loose vampire will naturally follow a vampiric scent trail if it stumbles on it, because there might be food on the other end." I took a map out of my folder and pointed to the red line veering its way through the streets. "This is a section of your patrol line. At least three vampires pass along this route every day. I'd say this is as strong a scent trail as you could get. Was the journeywoman patrolling that route when she fainted and dropped the vampire?"

"Correct." Ghastek was watching me with acute interest. "Since the vampire was already following the scent trail, I felt it was unlikely she would deviate from its course. Your office sits right under our outer patrol line. The building itself is in the Pack territory, but the parking lot is in ours. I'm sure it was by design."

It was. The location of my office had put me into a perfect position to watch the border with the People. Curran and I had discussed it at some length. That was part of the reason why my door could withstand concentrated bombardment from a tank. In case the shapeshifters got in trouble in their midnight adventures in vampire land, they could hightail it to my office and hide behind my sturdy door.

"It was a smart move on the Pack's part," Ghastek said. "The cooperation agreement forbids any fortified Pack or People structures within one mile of the border, but it doesn't forbid a business licensed by either party."

"And I'm sure you license several businesses near the border."

"It wouldn't be in my best interests to confirm or deny." Ghastek permitted himself a small half smile.

Here came the hard part. I had to say enough to hold his interest but not too much to betray the Red Guard's confidentiality. "I'm working a case in Sibley. During my investigation, I encountered a ward that disappeared."

Ghastek leaned forward. "What do you mean, disappeared?"

"It vanished, as if it'd never been there." I turned the map and pointed to Johnson Ferry. "This bridge is one of the two primary ways out of Sibley and into the city. Yesterday the wards guarding the Bridge Troll also disappeared." I trailed Johnson

Ferry until it crossed the red line of the vampire patrol. "I'm guessing this is the point where your girl dropped the vampire."

Ghastek said nothing.

"Something passed this way out of Sibley, over the bridge, and along this street. Something that ate the wards and tainted your vampire. Your own journeywomen told me that they couldn't grab its mind. I think that it took all of your power to hold it." That was why he made it curtsy and put on a show. It was a huge, shocking bluff.

Ghastek laughed softly.

"The thing that ate the ward left Sibley on a cart or a car, and your girl probably saw it just before she fainted. I need to know what that vehicle looked like."

Ghastek considered it. "I'll think about it."

I'd saved his life. Apparently it wasn't worth a tiny crumb of information. Thrashing Ghastek in his own office was out of the question. First, he had two vampires with him, and second, I would cause an interfaction incident. I rose. "Do that."

I was almost to the door, when he spoke. "Kate?"

"Yes?"

"I liked you better as a merc."

"I did, too." I could kick people and say what I actually thought without causing a diplomatic disaster. "But we all have to grow up sometime."

WHEN OUR TWO-JEEP PARADE ARRIVED AT THE office, Andrea was already there. I knew this because there was a new pile of steaming dog puke three feet outside our side door.

The two teenage shapeshifters pondered the puke.

I pointed to the spot in front of the door. "Ascanio, stand right here."

He moved to the spot. "Why?"

I stepped to the side and opened the door. One hundred pounds of Grendel caught in intense canine joy burst through the door. The attack poodle launched himself into the air. Ascanio grabbed him and clamped Grendel tight.

Good reaction time.

Ascanio stared at the poodle. "What is this?"

"A faithful canine companion."

"He stinks like a sewer."

The mutant poodle squirmed and licked Ascanio's chin.

"Ugh. What do I do with him?"

"Bring him inside."

I stepped into the office. Behind me Derek said, "I'd sterilize my face if I were you."

"Mind your own business, wolf."

The office smelled like coffee. Inside, Andrea raised her head from a small laptop sitting on top of paperwork spread on her desk. "What took you so long?"

"Good morning to you too, sunshine." I dropped my bag by my chair.

Andrea tossed an envelope at me. I glanced at it. The Order's shield logo marked the top left corner. Uh-oh.

"What is this?"

"It's Shane," she growled. "He wants me to 'cease my efforts' to get my weapons, because they are currently being used to apprehend real criminals."

Ha, I thought it was something dire. "He's just jerking your chain. If you want, I'll get Barabas to draw up a letter with his lawyer credentials on it. We'll send it to the Order and you'll get your weapons back. Shane can't hold your property."

"I know that. I'm still pissed off. It's your duty as my best friend to be outraged with me."

"I'm outraged!" I snarled. "That bastard!"

"Thank you," Andrea said.

Ascanio cleared his throat. "Consort? May I put him down now?"

I turned. He was still holding Grendel, who seemed to be enjoying it, judging by the way he kept licking Ascanio's shoulder. Behind him, Derek was trying to choke off a laugh.

"Yes."

Ascanio set Grendel on the floor.

Andrea peered at Derek. "What are you doing here?"

"I hired him," I told her.

Andrea's blond eyebrows crawled up a fraction of an inch. "And him?"

"Him, too."

Andrea pointed at Ascanio with her pen. "How old are you?"

"Fifteen."

"He can't work here. He's too young."

I shrugged. "The legal age for employment is fourteen."

"Yes, with the exception of hazardous jobs."

"He will be an office helper. How is that hazardous?"

"Kate! Would you like to go outside and look at the bullet holes in the pavement?"

"He isn't a full-time employee. He's an intern."

Andrea looked at me for a long moment. "I don't think you understand this whole business thing. Clients produce money. Employees cost money. We want fewer employees and more clients, not the other way around. We don't need teenage bouda sex fiends as interns."

"How do you know he is a sex fiend?"

Andrea looked at me like I was mentally challenged. "He is fifteen and he is a bouda. Hello?"

Good point. I nodded to the boy wonder and the sex fiend. "Pull up some chairs."

When I came back from the kitchen with a carafe of coffee and four mugs to pour it into, everyone had gathered around Andrea's desk.

I opened the file with the case and ran through it. By the time I finished, Derek was frowning. A crazy glow lit up Ascanio's eyes. "Do you think people will try to kill us?"

"Yes."

"Cool."

Cool. Right. "There is a freezer in the back room with de Harven's body in it. Go and examine it. Look at his face and memorize the scents. After you do that, walk through the office so you know the layout."

They took off.

"What's eating you?" Andrea asked.

"I had a fight with Curran."

"What about?"

"He's managing me."

Andrea raised her eyebrows.

"He maneuvers events, taking away my choices until there is only one possible solution to a problem. It pisses me off."

"That's what alphas do." Andrea grimaced. "I got a note from Aunt B last night."

Warning, warning, spiked traps ahead. "And?"

"She wants to meet. For a 'nice chat.'"

I knew exactly what this chat would be about. Andrea was a shapeshifter, and no shapeshifter could exist within Atlanta without becoming a member of the Pack's furry horde. Before, Andrea was a member of the Order, and the boudas kept her secret. Now she was unattached. Andrea would have to make a choice: enter the Pack and become one of Aunt B's boudas or move. After her childhood, Andrea would rather cut her arm off than become a bouda.

"I'm not going," Andrea said suddenly.

Aunt B wouldn't just let it go. Of all the alphas in the Pack, two gave me pause: Mahon, the Pack's executioner and the head of Clan Heavy, and Aunt B. Screwing with Aunt B was like sticking your hands into a meat grinder. She was all sweetness and cookies, and then giant claws came out and people's guts ended up as garlands on the chandelier.

"It's a courtesy," I told her. "She's letting you come to her on your terms. You blow her off too many times, and she'll have you brought to her."

"I know." Andrea locked her teeth. Right. No intelligent life there. Arguing about it would just make things worse.

The two shapeshifters trotted back and took their seats at the table.

I explained about Chernobog, Adam's last name, and the fact that he likely had ties to a Russian community.

Andrea frowned. "A sacrifice gives the priest a magic boost."

I nodded. "It only lasts a couple seconds, but yes."

"Could he grab Adam and his doohickey, and teleport out?"

Now there was a thought. "If he was a really, really powerful volhv, probably. But why would the volhvs need Adam?"

"I don't get it," Derek said. "Why can't we just go to talk to them directly?"

"When I was a merc, I took a job to guard a man. He had stolen something from the volhvs, and I kept them from killing him. They won't talk to me or anyone associated with me," I paused to make sure I had their attention. "Volhvs throw around heavy-duty magic. Once we start asking questions, they will be on us like white on rice. We need a security protocol in place."

I looked at Derek. *Start earning your keep, boy wonder.*

He pushed away from the edge of the desk. "From this point on, we're on high alert. We leave together, we arrive together. This office is a small fortress." Derek pointed at the door and looked at Ascanio. "While in the office, that door stays locked. The back door is reinforced with a metal grate. That door stays locked and barred at all times as well. We do not open the doors unless we know the person on the other side and they smell right. If you have to leave, let someone know where you're going and when you will be back, unless it's an emergency."

The phone rang. I picked it up.

"Kate?" Ksenia's voice said. "Evdokia says meet her at John White Park. I'd run, not walk, if I were you."

"Thanks." I hung up. "I have an audience with the witches."

"We divide and conquer." Andrea rose. "Derek, you and I need to dig into de Harven's background. His house, his neighbors, history, everything we can get."

"What about me?" Ascanio asked.

"You hold the fort," I told him.

"But . . ."

"This is the point where you say, 'Yes, Alpha,'" Derek said.

Ascanio shot him a look that was pure murder. "Yes, Alpha."

This wasn't going to end well, I just knew it.

CHAPTER 9

IN ANOTHER LIFETIME, JOHN WHITE PARK HAD housed a golf course flanked by a nice middle-class neighborhood of brick houses and arbitrarily curving streets. The houses still survived, but the park had gone to hell some time ago. Dense underbrush flanked the crumbling asphalt road, and past it tall ashes and poplars reached their way to the sky, vying for space with mast-straight pines.

The pre-Shift maps put the park at around forty acres. The recent Pack map, which was the envy of every law enforcement official in the area and of which I was now a proud owner due to being the "Consort," put it closer to ninety. The trees had eaten a chunk of the subdivision south of Beecher Street and chomped their way through Greenwood Cemetery.

Ninety acres of dense woods was a lot of ground to cover.

I turned the corner. A large duck sat in the middle of the street. To the left of the duck, a deep ditch took up half of the road. No way through.

The magic was up and my Jeep made enough noise to give a thunder god a complex. You'd think the stupid bird would move. I honked the horn. The duck stared at me, ruffling its brown feathers.

Honk-honk. Hoooonk!

Nothing.

"Move, you silly bird."

The duck remained unimpressed. I should get out more. This mated life made me too soft. I couldn't even scare a duck off the road.

I got out of the Jeep and walked over to the duck. "Scoot!"

The bird gave me an evil stare.

I nudged her gently with my boot. The duck rose and flopped on my foot. The bill pinched my jeans and the bird tried to pull me to the left. One of us was nuts and it wasn't me.

"This isn't funny."

The bird turned left and let out a single loud quack.

"What is it? Did Timmy fall down a well?"

"Quack!"

I took a few steps forward and saw a narrow gap in the wall of green. A path, diving deep into the park. I peered at the forest. It didn't give off an "I'll kill you with my trees" vibe the way Sibley did, but it didn't look welcoming either.

The underbrush was too dense for a duck flight. Hard terrain to cross on foot, especially if you have to waddle.

"How am I supposed to follow you in there, you demented bird? You can't fly through that wood. Unless you're planning on dropping ten pounds . . ."

The duck shivered. Feathers crawled, sinking back into flesh, folding on themselves. My stomach lurched. Dense fuzz sprouted as the duck's body flowed, reshaping itself. The blob that used to be duck stretched one last time and snapped into a small brown bunny.

I closed my mouth with a click.

The bunny swiped some nonexistent dust from his nose with both paws and hopped down the path.

I went back to the Jeep, shut off the engine, and chased the duck-rabbit down the path into the dense thicket of the John White woods.

THE FOREST TEEMED WITH LIFE. TINY SQUIRRELS dashed up and down the trees. A ruffed grouse shot from the forest floor. Somewhere to the left a feral pig grunted. Three deer watched me pick my way down the path from a safe distance. I sank into the quiet measured gait I used when walking through the woods: quiet and deceptively unhurried. The little rabbit fell in step and scampered down by my side.

A bowstring snapped. I jerked to the side and jumped behind an oak. The rabbit crouched by my feet, shivering.

I leaned out just enough to see. An arrow sprouted from the ground where my foot had been a second ago. The angle was high. I looked up. Across the path, a man crouched in an old tree, poised in a spot where the trunk split into two massive branches. Young, mid- to late twenties. Tattered jeans stained with brown and green, plain brown T-shirt. Looked like Army issue. Hair cut short. The branches obscured his face and most of his chest. No place to sink a throwing knife.

When unsure of the stranger's intentions, the best policy is to open a meaningful dialogue. "Hey, dickhead! Who taught you to shoot, Louis Braille? That arrow missed me by a mile."

"I was aiming at the rabbit, you stupid bitch."

"You missed." If I pissed him off enough, he might move to get a better shot at me. My throwing knives couldn't wait to say hello.

"I see that."

"I figured I'd let you know, since you must be blind. Maybe you could practice by aiming at a barn."

A bowstring twanged. I ducked back behind the tree. An arrow sliced the leaves a hair left of the oak. He was good, but not great. Andrea would've nailed me by now.

"You alive?" he called out.

"Yep. Still breathing. You missed again, hotshot."

"Look, I have no problem with you. Give me the damn rabbit and I'll let you go."

Fat chance. "This is my rabbit. Get your own."

"It's not your rabbit. It's the witch's rabbit."

Figured. "You got a problem with the witch?"

"Yeah, I got a problem."

If Evdokia wanted him dead, he would be dead by now. This was her forest. She hadn't killed him, which meant she was amused by his antics, or worse, he was a relative or a son of a friend. Injuring him was out of the question, or I could kiss good-bye any chance of cooperation from Evdokia.

"Last chance to give me the rabbit and walk away from this."

"No."

"Suit yourself."

A shrill whistle burst through the woods, lancing my eardrums. It drowned all sound and shot up, higher and higher, to an impossible intensity. I clamped my hands over my ears.

The whistle built on itself, slicing the petals off wildflowers to the left and right of the oak, stabbing through my hands into my brain. The world faded. I tasted blood in my mouth.

The whistle stopped.

The sudden quiet was deafening.

Russian fairy tales talked of a Nightingale Bandit, able to bend trees with his whistling. I seemed to have run into the real-life version.

"You alive?" he called out.

Barely. "Yep." I dug in my brain, trying to recall the old Russian folk tales. Did he have any weakness . . . if he had, I couldn't remember any. "You whistle so prettily. Do you do weddings?"

"In five seconds I'm going to split that tree down the middle and you with it. Hard to make jokes with your lungs full of blood."

I slid a throwing knife from the sheath on my belt and sneaked a glance. He sat in a tree, one leg under him, the other dangling down. Relaxed and easy.

"Fine, you got me. I'm coming out."

"With the rabbit?"

"With the rabbit." I slipped a throwing knife in my hand, flipped it, and rustled the weeds to my left with my foot. The Nightingale leaned to the side, trying to get a better look. I lunged right and threw the knife. The blade sliced through the air. The wooden handle smashed into his throat. The Nightingale made a small gurgling sound. I sprinted to the tree, grabbed his ankle, and jerked him down. He crashed to the ground like a log. I hit him in the throat a couple of times to make sure he stayed quiet, flipped him on his stomach, yanked a plastic tie from my pocket, and tied his hands together.

"Don't go anywhere."

He gurgled something.

I circled the tree and ran into a horse tied to the branch, its head swaddled in some sort of canvas. A coil of rope waited on the saddle. Wasn't that nice.

I snagged the rope and hauled the Nightingale upright against the tree, facing the bark. He was short but well-muscled, his dark hair cut down to a mere fuzz on his head.

A hoarse gasp issued from his mouth. "Bloody bitch."

"That's nice." I finished tying him to the trunk. He couldn't even turn his head. "Just remember, it could've been the other end of the knife."

I stepped back. He looked secure enough. I sliced the tie off and dangled it by the bark so he could see it. "I'm going to go see the witch now. In your place, I'd try to get free. I might be in a bad mood on my way back. Come on, bunny."

The rabbit hopped down the path and I followed it, listening to the sweet serenade of curses.

THE STICK WAS SIX FEET TALL AND TOPPED WITH A grimy human skull, decorated by a half-melted candle. It jutted on the side of the road, like some grisly path marker. A few feet past it another yellowed skull offered a second candle. Some people used tiki torches. Some people used human skulls . . .

I looked at the duck-bunny. "What have you gotten me into?"

The duck-bunny rubbed his nose.

The skull looked a bit odd. For one, all the teeth were even. I stood on my toes and knocked on the bony temple. Plastic. Heh.

The bunny hopped down the trail. Nothing to do but follow.

The path opened into a garden. To the left, raspberry bushes rose next to gooseberry and currant. To the right, neat rows of strawberries sat, punctuated by spears of garlic and onion to keep the bugs off. Trees rose here and there, surrounded by herbs. I recognized apple, pear, cherry. Past it all, at the end of a winding path in the middle of a green lawn, sat a large log house. Rather, the back of the large log house. A couple of clean glass windows stared at me above a wraparound porch rail, but no door was visible.

We stopped at the house. Now what?

"Knock-knock?"

The ground shuddered under my feet. I took a step back. The

edge of the porch quaked and rose, up and up, rocking a little, and beneath it huge scaled legs dug into the ground with talons the size of my arms.

Holy shit.

The legs moved, turning the house with ponderous slowness ten feet above the ground: corner, wall, another corner, Evdokia in a rocking chair sitting on the porch.

"That's good," the witch said.

The house crouched down and settled back in place. Evdokia gave me a sweet smile. Middle-aged, she was plump and looked happy about it. Her face was round, her stomach was round, and a thick braid of brown hair snaked its way over her shoulder down to her lap. She was knitting some sort of a tube out of strawberry-colored yarn.

There was only one person in the entire Slavic mythology who had a house on chicken legs: Baba Yaga, the Grandmother Witch, the one with a stone leg and iron teeth. She was known for flying around in a mortar and for casual cannibalism of wandering heroes. And I'd walked to her house on my own power. Talk about delivering takeout.

Evdokia nodded to the chair next to her. "Well, come on. *V nogah pravdi nyet.*"

No truth in legs. Right. *Will you walk into my parlour, said the spider to the fly . . .*

Her smile got wider. "Scared?"

"Nope." I walked up the steps and took the chair. The house jerked, my stomach jumped, and the garden dropped down below. The house had straightened its chicken legs. Trapped. No matter. "Besides, I'm all gristle and tough meat anyway."

She chuckled. "Oh, I don't know, you might be just right for a nice big pot of borscht. Throw some mushrooms in there and mmm."

Borscht, bleah.

"Not a fan?" Evdokia reached to the small table between us, poured two cups of tea, and handed me one.

"No." I sipped. Great tea. I waited a moment to see if I turned into a goat. Nope, no horns, clothes were still there. I raised the cup at her. "Thank you."

"You're welcome. You hate borscht because Voron never

made it properly. I swear, anything you gave that man, he'd turn into mush. It took me the longest time to get him to eat normal food. For a while it was all 'borscht and taters.'"

The bunny hopped onto her lap. Her fingers brushed the dark fur. Flesh and fur seethed, twisting into a new body, and a small black cat rolled on her back on Evdokia's lap and batted at her fingers with soft paws.

For a moment the witch's control slipped, and I glimpsed magic wrapped around her like a dense shawl before she hid it again. If this went sour, getting off this porch alive would be a bitch.

"Now, go on," Evdokia said. "You're tangling my yarn."

The kitten rolled off, jumped to the porch rail, licked her paw, and began washing herself. An all-purpose pet. How do you turn a duck into a bunny? I didn't even know where to start.

The needles clicked in the older woman's hands. "Had any trouble finding your way?"

"Not really. Ran into a Nightingale Bandit, but that's about it."

"Vyacheslav. Slava, for short. He's angry because I won't let him rob people on my land. Slava talks a big game but he's harmless."

He split solid trees into splinters and made people's ears bleed with a supersonic whistle, but of course, he was completely harmless. Silly me, worrying for nothing.

Evdokia nodded at the platter of cookies. "Have one."

In for a penny, in for a pound. I snagged a cookie and bit into it. It broke in my mouth into a light powder of sweet vanilla crumbs, melting on my tongue, and suddenly I was five years old. I'd eaten those before when I was very little, and that taste jerked me right back into the past. A tall woman laughed somewhere to the side and called me. *"Katenka!"*

I shrugged her out of my mind. No time for a trip down the memory lane.

For a couple of minutes we sat quietly. The air smelled of flowers and a hint of something fruity. The tea was hot and tasted of lemon. It all seemed so . . . nice. I sneaked a glance at the witch. She seemed absorbed in her knitting. I needed to get on with the volhv questions.

Evdokia glanced at me. "Have you heard from your father? He isn't going to let his sister's death go."

I dropped my cup and caught it an inch from the porch boards.

"Nice catch." Evdokia pulled her yarn to give herself more slack.

My mouth was dry. I set the cup very carefully on the table. "How did you know?" *How much do you know? Who else knows? How many people do I have to kill?*

"About your father? You told me."

I chose my words very carefully. "I don't recall that."

"We were sitting right here. You had sugar cookies and tea and you told me all about how your daddy killed your mom, and how you had to get strong and murder him one day. You were all of six years old. And then Voron came and made you run laps around the garden. Do you remember me at all?"

I strained, trying to dig deep into my memories. A woman looked down at me, very tall, with bright red hair braided into a long plait over her shoulder, a black cat rubbing on her feet. Her eyes were blue and they laughed at me. A hint of a voice came, happy, offering me a cookie in Russian.

"I remember a woman . . . red hair . . . with cookies."

Evdokia nodded. "That was me."

"There was a cat." I vividly remembered a leather collar with the Russian word for "Kitty" written on it in black marker. I'd written it.

"Kisa. She died seven years ago. She was an old cat."

"You were tall."

"No, you were a short little thing. I was the same size, except I was skinny back then. And I dyed my hair fire-red so your stepdad would like me. I was a lot dumber in my youth. Voron, he seemed a proper man." Evdokia sighed. "Very strong, handsome. Dependable. I really liked him and I tried. Oy, how I tried. But it wasn't meant to be."

"Why not?"

"For one, it was all about your mother. A living woman I could handle, but fighting for your father with a dead one, well, that was a fight I couldn't win. For another, your father wasn't the man I thought he was."

"What do you mean?"

Evdokia raised the teakettle and refilled my cup. "Sugar?"

"No, thank you."

"You should have some. I'm about to speak ill of the dead. Sugar helps with the bitter."

She and Doolittle were separated at birth. Every time I suffered a near-death experience, he brought me syrup and claimed it was iced tea.

The older woman leaned back, gazing at the garden. "When I first saw you, you were two years old. You were such a cute, fat baby. Big eyes. Then Voron left and took you with him. I saw you again when you were four and then some months after, and then again. Every time I saw you, you got harder and harder. I'd braid your hair and put you in a pretty little dress and we'd go to Solstice Day, or out to our coven, and you would be so happy. Then he'd return and make you take it all off, and send you out to hunt feral dogs with a knife. You'd come back all bloody and sit by his feet like some sort of puppy, waiting for him to tell you that you'd done well."

I remembered that, sitting by Voron's feet. He didn't praise me often, but when he did, it was like I'd grown wings. I would've done anything for that praise.

"Finally Anna Ivanovna called me to come and see her. You were seven then and she was an Oracle Witch at the time. Old, old woman, frightening eyes. I took you with me. We visited at her house and she looked at you for a while, and then she said that it wasn't right what Voron was doing to you. It never sat well with me, and I'm not one to hold my tongue, so I cornered him that night over dinner and told him so. I told him that you were a little girl. An innocent. That if you were his own flesh and blood, he wouldn't be treating you this way."

If this was true, she stood up to Voron for my sake. Few people would. "He made me this way so I would survive. It was a necessity."

Evdokia pursed her lips for a long moment. A shadow darkened her eyes. Something inside me clenched, as if expecting a punch.

"What did Voron say?"

Evdokia looked down at her knitting.

"What did he say?"

"He said that you *weren't* his flesh and blood, and that was the whole point."

It hurt. It was the truth and I'd known it all my life, but it still hurt. He was my father in everything but blood. He cared about me, in his own way; he . . .

"I told him that the Covens would take you in," Evdokia said. "He said no. So I asked him what did he think would happen when you and Roland finally met. He told me that if he got lucky, you'd kill your father. If his luck ran out, then Roland would have to murder his own daughter and that was enough for him."

A sharp pain stabbed me somewhere right below the heart. My throat closed up.

It wasn't true. That conversation never took place. Voron loved my mother. She died for me. He trained me to make me stronger so that when the final confrontation came, I'd hold my own against my real father.

Anger vibrated in Evdokia's voice. "I told him to get out. I thought he'd cool off and I'd persuade him to give you to me. But he vanished and took you with him. The next time I saw you, you came to ask for a favor in the Belly of the Turtle. I almost didn't recognize you. It's not what we wanted for you. I know it wasn't all him. Kalina had ruined him, but I blame Voron all the same. It was his fault as well."

I struggled to speak, but the words wouldn't come out. I felt helpless, as if I were stuck in the middle of some void and couldn't break out of it.

"You were one of ours. We would've taken you in and hid you and taught you, but it was not to be. It gnaws at me to this day that I couldn't get you away from him."

My mouth finally managed to produce a sound. "What do you mean, one of yours?"

"Because of your mother, of course."

I stared at her.

Evdokia gasped. "He didn't tell you, that *pridurok*. Kalina, your mother, she was one of ours. An old Ukrainian family. Your grandmother's sister, Olyona, married my uncle Igor. We're in-laws."

The world jumped up and kicked me in the face.

CHAPTER 10

———◆———

"THEY'RE FROM A SMALL SETTLEMENT ON THE BORder of Ukraine and Poland," Evdokia said. "Zeleniy Hutir. It has been a bad place to live since antiquity. The border there jumps back and forth; one generation they'd be Polish, the next Russian, then Turkish, then something else. Legend says, in savage times, back when Ukraine was home to Slavic tribes, they made war with the Khazarian Empire to the east. During one of those raids, all the men from the village were taken. Magic was still in the world back then, although it was growing weaker, and the old ways were strong in the area. The women worked a charm on themselves, the power of enchantment, to make people want to please them. They got their men back. The power came with a huge price—most of them went barren after that—but if they wanted the shirt off your back, all they had to do was smile and you'd give it to them. That's where your mother's power comes from."

That sounded suspiciously familiar. "There is a woman working for the People. Her name is Rowena."

Evdokia nodded. "I've seen her. Same ancestry, but watered down. Her magic is like a fireplace; if you stand real close, you'll feel the warmth. Nothing to write home about. Your mother's magic was like a bonfire. It didn't just warm, it burned."

That would be a hell of a power.

"A lot of us, the old families that came over here from Russia and Ukraine, have known we were magical," Evdokia continued. "Even when the technology was at its peak, just before the Shift, a tiny trickle of magic still remained in the world and we saw its effects and we used it, in the small ways. The old women would spell a toothache away, find the drowned bodies, or meddle in people's love lives. I had a friend whose mother once dreamed that their house would catch on fire. Two days later her senile grandfather poured kerosene into their stove to get the fire going. Almost burned the whole place down. Small things like that.

"Your grandmother had the power but didn't use it. She got a doctorate in psychology and didn't truck with any of the old superstition, as she called it. She pushed Kalina the same way, except by the time your mother finished all her degrees, the magic was here to stay and she'd come into her power. She was very good at what she did. She used to lecture all over the country. Universities, military, cops. She did all that."

A light went on in my head. That had to be how she met Greg, my guardian. "Did she work with the Order?"

Evdokia nodded. "Oh yes. They tried hard to recruit her, too. Then she met your father, your real father, and all that went by the wayside. She vanished."

"Do you think she loved him?"

"I don't know," the old witch said. "We were never too close. Kalina's magic leaked, even when she kept it in check, and I don't take kindly to having my emotions jerked around. I'd seen her once since she went to stay with Roland—she'd come back for her mother's funeral. She seemed happy. Secure, like a woman who is well taken care of, loved, and isn't too worried about tomorrow."

I couldn't keep the bitterness from my voice. "That didn't last."

"No, it didn't. She must've been desperate to save you."

"She was. She stayed behind and sacrificed herself for my sake, because as long as she lived, Roland wouldn't stop chasing her. Voron took me."

Evdokia grimaced. "And that is the root of it all. I would do anything for my child. Kalina would do the same. Any sane woman would. She was trapped and with child, and she knew Roland would keep looking for her even if she ran to the ends of the Earth. She had to find someone to protect you, someone strong who knew how Roland's brain worked. She found Voron. He was strong and ruthless, but he was loyal to Roland."

The witch's blue eyes brimmed with regret. "She fried him, Katenka. She had time to do it, and she cooked him so hard, he left Roland for her and spent the last years of his life raising you. I should've seen it sooner, but love is blind."

No. No, they loved each other. Voron loved my mother. I'd seen it in his face. When he spoke of her, his whole demeanor changed. He became a different man.

If Evdokia was right, my mother would've worked on him for months, adjusting and realigning the emotional patterns just right, so that when Voron and I were alone, he wouldn't carry me back to Roland or throw me into some ditch.

In my head, my mother was a god. She was kind and wonderful, beautiful and sweet; she was all those things I wanted in a parent as a child. All those things that were ripped away from me. Unconditional love. Warmth. Joy. My mother was guilty of nothing except being naive and falling in love with the wrong man. She found herself trapped, and Voron saved her, because he loved her.

Nobody was like that. People weren't like that. I knew this wasn't how the world worked. I wasn't a child anymore; I'd seen the grit, savagery, and cruelty; I'd tasted my fair share of it and dished it out.

So why had I never doubted this rosy picture before? Why did I think my mother was a princess and Voron served as her knight in shining armor? I'd never questioned it. Not once.

Evdokia was talking. I barely heard her. The bright and shiny temple I'd built to my mother in my mind was falling to pieces and the noise was too loud.

". . . what she did is forbidden for a good reason. It never ends well. Kalina was conscientious. She must've felt it was the only way."

I held my hand up. The older woman fell silent.

Bits and pieces of forgotten memories floated to the surface: Evdokia's face, much younger. The little black cat. Going to a party in the woods, wearing a pretty dress. Some woman asking, *"How old are you, sweetie?"* My own voice, tiny and young, *"I'm five."* A little doll someone gave me, and Evdokia's voice, *"That's your baby. Isn't she pretty? You have to take care of your baby."* Voron, taking away the doll. *"We have to go now. It's extra weight. Remember, only take what you can carry."*

My whole childhood was a lie. Even Voron's thirst for vengeance wasn't real. It was implanted in him when my mother's magic had seared his brain. Was there anything at all real in my past? Anything at all would do at this point.

So pathetic.

All those times I drove myself into exhaustion to please Voron. All those times I did as I was told. People I killed, things I mourned, all the shit he put me through. All of it was so when my father and I met, we could kill each other, and Voron would have the last laugh.

Fury exploded in me in a raw torrent. I wanted to rip his grave apart, pull his bones out and shake them, screaming. I wanted to know if it was true, if all of it was true.

"I warned you," Evdokia said softly.

"He is dead," I said. My voice had no inflection. "He's dead and I can't hurt him."

"Now, don't be like that," Evdokia murmured. "He was human, Katenka. He was proud of you in his own way."

"Proud of what, an attack dog he made? Point me in the right direction, take my muzzle off, and watch me rip things apart for a meager crumb of praise."

Evdokia reached over and held my hand.

I was the biological by-product of a megalomaniac and a woman who magically brainwashed others into doing her will, and I was raised by a man who reveled in the knowledge that my biological father would one day kill me. All those years, my life, my accomplishments, any feelings I had for him, everything I was, Voron would've traded all of it for a chance to see the look on Roland's face when he slit my throat. And my mother made him that way.

Magic splayed from me, fueled by my rage.

On the porch rail the cat arched her back, her fur standing on end. The floor beneath my feet shuddered.

"Easy, easy now," Evdokia murmured. "You're scaring the house."

Get over it. Just get over it. Put it away, shove it aside, so you can deal with it later.

The magic filled me, threatening to burst out. The house rocked. Cups clicked against each other on the table. Evdokia clenched my hand.

I had to get out of here alive. If I let it all go now, Evdokia would fight me to save herself. I needed a clear head.

Put it away.

I could do it. I was strong enough. I had Voron to thank for it.

I pulled the magic back. All the anger, all the pain, I collapsed it on itself and stuffed it away. It hurt.

I took my hand out of Evdokia's fingers and picked up my teacup. Lukewarm tea touched my lips. "It's cold. I think I need a refill."

Evdokia looked at me for a long moment. *That's right. Barely human, you got it.* I had a chance when I was five. Now it was too late.

"You never said what you would do about your father," the witch said.

"Nothing has changed. It's still him or me."

"You're not strong enough," Evdokia said. "Not yet. I can make you stronger."

"At what price?"

She heaved a sigh. "No price, Katenka. You are one of our own."

"If I'm one of your own, why did you wait till now? Why didn't you help me when my aunt almost murdered me?" *Where were you when Voron died and I had no place to go?*

Evdokia pursed her lips.

I fixed her with my stare. "What do you want from me?"

The witch's magic flared. She set her cup down. "Sienna has foreseen a tower over Atlanta."

Towers were Roland's trademark. "Sienna of the Witch Oracle? Does the Oracle know who I am?"

Evdokia nodded. "Yes."

"Who else knows?" The list of people to murder was getting longer and longer.

"Just us." Evdokia matched my gaze. Her blue eyes turned hard. "We've kept it to ourselves, too."

"Why?"

"Because we govern ourselves. Nobody tells us what to do."

I smiled at her. It wasn't a pleasant smile. The cat leaped off the porch rail into Evdokia's lap and growled, puffing its fur.

"I get it. You have power. Status. Respect. You know Roland is coming one way or the other. And Roland doesn't tolerate any government except his own. He doesn't have allies or friends. He has servants."

Evdokia narrowed her eyes. "That's right. I've earned my place in this world; with backbreaking work I've earned it. I won't be bending my knee to anyone, not to a government, not to a judge, not to that cursed tyrant."

I rose and leaned against the porch post. "I'm your best bet to keep Roland from taking over."

"Yes."

"Young, in need of being taught . . ."

Evdokia crossed her arms. "Yes."

"Easily manipulated? Emotionally compromised? Are these my best qualities?"

Evdokia threw her hands up in exasperation.

"I would just like to know the score from the start. So I have no disappointments later."

"Boginiya, pomogi mne s rebyonkom."

"I doubt the Goddess will help you with this child. The last time I came across a goddess, she decided she didn't want any."

Evdokia shook her head. "You are what you are, Kate. You can't run away from yourself. Do you think your lion didn't consider who you were before he swept you off your feet? All those years, all those women, and you are the one he mated with. He was interested in more than your bed, I can tell you that."

Ouch. "Leave Curran out of this."

"The man isn't a fool. And neither are you. Now is the time to build alliances and learn, because when your papa shows up here, it will be too late. I'm offering power. Knowledge. Things you will require. I can help you. You don't even have to do anything in return."

I would take her up on it. I would come back here, and sit,

and drink tea, and eat cookies. I'd bring Julie with me and watch her play with the mutant cat-rabbit-duck thing. But not yet. Not now.

I took the picture of de Harven's body from my pocket and passed it to her. Evdokia glanced at it, spat three times over her left shoulder, and knocked on the wooden rail.

"Chernobog's volhv. Grigorii. That's his work."

"This picture was taken in the workshop of a Russian inventor. Name is Adam Kamen."

"Ah! Adam Kamenov. Yes, I've heard about that. Smart boy, no common sense. He was building something vile. Had all the elder volhvs tied up in knots. Whatever it was, they told him not to build it. I gather he built it anyway."

"He's missing."

"They have him, then." Evdokia shrugged.

"The volhvs sacrificed someone to teleport him out."

The old witch grimaced. "It doesn't surprise me. They are men. They solve things directly. Grigorii needed power, so he took it. Give me a coven of thirteen witches and I could've teleported him too, and without blood. We'd channel the magic through us, pull it from nature through our bodies and focus it on the target. Grigorii's way is to take everything from one. Our way is to take a little bit from each of us, so everyone can recover."

"I need to find Adam."

She raised her chin. "I'll ask around."

She wouldn't do anything that put her in conflict with the volhvs. She would teach me, and she might throw me a crumb of information now and then, but she wouldn't fight my battles for me. That was fine.

I started down the porch stairs. "Thank you for the tea."

"Don't mention it."

The house crouched down and I stepped onto the path. The moment my feet touched the ground, the porch rose back up.

"Think about what I've said, Katenka," Evdokia called from above. "Think carefully."

WHEN I WALKED OUT OF THE WOODS, A MAN STOOD by my Jeep, leaning on a tall unfinished wooden staff with a thick top. It looked like he had just cut a thick sapling, haphaz-ardly chopped off the branches, stripped it of its bark, and made himself a walking stick.

A black robe hung from his shoulders down to just below his knees, revealing leather boots. Silver embroidery ran along the wide cuffs of the robe and along the hem. A wide leather belt caught the robe at the waist, and small canteens and charms dripped from it on chains and cords. A deep hood hid most of his face.

A volhv. If the staff hadn't given him away, the charms on the belt would have. Judging by the embroidery, not a light-weight, but not one of the really old ones either. The younger volhvs couldn't afford hand-stitched silver, and the older ones didn't bother with it.

"I have a real problem with people in hoods," I said.

"That's too bad." He had a rich voice, deep and confident. Yep, a fun and exciting storm of magic was about to come my way. Why was it I never got a tech shift when I needed one?

The volhv pulled the hood back. Large eyes, dark like mol-ten tar and framed in thick black eyelashes, looked at me with wry amusement. His features were well cut: high cheekbones, strong masculine jaw, and an aquiline nose, made more promi-nent because the hair on the sides of his head had been shaved off past his ears. The rest of his jet-black hair fell down his back like a horse mane. His mustache was black, too. His beard was nonexistent, except for a carefully trimmed goatee that met his mustache on both sides of his mouth. His full lips curved into a half smile.

The overall effect was decidedly villainous. He needed a black horse and a barbarian horde to lead. That or a crew of cutthroats, a ship with blood-red sails, and some knucklehead heroine to lust after. He would fit right into Andrea's romance novels as some evil pirate captain. If he started stroking his beard, I'd have to kill him on principle.

"Grigorii?" Probably not.

"Grigorii doesn't bother with the likes of you."

As expected. "Look, I've had a bad day. How about you just walk away from my Jeep?"

The volhv smiled wider, flashing even white teeth. "You went to see the witch. What did she tell you?"

"She said your dress was so last season."

"Oh? Is that so?" He raised his hand to his goatee.

That does it. "Yeah. And what's with the beard and the horse mane? You look like Rent-a-Villain."

The volhv's eyes widened. He waved his hand at me. "Well you don't look . . . female . . . in your pants."

"That's a hell of an insult. Did you think of it all by yourself or did you have to ask your god for help?"

The volhv pointed at me. "Now, don't you blaspheme. That's not nice. Tell me what the witch said, hmm? Now, come on, you know you want to tell me." He winked at me. "Come on, share. You tell me, I don't kill you right away, everybody's happy."

I pulled Slayer out of its back sheath.

The volhv blinked. "No? Don't want to tell me?"

"Step away from my vehicle."

"I didn't want to do this, but fine." He raised his staff and struck the pavement. The thick wood at the top of the staff flowed, morphing. A vicious wooden beak emerged from the shaft, followed by savage round eyes.

"Safety's off," the volhv said. "Last chance to tell me what the witch said."

In my head I charged, Slayer ready to strike. But my knee popped with a dry crunch, my leg snapped, and I rolled onto the pavement just in time to see the end of the volhv's staff as it punctured my chest. Great. No running. Doolittle had performed medical miracles and the knee didn't hurt, but I didn't want to take chances. I needed to save the leg for the close-up fighting. I'd have to rely on magic until I got within striking range. And if I did kill him, I'd have a volhv stampede on my doorstep. They'd race each other to take a shot at me. I'd start the war between the volhvs and the Pack and kill Adam Kamen with one fight. Oh goody.

I strode toward the volhv, broadcasting as much menace as I could muster. Maybe he'd panic and drop to his knees with his hands in the air.

Fat chance.

The volhv watched me. "Hurry up. At least put some effort into it!"

"For the likes of you? Why bother?"

The volhv spun in place, his staff slicing through the air. The wooden beak gaped open with a creak and belched a swarm of tiny black flies. Probably poisonous. Great. This fight was in the bag.

I jerked a bag of rosemary powder from my belt and ripped it open, chanting under my breath.

The swarm shot to me.

I tossed the dust into the air. My magic clutched it and it hung motionless like a cloud frozen in midmotion. The swarm pierced it. For half a second, nothing happened and then the flies and rosemary rained to the ground.

Sweat drenched my hairline. That took a wallop of magic. I kept walking.

The volhv planted the staff into the pavement and let go. It remained upright. He jerked a twig charm off his belt, snapped it in half and tossed one part into the street, clutching the other in his fist. The twig exploded into thick black smoke and coalesced into a mastiff-sized dog. Rivulets of smoke slid and curled along its sable fur. Pure white eyes stared at me, like two stars caught in a storm cloud.

I fed magic into my saber. The opaque blade shimmered slightly and hissed, perspiring. Thin tendrils of smoke rose from the blade.

The volhv's eyebrows rose. He snarled a single word. The dog's maw opened, releasing glowing fangs. The smoke beast charged.

It came at me, massive paws pounding the pavement. I stepped into its charge and sliced. Slayer's blade severed the dog's neck in a clean precise cut. No resistance. Shit.

The smoke along the cut swirled, sealing it. The dog snapped at my left leg, but I was already moving. The glowing fangs barely scraped my jeans just above the knee. A thin line of pain cut my thigh, like a hot wire. Wet heat drenched my skin—blood. I spun and sank Slayer's blade into the dog's molten eye. The enchanted saber slid halfway in. Nothing. I jerked it and danced away as the dog's fangs clicked closed a hair's breadth from my arm.

If only I had a portable fan with me, I'd be all set. Maybe if I huffed really hard, it would disperse.

A hot dark stain soaked my left pant leg. I was bleeding like a stuck pig.

The volhv moved his fist. The dog backed up, snapping its

teeth. He was controlling it like a puppet with the other half of the twig in his hand.

"Ready to talk?" the volhv asked.

"Not a chance."

The volhv jerked his fist. The dog rushed at me, smoke paws striking tiny wisps of steam from the pavement.

I stuck my hand into the cut in my jeans. It came away slicked with crimson. My blood's magic prickled my skin.

I had only a fraction of a second to pull this off.

The dog leaped. I shied right and stuck my hand deep into the coils of smoke on its side. Magic pulsed from my hand, bristling my blood into a dozen sharp needles. Crimson spikes pierced the dog. Across the street the volhv screamed, cradling his fist with his other hand. The twig rolled from his fingers. The smoke collapsed on itself, sucked into a small twisted branch on the ground. I stomped on it, crushing it into pieces.

The spikes shriveled into black dust and fell off my fingers, melting into dust. My hand felt like I'd stuck it into boiling water.

"Fuck, that hurts." The volhv bared his teeth at me.

Twenty feet between us. I ran.

He spun his staff, chanting.

Ten feet. I flipped Slayer in my hand, reversing the blade.

Six.

The volhv swung the staff, aiming to hit me from the left. I blocked the strike with my sword, grabbed his right wrist with my left hand, forcing the staff sideways, and smashed the dull edge of Slayer's blade into his right side. Ribs crunched. I bashed the volhv's right arm with the flat of the blade. He dropped the staff. I let Slayer slide from my fingers, dropped into a half crouch, pulled my arms to the sides of my body, and straightened my knees, driving both fists up into the soft underside of his jaw. The volhv's head jerked back, his body wide open. I sank a punch into his solar plexus. All of the wind rushed out of his lungs in a single, painful breath. The volhv doubled over, and I grabbed his left arm, jerked him forward, and swung my right arm in a wide arc, smashing my fist into the back of his head. The volhv's eyes rolled up and he went down.

I danced back on my toes, light and ready, in case he decided to get up.

The volhv lay still. His staff snapped its beak at me in impotent fury.

It was over. I still had all this anger to work out, but it was over. Damn it.

I stopped dancing and felt his pulse. Alive and well. Sleeping like a baby, except babies didn't usually wake up to a world of hurt.

I swiped Slayer off of the pavement. "Sorry."

If the sword resented being used as a stick, it didn't say anything.

The magic drained from the world. The ferocious monster on the volhv's staff faded back into ordinary wood.

I raised my arms and stared at the sky. "Really? Now? Would it have killed you to end fifteen minutes ago?"

The Universe was snickering at me.

I sighed and headed to my Jeep to get medical supplies, rope, and gasoline. My blood was all over the street, screaming my identity to anyone who'd cared to listen, and I needed to set it on fire.

CHAPTER 11

———◆———

WHEN I RETURNED TO THE OFFICE, ASCANIO OPENED the door and hit me with a thousand-watt smile. The smile evaporated with his next breath.

"I smell blood."

"It's nothing. Where is everybody?"

"The wolf and Andrea haven't come back yet."

"There is a bound man in the back of my Jeep. I need you to carry him in and lock him in the loup cage. Don't untie him. If he comes to, don't speak with him. He's a powerful mage and he'll try to conjure painful things."

Ascanio took off. I walked to my desk. A neat stack of files sat in its center, each beige folder marked with the Pack's paw. Next to them waited a binder filled with papers. I opened it.

Article Seven, Section A. Clan Land and Property. All real property, as defined by **Article 3, Section 1.0**, is jointly owned by the Pack, with rights of survivorship. Each Pack member has a right to use and enjoy the entire property, but may not prevent another Pack member from also doing so. The real property subject to a lease between a Clan and the Pack must be for the Clan's official meeting house, exclusively. Any nonconforming use is a breach of the lease agreement and will function as the immediate revocation of a Clan's lease. Any personal property located on real property leased by a Clan shall be deemed the sole property of the Clan . . .

What the hell?

Ascanio maneuvered the volhv's body through the door, carrying him over his shoulder like a sack of potatoes, and brandished the volhv's staff at me. "What should I do with the stick?"

"Lock it in the closet. And be careful; when magic is up, it bites."

Ascanio nodded and took the volhv to the loup cage. I pondered the phone. Sooner or later, I'd have to call the volhvs and tell them that I had their boy hog-tied in my back room. Best-case scenario, they would trade Adam Kamen for him. Worst-case scenario, we all die agonizing deaths. Hmmm. Whom to call and what to say?

Ascanio came back. "What happened to him? He looks like he got his ass run over by a car."

He was run over by my fist. "What are these files?"

"Barabas left them for you. He said to tell you that the Beast Lord is gone on an important errand."

Yes, hunting Leslie before she did any major damage.

"And that you will be handling the petitions tonight."

Full stop.

There were two things I hated: being on display and making decisions about other people's lives. Hearing petitions involved both. When a shapeshifter had a problem with someone within the Pack, it went up the chain to the alpha couple, who acted as arbitrators. If two different Packs were involved, two sets of alphas had to come to a decision. If a decision couldn't be reached, the matter went to Curran and, because I was his mate, also to me.

My original plan was to avoid the petitions altogether. Unfortunately, Curran had explained to me at great length and in a lot of detail how this was one of the burdens of the alpha and how he was disinclined to suffer it by himself. Which was why once a week, I ended up sitting next to His Majesty behind a very large desk in a very large room, providing a convenient eye target for the audience of shapeshifters. Up to now all I'd had to do was look like I was paying attention and hope that Curran didn't have to cut any babies in half. Dealing with petitions by myself was *not* on my agenda. I didn't even know which cases were scheduled for the hearing or what they were about.

I tapped the binder. "Those are petitions, what is this?"

"Barabas said that they're essentially CliffsNotes from the Pack's code of law relevant to the hearing."

I swore.

"Barabas said you might say that. I'm supposed to tell you this." Ascanio cleared his throat and produced a remarkably accurate impression of Barabas's tenor. "Courage, Your Majesty."

"I will kill him."

"The Beast Lord or Barabas?"

"Both." I rubbed my face and glanced at the clock on the wall. Ten past four. The petitions were scheduled at eight, and it would take me an hour to get from here to the Keep, which meant I had a grand total of three hours to cram this stuff into my head. Argh. I so didn't want to do this. The volhv would have to wait until I sorted this out. Well, he wasn't made out of ice cream; it wasn't like he'd melt.

"Any messages from the Keep?"

"No, Consort."

"Don't call me Consort. Call me Kate."

No news of Julie. Damn it, how long did it take one kid to walk a hundred miles? If Curran's trackers didn't report in by tomorrow evening, I'd go and look for her myself. Rene and her world-ending gadget would just have to wait.

I gathered the files and the binder. "I'm going upstairs. I don't care who comes to the door, unless there is blood or fire, I'm not to be disturbed."

Ascanio clicked his heels together and snapped a crisp salute. "Yes, Consort!"

Some days I understood why Curran roared.

READING THROUGH PETITIONS MADE MY BRAIN hurt. I knocked the first two out in an hour, and then I hit a property dispute between the two clans and got stuck. Sorting out who was who and what belonged to whom was like untangling a Gordian knot. If I shook my head and bits and pieces of the Pack's Law fell out of my hair, I wouldn't be surprised. I would carefully sweep them up and put them back in Barabas's binder, but I wouldn't be surprised.

It didn't help that my memory kept replaying the conversation with Evdokia. *Do you think your lion didn't consider who you were before he swept you off your feet?*

What she had told me about Voron and my mother hurt. For the first fifteen years of my life I had trusted Voron completely, without any reservation. If I was in trouble, he would drag me out of it. If he made me endure something, it was necessary for my survival. I didn't have a mother, but I had a father. He was a god of my childhood. He could do anything, he could fix anything, he could kill anyone, and he loved me because I was his daughter. Because that was what fathers did.

It was a lie. A betrayal so deep, it cracked something vital inside me and now I was full of rage. I wasn't his daughter. I was a tool to be used. If I broke in the final battle, no big loss, as long as I did the damage.

It hurt. Seeing it now with adult eyes hurt. I needed to scream, to punch and kick and hit something until my pain went away. If I sat still and really let myself think about it, I would lose it. But whatever had happened between my mother and Voron happened in the past. I'd wrestle with it and then I'd get over it. I couldn't change it; it was done.

Curran and I were happening now.

When I was seventeen, with Voron dead for two years and Greg acting as my guardian, I met a guy. Derin was a few years older, handsome, funny. I wasn't exactly in love, but I was in something. For my first time, it could've been worse. The morning after, I walked out of his apartment and walked right into Greg waiting for me on the street.

I'd thought there would be screaming. Voron had a lot of patience, but he'd screamed on occasion. I should've known better. Greg never screamed. He just explained things in a logical, unhurried manner until he made you scream instead.

Greg took me to the Sunrise House to have breakfast. He bought me one of those giant pancake combos with jam and whipped cream and while I ate, he talked. I could still remember his patient calm voice. "Sex is a human necessity. It's also an issue of trust, for you more than for other people. Intimacy puts you in danger, Kate."

I shrugged. "I can take Derin. He's not all that."

Greg sighed. "That's not what I mean. Physical intimacy leads to emotional intimacy and vice versa. If you have a relationship with Derin, even if you intend for it to be purely physical, sooner or later you will let down your guard. Tell me, what's the worst thing that can happen if Derin realizes how powerful you are?"

I stuffed a huge chunk of my pancake into my mouth and chewed it slowly, just to irritate him. "He'll connect the dots and sell me out to my real father?"

"That would be unfortunate, yes. But that's not the worst thing that can happen."

"If you're talking about transference, we used protection. I'm not an idiot, Greg."

He shook his head.

"Well, then I don't know."

Greg's blue eyes fixed on me. "Derin is an ambitious sort. Perfect grade point average, valedictorian, the first of his class to be promoted to Apprentice Level Two by the Mage Academy."

"Been spying on me?"

He brushed the barb aside. "Derin aims to go far in life. He wants it all: money, prestige, respect, power. He wants it so badly, he can almost taste it. And you are vulnerable, Kate. You miss your father and you dislike me. You're desperate for acceptance. If you persist, sooner or later—and I believe sooner—Derin will recognize your potential. He'll become the best boyfriend you could ever hope to find: kind, gentle, understanding. You'll fall in love or at least become infatuated. It's natural: if someone makes you feel better, you want to be with that person. Then Derin will ask you to do something for him. It will start small. Perhaps he has a problem with another student. Or he needs to impress a professor to get a scholarship. A small thing. Nothing really.

"It might require you to use your magic or perhaps just a drop or two of your blood. You'll do it, because you love him. Then he'll ask something else. And then something bigger. And every time you comply, he'll pamper you and make you feel as if you're the only woman on Earth. And then one day you'll wake up and realize that you've been used, that you've chained yourself to this man who seeks only to further his own interests at the expense of your feelings and safety, and that his careless use of your power has drawn the attention of your father. Now you must defend him and yourself and you're not ready. Then, when the opportunity presents itself, he'll betray you to save his own skin. This is the worst thing that can happen. Even if you escape, this experience will scar you and emotional scars never heal completely. You'll never recover."

I stared at him, pancakes forgotten.

Greg drank his coffee. "You have a problem, Kate. If you form a relationship with someone weak, he'll be a liability. He'll feel inadequate and you'll deny yourself the satisfaction and joy of a true companionship. If you form a relationship with someone powerful, you run the risk of exposure or of being manipulated and used. Don't ever think that a man in a position of power won't tear down every wall in his way to form an alliance with you. Your magic makes you a priceless asset. How can you tell if someone loves you or craves your power?"

"I don't know."

Greg nodded. "Neither do I. A one-night stand with no strings attached is the safest option for you. It's not fair, but such is your reality. It's your life, Kate. I will advise you, but I won't force you to follow my advice. I do urge you to consider what I've told you. You've come this far. I'd hate to see it all go to waste."

I'd gone back to Derin right after breakfast. We holed up in his apartment, drank cheap booze, and had sex for two days. At the end of the long weekend, I decided to take a shower. When I came out, Derin was holding my sword. He'd never seen anything like that before. Could he take some samples? He was doing an independent study for the Mage Academy. It would really help him out.

I told him I'd trade samples for a chicken burrito. The closest place that sold them was a couple of miles away. He complained, but I wouldn't budge. The moment he left, I called Greg. It took Greg twenty minutes to get to the apartment, and by the time he got there, I'd shaken the sheets and pillowcases over the balcony, loaded them into the washing machine, swept the floor, and drowned the dishes in the sink. I wiped down the furniture and cleaned the shower drain. I removed all trash, every tissue, every stray hair, everything that could possibly betray me. Greg purified the apartment, searing it with his power. If any residual trace of my magic remained, it would be hidden. If Derin m-scanned the apartment, the m-scan would register only the blazing blue explosion of diviner power. Then we and the trash bags left the building. Forty-eight hours later I was on my way to the Order's Academy, and I didn't know if it was because I wanted to get away from Derin or to get away from Greg, because he'd turned out to be right.

I stared at the files marked with the paw print.

Curran was paranoid. He valued his safety and the safety of the Pack; hell, he dedicated himself to preserving it. I always thought I put him in danger, and I told him so. He wanted me anyway. That meant everything to me.

But Curran was also a manipulator. If I sat there and objectively looked at the situation, the picture didn't look pretty. Roland had marked the Pack for elimination. Curran had grown too powerful, and my father wanted to destroy him now, before the Pack grew any stronger. He had attacked it with rakshasas, and when that failed, he sent my aunt to decimate the shapeshifters. One way or the other, the clash between Roland and the Pack was coming. What did Curran have to lose by mating with me?

I wanted him so much that I'd never considered he might want to use me. All this time I'd been focused on worrying that my ancestry would keep him from being with me. It'd never crossed my mind that he could view it as an asset. It was time to take the blinders off.

When I looked into his eyes, I knew he loved me. He came for me when I had given up all hope of surviving. He rescued me from a horde of demons. He wanted to protect me. He never actually said it, but it felt like he loved me.

Also, Voron was a great father, and my mother was a saint. And pink unicorns would fly around on rainbow wings over hills made of chocolate and rivers of honey.

I pushed away from the table. I was driving myself crazy. This brooding wasn't me.

The door creaked. Probably Andrea and Derek. Good; if I sat here with my own thoughts for another minute, I'd need a straitjacket.

CHAPTER 12

————◆————

THE MOMENT I STEPPED DOWNSTAIRS, ANDREA grabbed me. A pink flush painted her cheeks. She seemed agitated. Agitated wasn't good.

"We need to talk. Derek, you, too."

Everybody needed to talk to me. I was getting sick of talking. "Before we do that, I've got something to show you."

I led her to the loup cage. The volhv sat upright, tied to the chair. His eyes were closed. He looked passed out.

Andrea's eyes widened. "Who is that?"

"That's a volhv,"

The volhv's eyelashes trembled. Wakey, wakey.

"The one who kidnapped Kamen?"

"No. The one who kidnapped Kamen was an elder volhv. This one is more like middle management, powerful but not up there yet."

Andrea arched her eyebrows. "Aha. How did he get all beat up?"

"He hassled me about meeting with Evdokia."

"Were you in a bad mood or something?"

You have no idea. "Yeah. You might say that."

Andrea pursed her lips. "Why does he look like a hidalgo pirate? I thought Russians were blond."

"And we all carry a bottle of vodka in our pocket and wear a fur hat year-round." The volhv opened his black eyes. His gaze snagged on Andrea. He blinked and stared, stunned.

Oh boy.

"Pretending to be passed out," I said.

"Just resting my eyes." He was still looking at Andrea. "It's nice in here. Peaceful." A slow smile bent the volhv's lips. "Although if you would like me to model a fur hat for you instead, we could come to an understanding."

Andrea barked a short derisive laugh and left the room.

"Does she work here with you?" the volhv asked.

"You—never mind," I told him, went out, and locked the door behind me for good measure.

Andrea crossed her arms. "The nerve. Did you see those eyes. Pow!"

Yeah, pow. "You wanted to tell me something?"

"Yes. Derek, too. Kitchen?"

"Yeah."

The three of us landed at the kitchen table. Ascanio sauntered in and leaned against the wall.

"De Harven's records are pristine," Andrea began "Everything checked out. He did four years in the Army. I found his DD214, the discharge papers, and called it in to the National Personnel Records. They said it would take two months to confirm, so I called it in to a buddy of mine in the Military Supernatural Defense Unit. He says everything on MSDU's end comes up roses. I also found de Harven's NCO evaluations and his pay stubs."

A man might falsify his discharge papers, but he'd have to go an extra mile to fake pay stubs and performance reports.

"Orlando PD confirmed he was a cop," Derek said. "I talked to two people who knew him. They said he was a good cop. Dedicated."

"We went through de Harven's apartment." Andrea opened an envelope and pulled a Polaroid out. It was a picture of a digital painting. A sunrise died down over the sea, leaving ragged gray clouds in its wake. In the center of the picture a lone rock jutted from troubled water, supporting a white spire of a lighthouse that sent a brilliant beam of light toward the horizon. The caption under the image said, DARKNESS REIGNS AT THE FOOT OF THE LIGHTHOUSE.

"Is this supposed to tell me something?" I asked.

"It's a lighthouse," Andrea said in the same voice in which people usually said, "It's a murder."

"It's a very nice lighthouse. Lots of people have paintings of lighthouses." Where was she going with this?

Andrea dug in the envelope and pulled out a picture in a frame. Two rows of teenagers stood in their graduation robes. Andrea pointed to a dark-haired kid on the left. "De Harven." She stabbed the blond kid on the far right. "Hunter Becker."

I waited to see if she shed any more light on it.

"Hunter Becker!" Andrea repeated. "They were in the same high school class!"

"Who is Hunter Becker?"

"Becker the Gory? Lighthouse Keepers? Boston?"

"I would've preferred Becker the Easily Surrendering or Becker the Quite Reasonable, but beyond that his name tells me nothing."

Andrea sighed. "The Order suspects the existence of a secret society called the Lighthouse Keepers. They're well organized and really well hidden."

"A secret society?" Derek frowned. "What, like Masons?"

Andrea huffed. "Yes, just like Masons, but instead of getting together, putting on silly hats, and getting drunk and sponsoring charity events, they get together and think up ways of killing people and destroying government buildings. They hate magic, they hate magic users, they hate magic creatures, and they would love to exterminate the lot of us with extreme prejudice."

Well, that pretty much covered everyone in this room.

"Why?" Derek asked.

"Because they hold technological civilization to be the perfect state of humanity. They think magic is dragging us into barbarism and they must preserve the light of progress and technology. Without it, we would all descend into darkness." Andrea shook her head. "Three years ago Hunter Becker blew up a medmage hospital in Boston. Dozens dead, hundreds injured. They tracked him down and he walked out straight into a SWAT unit, clenching a gun in each hand."

Suicide by cop. Always a good sign.

Andrea held up the Polaroid, pointing to the caption. "This

was written on the wall of his safe house. That is what in our business is called a 'clue.' "

Thank you, Miss Smartass. "Excellent work, Miss Marple."

She bared her teeth at me. "Kate, these people are fanatics. That stunt in Boston took a lot of teamwork. The hospital was developing an experimental magical treatment for the blue flu. They had several virulent variations of it in their labs, guarded better than Fort Knox."

She counted off on her fingers. "Someone built several bombs with an elaborate fail-safe. Someone bypassed three levels of security. Someone distributed the bombs on separate floors in restricted areas with limited access. Finally, someone had given Becker access to the building across the street, which was the local police station. It was estimated that at least six people were directly involved in the bombing, some of whom had to be hospital personnel. Nobody except Becker was ever discovered, and the only reason they found Becker was that he had been injured by debris and left a blood trail. None of the people were planted, Kate. They actually worked there. Since then, the Order has found two other instances of terrorism, all involving teams of covert operatives. That's how these people operate: they recruit young and activate their members as the need arises."

Sleeper cells of domestic terrorists. This investigation was getting better and better. "How do you know all this?"

Andrea bit her lip. "Becker was a knight of the Order."

If the Keepers infiltrated the Order, it would be impossible to find them. With their anti-magic attitude, they would fit right in. Someone like Ted would welcome them with open arms. Hell, Ted could be one of them. I would have to be very careful now, because I very much wanted Ted to be involved. So much so that if I wasn't careful, I'd twist reality to implicate Ted, whether he was guilty or not.

"They infiltrated the Order and the PAD," Derek said. "De Harven was a cop before he was a guard."

"It could literally be anyone. It could be Rene." Andrea waved her arms. "It could be Henderson. Anyone."

"Not anyone," I said. "I'm not one, you're not one, neither is Derek. I'm reasonably sure we can exclude Curran and the kid as well."

Ascanio grinned.

Andrea stared at me. "You're not taking me seriously!"

"That's probably because you're not excited enough," Derek said. "You should clench your fists like they do in the movies, shake them, and yell, 'This is bigger than any of us! It goes all the way to the top!'"

Andrea pointed her finger at him. "You shut up. I don't have to take shit from you. From her, maybe. But not from you."

"I trust your professional judgment," I said. "If you say there is a secret society, then there is one. I'm simply trying to define the boundaries of our paranoia. Did all the other incidents involve more than one person?"

"Yes."

I thought out loud. "If de Harven was a member of the Lighthouse Keepers, then he'd been activated to obtain Adam Kamen's device, which means we can expect there to be an entire cell."

"Probably."

"The optimal size of a terrorist cell ranges between seven and eight members," Derek said. "Groups below five members lack sufficient resources, manpower, and flexibility, while a group above ten begins to fracture due to specialization. Larger groups require managerial oversight to remain cohesive. That's difficult to do while the cell is in sleeper status."

I closed my mouth with an audible click.

Derek shrugged apologetically. "I spent a lot of time with Jim."

"So we can expect between five and ten people?" I asked.

"Probably closer to five," Derek said. "Especially since de Harven is dead. However, that's assuming that we're dealing with a single cell. They may have more than one cell in a city the size of Atlanta, and they also may mobilize neighboring cells if their goal is vital enough."

Nobody would awaken a sleeper cell for something minor, not when its members have been dormant for years. "How many people can we expect if they threw caution to the wind and moved all available cells in?"

Derek frowned, concentrating. "I'd guess between fifty and three hundred. The more people, the less cohesive the group.

If I were them, I'd rely on hired muscle. Not every job has to involve the entire cell. Some targets can be eliminated by a contract killer, for example. It minimizes the risk and the exposure—if the job goes sour, the killer can only betray one member of the group."

Andrea rocked back and forth. "What the hell was Kamen building in that workshop?"

"I don't know. But I know someone who does. He's tied up in our loup cage."

I strode to the loup cage, Andrea, Derek, and Ascanio in tow. I took the key off the hook in the wall and unlocked the door.

The loup cage stood empty. Perfectly intact rope lay in coils on its floor. It was still tied.

Derek looked slightly ill. I'd seen this precise look on Jim's face when a teleporting thief stole the Pack maps a few months ago. "How the hell . . ."

"Magic," Ascanio said.

"The tech is up." I tried the cage door. Locked. "Neat trick."

"Next time we'll chain him to the wall," Andrea said.

"There won't be a next time." He wouldn't let himself get caught again. At least, not this easily.

Derek walked off. "The back door is unlocked," he called out.

Well, at least we knew he didn't evaporate into thin air.

We'd failed to find Kamen, we'd failed to recover the device, and the only person who could shed light on what was happening had disappeared from a locked cage while in our custody. It was good that I owned the damn place, or I might have had to fire myself.

"His stick is still here," Ascanio said, holding up the volhv's staff.

Ha! Gotcha. "Bring it here." I headed to the back room, opened the door of the body freezer, and stuffed the staff into it.

"What are you doing?" Andrea asked.

"A volhv without his staff is like a cop without a gun. He'll come back for it. The office is a fortress, so he won't be able to get in during tech. He'll return during magic, when he's at his strongest. I've warded this freezer so hard, it would take MSDU to get through it. When he returns, we nab him." And this time he would stay put.

•   •   •

THE TRAFFIC HOME WAS MURDER. IT WAS SEVEN fifty-five by the time I pulled into the parking lot and sprinted across the yard. I conquered the hallways, and I and my files headed downstairs, two steps at a time.

I was almost to the landing when Jezebel, the second of my boudas, barred my way. Her eyes blazed bright red. She looked ready to spit fire.

"I know, I'm late." I put some speed into it, hoping my knee held up.

Jezebel chased me, keeping up with ridiculous ease. "I'm going to rip their heads off and skull-fuck them."

That would be something to see, especially since she didn't have a penis. When Jezebel got worked up, getting her to explain things was next to impossible. I'd been learning to guess. "Who?"

"The wolves," she snarled.

Not again. "Which of the wolves?"

She bared her teeth. "I'll cut her legs off."

So Jennifer was involved. Of course. During my aunt's rampage, Jennifer, the female half of the wolf alpha pair, made an executive decision not to evacuate. My aunt attacked the wolf safe house in the city while Jennifer was out, and her magic caused the whole house to go loup, including Jennifer's twelve-year-old sister Naomi. When I ran into the house, hoping to kill my aunt, Naomi attacked me and I ended her life. Jennifer blamed me for her sister's death. The wolves went out of their way to stick it to me whenever they could. They turned it into almost a game.

The auditorium door loomed before me. Two minutes to eight. "We'll talk about it after."

"Kate?"

"After."

I took a deep breath, opened the door, and strode in, Jez behind me. An enormous auditorium stretched before me. Rows of ledges crossed it, offering a place to lie and sit, all facing a wide stage lit by electric lamps and braziers cradling open flame. A giant desk with a chair waited in the middle of the stage. Usually it was flanked by two chairs. Only one chair this time. My chair.

The bottom rows were filled. Shapeshifters sprawled here and there, some by themselves, some in couples. At least a hundred people, maybe more. Petitions rarely attracted that kind of audience. Something was up.

I raised my head, walked across the stage to the desk, and sat. To the left, just below me, a second desk stood perpendicular to the stage. The desk was occupied by a dark-haired woman about my age. She had curly brown hair, large dark eyes, and an infectious laugh. She also introduced herself as George. George's full name was actually Georgetta, and she tended to break people's bones when they used it. Her parents were the only two beings on Earth able to say it without consequences, and since her father was Mahon, the Pack's Executioner, I didn't want to try my luck. During petitions, George acted as the neutral third party, who prepared summaries of the cases and ran the hearings.

George rose and rang the bell. "We're now in session."

The crowd quieted.

Damn, there were a lot of people here. Shapeshifters gossiped like old Southern ladies at church. If they got hold of some juicy rumor, they showed up in droves to watch it unfold. So far today I'd been cut, burned, bruised, advised that we were facing a secret society, and emotionally compromised. I didn't need any more bloody surprises.

"Case of Donovan versus Perollo," George announced.

Two shapeshifters rose from the audience and went down to the first row.

I opened the first file.

The first four cases were routine. A dispute over an abandoned car on the border of the rats' territory. One of the cats had found it and spent a few hours hauling it out of the ravine. Technically all of the shapeshifter territory was Pack territory, but each clan house had a few square miles of exclusively their land, so the clans could meet in private. The car went to the rats. I ruled that the cat had no business on their land in the first place.

The second case was a domestic dispute between ex-spouses belonging to different clans. When the couple had divorced, the rat father took the children, and the jackal mother claimed that she didn't have to pay child support because both kids turned into rats. I decided she did.

The third and fourth cases involved a business jointly owned by Clan Heavy and Clan Jackal. It was long and complicated, and I had to check my notes more times than I could count. When all interested parties finally sat down, I had to squish the urge to collapse in relief on my desk.

Another couple stepped up. The man's right arm was in a sling and he held himself like he was spoiling for a fight. He looked to be in his early twenties. Hard to say for sure—shapeshifters were long lived, and some people I could've sworn were in their late forties were pushing seventy.

The woman appeared to be about the same age. Slender, she had a pretty face framed by a waterfall of blond hair that spilled below her waist. She seemed on edge, as if she expected me to throw something at her at any moment.

The man raised his head. "Kenneth Thompson, Clan Wolf, petitioner."

The woman squared her shoulders. "Sandra Martin, Clan Wolf, defendant."

A warning bell went off in my head.

Ken looked at me. "I exercise my right of individual appeal. I appeal to have my petition judged by the Consort."

That meant that he wanted me to make the judgment. If Curran were here, he could offer his opinion, but the decision was my responsibility. Except Curran wasn't here.

"I'm the only person here," I told him. "I have to judge your case by default."

Ken looked a bit confused. "I was told to ask for direct appeal."

I glanced at George. She made a winding motion with her left hand. *Keep going.* Right.

Barabas had made me memorize the protocol, so at least I wasn't completely lost. I looked at Sandra. "Do you have any objections?"

She swallowed. "No."

"The request for individual appeal is granted," I said.

The audience focused on me. So this was it. That was why every busybody in the Pack was here. I glanced at the wolf alpha couple. Daniel was impassive and Jennifer had a small smile on her long face.

Okay. You want a fight, you'll get one. I opened the file and pulled out the summary—two typed pages. With Andrea and her conspiracy theories, this was the one case I had failed to preview.

George gave me a reassuring wink from her desk.

I scanned the summary. Oh boy.

"These are the facts of the case: You, Kenneth, were romantically pursuing Sandra. In an effort to court her, you broke into her house on Friday. She woke up, found you in her bedroom, and shot you with a Glock 21, damaging three of your ribs and shattering the bones of your right arm. You feel that her reaction was excessive and want compensation for the pain and suffering and medical bills. Is this correct?"

Ken nodded. "Yes, Consort."

I glanced at the summary. "It says here that when Sandra woke up, you were nude and carrying a bouquet of sticks."

Ken turned a shade redder, but I couldn't tell if it was from embarrassment or outrage. "They were roses. I tore the petals off and put them on the carpet."

If Curran were here, he'd be closing his eyes and counting to ten in his head.

"Can I say something?" Sandra asked.

I looked at her. "No, you can't. You have to wait your turn."

She clamped her mouth shut.

I turned back to Ken. "Did Sandra encourage your . . . courtship? Did she give you any indication that she liked you?"

"Some," Kenneth said.

"Be specific," George said.

"She told me that I looked nice. I've been trying to get her for a while, so she knew I liked her."

"Can I say something?" Sandra asked.

"No. And if you ask me one more time, I'll have you removed and we'll proceed without you."

She blinked.

I looked back at Ken. "What else did Sandra do to encourage you?"

Ken considered. "She looked at me."

Great. Just peachy.

"So because Sandra looked at you and said that you looked nice, you decided to break into her house and surprise her in her bed naked?"

A light laugh ran through the audience. I glared at them. The laugh died.

Ken turned bright red and turned back to glare at the shape-shifters in the stands. All we needed now was for him to go furry and rip into our spectators.

"Kenneth, look at me."

He snapped back to me.

"It says here that you and Sandra work together in the Northern Recovery office. Is that correct?"

"Yes."

"Aside from what happened on Friday, would you say Sandra is a friendly person?"

Ken puzzled it over. He wasn't sure where I was heading. "I suppose so."

"Could it be that when Sandra told you that you looked nice, she might have just been trying to be friendly?"

"No."

"So you had never seen her compliment anybody else in the office?"

He paused. "Well, yes, she does say nice things sometimes to people, but I mean, I'm the only guy there, so it's different."

This was so not my thing. I just wanted to hop on the table, knock him upside the head, and be done with it. "But it is possible that you might have misinterpreted Sandra's comment?"

It took a few more seconds, and then he finally said, "It's possible."

Hallelujah. "Suppose there were a man working in your office. A much larger, stronger man. Let's say a render. He came into the office wearing a new leather jacket. You had a friendly chat, you complimented his jacket, and that night you woke up with the man standing over you, nude and holding a bouquet of roses."

Kenneth's eyes went wide. "But I'm not gay!"

"It's not about being gay; it's about being confronted by someone larger and stronger than you are when you are at your most vulnerable. If you were to find this dude standing in your bedroom, would you be upset?"

"Hell yes, I'd be upset. I'd tell him to get the fuck out. But she didn't tell me to get out. If she had said, 'Ken, get the hell out!' I would've left. She shot me eight times."

Oh, screw it. "She is smaller and weaker than you are. She woke up, saw you naked and ready for action, and probably thought you were going to rape her. She was scared, Ken. You scared her half to death."

"She didn't have anything to be scared about! I wouldn't have done anything."

"She didn't know that. You already broke into her house, so you have no respect for her property. What would make her think that you would respect her as a person and just walk away if she told you to leave?"

Muscles played along Ken's jaws. "That's the way the shape-shifters do it. Everybody knows that you didn't encourage the Beast Lord, but he broke into your apartment and you didn't shoot him."

The audience got so quiet, I could hear myself breathe. So that was it. That was what Jennifer was after.

"I see." My voice went quiet. "Is that why you decided to appeal directly to me?"

"Yes."

"Who suggested it?"

"My alpha."

Jennifer wanted to embarrass me. Well, if she expected me to wilt, she'd be waiting until hell sprouted roses. I turned and looked at Jennifer. She smiled back at me. Half a second to clear the desk, two seconds to cross the room and I could be sinking my fist into her face. Cure all her ills and mine.

"I had no idea that Clan Wolf's alphas kept such a close eye on my relationship with the Beast Lord. I'll have to check under our bed tonight to make sure no little wolf spies are hiding under there."

Somebody snorted and choked it off.

"Do you know what I did after I discovered the Beast Lord in my apartment?"

Ken realized he was on shaky ground. "No."

"I put a knife to his throat," I said. "And I changed the lock on my door. Besides that, I had encouraged the Beast Lord prior to him breaking in. I flirted with him, I kissed him, and I paraded around in front of him in my underwear."

I was almost done. I just had to keep from pummeling Jennifer for a little bit longer. "Did Sandra ever do any of those things?"

"No."

Let's get it all out there. "Did she ever make out with you in a hot tub or offer to serve you dinner naked?"

My face must've gotten darker, because Ken gulped. "No."

I turned to George. "Does the Code of Pack Law have anything to say about courtship?"

George cleared her throat. "Article Five, Section One states that no member of the Pack may threaten or assault another member with the intention of forcing sexual congress."

"What's the punishment for rape?" I asked.

"Death," George answered.

Ken turned white.

"Your actions can be construed as a prelude to sexual assault. It's alarming that your alphas didn't realize that, since it's their job to know things like that and impress that understanding onto the members of their clan. Is forced mating common in Clan Wolf?"

The audience turned to look at the wolf alphas. Daniel startled. Jennifer clenched her teeth.

Ken showed all the desperation of a man trapped on a chunk of ice in the middle of a raging river. "No."

"So your alphas do not encourage rape, to the best of your knowledge?"

"No!"

"Very well. I'm ready to rule." I looked at Sandra. "You may say something if you would like."

She shook her head.

I looked at Ken. "You acted like an idiot and got eight bullets for your trouble. Count yourself lucky that she didn't shoot you where it counted. If it had been me, I would've cut off your head and filed a police report after you were done bleeding out on my carpet. Suck it up, learn from it, and move on. You get nothing. Apologize to Sandra for scaring her and then causing her a load of embarrassment by having this matter dragged before the Pack assembly."

He stared at her wild-eyed. "I'm sorry."

"This proceeding is over." I glanced at the wolf alphas. "Would the alphas of Clan Wolf please see me on their way out."

The auditorium cleared in record time. I leaned back in my chair.

Daniel and Jennifer approached my desk.

Both of my boudas moved closer.

"Jezebel, Barabas, leave us," I said. The fewer witnesses we had to this, the better.

Barabas reversed his course in midstep and went out the door. Jez hesitated, snarled something under her breath, and followed him out.

Just me, Jennifer, Daniel, and George.

"It's been fun," I said. "The game ends now."

"What game?" Jennifer asked.

I shrugged. "You have three choices. First, you can quit fucking with me and walk away. Second, you can challenge me, and I'll kill you. It would be good for me. I need the practice."

Jennifer bared her teeth. Daniel put his hand on her forearm. I could take her alone. Both of them with magic down would be hard.

"Third, you can keep pestering me, in which case at the next Pack Council I'll move for your removal. I can do that, can't I, George?"

"Yes, you can," George said with a big smile.

"On what grounds?" Jennifer snarled.

"Incompetence. I'll cite this proceeding as evidence. This matter concerned two members of the wolf clan, which placed it under your authority. So either you didn't know how to deal with it, or you didn't want to deal with it, due to laziness or due to actively condoning rape. Either way, you should be removed and an investigation must be launched into the mating practices of the wolf clan."

"They'll find nothing," Daniel said.

"Five hundred wolves, of which there are probably at least what, a hundred and fifty couples? How do you think they'll react to having their mating rituals examined?"

"You can't do that!" Jennifer spun to Daniel. "She can't do that."

"Technically, she can," Daniel said. "It's over, Jennifer. You can't win this."

Jennifer's eyes went completely green. "What the hell would you even know about being an alpha? You're a human. The only reason you're here is because you're fucking Curran."

Nice. "I don't know much, but I'm learning fast." I rose.

"And I'm here because I killed twenty-two shapeshifters in two weeks. I've earned my place. How many challenges did you have, Jennifer? Oh, that's right. None. Enlighten me, how did you become an alpha again?" I turned to Daniel. "Help me out here. Who was she fucking, Daniel? Was it you? It must be especially good for you, because that's the only way you'd have gone along with this for so long."

I barely saw Daniel move. One second he was standing there, loose, and the next he clamped Jennifer in a hug. It was a very careful hug—it looked gentle, but I could tell she couldn't move an inch.

"We apologize for any offense to the Consort. We meant no disrespect," he said.

"Apology accepted."

"Stop talking like I'm not here," Jennifer ground out.

"We look forward to working with you in the future," Daniel said. "With your leave?"

"Please. Have a pleasant evening."

Daniel moved, and Jennifer moved with him. Together they walked out of the auditorium.

I waited until the door closed and fell into my chair. George stared at me. "Oh my freaking God. I can't believe she went that far."

I closed my eyes.

"Are you okay?"

"I'm tired. My knee is hurting again and I'm trying to teleport myself upstairs."

"Um, Kate, you can't do that."

"I know. But I'm trying very hard. Let me know if I start fading?"

Sadly, teleporting didn't work. I climbed the stairs, got into the shower, washed off the dirt and blood, and put on clean clothes.

The rooms felt empty without Curran. I stood in the doorway of the bedroom for a while and looked at the bed.

I didn't want it all to turn out to be one big lie.

A small part of me wanted to leave. Just leave now, without any explanations and disappointments. Disappear. That way if this was a lie, I'd never know.

But then I didn't run from my challenges. I met them straight on and bashed my head against them, until it left me hurt, bloody, and dazed.

I hugged myself. When I was with Curran, he filled the empty space. If I was sad, he'd make me laugh. If I was pissed off, he'd invite me to spar. I was forgetting what it was like to be on my own. And I was on my own. Aside from Roland, there wasn't another human being this screwed up for thousands of miles.

If tomorrow I woke up and Roland waited on the Keep's doorstep, I would die. Pretty quickly, too. Evdokia was right. I had all the training with the sword I would ever need, but when my father and I met, the fight wouldn't be decided by the sword. I needed magic training and a lot of it. And I had no idea how Curran would react to it. *Hey, baby, you don't mind if I practice turning a vampire inside out on the Keep's grounds, do you? Please ignore the torturous screams of your people when things go horribly wrong.*

It was one thing to know you had mated with Roland's daughter. It was another thing entirely to have your nose rubbed in it.

Ultimately, I didn't have to figure out whether Curran truly loved me. All I had to know was whether I loved him enough not to care why he was with me. I knew the answer. I just didn't want to admit it. If he called right now, hurt, I would find him and save him, even if it cost me my life, whether he loved me or not. This was all sorts of screwed up.

No. I was wrong. If he was with me because he needed me to fight Roland, I had to leave. I couldn't stay here, sleep next to him in this bed, touch him, kiss him, knowing that he didn't truly love me but was bound by the need for survival. I would still love him, but I couldn't stay. Had he laid it out for me from the start, before I had a chance to fall in love, I might have joined forces with him anyway. I wouldn't have slept with Curran, but an alliance with the Pack would have strengthened me, and he and I might have gone for some sort of business arrangement. It was too late now. I wanted love or nothing.

I stole my pillow off the bed and curled up on the couch, wrapped in a spare blanket. Eventually he'd come home. Then we'd talk.

CHAPTER 13

———◆———

THE ALARM WENT OFF AT SIX A.M., SIGNALING THE end of night and the absence of magic. My back and sides had decided to develop an ache overnight. I rolled off the couch, feeling every knot and snarl in my muscles, pulled on my sweats, and padded downstairs to the gym. Forty minutes later I felt much better. I still didn't know where Curran and I stood, but for now it couldn't be helped. I still had people to kill and a Doomsday Device to find.

I made the trip to the guard desk. "Any messages for me?"

Curtis, an older dark-haired werewolf, offered me two scraps of paper. "There is also a message from the Beast Lord, Consort. It's in your private box. You can access it from your quarters by dialing 1000."

He called but didn't talk to me. Chicken. "When did he call?"

"Twelve minutes past midnight."

"Why didn't you wake me up?"

Curtis looked uncomfortable. "He instructed us that you shouldn't be disturbed."

Should I be pissed off because he didn't want to talk to me

or touched because he'd thought about letting me rest? I wasn't sure.

I glanced at the top scrap of paper. The message stated that the trackers had found Julie's scent on the outskirts of the city. At least she hadn't been kidnapped.

The second message had a number and a name. Roman.

I took my scraps of paper, headed upstairs, and dialed 1000. Curran's voice filled the room. "Hey. It's me."

I landed in the chair. Hearing him was like coming home in a downpour and finding the lights on and the house warm. I was in so deep, I couldn't even see the surface anymore.

"They said you're asleep. I'm glad you're home safe. I'm stuck in some hellhole in the Southside. Leslie's been running all over the city. No rhyme or reason to it. We'll catch up to her eventually. She can't run forever."

And when they did, there would be a bloodbath.

"I thought about what you said. Fair enough. I do things this way because it usually works and I've done them this way for a long time. But I wouldn't want it done to me."

Ha! I'd won one.

"But we agreed that we wouldn't do the not-talking thing and you hung up on me twice. If our agreement changed, I didn't get the memo."

He had me there.

"Anyway, I'm getting pretty sick of chasing the render around, so I'm going to catch her tomorrow and come home. I want to know if we're cool. I'll try to call you at work when I get done. Bye, baby."

I played the message again. It didn't say anything different.

He wanted to know if we were cool. That made two of us.

I dialed the number on the message from Roman, whoever he was. A familiar male voice answered. "Hello?"

Ha! The volhv. "Morning."

"You should give the staff back to me. I can come to your office and pick it up. I promise, no tricks even. Nobody will die."

"You got that right."

"Are you going to be a hardass about this?" he asked.

"I'll trade you the staff for Adam Kamen."

"No."

"Those are my terms."

He heaved a dramatic sigh. "We could do this like civilized people. But no, now I'll have to go to your office and unleash plagues on things, and set things on fire, and condemn things. Nobody wants that. Just give me the staff and we'll call it even. I am trying not to be a bad guy here."

As soon as the magic wave hit, I'd have to reinforce the wards, just in case. I'd taken him down, but it was mostly luck and surprise. This time he would be ready.

"An hour with Kamen, and you can have your stick back."

"*Chyort poberi*, you are a stubborn woman."

"You're a pagan. Saying 'Devil take you' is a Christian curse. How does this work exactly?"

"That's a funny thing about Christianity; when the dead God's priests came to Europe, they made all the old gods into devils. So technically when I am saying *Chyort*, I'm appealing to the Black One. Anyway, I'll see what I can do."

"Wait. When you snagged Adam from his workshop, did you take the thing he built with you?"

Roman paused. "Hypothetically, if we had taken such a thing, it would no longer exist. It would be as if it had never been built. An urban legend."

"So is it? A legend?" If they had gotten hold of the device, they would've destroyed it by now.

"Not so much."

He hung up. Starting the day with a philosophical debate with a priest of the Embodiment of All Evil. It could only go downhill from here.

I took a shower, got dressed, got a sandwich, and went down the stairs, eating it on the way. No shapeshifters assaulted me and tried to take my food. No wolf alphas sprung any surprise attacks. Nobody even offered me a bouquet of headless roses. The lack of drama was downright disheartening.

Outside, the sunrise split the horizon, sudden and bright, like a gush of blood from a knife wound. Both of my vehicles were idling in the yard. The boy wonder had started my car for me and now waited by his Jeep. He wore a dark hooded sweatshirt and beat-up jeans. If you didn't see his face and didn't pay attention to the broad shoulders, you'd think he was just a kid, fifteen, maybe sixteen. Knowing Derek, he did it on purpose.

The younger he appeared, the less his potential opponents would think of him. Except he was filling out. Another year at this rate, and he'd have to update his wardrobe.

"Thanks for starting the car."

He grinned, a quick flash of teeth.

"Where is the bane of my existence?"

"He knows the time. I'm not his nanny."

"What did you think of him?"

"Not much. He's a spoiled baby." He shrugged. "You give boudas a young male and they fall over themselves to pamper him."

A side door opened and Ascanio emerged, followed by a familiar plump woman. She looked to be in her early fifties, with graying hair rolled into a bun, and a kind face, like a young grandmother. You half expected her to start handing out school lunches and tell you to play nice with the other kids.

She waved at us. "Kate!"

Oh crap.

I cleared my throat. "Aunt B, good morning."

Aunt B hurried over, Ascanio in tow. "I have to go to the city. So I thought, why don't I just catch a lift with you? We can catch up and chat."

I'd rather give a lift to a rabid tiger. "Of course."

"Wonderful." Aunt B hopped into my passenger seat.

Derek hesitated for a long moment. He plainly didn't want to leave me alone with Aunt B, but the Jeep could only seat two. He made a follow motion to Ascanio, and without waiting he turned slowly and went to his own vehicle.

We drove out of the Keep's yard and headed toward the city.

"I heard about your run-in with the wolves," Aunt B said.

Thank you, George. "It wasn't much of a run-in."

"Not the way I heard it. Well handled, dear. Well handled. Jennifer isn't a bad sort, but she is young. She has been an alpha for barely two years. She's still establishing her place, and of course losing a loved one, especially so young, it can mess with your head. She'll come around."

That would be the day. "You have a lot of faith in her common sense."

Aunt B smiled. "Oh no, dear. I have a lot of faith in Daniel. He fought hard for his spot at the top. He won't let anything jeopardize that, not even her. Speaking of sweet young things, how is my boy fitting in?"

Like a square peg into a round hole. "We're working on it."

"It's so rare, you know, for the boudas to make it through puberty without loupism. That was the problem with my first two boys. They were just like Ascanio: handsome, funny, charming . . ."

Undisciplined, spoiled, cocky . . .

"He has so much potential. I haven't seen such good half-form at such a young age in years. Almost as good as my Raphael."

Oh wow. She really liked him, if she was comparing him to her son. "So why give him to me?"

Aunt B sighed. "He hasn't grown up in the Pack. His mouth gets away from him. He pushes things too far, sometimes in public. I'd hate to kill him. I'd do it, of course, but it would break my heart."

There you go, that was Aunt B for you. *Please hold the wheel, while I jump out of this moving vehicle and run for my life.*

"And his mother is such a nice girl, too. It would devastate her. Of all the places he could be, he's safest with you. You're much too softhearted to murder children."

I stared at her.

"Mind the road, dear."

I swerved to avoid a fallen tree. "What's his story? If I have to take care of him, I might as well know the whole thing."

"It's all very, very sad. Martina, his mother, met his father while she lived in the Midwest. Not a lot of boudas out that way, so when she found him, she didn't look too closely at the quality of his character. And he seemed like a good enough sort, a proper bouda, on the passive side, but our men sometimes go that way. They had their fun, she conceived. She was thrilled. He was not."

"Didn't want to be a father?"

Aunt B rocked her head from side to side. "Not exactly. Turns out to be that he was on his 'pilgrimage.' He grew up in a religious community out in the boonies led by some prophet, and they sent him out to see how the 'heathens' live. He wasn't supposed to be getting his jollies on and seek carnal pleasures." She raised her eyebrows at "carnal."

"So what happened?"

"He stayed with her. Martina thought they were a family. She gave birth. It was a hard birth. The hospital had sedated her—they were afraid she might snap from the pain. When she woke up in the hospital bed, the baby and the father were gone. He'd left her a note. He was going to raise the baby in the 'proper' way. The baby was an innocent, but she was unclean, because they'd sinned and had intercourse without the blessing of the prophet, so she couldn't come. Martina barely got to hold the boy. A dim memory, that's all he left her. She can't tell the story without breaking into tears."

I would've found him. I would've found him and killed him and took my baby back. "Did she chase him?"

Aunt B nodded. "She did. But she was weak and he was very good at covering his tracks. She floated about for a few years like a broken ship without a rudder until she came here and we took her in. She is a good person. Just had to get her head on straight. She swore off having children, and we can't afford to do that, not with our numbers."

"What happened to Ascanio?"

"His father brought him back to his sect." Aunt B grimaced. "The way the boy tells it, it was one of those sects where the prophet starts receiving messages from some celestial flimflam god, who tells him to sleep with all the women. Especially the younger prettier ones. This prophet wasn't that keen on Ascanio's father returning."

"Eliminating the competition," I guessed.

"That's right. Most young men didn't come back after the pilgrimage—why would you? You'd have to take a wife eventually, and how can you do that knowing she leaves every night to go sleep with this prophet? But Ascanio's father was too stupid to think for himself. When Ascanio was about seven or eight, he died. A hunting accident."

"Aha. I'll buy that for a dollar." What kind of a hunting accident would it have to be to kill a damn bouda? Were they hunting an elephant and it fell on him?

"The boy was sort of collectively raised," Aunt B continued. "The sect mostly consisted of women, the only men being the prophet, a few old-timers too creaky to leave, and the prophet's progeny. They spoiled him rotten, but eventually he grew up. You've seen the way he looks. He got to sowing some wild oats. The prophet started getting messages that Ascanio was unclean real quick. Except by that point, Ascanio was strong enough that the prophet was worried about confronting him directly. Ascanio's daddy had written the whole sordid account of his sin in a confession, so the prophet found the mother's name, looked her up, and called us. 'Come and get him before something bad happens.' So we came and got him. He is ours now. He has a good heart. He just doesn't know the rules and doesn't have an awful lot of sense in that pretty head of his."

So the only male role model Ascanio had ever had was a lecherous, murdering con man. Great. That explained a few things.

Aunt B stared into my eyes. "You will take care of my boy, won't you, Kate? I'd consider it a personal favor."

"I'll do what I can," I told her. "But I can't pull him out of the fire if he jumps into it after being warned."

"I don't ask for miracles," Aunt B said. "Just things within reason."

It would take a miracle to keep Ascanio in line. But now didn't seem like a good time to mention it.

AUNT B WANTED TO BE LET OUT HALF A MILE FROM my office, at some bakery. When we got in, Andrea was already there, sitting at her desk. The loyal hound took a running start and hit me in the chest. I could've used Grendel's company last night. But Andrea still needed him more than I did.

"Did you sleep here?" I asked.

She raised her chin. "Of course not."

Yep, she slept in the office. Sometimes being by yourself in an empty apartment, with nothing but your own craziness for company, was far worse than weathering a night in the office in an uncomfortable bed. At least in the office you could pretend you were still at work and keep busy. I'd been there.

Derek stuck his head into the fridge. "There is nothing to eat."

"Did you not eat before we left?"

Derek gave me a long-suffering look. "Yes, I did. But by

lunch we'll need food, and we can't afford to keep running out of the building for munchies."

He was right. We had three shapeshifters to feed, and every time one of us left the office, we became a target. "Fine." I opened the safe and handed him three hundred dollars. "There is a grocery down the street. Get something that will keep well."

"I'll go with him," Andrea said. "I need to walk the fur-face anyway."

They left, and I watched Ascanio bar the door behind them.

The box containing the evidence from Adam's house wasn't at my desk. If Andrea spent the night, she probably took it upstairs. I ran up the steps. There it was, spread out all over the floor into neat little piles: Polaroids on one side, Andrea's and my notes on the other, little baggie with dead ants in the middle. I sat on the floor. There had to be something here we could use. Something we were missing. So far all I had to work with were theories and suppositions. The volhvs had probably kidnapped Adam; Roman pretty much confirmed it. But unless he was lying, the device was still out there, somewhere. The Red Guard didn't have the device either, otherwise the Guardsmen wouldn't have hired us to look for it. Adam couldn't have moved the device by himself. It weighed a ton. That left the Lighthouse Keepers. They must've wanted both Adam and the device, but the volhvs snatched Adam from under their noses, so they took the device instead. And used some sort of vehicle to move it out of Sibley, leaving the trail of screwed-up magic. And I would know what that vehicle looked like if only Ghastek condescended to let me in on it. Ugh.

If the Keepers had Adam's gadget, nothing good would come from it. Of all the opponents I had to face, fanatics were the worst. Most people could be bribed, threatened, intimidated. None of the usual methods of persuasion applied to fanatics. They did things that defied logic.

And we still didn't know what the hell the device actually did. I sifted through the evidence. Adam had kept a journal, but it was missing, along with all his other notes.

Twenty minutes later I was no closer to solving anything. I picked up pieces of paper at random, marked in Andrea's neat, precise hand. LIST OF CLOTHES. LIST OF COOKING UTENSILS. LIST OF GROCERIES. She cataloged the entire house. I scanned the grocery list. Not like I had anything better to do. Cheese, milk, bananas, chocolate, protein shakes . . .

Wait a bloody minute.

Sugar, dried apricots . . .

I stared at the list. I'd seen this list of ingredients before. I'd watched them being put into a blender one by one: bananas, sugar, protein shake, chocolate, milk. It was a nauseating mix Saiman used to drink when he was about to change shape and expected to burn through a lot of calories in a hurry.

I double-checked the list. Saiman was Atlanta's premier expert on all things magic. He dealt in sensitive information, owned a part of an illegal martial arts tournament, and had fewer morals than the Norse gods he had descended from. He was a complete and utter egoist, focused solely on gratifying his own wants, and any dealings with him came with a giant price tag. A few months ago his egoism had finally gotten him into trouble. He maneuvered me into playing his escort for the evening and then displayed me for Curran's benefit to avenge a blow to his pride. Curran didn't take it well. In fact, I was amazed Saiman was still among the living.

Saiman also changed shape. Any human body type, any gender. Once he'd turned into a woman, seduced a pagan priest, stolen his magic acorn, and then hired the Mercenary Guild to keep him safe while the priest's friends and relations turned themselves inside out trying to kill him. The priest he'd seduced happened to be a volhv. And I was the idiot merc sent to guard him. He was the reason why I had to go to Evdokia instead of the volhvs and got my childhood smashed to pieces.

If Saiman was involved, he could've impersonated anyone. He could've been one of the guards or he could've pretended to be Adam Kamen himself. But why? What the hell did he want? Saiman was loaded. Maybe he was one of the investors . . .

A faint metal clang announced the bar being removed from the door. That was some fast grocery shopping.

"Hi there!" Ascanio's voice had the unmistakable overtone of a young guy trying to be smooth.

"Who are you and where is Kate?" Julie's voice asked.

CHAPTER 14

I GOT UP, PADDED TO THE RAIL, AND LEANED against the wall, hidden in the shadow. From here I had an excellent view of the main room. Ascanio barred the stairs. Julie stood in the middle of the room, with a determined look on her face. Her light hair was pulled into a ponytail. Good balance, light on her toes. Her hand was on one of my throwing knives. No matter how many times I took them away from her, she always managed to steal them.

"I'm Ascanio Ferara of Clan Bouda. The question is, who are you?"

"Move aside."

"I can't do that," Ascanio purred. "I'm under strict orders not to let anyone I don't know upstairs. And I don't know you."

At least in one respect the school had been good for Julie— they'd made sure she had frequent meals. She'd come a long way from the waif I found in the Honeycomb. Still slender and pale, she looked stronger now, and her legs and arms no longer resembled toothpicks. She was also pretty, a fact Ascanio noticed, judging by his killer smile and the light flexing of his arms.

One cute face and all my orders of not admitting strangers flew right out the window. The kid was hopeless.

"Move," Julie repeated.

"No. You see, I have a problem. Kate didn't tell me she was expecting an angel."

Bwahahaha.

Julie blinked, obviously stunned.

"I'd like to help you." Ascanio spread his arms. "I just can't. Kate is a very stern alpha."

Stern?

"She might put me in a hole. Or whip me."

No, but she might twist your head off for this.

Julie arranged her face into a shocked expression. "Whip you? Really?"

Ascanio nodded. "It's brutal. But if I had something, some small favor, I might take a chance on being punished."

"A small favor?" Julie nodded. "Like what?"

"A kiss."

Julie's eyes narrowed. "Maybe I'll come back later."

"She'll be leaving later and my memory is terrible. I might forget you were here and let her leave for the Keep. It's very difficult to reach her in the Keep. There are many guards."

Who would all fall over themselves to deliver her to me.

Julie stepped back. Ascanio stepped forward. She took another step. He followed, with a fluid shapeshifter grace. He thought he was stalking her. She was pulling him away from the stairs, giving herself room to work.

"Are you going to be nice if I kiss you?" Julie took another step back.

"Very nice."

"And no tongue."

"No tongue."

Kill me, somebody.

Julie motioned to him. "Okay."

Ascanio took a step forward. Julie stood on her toes and gently kissed him. Her right hand slid into a leather pouch on her belt. Ascanio leaned forward, gliding his hands over her shoulders. Julie jerked back and smothered a handful of yellowish paste on his face. Wolfsbane. Deep color too, almost orange—potent as hell.

Ascanio made a strangled noise and clawed at his face, trying to exhale the fire that suddenly exploded in his mouth and nose. Julie hooked his right leg with hers and shoved him back. He crashed like a log. His back slapped the floor, forcing all of the air out of his lungs in a hoarse breath. Julie grabbed his arm, twisted it, flipping him over on his stomach, landed on Ascanio's back, pulled a plastic tie from her pocket, and locked his wrists.

I wanted to jump up and down, clapping. We'd practiced this takedown over the Christmas break and she had done it perfectly.

Julie grabbed Ascanio by his hair, raising his face off the floor, and slid her knife against his throat.

An eerie hyena noise broke from Ascanio's lips, a ululating half groan, half laugh, laced with a hoarse snarl, like a creaky barn door swinging open inch by inch. Every hair rose on the back of my neck.

"I'll rip you apart!"

"Oh no." Julie clicked her tongue. "Did the mean human girl pick on you? Does the little bouda boy want his mommy?"

"Untie me!"

"Awww, the little baby is crying. Boohoo. Does the baby need his bottle and his teddy?"

That plastic tie looked too thin to hold a shapeshifter.

"When I get free, I'll—"

"Don't worry. Your teddy has to be here somewhere. I bet he is upstairs. You lie here like a slug while I go look for him."

Ascanio twisted. Hard muscles bulged on his arms. Julie took a step back.

The boy jerked. A ragged snarl tore out of his throat, his skin ruptured, and a monster spilled forth. The plastic tie snapped apart and a six-and-a-half-foot-tall bouda in a warrior form rolled to his feet. Dark stripes marked his massive limbs, dashing up to his shoulders, where the brown fur flared into a long thick mane. A brown hyena. Interesting. I had only seen one of those before.

Red eyes stared at Julie from a shockingly inhuman face. She raised her knife.

Ascanio lunged. His clawed fingers caught her wrist. He plucked the knife out of her hand and dropped it to the floor.

That was just about enough of that. I opened my mouth.

The front door swung open and Derek walked into the office. Ascanio and Julie froze, her arm still caught in his grip.

Derek's eyes sparked with a lethal yellow glow.

I moved to the stairs. Julie jerked her arm away from Ascanio.

Derek's voice was iced over. "Julie, go upstairs."

Julie sidestepped Ascanio and swiped her knife off the floor.

The bouda's mouth gaped open. Mangled words came out, shredded by his fangs. "Gorna dooo what he said, huh?"

Surprise, surprise. He could speak in a half-form. That took real talent.

Julie stuck her tongue out, went to the stairs, and saw me. Her face fell. *That's right. You're so busted.*

Derek shut the door and looked at Ascanio.

Ascanio spread his arms, his voice dripping with derision. "What? What? What arrrre you gorna dooo?"

"I'm going to teach you a lesson." Derek shrugged off his sweatshirt and draped it over the chair.

Ascanio snapped his huge teeth. "You won't teach me anything, but I give you a few morr scarrrs. You'rrrre tooo prretty."

Derek took a few steps forward and motioned to Ascanio with his hand. "That's a nice half-form. Let's see what you can do with it."

"I'm waiting for yoooo to turrrrn, woof. I drrrag your bloody brrrroken carcass to Kate. At least trrrry to poot up a good fight."

Derek smiled. It was a cold humorless smile that bared the edge of his teeth. "I can't wait."

Ascanio leaped.

THE BOUDA FLEW THROUGH THE AIR, HUGE CLAWS poised for the kill. Derek shied out of the way. Ascanio hurtled past him and whipped around.

"When you're airborne, you can't change your direction," Derek said. "Try again."

Ascanio snarled and charged him.

Derek stepped into the charge, pivoted on his left foot, and kicked. The lower part of his right shin connected with

Ascanio's ear. Ascanio rolled sideways, crashed into a wall, and surged up.

"Mind your flanks," Derek said. "You have peripheral vision for a reason."

"I fucking kilr you!"

"Left foot, right foot, left foot." Derek raised his arms. "Watch."

Ascanio lunged. "Left foot." Derek met him halfway and sank a vicious left kick into the bouda's stomach.

Ascanio staggered back.

"Right foot." Derek took a quick step, building momentum. "Left foot." He jumped and hammered the ball of his foot into Ascanio's forehead. Like taking a sledgehammer to the face.

The impact sent Ascanio flying. He smashed into my desk with a wicked bone-snapping crunch.

"Go easy on the furniture," I said.

"My apologies, Alpha."

With a brutal cry, Ascanio launched himself off the floor.

"Left kick. Right kick. Uppercut. Arm bar. See, now I control your head. That's not good, because I can do this. Oh, and now while you're lying there, your opponent can kick you like this."

Julie winced. "He'll kill him."

"Derek's being very careful. What did I tell you about plastic ties?"

"Only for humans," Julie murmured.

"If you don't listen to me, I can't teach you anything."

Derek rolled his head left, then right, popping his neck. "Come on, shake it off. Back on your feet. You're a shapeshifter. You can take a lot of punishment. It will all heal, but meanwhile it hurts doesn't it? Kick—groin, elbow—throat. No, don't raise your hands up, you leave your stomach exposed. Side kick."

Ascanio hit the wall. The building shook.

"You know who doesn't heal as well as you do? Humans. They are smaller and weaker than you are, and they break easily and stay broken. That's why we don't put our hands on humans. Especially girls. And never ever *that* girl."

Ascanio's claws fanned Derek's throat. The boy wonder

grabbed the bouda's left arm and twisted. With a soft crunch the arm popped out of the socket.

"You're done." I walked down the stairs.

Derek raised his hands and took a step back.

Ascanio moved to chase him. I snapped a single punch to the back of Ascanio's neck. The boy crashed down to the floor.

I grabbed his left arm and jerked sharply, popping the shoulder back into place. Ascanio gasped. I flipped him over and stared into the red-hot eyes. "It's over."

He bared his teeth at me. I slapped his nose. "I said, it's over. Or you'll find out what the loup cage looks like from the inside."

The red glow in Ascanio's eyes died down.

I glanced at Derek. "Where is Andrea?"

"She said she had an errand. She's coming back to the office right after."

"Wash up." I nodded at his bloody knuckles and turned to Ascanio. "You—come with me. We need to talk."

Ascanio followed me to the side room.

I pointed at the chair. "Sit."

He landed his shaggy body into it.

"Do you know why you're here?"

He shrugged.

I sat in the other chair. "People practice for years to create a good half-form. You're barely fifteen and you already have it. And you can speak in it. That takes talent, the kind that's rare and difficult to come by. Normally when a young shapeshifter displays talent like that, there is a bidding war. Curran's guard wants him. Jim's security people want him. And the warrior trainers want him. Nobody wants you. Not even your own alpha."

"My apha ikes me!"

"Of course, Aunt B likes you. You're witty, and handsome, and a smartass. She buried two sons, boys just like you. She has a soft spot for you. That's why she sent you off to me."

Ascanio opened his mouth.

"She can't control you and she's worried you'll cross the line in public and she will have to kill you."

The bouda's jaws clicked shut, flinging drool onto the table.

"It would devastate her, but don't think for the tiniest second that she won't do it. Aunt B's been alpha longer than I've been alive. She didn't stay in power because she bakes great cookies."

Ascanio stared at the table in front of him.

"You ended up here because of all the people in the Pack, I'm the least likely to kill you." I dipped my head so I could look into his eyes. The monster at my table looked ready to cry. I'd managed to make a teenager depressed. Maybe I could shoot some fish in a barrel for an encore.

"What were your orders?"

He didn't answer.

I didn't say anything. The silence lay empty between us. Eventually the need to fill it won.

"To guarrrd the doorr."

"And?"

"To keep people I don't know ouoot."

"And you let Julie in. You had no clue who Julie was, because if you had known she was my ward—"

Ascanio's head snapped up.

"—you wouldn't have put your hands on her."

He stared back at the table. *That's right, you just physically assaulted the Pack princess. Not that she didn't give back as good as she got.*

Poor kid. His day had gone from bad to worse.

"Derek was trained by Curran," I told him. "After that, he worked for Jim. He was his best cover agent. After that, he ran Curran's personal guard. Derek thinks of Julie as his little sister. He wanted to skin you alive. He didn't do it, because you belong to me and he respects my authority, but he could've. It wasn't a fair fight. He kicked your ass and there is no shame in that. In terms of power, the gap between you and him is about as big as the gap between you and Julie." I crossed my arms. "Julie also kicked your ass. If she'd had a thicker tie, or if she'd jammed her knife between the vertebrae of your neck while you lay there kissing the floor, it would've been all over. If I chop off your head, you won't grow another one. Not to mention, she could've been some creature dressed in human skin. You endangered everyone in the office by letting her in."

I rose. "Your way of doing things isn't working. Time for a new strategy. The only difference between you and Derek is discipline and training. Either you can work on both, or you can keep thinking with your balls. It's your choice. Say 'pop.' "

"Pop?"

"That was the sound of me pulling your head out of your ass. If you stick it back up there again, there is nothing I can do about it. This is the only lecture you'll ever get from me."

I headed for the doorway.

"Can I beat him?"

I turned. "Derek?"

He nodded.

"Yes. You'll have to work your ass off in the gym and learn the rules of the Pack, so you don't get killed in the meantime, but yes. You can."

I went out the door. One chewing-out of a teenage misfit down, one to go.

JULIE HAD ARRANGED HERSELF AT THE TABLE UPstairs. She couldn't quite figure out if she would be better off with defiant or pitiful, so she had managed an odd mix in between: her lip was seconds from quivering, but her eyes could've shot laser fire.

I sat in the other chair. "Knife."

She pulled her knife out and put it on the table. I picked it up. Yep, one of my throwing knives, painted black. Two scratches marked the blade near the hilt where something had scraped the paint off the metal.

"Where did you get this?"

"I pulled it out of the tree."

Ah. So it was that knife. When she was first having trouble in school, I'd tried to help her with her street cred by staging an appearance. It was a dramatic affair, involving black horses, Raphael in black leather, and my throwing this knife into a tree from horseback. It was a good throw and the blade had bitten deep into the bark.

"You pulled it out by yourself?"

She hesitated for a second. "I used pliers to loosen it."

Explained the scratches. "Why clamp the blade and not the handle?"

"I didn't want it to break off."

"Where did you get the pliers?"

She shrugged. "Stole them from a shop."

You could take the kid off the street, but getting the street out of the kid was a lot harder. "And wolfsbane?"

"I made it in the herbalism class. We had to have a project where we harvested an herb with magic properties and found a practical application."

She'd found a practical application, all right. "When did you harvest it?"

"In September. I kept the paste in a zip-lock bag in the freezer so it wouldn't go flat. In case of an emergency."

"Like what? Wild shapeshifters attacking the school?"

Her chin rose. "Like shapeshifters taking me back to school."

And here we go. "I thought I made it clear: you couldn't get that knife until you graduated."

"I did. Graduated."

"Aha."

"I hate that school. I hate everything there. I hate the people, the teachers, the subjects. The kids are stupid and ignorant and just dumb. They think they're cool, but they're a bunch of idiots. The teachers want to be friends with the students and then they say mean stuff behind their back."

"Who is 'they'? The teachers say mean stuff or the students?"

"Both of them. I don't like the schedule, I don't like how much work they make you put into useless stuff, I don't like my room. The only good thing about it is going home."

"Don't hold anything back. Tell me how you really feel."

"I'm not going back there!"

"And you've made this decision on your own?"

Julie nodded. "Yes. And if you take me back there, I'll run away again."

I crossed my arms on my chest. "I can't take you back there. They kicked you out."

Julie's eyes went big with outrage. "They can't kick me out! I quit."

I lost it and laughed.

"They really kicked me out?"

"Refunded the tuition and everything."

Julie blinked a couple of times, coming to grips with that tidbit. "So what happens now?"

"I expect you'll be a bum. Homeless and jobless, begging on the street for a crust of bread . . ."

"Kate!"

"Oh alright, I suppose if you come by the office once in a while, I'll give you a sandwich. You can squat in the office on the floor when it gets too cold outside. We can even get you a little blanket to lie on . . ."

"I'm serious!"

"I am, too. It's an honest offer. I'll even put some real roast beef into your sandwich. No rat meat, honest."

She stared at me with a martyred expression. "You think you're so funny."

"I have my moments." I leaned forward and pushed the knife to her. "Keep it. Wolfsbane, too. You'll need it, since you'll be staying at the Keep."

Julie eyed the knife. "What's the catch?"

I sighed. "No catch. I put you into that school because it was a good place. A safe place."

Julie shook her head, sending the blond hair flying. "I don't want to be safe. I want to stay with you."

"I've gathered that. Curran and I are looking into schools in the city. There are a couple that might be a better fit. You'll stay in your room at the Keep, ride into the city with me when possible, and go to school. When done, you'll come back to the office and someone will take you back to the Keep. You will be good and you won't take any stupid chances. While you're at the office, you're my slave. You'll run errands, clean the place, work out, file . . ."

Julie came over and hugged me. I hugged her back. We stayed like that for a long moment, until the door swung open downstairs and Andrea walked inside, asking why the place stank of wolfsbane.

CHAPTER 15

———◆———

BY NOON, RAGGED CLOUDS FLOODED THE SKY. THE world turned dim and hazy, and as Derek and I approached Champion Heights, the lone tower of the apartment building and the ruined city around it seemed little more than a mirage, knitted from fog and shadows.

Derek scowled at the high-rise. "I hate him."

"I know," I said.

We had three leads, of which Saiman was one. The volhvs were the other. The third lead concerned de Harven and the Keepers. Since we could do nothing about the volhvs, Andrea called Rene, notified her of de Harven's possible secret-society whack-job status, and requested the detailed files on all the Red Guardsmen who'd ever worked with de Harven. Rene had a very controlled fit of apoplexy and promised to deliver the files, with a Red Guardsman who would stand over Andrea as she went over them and take them back when she was done. The plan was for me to go and see Saiman on my own and for Derek to help Andrea look for patterns and possible accomplices.

And that was when both Derek and Andrea dug their heels in.

"No." Andrea nodded for emphasis. "Hell no."

"It's not a good idea," Derek confirmed. "I should go with you."

"You despise Saiman. Why in the world would you want to go with me?"

"Because your rabid honey-bunny and Saiman had a giant fight over you." Andrea spoke slowly, as if to a child. "You said yourself, Saiman's ego is so big, he has to rent a separate building for it. Curran made him run away like a scared rabbit. You have no idea how he'll react when he sees you."

"She's right," Derek said. "It's a safety issue. The office is well protected, so Andrea doesn't need me here. You will be out in the open and two is better than one. Besides, you're alpha."

"And that means what?"

"It means that you must be above reproach and avoid even the appearance of impropriety. Saiman's a degenerate pervert. You should bring an escort."

I crossed my arms on my chest. "So I can't be trusted to see him without supervision?"

Andrea shook her head. "Kate, it's not personal. It's protocol and it's common sense. You don't challenge people under you, you don't get to skip formal dinners, and when you go to see an unstable coward who screwed half of Atlanta and propositioned you in public, you bring an escort. Deal with it."

"Three weeks ago a woman from the city came to see Curran," Derek said.

"Yes, an attorney about the road. Lydia something." For some reason, Curran had insisted that I needed to attend a boring meeting about the repair of some road owned by the Pack. I hadn't wanted to go, so I'd decided not to cut my workout short. I hadn't realized that he held up the meeting until I deigned to make an appearance, so when I'd walked into the meeting room, almost an hour late, he, Lydia, and the two alphas of Clan Heavy were all patiently waiting for me. Mahon had dosed off, his wife had knitted half a sock, and Lydia had shot me a look of pure hatred. I'd felt like a total moron. The meeting had lasted a total of fifteen minutes and neither I nor the alpha couple of Clan Heavy needed to be there anyway . . .

Oh.

The light dawned. "She was one of Curran's ex-girlfriends?"

Derek nodded.

Curran had followed the protocol. I would do the same. "Fine."

Derek nodded again. "I'll get my jacket."

An hour later we stared at Champion Heights, where Saiman made his not-at-all-humble abode. During the magic wave, chunks of the tower would fade into hard red granite, complete with old moss—the result of spells shielding the building from the magic's jaws. Right now it was all brick, mortar, and glass, foreboding and dark.

Neither one of us wanted to go in.

Sitting in the Jeep would accomplish nothing. I parked the vehicle in the tower's parking lot and we climbed the wide concrete stairs to the glass-and-steel entrance. Despite everything that happened, Saiman still hadn't changed the code word. It took us less than a minute to get through security and ride the elevator up to the fifteenth floor. The elevator vomited us up into a hallway lined with criminally luxurious carpet.

Derek's frown had graduated to a full-blown grimace. A furious yellow light sheathed his irises.

"Try to look less disgusted."

He shrugged. "Are you worried I'll offend him?"

"Your eyes are glowing, and your upper lip is trembling like you're about to snarl. I'm worried Saiman will panic, and that door is hard to break. Make an effort to look less deranged and threatening. Think of rainbows and ice cream; it will help."

Derek sighed, but the glow in his eyes dimmed.

I knocked on the door.

No answer.

I knocked again.

Nothing.

"He's in there," Derek said. "I can hear him moving."

"I'm deciding if I should let you in," Saiman's smooth voice called through the door. "Our meetings never go well, Kate. You'll forgive me if I'm less than enthusiastic."

"Adam Kamen," I said.

The lock clicked and the door swung open. Saiman wore his neutral form, a bald man of slight build and indeterminable age, somewhere between twenty and fifty. He was a blank canvas, hairless, colorless, without any distinguishing features. If you bumped into him on the street and didn't notice the sharp intelligence stabbing through his eyes, you'd never remember him.

Saiman's face wore a martyred expression. "Come in, come in . . ."

I stepped inside and froze. Chaos reigned around me. Usually Saiman's apartment was a highly controlled environment of white rugs, stainless steel furniture, and ultramodern curves. Not a single carpet fiber was out of place. Today the couch held a variety of clothes folded into neat stacks. Wooden crates littered the floor, half-filled with books and linens. The door to Saiman's state-of-the-art laboratory stood wide open, and through the doorway I could see more boxes.

"What are you doing?"

"I'm playing golf, Kate. What does it look like I'm doing?"

He was in rare form today. "Why are you packing?"

Saiman rubbed his forehead. "Are we playing the obvious question game? I so apologize, nobody told me the rules. I'm packing, because I intend to move."

"Watch your tone," Derek said.

"Or what?" Saiman spread his arms. "You shall tear me to pieces? Spare me your threats. I assure you, under the present circumstances, they will have no effect."

I glanced at Derek. *Let me handle it.* Derek nodded very slightly.

I stepped closer to Saiman. The odor of scotch floated to me. "Are you drunk?"

The last time he got drunk I had to drive like a maniac across a snow-strewn city while an enraged Curran chased us across the rooftops.

"I'm not drunk. I'm drinking, but I'm not drunk. Kate, stop giving me that look; I've had two inches of scotch in the last two hours. With my metabolism, it's a drop in the bucket. I'm functioning at maximum capacity. The alcohol is merely the grease for my wheels."

"You never told me why you're packing," I said. Saiman was the last person I expected to move. He loved his ridiculously overpriced apartment in the only pre-Shift high-rise still standing in Atlanta. All his business contacts were tied to the city. He had half a dozen aliases, each with his or her fingers in a different pie.

Saiman rocked back on the balls of his feet. "I'm moving because the city is about to die. And I do not intend to go down with the ship."

"MOVE THE CLOTHES IF YOU WANT TO SIT DOWN." Saiman walked to the bar, retrieved a crystal goblet and a thick glass, and splashed amber-colored scotch into it.

Neither Derek nor I moved.

Saiman sipped his drink. "It started with Alfred Dugue. French-Canadian. An unpleasant violent man, very conflicted about his sexuality. His sexual practices were . . . odd."

Dear God, what would Saiman find odd? Never mind, I didn't want to know.

Saiman seemed to study his scotch. "I understand that realizing your preferences are in conflict with established norms can be traumatic, but Dugue was engaged in extreme self-loathing. Somehow between bouts of whipping himself and performing bizarre erotic rituals, he managed to build a successful enterprise shipping goods down the Mississippi. I wanted a piece of the action. I assumed the shape consistent with Dugue's type, charmed him, seduced him, and permitted him to take me home. I should've been more thorough in my research."

"Didn't go well, did it?"

Saiman's eyes brimmed with outrage. "He served me poisoned wine. When that failed, he tried to strangle me. I snapped his neck like a toothpick. It was a distasteful affair."

"I'm sure."

"I was going through his papers when I stumbled on his notes on Kamen's research. At first I dismissed it as a pipe dream. However, after running Dugue's operation for a few weeks . . ."

Of course. Why was I not surprised?

"You turned into the man you killed?" Derek couldn't keep derision out of his voice.

Saiman shrugged. "He was already dead. He couldn't benefit from his company, and it couldn't be left unsupervised. I'll have you know I've greatly improved on it since it came into my possession. For one, his teamsters are now paid a living wage. Consequently, the incidents of theft are down thirty-seven percent. Soon, I shall simply sell the entire enterprise to myself, eliminating the need to perpetuate the Dugue impersonation. But I digress. I realized that Dugue wasn't fond of bets; if he invested in something, it was a sure thing. Given the obscene amount of money he'd sunk into Kamen, I revisited the matter. I went to see Adam."

"While he was under the Red Guard's supervision?"

"Of course."

So much for no visitors. I knew it was a shit job from the start. I knew Rene had denied me information. I could deal with it. But an outright lie went over the line. Strike one against Rene. "Go on."

"We chatted. Kamen was deeply damaged by his wife's death, a genius in his work, but practically nonfunctioning in all other areas of his life. It took me two visits to realize the machine was real. For a brief period I considered using it for my own means, but I've since come to my senses. It has to be destroyed."

I raised my hand. "Saiman, what does it do?"

He stared at me for a long moment. "You don't know?"

"Who is asking obvious questions now?"

Saiman leaned forward. "It destroys magic, Kate."

What? "You can't destroy magic. It's a form of energy—you can convert it, but it doesn't just disappear."

"You can also contain it," Saiman said. "Adam Kamen has built a device that collapses the fabric of magic in on itself. When activated, the device causes the magic around it to implode, converting it into a dense concentrated form. Think of it in terms of gas and liquid; if the magic's normal state in our world is gas, then Kamen's device pressurizes it into a liquid state."

He was crazy. "By what means?"

Saiman sighed. "I don't understand most of it. To be brutally simplistic, the apparatus is basically a cylinder with a reservoir within its core. The device must be permitted to charge during a magic wave for a certain period of time. Once the device is charged, it goes active. The actual process of magic cleansing takes very little time. Kamen's first prototype cleared an area half a mile across under ten minutes.

"The device pulls the magic inside its core, affecting a large radius directly around it. The magic enters the device and passes through a series of chambers. Each successive chamber causes it to implode further and further upon itself, so by the time it reaches the reservoir at the core, the magic is 'liquid,' very dense. It occupies a very small volume in this state. When the next magic wave floods, the area affected by the device remains magic-free. I don't know why. I just know that it works."

My brain struggled to digest this. "We were told it was never tested."

Saiman shook his head. "Kamen tested a small table model, the very first prototype he built. It was the size of a wine bottle and it cleared the magic in a half-mile radius. There is a spot in Sibley where there is no magic, Kate. I've stood on its edge and walked through it. I can give you the coordinates. The second prototype he had built was supposed to affect an area with a diameter of two point seven miles . . ."

If the prototype I had seen in Rene's picture were activated, it could wipe out a small town. "What happens to people caught in the implosion?"

Saiman drained his glass. "I don't know. I can only tell you what Kamen told me, and so far he hasn't been proven wrong. He theorized that during the implosion anything that uses magic dies."

Ice slid down my spine. "Define 'anything.' "

"Necromancers, vampires, creatures, your precious shape-shifters, you, me. Anyone with any significant amount of magic. We. All. Die."

Fucking shit. The entire city wiped out. Men, women, children . . . By the latest estimates, at least thirty percent of the population used magic or depended on it. If the Lighthouse Keepers had the device, they would use it. It destroyed magic— they would fall over themselves in a rush to activate it and they could strike anywhere. If they turned that thing on near the Keep, Atlanta would be free of shapeshifters. Curran, dead. Julie, dead. Derek, Andrea, Raphael, Ascanio, dead, dead, dead.

I stared at Saiman. "Why would he build something like this?"

"Kamen's wife required dialysis to live," Saiman went on. "Three times a week. When the magic interrupted the process, one of the nurses had to hand-crank the machine to return the blood to the patients. One day the magic wave caused several patients to go into cardiac arrest. While the nurse tended to them, Kamen's wife bled out and died. He wanted to create a small model of the apparatus that would generate a magic-free zone in which technology could work unhindered. And once he did that, he had to build a bigger machine, just to see if he could improve on it."

"You knew what it was and you let him build it? What the fuck is wrong with you?"

"I didn't!" Saiman hurled his glass across the room. It shattered against the wall. "I was too closely supervised to bring in a weapon, so I tried to poison him. He survived. Then I hired half a dozen men, trained, expensive professionals. They were supposed to cut through the Red Guard and destroy everything: Kamen, plans, prototype. Everything. I supplied them with enough plastique to make a crater the size of a football field."

"What happened?"

"They never got to the Red Guard. They were met in the woods by someone and the next morning their heads were delivered to my doorstep in a garbage bag."

"Could one of the other investors have done it?" Derek asked.

Saiman shook his head. "His other investors are Grady Memorial and the Healthy Child, Bright Future charity fund. They are actually what they pretend to be—do-gooders."

The volhvs wouldn't have dumped the heads at his door. They would've just made the hired muscle disappear. No, that was a terrorist tactic designed to frighten and intimidate. It had to be the Lighthouse Keepers. Killing Saiman would've created too much noise. He maintained damaging files on every prominent person in the city. If he died, they would panic. Every law enforcement agency would be crawling all over his murder. The Keepers didn't want noise, not yet.

"What do you know about the Lighthouse Keepers?"

Saiman's face fell. "That would explain volumes."

Crap.

"What happens if the device is broken?" Derek asked.

"The magic escapes in a huge burst," Saiman said. "Theoretically, if the machine is activated, the people in the immediate area would survive the longest. Those on the perimeter would die first, because the magic would stream from the perimeter toward the device. Standing next to the device would be like standing in the eye of a storm, so it is possible to interrupt its operation. However, the individuals who stole it are unlikely to permit any such interruptions. The six heads in the garbage bag testify to their resolve." He paced back and forth. "These people had me monitored, they killed my mercenaries, and they've taken the machine from under the noses of an elite Red Guard unit. This indicates to me that they're both competent and highly motivated. If they are, indeed, the Lighthouse Keepers, they will use the device where it will inflict the most damage. They have to use it. The destruction of magic is the entire purpose for their existence. I need to resume my packing."

I exhaled rage. The entire city was about to die and he was packing. God damn selfish asshole. "Why didn't you come to me? I have fifteen hundred shapeshifters at my disposal."

"I had a perfectly good reason."

"I'm dying to hear it."

"Please, allow me to demonstrate." Saiman turned to the giant flatscreen, plucked a DVD case from the shelf, and slid the disk into the DVD player's slot.

The screen ignited, showing an inside of a large warehouse, filmed in high definition from above. Cars sat in two lines: a Porsche, a Bentley, a Ferrari, a Lamborghini, something sleek I didn't recognize . . . I'd never seen so much horsepower crammed into one place.

I glanced at Saiman. "What is this?"

"These are the contents of the *Merriweather*, one of the vessels in my shipping company." Saiman braided his long fingers. "This fleet of cars was purchased in Europe, brought over to Savannah at considerable expense, and then shipped up to Atlanta to one of my warehouses."

We looked at the cars. The cars looked back at us.

"After the events of that unfortunate night at Bernard's, I expected immediate retribution from the Beast Lord. When it didn't come, I called you to check on your well-being. You confirmed that you were in good health. I began to believe that perhaps I had dodged a bullet."

"Let me guess, you didn't dodge?"

"Keep watching," Saiman insisted.

We stared at the cars.

"I don't get it." Derek frowned. "None of them are water-modified. What's the point of having a vehicle that's not drivable during magic?"

"To experience speed," Saiman said. "Have you ever driven a luxury car at a hundred and sixty miles per hour? It's a feeling you never forget."

The door in the wall opposite the camera opened. Curran walked into our view. He moved in an unhurried way, almost relaxed. The camera locked on to him, zooming on his face. His eyes were dark. The digital clock in the corner of the movie said 10:13 a.m. Twelve hours after Saiman had delivered a monumental insult to Curran while the Pack's elite watched. An hour since Saiman had called and Curran listened to our phone call, rolling one of my metal plates into a tube. Forty-five minutes after I refused to go with him to the Keep to announce that we'd been mated and His Furry Majesty had walked out on me in a huff.

Alarm prickled my fingertips.

A large man in a dark uniform approached Curran from the right, brandishing a baton. "Hey, buddy. You can't be here."

Curran kept walking.

"Why a baton?" Derek asked.

"Because I'm not about to give security guards a weapon that could make holes in my merchandise."

"Stop!" the guard barked. A streak of light dashed along the baton's length.

"That's not a baton." I leaned to the screen. "That's a torpere. An electric stun weapon. It was the top of the line in crowd control just before the Shift."

"Quite right. A typical stun gun delivers its voltage in short bursts to avoid the death of the target," Saiman said. "This is a modified model. When triggered, it emits a powerful uninterrupted electric current for up to twelve minutes. It has been shown to induce cardiac arrest in two."

"Stop!" The guard swung the baton at Curran's back.

Curran whipped about, too fast to see. His hand locked on the baton. Metal crunched, sparks burst, and the crushed mess of metal and electronics fell to the floor.

The guard took a step back. His lower jaw dropped. He looked at the torpere, looked back at Curran, and took off for the door.

Curran turned around.

Behind him a second guard edged outside.

What are you doing, Curran?

The Beast Lord surveyed the cars. His face was calm and cold, as if carved from a glacier. The amount of money tied up in those cars had to be enormous. The warehouse would have to have been well protected from the outside. I wondered how many guards he had chased off.

A muscle in Curran's cheek jerked.

His eyes burst into gold. Curran grabbed the Porsche on his left, ripping the car door off as if it were tissue paper. He grasped the car from the bottom. Monstrous muscles bulged on his arms. The Porsche went airborne. It flew up, flipped over twice, and crashed atop the red Lamborghini. Glass snapped, steel groaned, and a car alarm went off in a sharp-pitched wail.

Holy shit.

Curran lunged at a silver Bentley. The hood went flying. He thrust his hand into the car. Metal screamed, and Curran jerked a twisted clump out of the hood and smashed it into the nearest car like a club.

"Did he just rip out the engine?" I asked.

"Yes," Saiman said. "And now he's demolishing the Maserati with it."

Ten seconds later Curran hurled the twisted wreck of black and orange that used to be the Maserati into the wall.

The first melodic notes of an old song came from the computer. I glanced at Saiman.

He shrugged. "It begged for a soundtrack."

Curran ripped the remains of a car in two. He raged through the warehouse like a tornado, smashing, crushing, tearing into the metal and plastic, so primal in his fury that he was frightening and hypnotic at the same time. And while we watched him rage, some long-gone man sang about being kissed by a rose at someone's grave.

The song ended and still he kept going. Saiman's face remained passive, but his eyes had lost their usual smugness. I looked into them and saw a shadow of fear hidden deep beneath the surface.

Saiman was terrified of physical pain. I'd seen it firsthand—when injured, he panicked and lashed out with remarkable violence. He had watched the recording, soaked up the full extent of the devastation Curran could unleash, and waited, wondering when the Beast Lord would show up on his doorstep. He'd watched the recording over and over. He'd attached a lyrical soundtrack to it, trying to diminish its impact through the sheer absurdity of it. One glance at his expression told me it hadn't helped: the cold face kept relaxed by sheer will, the haunted eyes, the tense mouth. Curran had made Saiman paranoid, and it wore him down. He would do anything to avoid Curran's wrath.

Curran stopped. He straightened, surveying the heap of tortured metal, ruined plastic, and torn rubber. He turned around. Gray eyes looked directly into the camera. The cuts and gashes on his hands and face knitted closed.

Curran's clear, cold voice rolled through the room. "Don't call her, don't talk to her, don't involve her in your schemes. She doesn't owe you anything. If you hurt her in any way, I'll kill you. If she gets hurt helping you, I'll kill you."

It was about me. This epic devastation was all about me. Curran must've thought Saiman had something on me and was using it to force me to help him, so he'd sent a message.

The Beast Lord walked out of the warehouse. The screen went dark.

My knight in furry armor.

Saiman opened his mouth. "This is why I didn't. Personally, I think your smile is inappropriate."

I caught myself and switched to a scowl. "Give me the recording, and I'll mend this fence."

"At what price?"

"You will tell me everything you know about the device and Adam Kamen. You'll turn over all documents, notes, everything, and you will help us find it."

Saiman braided the fingers of his hands together and rested his chin on his fist, thinking. "That homicidal maniac you're in lust with will want more."

"If he does, then I'm sure the two of you can come to an

understanding," I ground out. "In Atlanta, you're a person of substance. Outside it, you're an unknown. You'll have to start over. It's in your best interests to stop the destruction of the city. I will intercede on your behalf with Curran. Take it, Saiman, because that's all I'm offering."

Saiman frowned. A long minute passed. He rose, pulled the disk out, slid it into a thin plastic sleeve, and held it out. "Deal."

I took the disk and slipped it into my pocket. "The documents?"

Derek grabbed us and dived to the floor, knocking over the couch.

The door behind us exploded.

CHAPTER 16

BULLETS BIT INTO THE COUCH, CHEWING THROUGH the steel and cushions. The world went white in a blinding flash. Thunder slapped my ears, shaking the brain in my skull. All sound faded. Derek jerked, clamping his hands over his ears.

A stun grenade.

Next to me Saiman trembled, hugging the floor.

Steel shutters dropped, covering the floor-to-ceiling windows—Saiman's defense system kicking into high gear.

The electric lamps on the ceiling shone bright, illuminating us. The couch wouldn't hold. We had to move.

To the right, the lab door gaped wide open. Twelve feet. If we had a distraction, we could make it. I looked around, trying to find something to throw. Clothes—no, too light—clothes, more clothes . . . Table. The heavy glass-topped table.

I lunged for it and tried to lift it. Too heavy. I could heave it upright and maybe throw it a couple of feet. Not far enough, and they would cut me down while I struggled to lift it.

The roar of the gunfire penetrated the wall in my ears, soft like the noise of a distant waterfall.

A dark canister rolled into the space to the left of us, between the couch and a bar, and belched a cloud of green gas. Shit. I held my breath. Derek pressed his hand over his nose. Tears streamed from his eyes.

Derek's shapeshifter senses couldn't take it. We had to go now.

I grabbed Derek's shoulder, pointed at the table, and made a throwing motion with my arms.

He nodded.

"Saiman!" My voice was a faint echo. "Saiman!"

He glanced at me and I saw a familiar blank look in his eyes. He would snap any second. I grabbed his arm. "Run or die!"

Crouching, Derek grasped the table and hurled it at the muzzle flashes.

I jerked Saiman to his feet and ran.

Behind me glass shattered in the hail of gunfire. I leaped inside and spun around in time to see Saiman dive through the doorway, with Derek a hair behind. Derek slammed the thick reinforced door shut and stumbled, like a blind man, his eyes wide open, tears streaming down his face. Blood gushed from his leg, staining the jeans inside out.

Slowly, as if underwater, Saiman locked the heavy metal door.

To the right, a decontamination shower loomed in the corner. I pushed Derek into it and pulled the chain. Water drenched him. He shuddered and raised his face to the stream, letting the water run into his eyes.

"How bad are you hit?"

"The bullet went through. It's nothing."

Bullets pounded into the door with sharp staccato. It wouldn't hold them for long.

If I had a lab, I'd have the fuse box nearby in case I had to shut things down in a hurry. I looked around and saw the dark gray rectangle of the fuse box in the wall between two cabinets. Perfect. I pried the cover open and pulled the main fuse.

The apartment went pitch-black. For a second I was blind and then my eyes adjusted, picking up faint light from the digital clock on the wall. Must be battery operated.

Next to me the sound of ripping fabric announced the werewolf shedding his clothes and human skin. Yellow eyes ignited six and a half feet off the ground, like two moons.

Saiman took a deep, shuddering breath.

"Hide or fight," I whispered to him. "Just don't get in my way."

The rain of bullets halted. Not good. They'd decided they couldn't shoot their way through the door. The next step was explosives. I dashed to the left side of the door and pressed myself against the wall in the corner.

Across the room the enormous shaggy monster that was Derek leaped onto the counter. A clawed paw swiped the butane lab lighter and raised it to the sprinkler. A tiny blue flame flared at the end of the lighter. It licked the sprinkler, once, twice, and then water rained down in a stinging spray.

Bye-bye gas.

A high-pitched whine tore through the quiet.

The explosion shook the door, slapping my ears. The metal door screeched and fell into the room. A flashlight beam sliced through the darkness, searching for targets.

I squeezed the hilt of my saber. It felt so comforting, like shaking hands with an old friend. Water soaked my hair.

Derek sank his claws into the paneling, leaped, and crawled across the ceiling with terrifying speed, grasping steel beams for support.

The door burst open. I slid down into a crouch.

The first man edged into the room, his black handgun gripped in both hands in a time-honored shooter stance. The bulletproof vest made him appear almost square. The man spun right, spun left, turning the gun barrel two feet above me, and advanced into the room.

A second man followed, holding his flashlight and gun in a Chapman hold: the gun gripped in the right hand, the flashlight in the left, the hands clenched together. He turned, his flashlight sweeping the length of the room.

Come in, there is nothing to fear. You're big and strong, and your gun will protect you.

The bright beam glided over lab tables, biting at darkness broken by streams of water. Left, right . . .

The third man stepped into the room, covering the man with the flashlight. Classic.

The beam slid up. A nightmare looked into the light: a huge man towering eight and a half feet high, his colossal muscles bulging in hard ridges on his immense frame. His skin glowed in the light, pure white, as if he were molded out of snow. A blue mane cascaded down his shoulders, framing a cruel face, and on that face two eyes blazed, pure translucent blue, like ice from the deepest part of a glacier. Looking into them was like staring back in time, at a thing that was alien and ancient and very, very hostile. Saiman had taken his true form.

The men froze for half a second. They expected a man, a woman, and Saiman. They didn't expect their flashlight to find an enraged ice giant in the darkness and they gaped, just as the ancient Scandinavians had done ages ago, gripped by a paralysis of awe and fear.

I sliced the inside of the closest man's thigh in a sharp upward thrust, severing muscles and the femoral artery, stabbed him in the heart, pulled the blade out, and sliced the neck of the second man in a fluid easy movement—the blade was so sharp, the cut was almost delicate.

The man with the flashlight fired once. Saiman's enormous hand slapped the firearm out of his fist. Massive fingers clenched him and the man vanished into the darkness. A hoarse scream cut through the silence, full of pain and pure terror.

Derek dropped to the floor and bounded over the bodies into the living room. I followed him.

Behind us the man kept howling, no longer desperate, just hurting.

A gun spat bullets to the right, wood snapping—someone firing blindly in panic. I waited four seconds until he emptied his clip, and then I ran across the room, stepped behind him, and sliced: one cut left to right, the second straight across the spine, just under the bulletproof vest. He went down.

Something moved behind me.

I spun, slicing, the man behind me a mere shadow in the gloom. Slayer crashed against a thicker blade. The man snapped an angle kick to my left side. His shin hammered my ribs in a burst of pain. A Muay Thai fighter. Fine. I spun with the impact, whipped around, and kicked him, heel to solar plexus, putting all of the power of my spin and my thigh into it.

The impact knocked him back. My knee crunched. Ow.

I chased him, leaping over boxes. The fallen man rolled to his feet in time for me to split his stomach open. I tugged Slayer free, sank the blade between the lower ribs of his right side, for good measure, and withdrew.

The screaming stopped.

"Cleearr," Derek's mangled voice said.

"Saiman! Flip the fuse."

A long moment passed. The electric light came on, sudden and harsh, like a sucker punch. Five bodies lay broken and twisted in the living room, their blood ridiculously vivid against the monochromatic backdrop of black floor and white furniture. The massive shaggy beast that was Derek straightened, scarlet dripping from his claws, and dropped a mangled body to the floor. He raised his muzzle. A long wolf howl rolled through the apartment, a song of hunt and blood and murdered prey.

Saiman emerged from the lab, stooping to fold his frame through the doorway. A thing dangled from his hand. It might have been a man at some point, but now it hung, limp and boneless, like a sack of human meat pierced here and there by shards of its bones.

"It's over." I kept my voice soothing. "Put it down."

Saiman shook his victim.

"Put it down. You can do it. Just let go."

Saiman released his victim. The body fell with a sickening wet thud. The ice giant slumped against the wall and slid down to sit on the floor.

I walked past the overturned couch to the man whose stomach I'd cut. He was still breathing, clutching at his wounds, his heavy tactical sword lying next to him. Thick blood wet his fingers in a dark, almost tar-like stain. Yep, hit the liver. A ski mask hid his face. I pulled it off. A familiar brutish face stared at me with pale eyes.

Blaine "The Blade" Simmons. Blaine used to work for the Guild. About four years ago he decided the Guild wasn't hardcore enough for him and struck out on his own. Word on the street was, Blaine hired killers and liked wet work. The nastier, the better. Any gig, any target, as long as the money was right. That must've been his crew.

I crouched by him, my sword still bloody.

Blaine's breath was coming in quick ragged gasps.

"Who hired you?"

He wheezed, his fingers shaking.

"Who hired you?"

"Go to hell!"

Blaine's eyes rolled back into his skull. He went rigid and sagged down. His hands stopped shaking.

"I have a laaive one." Derek picked up a body off the floor. The man shuddered in his grasp. His right leg hung at an unnatural angle—broken femur. A huge cut gaped across his back, where Derek's claws ripped through his flesh. Derek turned him, so I could see his face. Pale, terrified eyes looked at me.

"If you stay as is, you'll live. Tell me what I want to know, and I won't make it worse," I said.

The man swallowed. "I don't know! Blaine made the contracts!"

"What were your orders?"

"We had to sit on this apartment. If law or any PIs showed up, we had to hit it fast."

"Did you have specific orders to attack if you saw me or Derek?"

The man nodded. "You—yeah. But not him. Blaine had pictures of you and the blonde."

They knew who Andrea and I were, which meant they knew where the office was. If they'd hit us here, they'd target the office. I would.

"Why did you use a concussion grenade instead of shrapnel?"

The man gulped. "Blaine said the freak had money. He said nobody would care when or how he got dead, as long as he got dead in the end. We'd just hold him for a bit, get him to give us the money, and then terminate him. Blaine said it would be a bonus."

Nice. "Did you kill some people in Sibley?"

"Us and some other guys. We knew exactly when and where they would be coming from. We wiped them out. Shot them all to hell. It was easy."

Mystery solved. "Drop him."

Derek opened his fingers and the man crashed to the floor.

I walked to the phone and dialed Cutting Edge. Julie's voice popped on the phone. "Good afternoon, Cutting Edge. How may I help you?"

"Hey, it's me. Put Andrea on the phone."

"She isn't here."

Damn it. "Where is she?"

"Some boudas came to talk to her. She said she would be right back and left."

Aunt B. Just couldn't wait, could she, old bitch, had to speak to Andrea right that minute.

"Joey is staying with us."

I struggled to put the name to a face. Joey, Joey . . . My mind served up a man in his early twenties, his hair dark, nearly black. "Put Joey on the phone."

A young male voice said, "Why hello there, Consort. And how are you?"

"We're under attack. Bar the door, do not open it to anyone you don't know. Make sure the kids understand. I'll be there in half an hour. Stay put, do you understand?"

All mirth vanished from his voice. "Yes, Consort."

I hung up and punched in the number for the Keep's Guard Station. "I need access to Jim. Now."

"He's out in the city," a female voice began.

I sank enough menace into my voice to terrify a small army. "Find him."

The phone went silent. I waited. The Lighthouse Keepers had hired a crew of killers. Made sense; their own people were embedded and too valuable to risk. We had to assume they already knew that the attack on the apartment had failed and what little cover they had was blown wide open. They would be coming for Saiman.

The phone clicked and Jim's voice came on the line. "Kate, I'm a little busy here."

"There is an anti-magic secret society in the city. They have a bomb. When activated, it kills anything that uses magic in a radius of several miles."

Jim didn't miss a beat. "What do you need?"

"I'm at Saiman's apartment. We've been attacked; there are seven bodies, one survivor. I need to know where the attackers came from, who hired them, anything you can get. I'm sending Derek with Saiman to the western safe house. Saiman has the documentation describing the device, and he is now their primary target. I'm going back to my office. Julie and Ascanio are in the office and I need to get them out to the Keep."

"We're on the Southside, near Palmetto," Jim said.

Across the city. Great.

"I'm sending an escort now. It will be there in an hour."

"Is Curran there with you?"

"He's out in the field, but I'll get hold of him."

"Tell him . . ." *Tell him I love him.* "Tell him I'm sorry we didn't see each other last night."

"Will do."

I hung up and looked at Derek. "Take Saiman and the documents to the western safe house. Keep him protected; we need the knowledge in his head."

Derek's muzzle gaped, like a bear trap swinging open. "Yeshh, Conshort."

THE MAGIC HIT ONE MILE FROM THE OFFICE. THE Jeep's gasoline engine faltered and died and I guided it to a slow stop at the curb.

The worry that had sat in the pit of my stomach since the phone call grew stronger and stronger until it blossomed into full-blown anxiety. Something was wrong; I felt it.

The kids were fine. They were in a fortified office. They had a full-grown bouda with them. Reinforcements were on the way.

I stared at the wheel. It would take me fifteen minutes to chant the water engine into life.

They were fine.

Screw it.

I jumped out of the car, locked it, and took off down the street at an easy jog. My knee protested, sending a warning spike of pain into my thigh with every step. A nagging ache gnawed at my ribs. It was a good kick, but in retrospect I should've punched him instead.

The streets rolled by. I was doing a seven-minute mile. Still faster than warming up the car. I turned onto Jeremiah, passing a couple of delivery trucks, blocking most of the street. Not too far now.

Something lay in the street in front of the office. Something small and wrapped in fabric.

My heart hammered. I sped up.

A child mannequin rested on the pavement, swaddled in a grimy sweater. Blood stained its clothes and plastic face.

The door of the office stood ajar. Ice rolled down my spine.

I pulled Slayer from its sheath and forced myself to slow down. I'd need my breath. The door was intact. Someone had opened it. I tested it with my fingertips and it swung, revealing the office. My desk lay on its side, a flurry of papers scattered on the floor. Red stained the wood, where someone's bloody hand had gripped it.

A nude body sprawled on the floor on my right. It lay on its back in a puddle of blood, its chest a forest of bone shards where someone had wrenched ribs out of their place. Male. A hole marred his neck and left shoulder. Something had bitten him with preternatural teeth. The head was a mess of blood and battered tissue. A chair leg protruded from the stomach, where someone had pinned the corpse to the floor like a butterfly.

I approached the body, sword ready, and saw a shock of spiky black hair on the right side of the corpse's skull. *Joey.*

An enraged growl shook the office. Something clanged, once, twice, a ringing of metal being struck.

I dashed to the back.

The door to the back room lay in shards on the floor. I leaped over it. A section of the wall had been ripped open, and through the gap I saw a female shapeshifter in warrior form. Huge, at least seven feet and sheathed with beige fur with dark spots, she was all claws and teeth, pounding the loup cage with the rest of the chair. Tufts of black hair crowned her monstrous ears. A lynx.

The pieces snapped together in my head. Leslie, the missing render that Curran had been hunting.

Inside the cage, a bouda in warrior form cradled something, shielding it with his body. Deep gashes scoured his back, marked with thick bloody smears. The shape in his arms trembled. Two legs stuck out, deformed and twisted. Muscle bulged in odd places, sheathed by human skin and patches of beige fur.

Leslie saw me and froze.

Ascanio turned and I glimpsed the thing he was trying to

protect. A horrible face gaped at me, its lower jaw protruding, its face like a blob of melting wax, the eyes little more than tiny slits. It was the face victims of Lyc-V wore when the shape-shifter virus first infected their bodies.

The small brown eyes looked at me from the monster's face. Julie. Oh my God, *Julie*.

Leslie was trying to murder the kids.

I charged.

Leslie roared and hurled the shattered chair at me. I dodged and stabbed her in the chest, aiming for her heart. Slayer slid off the ribs—I'd punctured her lung instead. Like poking a normal human with a needle. Claws raked my shoulder. I sliced across her stomach. She leaned back and kicked out with both feet. I saw the kick but there was no way to avoid it. The blow took me square in the chest. I flew into the main room, curling into a ball. My back slammed into the wall. The world swam.

Leslie leaped at me through the gap, claws raised, giant teeth snapping.

I dodged. She hit the wall full speed and whipped around, carving the air, her claws like daggers. I dodged, left, left, right. She swung too wide and I lunged into the opening, turning Slayer into a metal whirlwind. Left thigh, side, right thigh, left shoulder, chest . . .

She snarled and backhanded me. I've been hit with a hammer. It hurt less. My head snapped back and she raked at me with her other hand. Pain cleaved my stomach. I stumbled back.

Blood filled my mouth. Leslie bled from a dozen places, but not enough to slow her down. She was fast, Lyc-V was healing her cuts, and my sword wasn't doing enough damage.

I kicked at her. She hammered a fist into my thigh. I swayed at the last moment and the fist grazed me. My femur screamed from the impact. She was aiming for my injured knee. I drove Slayer into her liver.

Leslie screeched and roared, "Die alrrrcady!"

I cleaved at her right arm, severing the tendon. Unless I won, the kids died. I would kill this bitch. I'd tear her limb from limb if I had to.

She grabbed at me with her left hand, clenching my shoulder, lifting me off the ground, and jerked me to her teeth. I pulled my throwing knife and stabbed her in the throat, quick, like hammering a nail. She gurgled, tore me off, and hurled me aside.

I hit Andrea's desk with my back, dropped to my feet, and started toward her. I hurt so much, the pain kept me from passing out.

Leslie grabbed a filing cabinet and hurled it at me. I dodged. She threw a chair. I ducked and kept coming. Leslie heaved a bookshelf. It would hit me; I had no place to go.

A black dog the size of a pony burst through the doorway. *Grendel, you stupid magic poodle.*

The dog hit Leslie in the chest like a battering ram. The render went down, knocked off her feet by the impact. I ran at Leslie. This was my chance.

Leslie clenched Grendel by the scruff of his neck and flung him aside. He crashed into the wall with a snarl.

Leslie leaped to her feet and bared her teeth at me. Blood dripped from between her fangs, stretching in long red threads to the floor.

Don't black out. I just had to stay conscious.

"Osanda." The power word left my mouth, tearing out a chunk of my magic in a flash of pain. I didn't care. I sank everything into it. *Kneel.* Kneel, you bitch.

She gasped. The bones of her shins snapped like toothpicks and she crashed to her knees. I swung Slayer. The sword's pale blade smoked, feeding off my fury. I cut, severing the spinal column. Leslie's head dropped to the side. I chopped at it again. It rolled to the floor. Her headless body toppled toward me. I kicked her head into the corner and dragged myself to the loup cage.

Julie whimpered in a thin tiny voice, her breath whistling through the space between her mangled jaws. Ascanio lay on his back. His eyes looked at me, flashing red. Still alive. They were both still alive.

I grabbed onto the bars. God, my chest hurt. "She's dead. It will be okay. It will be okay. Give me the keys."

Ascanio cried out and flipped onto his side. A rib had pierced his chest, sticking out. His hand opened, the key a gory bloody mess in his palm. He shut his eyes.

I thrust my hand through the bars, grabbed the slick, warm key, and unlocked the cage.

"Help us," Julie whispered. "It hurts, Kate . . . It hurts."

"I know, baby. I know." I had to get them to Doolittle. A quarter of Lyc-V's victims didn't survive their first transformation.

Tears slid from Julie's eyes. "The boy's dying."

I looked over Ascanio. Broken ribs, torn-up back. I touched Ascanio's neck. Pulse. Weak, but steady pulse. He opened his eyes slowly. "I trrrried."

"You did great."

The roar of an enchanted engine thundered outside. Jim's backup. I forced myself upright.

"Don't leave me!" Julie sobbed.

"Just to the door. To get help. I'll be right back."

I ran out into the living room, wrapped in my pain like a cloak, and saw a gray van pulling up in front of the office. The Pack didn't own gray vans.

I sprinted to the door.

The van door opened. An older man stepped out and leveled a crossbow at me. A tiny green spark winked on the end of the crossbow bolt. An exploding arrow head.

I slammed the door shut and barred it.

The explosion shook the building.

I pulled the internal shutter on the left window closed and dashed right. The crossbow bolt got there half a second before me and bounced off the grate, falling back. I pulled the shutter down. The burst of magic energy was like a wrecking ball. The walls groaned but held. A couple more direct hits and they would come down.

The kids couldn't move, not fast enough to outrun a vehicle.

Grendel limped to me. I hugged his shaggy neck and ran my hands along his back. Nothing was broken.

I had enough juice for one power word. It would buy us a couple of minutes, but I would pass out, and with the kids immobile, we were trapped.

"When the shit hits the fan, you hide, you hear?"

Grendel whined.

"Don't be a hero, dog."

I slid the cover in the door aside, exposing the narrow viewing window. The door of the van was open. Inside, the man in the tactical vest slowly, methodically loaded another explosive bolt into his crossbow.

We were done.

When they blasted through the wall, I would take a few of them with me. That was all I could do.

The crossbowman raised the bow.

A gray shape leaped off the roof. A massive beast, a meld of human and lion, landed on the roof of the van, crushing it.

Curran.

The giant claws gouged the top of the van, and he ripped the metal sheet away, as if opening a can of sardines. The crossbowman looked up in time to see the huge paw just before it cracked his skull like an egg. The enormous jaws of the leonine head opened and a deafening roar blasted forth in a declaration of war, drowning even the noise of the enchanted engine. The beast dipped his massive head inside, pulled a kicking body out between his teeth, pinned it with his paws, and ripped the top half of the body off.

He had come for me again.

Curran's body flowed, snapping into a more humanoid form. He plucked another man from the van, snapped his neck, hurled the broken body aside, and dove into the vehicle. The van rocked. Blood sprayed the windows, someone screamed, and he emerged from the van, bloody, his golden eyes on fire.

I unlocked the door. It swung open and he clenched me to him. I threw my arms around his neck and I kissed him, blood and fur and all.

CHAPTER 17

———◆———

HELL WAS DRIVING A BLOOD-SOAKED VAN LISTEN-ing to two children dying in the backseat, while Grendel whined as if something were killing him. Hell was watching Jezebel run out of the Keep's gates, her face a pain-distorted mask, clench Joey's mangled body, rock him like a child, and scream and scream and scream, as if it were Jezebel who was dying. Hell was seeing fear in Doolittle's eyes when Curran carried Julie, wrapped in the sheets from my office cot, into the Keep, and then sitting in the waiting room.

Curran spoke into the phone, biting off words. "Is anybody going to tell me why our own fucking render attacked my mate?"

Barabas walked into the room. The skin of his face stretched too tight over his features, making him look sharper and fragile. He came over and crouched by me. "Can I get you anything?"

I shook my head. Curran hung up the phone.

Barabas's eyes were watering. He looked feverish and unhinged. His quiet voice shook with barely contained anger. "Did she hurt before you killed her?"

"Yes," Curran said. "I saw the body."

"That's good." Barabas swallowed. His hands shook. Technical difficulties with controlling his rage. I could relate. "Jez will be glad to hear it."

"Was Joey a relative?" I asked. My voice squeaked. I could've given a rusty metal gate a run for its money in the creaking department.

"He was the youngest of our generation," Barabas said. "Jezebel used to babysit him. We all did, but she had done it the most."

The door swung open and Jim blocked the light. Tall, dark, grim, and wrapped in a black cloak, he looked like death walking in. Jim reached into his cloak and pulled out a thin gold chain. The light of the feylanterns clutched at the gold and slid down to a small pendant. A lighthouse. A tiny diamond winked from the spot where the lighthouse lamp would have been.

"Boyfriend had it," Jim said. "Leslie broke the chain. He was getting it fixed for her birthday."

Leslie Wren was a Lighthouse Keeper.

It wasn't the hundred-mile walk through rough terrain that had hurt Julie. It wasn't a freak accident or a render gone loup. No, it was my case. Had she not been in that office, she wouldn't have been attacked. Had I ordered the trackers to bring her back to the Keep . . .

"Leslie's father was an engineer in Columbia," Jim said. "Made good money. About fifteen years ago the man lost his shit, quit his job, and moved the family north of Atlanta, to the countryside. He'd inherited the house from his parents. Leslie had an older brother, but he stayed in Columbia. The locals say they never saw the family much. They remember Leslie— a quiet kid in threadbare clothes. She went to school, but the parents wouldn't leave the property."

"How did they survive?" I asked.

Jim put the pendant on the table. "Lived off the land. There are deer in the woods, raccoons, small game. They must've hunted a lot. Three shapeshifters need a lot of food."

Curran glanced at me. "Explains why Leslie made a good render. She probably spent more time in her fur than in her skin growing up. It's not good for children. Messes with your head."

Jim shrugged off his cloak. "She came straight to the Pack the moment she turned eighteen. She's been with us for nine years. She was squared away. No warning signs, no problems, nothing. In hindsight, I should've asked myself why there were no problems. Most renders miss a step once in a while. She never did. She was the go-to render when we had an issue."

I leaned back. "Why would you look for trouble, when there is none?"

"She was with us for a third of her life. We treated her well." Curran leaned on the table. "I want to know why."

Jim squared his shoulders. "Teresa, one of my people, tracked down Leslie Wren's brother. She came back this morning. We'd just missed her. She says that Leslie's father, Colin Wren, had a serious case of paranoia. The mother, Liz, was a go-with-the-flow kind of woman. The brother says she was passive, didn't like confrontations. They weren't the most stable couple."

A paranoid shapeshifter with a passive mate who'd do pretty much anything he wanted to avoid a fight. That was a recipe for disaster.

Jim kept going. "When Leslie was twelve and her brother was seventeen, their mother had an affair with Michael Waterson."

"Local cat alpha of Columbia," Curran said for my benefit. "Not a bad guy. Capable."

"The affair didn't last long," Jim said. "When Colin found out, he snapped. From the way the brother tells it, he took Leslie with him out of Columbia and went to his parents' house. He gave Liz a choice: if she didn't come with him, she'd never see Leslie again."

"Used his daughter as collateral," Curran said.

Jim nodded. "The brother says she was afraid he'd do something to Leslie, so she went with him. Waterson never followed her. He says she told him not to look for her and that she was going to save her marriage. They holed up in the house. Liz wasn't allowed to leave the property. The brother was in high school at the time; he stayed behind to finish the year out. He came to visit them on his break. The dad tried to kill him. Said he was competition."

Living in that house must've been pure hell. It didn't make me regret killing Leslie. "She must've blamed Lyc-V for driving her father crazy."

Jim nodded. "Yeah."

"Bullshit," Barabas spat. "Dozens of shapeshifters deal with affairs. Marriages break. People die. We carry on. We don't abuse our mates and children."

"When did the Keepers recruit her?" Curran asked.

"We don't know," Jim said. "Had to be early on."

Something awful had happened to Leslie Wren in that house. Something that convinced her that the shapeshifters were evil, that the very magic that made their existence possible had to be destroyed. She believed it so deeply that she joined the people who hated her kind, signing her own death warrant. She had a life with the Pack, respect, friendships, a future. But whatever happened had scarred her so deeply, she threw it all away when the Keepers called.

How? How do you go from taking Julie on a hunting trip to trying to murder her? I had killed dozens, but I could never bring myself to take a life of a child. It was beyond me.

The door down the hall opened. Sander, one of Doolittle's junior medics, a tall, thin man who looked like he would snap in half any second, came out and approached us. "The boy is awake."

ASCANIO LAY ON THE BED UNDER THE COVERS. HIS face was a bloodless mask. He looked weak and small, his eyes enormous, like two dark pools on the pale face. If he were human, he would've been dead. Sander said he had hairline fractures in both legs, serious blood loss, a punctured lung, and two broken ribs. Leslie had thrown him around like a dog shaking a rat. The Lyc-V would knit him back together. A few days and he would be up and walking. But meanwhile he hurt.

I sat on his bed. Curran remained standing.

Ascanio's gaze fixed on him.

"What happened?" Curran asked.

"Aunt B's boudas came," Ascanio said, his voice flat. "Three of them. They told Andrea Aunt B wanted to talk. Andrea said no. They said, 'You're coming with us one way or another.' I figured there would be trouble. Andrea looked at me and said, 'Someone has to stay with the kids.' So they left Joey. He was the weakest. Grendel really didn't like him. He kept trying to bite Joey, so Andrea took him with her. Then you called and

Joey told us to stay away from the damn door. Then he went upstairs, he said to sleep."

Damn boudas. I tell him he's under siege and he goes to take a nap.

"About half an hour later someone knocked on the door. A woman was screaming."

Ascanio swallowed.

"Keep going," Curran told him.

"Julie said, 'Come on, doorboy, aren't you going to see who it is?' And I said, 'I'm not a doorboy, and if you want to know so bad, go see for yourself.' She went." Ascanio closed his eyes for a long moment. "The woman on the other end yelled, 'Help me, they hurt my baby.' Julie looked out and screamed that it was Leslie. She knew her from the Pack, and Leslie was carrying a bloody kid. We knew the Pack was being attacked. We opened the door."

They saw a shapeshifter woman with a blood-smeared child and they let her in. Of course they let her in. I would've run out the door to protect her. I should've told them about Leslie. No evidence existed that the two were connected, and I didn't know. If I had, Julie wouldn't be losing her humanity right now.

Ascanio took a deep breath. "She was in warrior form when she came through the door. She knocked Julie aside. I shifted and hit her. She was too strong. I got some strikes in, but then she clawed me up. I thought she'd slice me to ribbons and then Julie jumped on her back. The cat pulled her off and bit her, hard. It happened so fast. And then Joey came running. The cat said, 'Step aside, weakling. You know you can't take me.' And Joey pulled his knife and told me to protect Julie."

Ascanio squeezed his eyes shut. "Julie was already messed up. I picked her up and I ran."

His legs were broken and he'd carried Julie anyway. Whatever he did from now on, I would never forget this.

"I knew if we went out the back, she'd chase us down, so I got into the loup cage and locked the door."

He gulped the air.

I wanted to kill Leslie again. I wanted to kill her slowly and take my time.

"The cat did something to Joey to keep him from moving, because we heard Joey cussing her out. The cat came to get us, but she couldn't get through the bars. It really pissed her off. Joey was screaming and cursing, telling her she should come and pick on someone her own size. The cat went back out. And then we heard Joey scream. I wanted to go and help him, but I couldn't get up. The cat was beating him to death and I couldn't get up."

"You did everything right," I told him. "You did great. You couldn't have done more."

Ascanio's hand shook. "He died to keep us alive. Why? Why would he do that?"

"Because that's what you do," Curran said. "That's what being in the Pack means. The strong defend the weak. Joey protected you, and you protected Julie."

"He didn't even know us!" He stared at us, his eyes wet. "I'm not like you. I don't want this. I don't want people dying for me. I don't want to walk around with it."

Curran leaned toward him. "Then get strong. Learn to be bad enough so others don't have to die to keep you safe."

A commotion broke out by the door.

A female voice barked, "You *will* let me in or I'll kill you where you stand!"

The door flew open. A muscular woman strode through, a harried expression on her face. Martina, Ascanio's mother. She saw us and halted.

"You have a brave son," Curran said. "A credit to your clan."

Down the hall the door of the emergency room opened. Doolittle walked out, wiping his hands on a towel. I slipped out of the room and marched to him. He saw me. His face wore a tight expression, like he was straining to keep things inside.

Whoever you are upstairs, please don't let him tell me that Julie's dead. Please.

I reached him. "How is she?"

"Julie has massive trauma to the shoulder, three rib fractures, and a Lyc-V infection in the third stage."

Lyc-V infection had five stages: introduction of the virus, beginning of shift, half-shift, advanced shift, and stabilization. Julie was in half-shift, which meant her body was fighting the virus to stay human.

His face was grim. Something bad was coming. I clenched up.

"Julie's bloom levels are very high."

My chest constricted. Lyc-V "bloomed" when its victim was

under stress, saturating the body in great numbers. Too much, and it would put Julie over the edge. Forty percent of all Lyc-V victims went loup during the fourth stage. Julie was bitten, she was an adolescent, and she was injured. Her stress level was through the roof and her body was flooded with hormones. Her chances of going mad were astronomically high.

Someone asked, "Is she going loup?" and I realized it was me.

"Too early to tell." Doolittle rubbed his face. "Her transformation came on too fast. In all my years I've never seen it happen that fast. She started to transform almost from the moment the virus entered her system. Julie is very magical. Introducing the virus to her body was like planting a seed in fertile ground. The first transformation is always the most volatile. In a case of stable infection, the virus should've leveled off. Julie is still blooming."

Oh no.

"Call to the Frenchman," Curran said. I almost jumped. He'd come up behind us and I didn't hear him. "I don't care what it costs, just get it."

"Get what?" I stared at him.

"The Europeans have an herbal concoction," Curran answered. "It reduces the chances of loupism by a third. They guard it like it's gold, but we know somebody who smuggles it out."

Doolittle's face was mournful. "I took the liberty of calling the moment she came in, my lord."

"And?"

Doolittle shook his head.

"Did you tell him who was asking?" Curran snarled.

"I did. The Frenchman sends his apologies. If he had any, he would immediately deliver it, but there is none to be had."

Curran clenched his fists and forced them open.

"What now?" I asked.

"She's under heavy sedation. The main issue right now is to make her feel secure. No loud noises, no alarming voices, no agitation. We have to keep her calm and safe. That's all we can do. I'm so sorry."

"I want to see her."

"No." Doolittle barred my way.

"What do you mean, 'no'?"

"He means you're so agitated, you'll spike her virus levels by just walking in there," Curran said. "If you want her to get better, come back and see her when you're calm."

Yelling that I was calm, damn it, would only hammer home his point.

Curran turned to Doolittle. "When will we know?"

"I'll keep her under for twenty-four hours. We'll try to wake her up. If she shows signs of loupism, we can sedate her for another twenty-four. After that . . ." Doolittle fell silent.

After that I would have to kill my kid. All strength went out of my legs.

I would have given anything for this to be a nightmare. All my magic, all my power, for a chance she'd wake up. "Is there any hope?"

Doolittle opened his mouth and closed it without saying anything.

I turned and marched down the hallway. The Lighthouse Keepers had to have a base. Someone had to have owned or rented that van. Someone supplied them with explosive bolts. The only time I'd ever seen them used was when Andrea put two of them into a blood golem controlled by my aunt. She had to have them special-ordered.

I would find the Keepers. I would find them and murder every single one of them.

Curran caught up with me. "Where are you going?"

"I have things to do."

He barred my way. "You look like shit. You need a medic. Let Doolittle fix you."

"I don't have time for this."

He leaned to me, his voice quiet. "This isn't open to negotiation."

I unclenched my teeth. "If I don't hurt something, I'll lose it."

"Either you let him mend you now or you'll run out of gas in the middle of a fight when it counts. You know your body, you know you're at your limit. Don't make me carry you."

"Just try it."

He bared the edge of his teeth at me. "Is that a challenge, baby?"

I glared at him. "Would you like it to be, darling?"

A hulking figure loomed in the hallway. Mahon.

Thick and barrel-chested, the alpha of Clan Heavy looked like he could step in front of a moving train and force it to screech to a halt. His black hair and beard were salted with gray. He didn't like me much, but we respected each other and since Mahon was the closest thing Curran had to a father, both Mahon and I went out of our way to remain civil.

Mahon finished maneuvering his massive frame near us. "My liege. Consort."

"Yes?" Curran asked, his voice rumbling with the beginnings of a growl.

Mahon fixed us with his heavy stare. "Unlike your quarters, this hallway isn't soundproof. Your voices carry. These are trying times. Our people look to you for guidance and example."

Doolittle held open a door to a side room.

Mahon inclined his head in a slow half bow. "Please, Consort."

Fine. Half an hour wouldn't make a difference anyway.

CHAPTER 18

———❦———

I AWOKE ON OUR COUCH. MY WHOLE BODY ACHED, deep down, all the way to my bones. Pain was good. Pain meant I was still alive and healing.

Curran leaned on the windowsill, silhouetted against the window, where the dusk or dawn bled crimson onto the sky. The sun was in the east. Morning then. I'd slept for several hours.

Muscles tensed across Curran's wide back. He knew I was awake.

No matter where I was or how much trouble I was in, he would come to get me. He would demolish the city to find me. I didn't have to go at it alone.

Several floors below, Julie was sleeping while her body worked to betray her. My Julie. My poor kiddo. Some people awoke to escape their nightmares. I awoke into one.

"Any change?"

"She is still asleep," Curran said.

"Doolittle sedated me, that old bastard."

He turned around. "No. He was chanting your wounds closed, and you fell asleep. I brought you up here. Does it hurt less now?"

I shrugged. "How do you know it hurt in the first place?"

"You held your breath when you walked."

"Maybe I was just pissed off."

"No." He came toward me. "I know when you're pissed off. It's the way you stand. I know the look."

He noticed the way I stood. What was I supposed to do with that? "Grendel?"

"He's in Doolittle's infirmary. Nothing serious. A few bruises and a sliver of wood stuck in his paw. Andrea returned to the Keep. She says they were eating and he took off on her with no warning. Went through the restaurant's window."

Silly poodle. How had he even known we were in trouble?

Muscles played along Curran's jaw. "We should've found Leslie. We'd tracked her all over the city. Her scent was less than three hours old in Palmetto. If we had found her, none of this would've happened. You can't save everyone. I've made my peace with that. We should've saved Julie . . ."

"I love you," I told him.

Curran stopped in midword and strode to me. I kissed him, sliding into his arms. "I don't want to talk," I whispered. My cheeks were wet and I knew I was crying. My voice didn't tremble, but the tears kept coming and coming. I'd lost my mother, my stepfather, and now in two days, my kid as well. It was time to pay the piper.

Curran kissed me, his lips sealing on mine. His tongue slid into my mouth, his taste so familiar, so welcome. I clenched his shoulders, pulling him closer, pulling his shirt off. He moved the sheets aside and broke apart from me for the tiniest second to peel my tank top off. I kissed his mouth, my fingers in his short hair, asking for his strength. His hands slid over my breasts, the rough skin of his palms scratching at my nipples. He lifted me to my knees and licked my left breast, the heat of his mouth piercing through all of the pain swirling inside me. I let go of it all and lost myself in him, kissing, licking, stroking, wanting to be one.

He rose above me, I wrapped my legs around him, and when he thrust inside me, the world took a step back. There was only me and him. We built to a smooth hard rhythm, faster and faster, each thrust lifting me higher, until finally heat blossomed inside me, drowning me in a cascade of pleasure. He shuddered and emptied himself. We stayed like that for a long moment, then he moved to the side, gathering me up to him. We lay, curled up together, as the day uncurled outside the window.

I refused to let Julie go. There had to be a way around it. There had to be something I could do. She wasn't a loup yet, damn it. There had to be a way.

"We'll kill them," Curran said, his voice laced with so much violence I almost shivered. "We'll stamp them out."

Yes. "A year from now nobody will remember they existed." There would be no more Lighthouse Keepers after we were done. It wouldn't help my kid. But it might keep other Julies from being hurt.

A knock resonated through the door.

"What?" Curran growled.

"Jim is here, my lord," Barabas said.

I pushed off the pillow.

"Tell him to wait," Curran said. He turned to me. Gray eyes looked into mine. "I love you, too."

Maybe he truly did. "Promise me that if we leave, nobody will touch Julie until we return."

Gold rolled over Curran's eyes and vanished. "Not if they want to live."

"Not even an alpha of a clan." I didn't know how dark the inside of Jennifer's head was.

"Not even an alpha. Julie is sedated and restrained in her bunk. The access to her room is restricted, and Derek is staying with her. He's gotten it into his head that if he and Ascanio hadn't gotten into it, the bouda kid would've put up more of a fight. Jennifer doesn't have a prayer of getting past him, nor would she try. That's not who she is."

He swiped his sweatpants off the floor.

I put my clothes on. "It wouldn't have mattered about Ascanio. She was a trained render. You could've killed her. B. Mahon. Jezebel, maybe. Jim . . ."

"Kate," Curran said. "And now the entire Keep knows it."

I stopped with a boot in my hand. He was actually proud of me. I heard it in his voice. Oh hell.

He was looking at me with a smile, like the cat who ate the canary.

"What did I do with my other shoe?"

"You're holding it."

"Ah." I sat down on the couch and put my boot on.

Curran slipped on his T-shirt and went to the door. I followed.

Curran opened the door, revealing Jim. His cloak was back on. Andrea stood behind him. The right side of her face was black and blue as if she'd been hit by a five-pound dumbbell. She looked ready to kill something.

Jim's face was grim. "The Keepers activated the device at Palmetto."

"When?" Curran snarled.

"Half an hour ago."

Curran swore.

THE JEEP BOUNCED OVER A METAL PLATE IN THE road, went airborne, and landed with a crunch. Jim drove the way he did everything—just on the edge of reckless but never out of control.

In the front seat Curran rolled the window down and leaned, trying to read a grimy road sign. "Three miles." He rolled the window up before the roar of the Jeep's enchanted motor made us all deaf.

The Roosevelt Highway rolled past the window, the trees one long greenish smudge. Next to me Andrea held her crossbow. We didn't have a chance to talk, but we didn't need to. We just needed a target.

"The Keepers brought the device in sometime during the night," Jim said. "The Spring Farm Fair is in town this week. That's where most of Palmetto makes a good chunk of their money. School is canceled for the week and all the church services are moved to eight o'clock to accommodate the fair. The Keepers set the thing up in the middle of a busy street and bailed. The Fair has two fields' worth of weird magic crap. Nobody would've given Kamen's device another thought."

The people of Palmetto had walked right past the ticking bomb and watched it charge. And then it activated and killed them.

"Why not hit the fair itself?" Andrea asked.

"Because they wanted witnesses," Jim said. "People will travel in for the fair, see a dead town, and rush back to spread the panic."

"So it's over?" I asked.

"Yeah," Jim said. "We had people combing through the town yesterday, looking for Leslie. This morning I sent a man from the Keep to brief them on the Keepers and tell them to clear out. They were on the road to Atlanta when they saw the light behind them. They stayed the hell away from it. From what they say, white light appeared above the town, glowed for several minutes like the northern lights, and vanished. The whole thing took about ten minutes."

To the left, four hyenas, two wolves, four jackals, and a were-mongoose burst from the brush and flanked the car. Barabas, Jezebel, and others. The entire bouda clan howled for blood.

"Our source says the device can't be moved by a water car," Jim called out over the engine's noise.

Good call not mentioning Saiman by name.

"He says it kills the enchantment in the water. And they can't carry it—too heavy. They have to move it by cart and horse. There are four roads out of Palmetto. Used to be five but Tommy Lee Cook Road is shut down. There is a gap across it a quarter of a mile wide. I have people on every road. The machine pulls magic in a circle starting from the perimeter and going inward. The perimeter of the blast zone is clearly visible. They aren't getting out."

"Can we enter the zone after the blast?" Andrea asked.

"The source said he walked through the blast of the first prototype. He seemed no worse for wear," I told her.

An old billboard loomed from between the trees, advertising some gun show.

Jim stood on the brakes, spinning the wheel. The engine sputtered and died. The Jeep's tires squealed and the vehicle veered left and screeched to a stop. Fourteen bodies lay across the road. Men, women, children, dressed in good clothes. To the right, a church rose, its doors wide open. A preacher lay on the stairs, his Bible still in his hand. On the other side of the road, in a wide enclosure, carts waited for the owners who would never come. Horses snorted and whipped their tails at flies.

"Dear God," Andrea whispered.

They must've been Seventh Day Baptists, going to church for the Saturday-morning service. Whole families. Adam Kamen was right. If you had enough magic, the shock of losing it killed you.

Why? Why the hell were the Keepers doing this? What the hell were they hoping to achieve?

A naked man ran out from behind the church and made a beeline for us. Short brown hair, lean build . . . Carlos, one of the rat scouts. He came to a stop next to us and bent over, out of breath. "Can't go into it in a half-form. Turns you human or animal. You're weaker, too."

Carlos strained. Fur sprouted along his back as bones snapped. A moment and a wererat stood in front of us. Carlos opened his long jaws. "Thank Goshhh. I wash worreed."

A distant wolf howl echoed through the air.

"South." Curran pulled off his clothes. His skin split. Muscle boiled, fur sprouted, and he dropped to all fours, dark stripes like whip marks over his pelt. Jim shrugged off his shirt and a jaguar in warrior form landed next to Curran.

The monstrous lion head opened its jaws and Curran's voice rolled forth, the words perfect. "We'll cut across the fields, along the edge of the blast zone."

"I'll take the car."

Jim threw the keys at me and I snapped them out of the air.

"Don't break the device," I said. "You break it, it explodes, we all find our wings in a hurry."

Curran growled. "Later, babycakes."

Babycakes. Asshole. "Good hunting, sugar woogums."

I jumped into the driver's seat. Andrea pulled a rifle from under the passenger seat and hopped in to ride shotgun.

Curran dashed into the field, powerful muscles carrying him off. The shapeshifters followed him in a silent flood. I turned the key and the gasoline-burning motor purred in response. No magic. Right.

I made a wide circle around the bodies and stepped on the gas. The vehicle shot forward, picking up speed.

"Whoa." Andrea rubbed her face. "It's like somebody put a bag over my head. I can't hear that well. I can't smell anything either."

"What happened to your face?"

"She made me leave," Andrea said through clenched teeth.

I glanced at her.

"Aunt B. We needed to have the talk. Oh no, she couldn't wait to have that talk. She had to have it right away, so she could explain to me in detail how I needed to become one of her girls. I shouldn't have gone, but I wanted to avoid a fight in front of

the children. We sat at Mona's and ate pie, while the render tore
the kids apart, so her ego would be satisfied. I told her this. You
know what she said? She said it was my fault because if I had
run over like a good little bouda when she first called me, we
wouldn't be in this mess. So I slapped her."

"What?"

"When we got to the Keep and I found out about Julie, I
walked up and slapped Aunt B in the face. In front of everyone."

Holy crap. "Have you lost your mind?"

"You should've seen the look on her. It was worth it." Andrea
threw me a defiant glance. "Then her face went all psycho. The
old bitch backhanded me. I don't actually remember being hit. I
just remember rolling down the stairs. I guess she knocked me
off the landing. She is fucking strong." A crazy light sparked in
Andrea's eyes. "I'd do it again. I'll make it my mission in life
to take her down."

And people said I was nuts.

Andrea raised her hand. "This is the hand that slapped
Aunt B."

"Maybe you should have it gold-plated."

"Here, you can touch it, since you're my best friend."

"Is your hand connected to your brain at all? Are you going
to keep attacking her until she kills you?"

Andrea shrugged. "I might kill her instead."

"And run the bouda clan?"

She blinked. "No."

"And how do you think Raphael would take it? I know you
still love him. You think he'll be happy his mother is dead?"

Andrea let her breath out in a long sigh. "Listen, me and
Raphael . . ."

"Your master plan has holes big enough to drive a truck
through."

"Now look, you . . ."

The trees ended abruptly as the road shot us into the center
of the town. Words died on Andrea's lips.

Bodies lay in the streets. Laborers. Mothers with their children. A group of men armed with crossbows, probably just
passing through. A cop, a short blond woman, her uniform
pristine, lying face down on the pavement two steps away from
her police horse.

Oh my God . . . We drove through it all, surrounded by death on both sides, as if gliding through Armageddon.

On the far right, a man stumbled, walking through the street, with a lost look on his face, trying to come to terms with his world ending. A child cried in the distance, a thin uncertain sound.

This wasn't just bad. It wasn't just criminal, or cruel; it was so deeply inhuman, my mind had trouble comprehending it. I've seen death and mass murder, I've seen people slaughtered out of bloodlust, but this had no emotion behind it. Just a cold clinical calculation.

Another howl broke the silence. Closer this time and to the east. Andrea swiped the map off her lap. "They're probably hitting Fayetteville Road. Turn left at the next intersection. Church Street."

I made a hard left at the next intersection. In front of us a crumbling overpass barred the way. I steered the Jeep on the side, over the overgrown hill, praying the tires didn't blow up, and rolled over the hill. The vehicle plunged down, its seat springs squeaked, and we landed back on the road. I stepped on the gas. The Jeep hurtled forward.

A subdivision popped up on our right side. I stared straight ahead. I'd seen as much of the dead as I could take. Now I just wanted to make some of my own.

The road veered left, cutting through a dense patch of forest. I took the turn. Something black and large lay in the road.

"Look out!" Andrea yelled.

I swerved, catching a glimpse of a massive equine body. A mad amber eye glared at nothing, now dull, from a head crowned with a single sharp horn.

The woods ended, jerked away suddenly like a green silk scarf pulled out of place. A ribbon of straight road unrolled in front of us, before diving into the woods again in the distance. On the left side, two giant open A-frames covered by tin roofs housed rows of flea market stalls. The stalls lay deserted. Half of their owners had fled. The few who remained sprawled in the dirt, their eyes dull and lifeless.

A group of riders emerged from the woods in the distance, pushing their horses hard. Behind them a pair of bays pulled a wagon. At least ten people. The forest on both sides of the road was too dense for the wagon to pass through. They were heading away from the magic and toward us, back into the blast zone.

I turned the Jeep sideways, blocking the road. Andrea eyed the nearest A-frame. It would give her a good vantage point. But the moment she started shooting, they'd turn back. We had to keep that cart from moving.

I held my hand out. "Give me a grenade."

Andrea pulled open her backpack and slid a grenade into my palm. "Wait until they start shooting the Jeep. Boom comes first, shrapnel flies second. Count to ten before you run in there. And don't blow the device up."

"Yes, Mother. It's not my first time."

"That's the thanks I get for trying to keep you alive, Your Highness."

I slipped out of the Jeep and dashed down through the under-growth on the right side of the road. Andrea leaped six feet in the air, caught the edge of the tin roof, and pulled herself up.

Twigs and branches slapped me. I kept moving, light on my toes. If Curran had been there, he would've chewed me out for making more noise than a drunken hippo in a china shop, but with the thudding of hooves the riders wouldn't hear me. Ahead the ground leveled off, the undergrowth of fuzzy pines thick enough to provide good cover but thin enough to power through in a hurry. About a hundred yards from the Jeep. Far enough. I dropped into a crouch.

The lead horseman rode past us and stopped a dozen yards ahead. The rest of the riders halted, forming two loose lines along the road, staggering themselves to minimize the target area. The cart came to a stop with a creak right across from me. A large canvas bundle bulged in the middle of it, secured with ropes. Wooden partitions protected the device from the back and front. Perfect.

"Miss Cray," the lead rider said. "Please remove the obstruction."

A woman rode up to the leader. "Sir?"

"Ride down to the vehicle, shift it into neutral, and push it off the road. Burgess, go with her. Santos, cover them. If things look suspicious, shout."

The three riders advanced toward the Jeep, two ahead, one lagging behind, his rifle ready. I waited until they cleared half of the stretch, pulled the firing pin, and lobbed the grenade behind the cart. The metal clanged on the asphalt two hundred feet away from the cart. Far enough. Heads turned. I dropped down and pressed into the forest floor.

The explosion shook the trees. Horses shied, panicking. The device showed no intention of exploding.

"Protect the machine!" the leader screamed. "Form—" His head jerked. Andrea's bullet took him in the back of the skull and came out just under his eyes, disintegrating his face into a mush of bone and bloody flesh.

Shots rang out like firecrackers popping—they fired blindly to the front and to the back. I charged through the pines. They were packed too densely for the saber. I drew a throwing knife. Another rider dropped, cut down by Andrea's shot.

A rider loomed. I jerked him out of the saddle, stabbed him in the kidney, grabbed a woman off a horse, slit her throat, and pulled another man out of the saddle. The black barrel of a .45 glared at me. I shied left. The gun barked. Heat grazed my shoulder. I stabbed him through the heart.

The cart driver snapped the reins, turning the cart around. The horses neighed and plowed through the brush, skirting the crater left by the grenade. The cart hurtled back down the road, out of the blast zone and into the magic, heading away from the Jeep. The remaining riders chased it. Damn it.

A huge gray lion leaped out of the woods, barring the cart's path, standing almost as tall as the horses. The great mouth gaped and a deafening roar shook the trees. The horses reared in sheer terror. The driver surged up and slumped over, as a red wound from Andrea's rifle blossomed in the back of his head.

The lion morphed, his fur melting, and Curran grabbed the loose reins with his human arm, calming the horses.

Shapeshifters spilled from the woods, swarming the riders. "Alive," I yelled. "We need at least one alive!"

TWO MEN AND A WOMAN KNELT ON THE GROUND, their hands on the back of their heads. Around us an empty field stretched. The blast zone lay just a few yards away, behind the tattered ribbon of the crumbling highway.

The boudas circled the captives like sharks. They wanted blood. I wanted blood.

Curran reached down and picked up the larger of the men by his throat. The man dropped his hands, letting his arms hang limp by his sides. Curran brought his face up close and peered into the man's eyes. The man shivered.

"Why?"

"Why not?" the smaller of the men said.

He didn't look like a monster. He looked perfectly ordinary, just like the hundreds of people on the street. Wheat-colored hair. Clear blue eyes.

"You killed the entire town," I said. "There are dead children lying in the street."

He looked at me. His face was calm, almost serene. "We simply turned the tables."

"How did these dead children hurt you? Enlighten me."

He raised his chin. "Before the Shift, our society functioned, because to gain power, you had to work. Success was paved with labor. You had to use your mind and your hands to climb the ladder, so you could live the American dream: work hard, earn money, live better than your parents. But now, in this new world, brains and hard work count for nothing, if you have no magic. Your future is determined by pure accident of birth: if you're born with magic, you can rise to the very top with no effort. The safeguards that were meant to keep the dangerous and unbalanced from gaining power have failed. Anyone can be in charge now. They don't have to go to the right college, they don't have to learn the rules, they don't have to prove that they are good enough to be welcomed in the circles of power. All they have to do is be born with magic. Well, I have no magic. Not a drop. Why should I be disadvantaged? Why should I suffer in your world?" He smiled. "We don't want to kill anyone. All we want is a chance to have the same opportunities as everyone else. To restore order and structure to the society. Those who can't survive in our world, well, they are regrettable casualties."

The boudas snarled in unison.

A woman walked out from behind the brush bordering the road. Her dirty dress waved about her, like a grimy flag. She came toward us, wiping her nose with a dirty hand. One of the wolves detached from the pack and moved to flank her.

I leaned closer. "One of your people attacked my office and tried to kill a child. My child. She had done nothing to you. Is she also a regrettable casualty?"

The man nodded. "It's tragic. But look at it from my point of view: your child will grow up and prosper, while me and my children will be forced to struggle. She is no better than me. Why should your child take my spot under the sun?"

Nothing I could say would penetrate his skull, but I couldn't help myself. "That's nice. They taught you very well. But in the end, you're scum. A common thug might murder a man for money, but you murdered dozens out of selfish hope. This better life you're hoping to get for yourself will never happen, or you would be living it already, magic or not. You can't think for yourself. You want an excuse for your failure and so you found someone to blame. If you survived, you would always be dirt, ground under someone else's boot."

The man raised his face. "Say what you want. I know my cause is just. You didn't stop us. You just delayed the inevitable."

He didn't do it because his religion told him to murder people. He didn't do it because he couldn't control himself. He did it out of pure selfish greed, and he didn't feel the least bit upset by it. I'd rather take on a demonic horde any day.

The woman reached us. She was past thirty, maybe thirty-five. I looked into her eyes and saw nothing. A painful empty void. She wasn't a threat. She was a victim.

The woman stopped and looked at us. "Is it them?" she asked. Her voice was hoarse. "Is it them who did it?"

"Yes," Curran told her.

She sniffed. Her gaze fixed on the three people kneeling in the dirt. "I want a turn."

Andrea stepped close to her.

"They killed Lance," she said. "They killed my babies. My whole family is dead. I want a turn."

Andrea put a hand on her arm. "Ma'am . . ."

"You give me my turn!" The woman's voice broke into a sob. She clamped her hand on Andrea's fingers, trying to wrench them open. "I've got nothing left, you hear! Nothing. My whole life's gone. You let me at these sonsabitches, you—"

Curran walked over to her. She went quiet.

"If you wait," he said, "I promise you'll get your turn."

She sniffed again.

"Come on," Andrea told her, leading her to the side gently. "Come with me."

"Where were you taking the device?" Jim asked.

The smaller of the men raised his head. "We'll tell you nothing. We are not afraid of death."

Curran glanced at the boudas. A large spotted hyena moved forward, her strides slow and deliberate. Jezebel. She dipped her head and stared at the three captives with unblinking predatory focus. She would kill them. We wouldn't get much out of whoever she attacked. She needed to avenge Joey. After she was done, nothing would be left of them.

I wanted to join her. I wanted to hurt them. I wanted to mince them to pieces, slice by slice, and watch them suffer. But if we didn't squeeze every drop of information out of them now, I'd have to look at more dead bodies.

No. No, this ended now. They might not be afraid of death, but they were terrified of magic, of being enslaved by those who wielded it. They'd given me all the ingredients for their own personal nightmare.

I looked to Curran. He raised his hand. Jezebel halted. She didn't want to, but she stopped.

I turned to Jim. "Which one of them is the least valuable?"

He glanced at the smaller man. "He probably knows the most."

I stopped before the larger man. "We'll start with him, then." Anticipation of the terror was always worse. I wanted the smaller man to stew in his fear a bit.

The captive stared at me. "What are you going to do to me?"

"You think we're abominations." I pricked my palm with the point of my throwing knife. A drop of red swelled. I squeezed my hand, letting the drop grow. "Let me show you just how abominable magic can be."

I thrust my hand at the larger man's forehead. My blood connected with his skin, and I whispered a single power word. *"Amehe."* Obey.

It hurt. Dear gods, it hurt, it hurt like a sonovabitch, but I didn't care. Julie in a hospital bed, Ascanio torn and broken, Joey dead, corpses in the streets, children in their best clothes lying in the dirt, looking at the sky with dead eyes . . . They would never rise again. They would never walk, never laugh, never be. The rage inside me was boiling over.

The man froze, the line of magic between him and me taut with power. I'd promised myself I'd never do this again, but some promises had to be broken.

"Rise," I told him.

He stood up.

"What did you do to him?" the female Keeper cried out, her voice squeaking.

Curran was watching me, his face unreadable like a slab of stone.

"Rope." I gave the man a mental push. Sweat broke out on my hairline. The magic drain crushed me. It felt like I was dragging a chain with an anchor on the end of it.

Slowly he walked to the cart, untied the knots, and pulled the rope from the device. I pointed to the ringleader. "Tie him."

Jim grabbed the ringleader's wrists and pulled him up. The larger man looped the rope around the man's waist.

"There is nothing you can do to me," the ringleader said. The Keeper woman watched us with open horror.

I picked up the other end and showed it to the larger man. "Hold."

He clamped it.

I glanced at the shapeshifters. "He'll need help."

Jezebel shed her fur and took the end of the rope. Good. The change would tire her out. She was strung out too high. She needed to burn off some of that edge.

"Give me room."

The shapeshifters parted. The ringleader stood by himself.

I took a deep breath. *"Ahissa."* Flee.

The shock of the power word nearly took me to my knees.

The ringleader screamed, a sharp high-pitched shriek full of animalistic, mind-numbing fear, and ran. On the left, one of the boudas dashed away in panic, caught by the edge of the magic.

The rope snapped taut. The man fell and clawed the dirt, kicking, trying to swim away through solid ground. His larger friend held him, a blank expression on his face. The ringleader raked the soil, again and again, trying to get away, howling in hysterical frenzy. The shapeshifters watched him with stone faces.

"How long does it last?" Curran asked.

"Another fifteen seconds or so."

Moments stretched by. Finally the man stopped digging, his screams fading to weak hysterical sobs, echoed by the woman crying behind me. His fingers were bloody stumps, his nails torn off. I closed the distance between us and leaned over him. He looked up, slowly, his eyes brimming with echoes of panic.

"I bet the people of Palmetto would've screamed too, if you had given them a chance," I said softly. "What do you say we do it again? I bet I can turn your hair gray before lunch."

The man scrambled away from me and sprang to his feet. He managed a good sprint for about three yards and then the rope jerked him down. Jezebel gripped it and pulled him back, dragging him across the ground.

"No!" the man wailed. "I'll tell you anything, anything!"

Didn't take much after all. I braced myself and let out another power word. *"Dair."* Release.

The larger man sagged on the ground, his mind suddenly free. For a second he just sat there, a sad, abandoned expression on his face, and then he collapsed, curling into a ball, and bawled like a lost child.

"They're all yours," I said to Jim, and forced myself to walk to the Jeep. Every step took an effort. Someone had filled my shoes with lead while I wasn't looking.

We had won. It had cost hundreds of human lives, but we had won. We had the device. We'd rout the Keepers. Maybe I'd catch a break and Julie would survive.

"We're building another one!" the man behind me yelled through the sobs.

The tiny hairs on the back of my neck stood up. I turned slowly.

He cringed on the ground. Curran leaned to him. His face unreadable, his voice almost casual. "Run that by me again?"

"We had a man, a man on the inside." The man's words came out too fast, tumbling over each other. "He copied the inventor's plans. We've been building it for weeks. We just needed a working prototype to fine-tune it. It's three times as big as this one."

Damn it all to hell.

"Range?" Curran asked.

"Five miles," the man stammered out.

Enough power to wipe out everything from the city center all the way to Druid Hills. They could kill most of the city. All they needed was a strong magic wave.

Curran pointed at Jim. "Tell that man everything you know. Location, time, names, everything."

Jim grabbed the man by the throat. His lips parted in a feral grin. "Don't keep anything to yourself."

"Barabas!" Curran roared.

The weremongoose stepped from the Pack. A hundred pounds, sheathed in reddish fur, Barabas opened his mouth filled with sharp teeth and licked his fangs. The narrow horizontal pupils slit his coral-red irises in half, making him look demonic.

"I need you human," Curran ordered.

Fur split, melting. A moment and Barabas stood in front of Curran, nude, his eyes still glowing with madness. "Lord?"

"Call the Conclave."

The Conclave started as a quarterly meeting between the Pack and the People, officiated by a neutral party, usually someone from the Mage Academy, and held at Bernard's, an upscale Northside restaurant. It gave the Pack and the People a chance to resolve problems before things spiraled out of hand. The last two times, representatives of other factions had attended to resolve their own issues. I had attended only one so far, because the meeting over the Christmas holiday had been canceled by mutual agreement.

"Should I schedule it at Bernard's?" Barabas asked.

"No. There." Curran pointed to a lonely Western Sizzlin' steak house sitting on a low hill. The building was all glass and stone. The tall windows overlooked the town. To get to the place, the leaders of the factions would have to ride through the graveyard that was Palmetto.

"When?"

"Four. Sunset is at six. I want them to see the town. Invite the mages, the druids, the witches, the Guild, the Natives, Norse Heritage. Invite everyone."

"Except the Order," I added. "The Keepers may have infiltrated it."

Curran nodded.

"And if the cops restrict access to the area?" Barabas asked.

Gold rolled over Curran's eyes. "Buy the place. They can't restrict access to our own land. Go."

Barabas took off running.

"The volhvs have the inventor," I said. "We need access. I need to make some phone calls."

"I'll take you," Curran said.

We walked to the car. I was so tired, I could barely move.

"Curran?"

"Yes?"

Today was apparently the day for finding out what mating with me really meant. I nodded at the men. "One of them has my blood on his forehead. The blood must be destroyed or it can give me away if someone scans it."

Curran gave me a look usually reserved for the mentally challenged. "Someone would have to find the bodies, first."

Behind him the sounds of enraged boudas tore through the silence, followed by a cacophony of screams.

"In that case, cut off his head," I said.

Curran gave me a look like I was stupid.

"My father made the damn vampires. I don't know what my blood will do to a dead body. Cut off the guy's head before you bury him."

"Should I stuff his mouth with garlic?"

"Curran!"

"Fine," he said. "I'll take care of it."

I got into the car and slumped against the seat. The fatigue mugged me. I was hanging by a thread and I clawed onto it, desperately trying to stay awake. I had paced myself, but three power words in a row equaled a lot of magic spent far too quickly.

The screams went on and on, and I was too weak to get my slice of the revenge pie. I just sat there and listened to them shriek. Finally the howls died down. Curran approached the car and got into the driver's seat. "It's done."

The woman in the dirty dress stumbled into our field of vision. Her hands were bloody. She swayed, wiped the red dripping off her fingers on her dress, forced her way through the old dried weeds onto the road, and kept going, back toward the town.

"She had her turn," Curran said.

CHAPTER 19

CURRAN DROVE BACK. I SAT IN THE PASSENGER SEAT, watching the brush roll by. Andrea and Jim had taken a different vehicle—he wanted to ask her some questions about the Keepers.

The magic had crashed shortly after we finished burying the bodies, and the steady hum of the gasoline engine set my teeth on edge. There was something mind-numbing about it; it conjured images of streets strewn with bodies. We had no idea where the second device would be activated. They could snuff out the entire Keep from four miles away. We'd never know what had hit us.

We'd stopped at a store on the way and I made four phone calls. One to Roman, to inform him that unless the volhvs delivered Adam Kamen by three o'clock to the Western Sizzlin' I would crucify them at the Conclave. I wanted a shot at Kamen before the rest of Atlanta took it. The second call was to Evdokia to let her know what I was doing about the volhvs and that if she wanted to come and sit in on it, I wouldn't mind. Next I called the Keep, to speak to Doolittle. The news was the same. No change. I thanked him and told him to send Derek with the volhv's staff to the Western Sizzlin'. The fourth call was to Rene. She didn't like what I had to say, and when she found out that the whole thing would be blown wide open at the Conclave, she liked it even less.

"When I hired you, I expected discretion." The phone clicked and small noises muffled the sound—she'd put me on speaker.

"When you hired me, I expected honesty. You told me you had no idea what Kamen's device did, but he'd tested the prototype in the forest. You told me he'd had no visitors, when one of the investors came to see him on multiple occasions."

There was a small pause, and then Rene's voice said, "What is she talking about?"

Henderson's baritone answered. "Sorry, Captain."

"'Sorry,' Sergeant?"

"It was above your pay grade. The orders came from above."

Rene's clipped voice snapped like a whip. "This conversation isn't finished." Then she spoke into the phone again. "Kate?"

"You have two choices: either you come to the Conclave and help, and we gloss over the fact that you've been guarding the creator of the Doomsday Device that's about to murder everyone in the city limits, and then lost him; or you don't show up, and I will tell it like it is." *That's right, I'll throw your ass right under the bus. Watch me.*

"We'll be there," Rene ground out, and hung up.

Now we were back on the road, going toward the steak house, and I was fighting the phantom images of dead Julie flooding my mind.

Curran reached into the glove compartment and pulled out a roll of worn-out bills. He peeled a dollar from it and held it out to me.

"What for?"

"A dollar for your thoughts."

"The usual price is a penny, not a dollar. Had I known how bad you were with money, I would've reconsidered this whole mating thing."

"I didn't want to go through all the haggling." He held the dollar in front of me. "Look, here is a nice dollar. Tell me what's brewing in your head."

I snatched the dollar out of his fingers. It was old. The ink had faded so much, I could barely make it out.

"You took the money. Pay up."

"All those people meant nothing to them. The Keepers killed a whole town for this bullshit promise of a better tomorrow. In a world without magic, only the deserving rise to the top? Really? Did they not read history books at all?"

"They're fanatics," Curran said. "It's like expecting humanity from a falling rock. It's not going to have a fit of compassion and not crack your skull open."

"I can wrap my head around demons or rakshasas hating anything human, but the Keepers are people. A thug robs someone for money. A psychopath murders because he can't help himself. They are perpetrating mass murder for no real immediate gain." I stared at him helplessly. "How can you do this to your neighbors? They would have to murder millions of people and for what? It's inhuman."

"No, it's human," Curran said. "That's the problem. People, especially unhappy people, want a cause. They want something to belong to, to be a part of something great and bigger, and to be led. It's easy to be a cog in a machine: you don't have to think, you have no responsibility. You're just following orders. Doing as you're told."

"I can't hate people that much. Don't get me wrong. I want to murder every last Keeper I can find. But that's not hate. That's vengeance."

Curran leaned over and squeezed my hand. "We'll find them."

We drove in silence.

"Why do you hold back?" he asked.

I glanced at him.

"You never let go," he said. "You can do all this magic but you never use it."

"Why don't you murder every man that annoys you and rape every woman you find attractive? You can—you're powerful enough."

His face hardened. "First, it's wrong. It's the complete opposite of everything I stand for. The worst thing that ever happened to me happened because someone did exactly what you've described. The loups murdered my father, took my mother and my sister from me, ripped apart my family and my home. Why would I ever permit myself to become *that*? I believe in self-discipline and order, and I expect it from others just as I expect it from myself. Second, if I randomly murdered and violated people according to my whims, who the hell would follow me?"

"My father murdered my mother. She was no prize, but this doesn't change things. Roland wanted to kill me. Because of him, my mother brainwashed Voron. Because of him I had no childhood and became this."

"This what?"

"A trained killer. I like to fight, Curran. I need it. It's a function of my existence, like breathing or eating. I am seriously fucked up. Every time I use Roland's magic, I take a step closer to being him. Why would I ever permit myself to become that?"

"It's not the same," Curran said. "Loupism is loss of control. Practicing magic is honing your skills."

"Taking over someone's mind makes me feel like I'm swimming through a sewer. As I recall, the last time I did it, some overbearing alpha insisted on cramming the consequences of doing it down my throat." *Chew on that, why don't you . . .*

"I gave you a protector."

I shook my head. "I don't want to do it again, unless I have to. Besides, it's a limited magic. I can make the person perform basic physical tasks, but I can't force him to tell me what he knows. If I can't picture it, I can't make him do it."

"Does it get easier if you do it more often?"

"Yes. Saying a power word used to knock me out. Now it just hurts like hell. I can manage two or three in a row now, depending on how much magic I sink into them." I leaned back against my seat. "I know what you're driving at. Magic is just like anything else; you get better with practice."

I closed my eyes. A vision of my aunt dead on the bloody snow flashed before me. "Before Erra died, she spoke to me. She said, 'Live long enough to see everyone you love die. Suffer . . . like me.' "

"Why are you letting the dead woman fuck with your head?" he asked.

"Because I don't think I will ever become Roland. It's not in the cards. But give me enough time, and I could turn into Erra." Fighting her was almost like fighting myself.

"And every time I turn into an animal, I have a small chance of forgetting that I'm human. Every time I heal or exert myself, I have a chance of turning loup."

What was this, I'll show you my scars if you show me yours? If he wanted to play the weird powers game, I'd beat his ass. "I can pilot vampires."

Curran glanced at me. "Since when?"

"Since I was about five."

"How many at a time?"

"Do you remember the woman we killed, when we hunted the upir? Olathe? Remember the horde of vampires on the ceiling?"

He stared at me.

"I was holding them in place," I told him.

"There were at least fifty undead on that ceiling," Curran said.

"I didn't say it didn't hurt. I couldn't do much with them. With that many, you have to mold them into a whole. Like a swarm." I checked his face. *Are you freaked out yet, baby?*

"So you could kill a vampire with your mind?"

"Possibly. The easier thing would be to just have it bash its head against a rock. I've had almost no practice, so I have no skill or finesse, but a crapload of power. If you ever have a war with the People, Ghastek will be in for a surprise."

Curran frowned. "Why no practice?"

"Playing in an undead's head leaves your mind's footprint in it. Someone like Ghastek could take it from the dead vamp, assuming it's fresh, and pull my image right out of its head. Then I would have to answer interesting questions. The fewer questions, the better."

"Any other surprises?" Curran said.

"I can eat apples of immortality. My magic is too old to be affected by them, so it's just like eating a regular Granny Smith. You can, too. I made you an apple pie with them once."

"Aha. Okay, the next time you decide to put magic apples into my pie, I want to be notified of that before I eat it."

"You liked it."

"I'm serious, Kate."

"As you wish, Your Majesty."

We fell silent.

"The blast zone turned the shapeshifters in warrior form human," I said.

Curran nodded. "It takes magic to maintain the warrior form."

"What if we brought Julie into it? The virus would disappear. She would be okay, right?"

Curran's face slid into his Beast Lord expression. "Bad idea."

"Why?"

"Carlos was able to shift after he came out of the zone, which means it doesn't destroy the virus, it just negates its effects. The moment Julie stepped foot out of the zone, it would hit her all at once. That's a guarantee of instant loupism. Besides, do you remember the way Julie looked when we brought her in?"

My memory served up a twisted wreck of a body: a mix of fur, skin, exposed muscle and bare bone, and a grotesque face.

"I remember," I said through clenched teeth.

"She is alive only because Lyc-V holds her together. A regular human body can't sustain that much damage. You move her into the zone, all her regeneration will vanish. She would die quickly and in a lot of pain."

I stared out the window.

"I'm sorry," Curran said.

"She isn't going to beat it, is she?"

Curran exhaled slowly. "Do you want me to lie to you?"

"No."

"There is a way to calculate the probability of loupism," Curran said. "It's called the Lycos number. An average shapeshifter has ten units of virus per blood sample. I don't know exactly how the units are determined, but Doolittle can explain it to you. The unit level fluctuates as the levels of virus rise and fall in a shapeshifter's body. An agitated shapeshifter might show twelve units; a shapeshifter in a fight post-injury might show as much as seventeen or eighteen. The number isn't the same for everyone. For instance, Dali shows sixteen units at rest and twenty-two when agitated. Her regeneration is really high."

I filed it for future reference.

"Next we have shift coefficient. A loup can't maintain a human form or an animal form," Curran continued. "They can't fully shift. This is where it gets complicated. A normal shapeshifter in either animal or human form is considered to have a shift coefficient of one. As the shapeshifter begins to change shape, the coefficient changes. Suppose you're going from human to animal. You turn twenty percent of your body animal, while the rest remains human. Your shift coefficient is two. Thirty percent—three. And so on, until nine. When you turn a hundred percent, you go back to one. With me?"

"Yes."

"The Lycos number is determined by multiplying shift coefficient by the units of virus by the time it takes you to shift completely. Let's take Dali. She can completely shift in less than three seconds. Her Lycos number is one multiplied by sixteen multiplied by point zero five minutes. Point eight. Anything under two hundred seventy is safe. Over a thousand is a guarantee of loupism. Dali isn't going loup anytime soon."

"What's Julie's number?"

Curran glanced at me. "Julie's fluctuating between thirty-two and thirty-four units. Her shift coefficient is six point five and she's been at it for sixteen hours."

Dear God, I'd need a damn calculator.

"Twelve thousand four hundred eighty," Curran said. "We stop counting after an hour if there is no significant change."

Twelve times the loupism limit. My mind struggled to comprehend it. I knew what he was saying—it was right there—I just couldn't force myself to believe it.

The realization hit me like a punch. "When did you know?"

His voice was hoarse. "Once Doolittle pulled her unit number. It took us forty-five minutes to get to the Keep. She had begun the transformation at least fifteen minutes prior. I knew that unless she shifted within the first hour, her chances were cut by three quarters, unless her unit number was below twenty."

My heart hammered, as if I were running full speed. "I've heard of first transformations taking hours."

He nodded. "That happens when the unit number is low. Not enough virus entered the body during infection, or something is inhibiting it, so you might get somebody with five units in his blood, sitting at twenty percent of the shift for an hour. Five by two by sixty is only six hundred. Then the virus blooms and he shifts."

I was grasping at straws. "What about Andrea? During the flare she was in a partial shift for at least a couple of hours."

"Andrea had an object in her body that interfered with her shift. Once they pulled it out, it took her half an hour to rebuild the virus and change shape."

Damn it. "Then why bother with sedation at all?" Doolittle must've done it for a reason. He must've had some glimmer of hope.

Curran reached over and covered my hand with his. "It's not for her. It's for you. Doolittle is using all of his skill to keep her alive and comfortable. He's giving you time to come to terms with it . . ."

I stared at the road through the windshield. They were waiting until I gave up and agreed to put my kid out of her misery.

Curran kept talking. "I brought her in wrapped up, so nobody except the two of us, Doolittle, and Derek know how bad she is. The kid won't say anything." His hands gripped the wheel, his knuckles white. His face was calm, his voice completely flat and measured, almost soothing. He must've expected me to fall apart, because he'd locked his emotions inside, asserting absolute control over himself. "Julie isn't in pain. She's sleeping. You can take your time. I know how much she means to you. You care for her. Sometimes it can be very hard. If it's too hard, I'm here. I will help her, if you need me."

"Please stop the car."

He pulled over. The outskirts of Atlanta had long ago succumbed to the magic's onslaught. Ruins surrounded the road on both sides. The long stretch of highway lay deserted.

I stepped out of the car and marched out into the crumbling wreck of some old building, singed from the inside, its walls black and draped with dead kudzu. I didn't know where I was going. I just had to be on my feet, so I paced back and forth, one wall to the other.

Curran followed me inside and halted at the gap in the wall. He didn't say anything. Nothing needed to be said.

I paced. There had to be something, some way. Death was forever, but Julie was still alive.

"I keep thinking that if I had made it in twenty minutes earlier, none of this would've happened. I wish I could . . ." I clenched my fists.

"Kill Leslie again?"

I looked at him and saw my own rage mirrored in his eyes.

He'd wanted to rip Leslie apart. He'd pictured it in his head more than once. She had become the Keepers in his head and in mine.

I spun on my foot, making a turn at the wall. "Leslie could've bitten me until the cows came home. I'd get a light fever and that would be the end of . . ."

A light went on in my brain. I stopped. My blood ate Lyc-V for breakfast and chomped vampirism for dessert.

Curran was right. Julie was hanging on by a thread. A direct transfusion of my blood would kill her.

"What?" Curran asked.

But my blood could kill Lyc-V. It could be done because Roland had done it before. I racked my brain. I knew the general gist of the story, but my memory didn't store any specifics. I needed to know exactly what Roland had done. Where had I read about it? No, wait, I didn't read it, I heard it. If I closed my eyes, I could recall a woman's measured voice reciting the words.

Elijah. That's right. The Chronicles of Elijah the Unbeliever. The Chronicles couldn't be written down; they had to be recited from memory. Who in the city would know them? Who . . .

The rabbis. The Temple was my best bet.

I stepped to Curran.

"Can you take me to the Temple?"

He raised his hand and showed me the car keys.

CURRAN DROVE UP THE STREET, HEADING TO THE Temple. To the right, remnants of houses, little more than gutted wrecks of bricks and stone, thrust from the street. Behind them Unicorn Lane raged, like a wound in the body of Atlanta, bleeding raw magic even in the middle of a tech wave. Hideous things hunted there among decaying skyscrapers, feral and hungry, twisted by the very magic that sustained them, poisoned by the sewage and eating tainted prey.

The Unicorn lapped at the half-shattered walls, leaving long yellow hairs of the Lane moss in its wake. They glistened on the exposed metal framework of the magic-ravaged houses, feeding on iron and oozing corrosive slime, heralding the advance of the Unicorn. The Temple sat at the very end of the street running right next to the Unicorn, and the rabbis had warded it to allow safe access to the synagogue. Lampposts guarded the street, each decorated with mezuzot, small pewter cases engraved with the letter *shin*. Each mezuzah contained a parchment inscribed with holy verses from the Torah. The city council had been trying to contain Unicorn Lane for decades. It kept growing, expanding like a cancer, despite everything the city had thrown at it. Yet here, the rabbis quietly held it back without any fanfare or napalm.

"Who was this Elijah?" Curran asked.

"He was a small-time bricklayer down in Florida. He was kind of a jack-of-all-trades, so he did whatever came his way: fixed cars, performed small repairs, but mostly built houses. Something must've happened to him because he had a wife and a son at some point and was doing enough business to pay the bills, and then suddenly he just started drinking. And not just drinking, he drank himself into a stupor. Eventually his wife left him."

"Great story," Curran said.

"It gets better. Every weekend Elijah would take his paycheck, go down to the local pub, and do his best to drink himself to death. When he got drunk enough, he started raving. Sometimes he'd be spitting chunks of the Bible, word for word; sometimes he told these weird fables; sometimes it wasn't even English. People pretty much dismissed him as a complete lunatic. One night a rabbi happened to be in a pub. He heard Elijah carry on and realized that he was listening to a section from *Sefer ha-Kabod*. It's a twelfth-century text written by Eleazar of Worms, one of the most important Hebrew cabalists. Elijah was functionally illiterate. He could barely write his own name."

Curran nodded. "It's like a kid in kindergarten suddenly spouting the *Iliad* in ancient Greek."

"Pretty much. So the rabbi stayed in town for a week and paid Elijah to ramble on, while he recorded him. At the end of the week, Elijah finished his last tirade and died."

"From what?"

"Organ failure. He stopped breathing. There are about eighteen hours of tapes. Some of it was pure nonsense, and some of it was prophetic. In the recordings, there are about two hours of fables. Every fable is about Roland."

Curran glanced at me. "Seriously?"

"Yeah."

"Why don't you own a copy of this book?"

"That's the best part of the story. You can't transcribe the tapes. Every time you do it, the next magic wave wipes them out. People have tried to write them down and put them in lead boxes, even. Doesn't work. Magic hits, the words disappear. Even copying the tapes doesn't work every time. The Temple is the largest synagogue in the Southeast. If they don't have a copy of the tapes, someone there must've heard them played."

Curran peered through the windshield. "What the hell is that?"

I glanced straight ahead. A massive clay golem blocked the road. The top half of the golem was sculpted into a muscular human body, topped by the face of a male with a long beard. The bottom half was an enormous ram, complete with four hoofed feet and a tail. The golem brandished a tall metal spear. It looked frozen in midstep, the left foot raised off the ground, the spear swinging as if the golem had been making a turn.

"It's one of the Temple's guards. Please don't knock it over. I'm on thin ice with the Temple as it is."

Curran braked. The vehicle rolled to a slow stop. The golem didn't move. The magic was down. Without it, the Temple protector was just a clay statue.

Curran shrugged. "I guess from here we go on foot."

The Temple sat at the very end of the road, a solid red brick structure with a white colonnade, flanked by some utility buildings and a wall decorated with enough names of angels and magic symbols to make you dizzy. We crossed the yard and walked up the white stair to the reception area. The woman behind the receptionist's desk saw me and paled. The mirror behind her offered me our reflection: we were both smeared with blood and dirt. A big red stain marked Curran's sweatshirt over his chest—he had taken a bullet just under the clavicle. Lyc-V would heal the damage, but I'd had to pull the bullet out and the wound had bled after he put the sweatshirt on. My pale green turtleneck was splattered with something that looked suspiciously like someone's brains, and a big print of a bloody hand marked my stomach, where someone's fingers had clearly dragged over the fabric.

"The Beast Lord and Consort, to see Rabbi Peter," Curran said.

The woman blinked a couple of times. "Will you wait?"

"Sure."

Curran and I sat in the chairs. The receptionist spoke in a hushed voice into the phone and hung up.

Curran leaned to me. "You think she's calling the cops?"

"I would."

"Just letting you know, I'm not in the mood to be arrested and if they try it, they won't like it."

Why me?

I picked up a copy of a cookbook from the side table and flipped through it. Chocolate rugelach. Hmmm. Chocolate, sugar, almonds . . . Curran might like those.

"We sell those," the receptionist said, her voice hesitant. "They are recipes from the congregation. Would you like to buy a copy?"

I looked at Curran. "Do you have any money?"

He reached into his pocket and pulled out a roll of cash. "How much are those?"

"Ten dollars."

Curran flipped through the bills.

I leaned to him and whispered, "What are you doing?"

"Looking for one that's not bloodstained. Here." He pulled a ten-dollar bill out.

I offered it to the receptionist. She took the money carefully, as if it were hot, and gave me a small smile. "Thank you."

"Thank you for the book."

Curran glanced toward the hallway. Someone was coming. A moment later I heard it too, a quick patter of feet. Rabbi Peter emerged into the lobby. Tall and thin, with a receding hairline, a short, neatly trimmed beard, and wearing large glasses, Rabbi Peter should've looked like a college professor. But there was something in his eyes; they brimmed with curiosity and excitement, and instead of an aging academic, Rabbi Peter resembled an eager young student.

He saw us and paused.

We stood up.

Rabbi Peter cleared his throat. "Um . . . welcome! Welcome,

of course, what can I do for, eh, you, Kate, and, eh . . . I'm sorry, I don't know how I am supposed to address you."

Curran's eyes sparked. If he told the rabbi to call him Your Majesty, wc could kiss cooperation with the Temple good-bye.

Curran opened his mouth.

I elbowed him in the side.

"Curran," he said, exhaling. "Curran will do."

"Wonderful." The rabbi offered him his hand. Curran shook it, and then I did. "So what may I do for you?"

"Are you familiar with Elijah the Unbeliever?" I asked.

"Of course. Here, why don't we go into my office. We'll be much more comfortable there."

We followed the rabbi down the hallway. Curran rubbed his side and gave me an evil look. I mouthed "Behave" at him. He rolled his eyes.

The rabbi led us into an office. Bookshelves lined the walls from floor to ceiling, bordering the single large window so tightly that it looked cut out of the thickness of books.

"Please sit down." The rabbi took a seat behind his desk.

We landed in the two available chairs.

"Would you like anything, tea, water?"

"No, thank you," I said.

"Coffee, black if you got it," Curran said.

"Aha! I can do that." The rabbi rose and took out two cups and a thermos from a cabinet. He unscrewed the cap, poured black brew into the cups, and offered one to Curran.

"Thanks." Curran drank it. "Good coffee."

"You're welcome. So Elijah the Unbeliever. Which particular part are you interested in, or is it the whole thing?"

"We need a certain fable," I told him. "The Man on the Mountain and the Wolf."

"Ah, yes, yes, yes. A very philosophical piece. In essence, the man on the mountain encounters a wolf who wants to be rid of his savagery. The man turns him into a dog through the sharing of his blood. There are several interpretations. We believe that when God created Adam and Eve, he made them using his own essence; this essence, *Neshama*, meaning 'breath,' is what separates humans from animals. In the fable, the wolf is feral. He lacks a soul, and thus he is consumed with rage. The man shares his blood with the wolf, forging a constant connection between them, just as God breathes a soul into each man and a woman. Since our soul gives us our conscience and takes us beyond the animal instincts, the wolf becomes a dog who will forever follow his master."

Peter slid his glasses up his nose. "There is a second interpretation, based on the teachings of Maimonides, who believed in the necessity of balance. According to Maimonides, one should always walk the King's Road, staying away from the extremes, neither surrendering completely to one's emotions nor rejecting them entirely. The wolf, being enraged, walks the extreme path, and to return to the King's Road, he ties himself to the man, becoming a dog. The dog still retains his primal savagery, but his rage is now tamed, so he achieves his balance. Were you looking for a particular interpretation?"

"We were looking for the exact wording. Do you happen to have a copy of the recording here in the Temple?"

"Unfortunately, we do not."

Damn it.

Rabbi Peter smiled. "But I happen to have studied the tapes extensively. Elijah is my area of study. I've committed the tapes to memory, so if you have a few minutes, I can recite the fable for you if you would like."

Yes! Thank you, Universe. "I'd be in your debt."

"Very well." The rabbi reached into the desk and produced three white candles. He struck a match, lit the first candle, and used it to light two others.

"Why the candles?" Curran asked.

"It is traditional when reciting Elijah's words. In one of the recordings, Elijah states that a candle is synonymous with one's wisdom. If you use one candle to light another, your light is now twice as bright. Just so when a teacher shares his wisdom with a student, both minds are enlightened. Since I am about to share Elijah's words with you, I shall light two new candles and our light shall be three times as bright."

The rabbi arranged the candles in the corner of the desk. "Now then. Fable number three. There once was a man of wisdom who lived upon a mountain. One day a rabid wolf blocked his path. The wolf was suffering, for he was full of rage and it drove him to murder and violence. The wolf begged the man to take away his rage, at any price. The man denied him, for it was too dangerous and could cost both of them their lives. The next day the wolf returned and begged the man once more to take away his rage. The man denied him again, for rage was in the wolf's nature. Without it, the wolf would no longer be a wolf. On the third day, the wolf returned once more and refused to leave. He followed the man, begging and crying, until the man took pity on him. He agreed to free the wolf of his bloodlust, but in turn the wolf would have to promise to serve the man till the end of all time.

"On the fourth day, the man and wolf climbed to the top of the mountain. The man chained the wolf to a rock with chains of silver and iron. Then the man cut open his arm and let his blood run free while a rain of needles fell upon the mountain. Seeing the blood, the wolf had become mad with rage and struggled to break his chains, but they held him fast. The man sliced the wolf's throat and pulled the living blood from the wolf's body into his hand. As the wolf lay dying, the man mixed his own blood with the fiery core of the wolf's soul. Then the man thrust the mingled blood back into the wound, spoke the words that bound the wolf to obey him forever, and fell to the ground, weakened. The man's blood purged the rage from the wolf. He sat by his master, guarding him while he rested, and when the man awoke, he found that the wolf had become a dog. That's the end of the fable."

The rabbi sipped his coffee. "The fable's philosophical value can't be denied; however, in recent years some scholars, myself included, have speculated that the fable is based on actual events. A large percentage of Elijah's teachings, first taken as allegories, proved to be fact. The fable has all the characteristics of such a teaching. It offers specific if somewhat cryptic details: the rain of needles, the mixing of the blood, the chains of silver and iron, where fables conceived as fiction typically speak in general terms. But of course, daring radicals such as myself have to resign ourselves to scorn from our colleagues." He smiled.

My aunt made flesh golems by pulling the blood out of her victims, infusing it with her magic, and somehow inserting the mixture into new flesh, creating monstrously powerful automatons completely under her control. Roland had done almost the same thing. He'd pulled the blood out of the shapeshifter's body, seared it with his magic, and put it back. And somehow both he and the shapeshifter had survived.

I didn't even know where to start. Roland had a hell of a lot more power than I did and it wiped him out, which meant I'd need a power boost. Just like the volhv who teleported Adam out of his workshop. I would not resort to sacrifice. Even for Julie. It was out of the question.

"Was it something I said?" Rabbi Peter murmured. "You look shocked."

"No," Curran said. "Everything is fine. Thank you for your assistance."

I forced the words out of my mouth. "We appreciate it."

The rabbi took off his glasses, cleaned the lenses with a soft cloth, and put them back on his nose. "Since I have shared my knowledge with you, perhaps you'd share yours with me. Why do you need the fable?"

I rose. "I'm sorry, I can't tell you that. But I could tell you the name of the wolf."

Rabbi Peter rose from his chair. "This is beyond intriguing. Yes, I would be most interested in learning the name."

"He is called Arez. The Sumerians knew him as Enkidu. He was the first preceptor of the Order of Iron Dogs, and he conquered most of Africa and a third of Eurasia for his master. He lived for four hundred years and would've conquered more, but the ancient Greeks began praying to him, and their prayers turned him into their god of war. Does that help?"

The rabbi nodded slowly.

"Thank you for your help." Curran and I headed for the door.

"What about his master?" the rabbi asked.

"That's a conversation for another time," I told him.

"I look forward to it," the rabbi called out as we stepped out into the hallway. "Enjoy the cookbook!"

CHAPTER 20

"NO." CURRAN STRODE TO THE CAR, HEADING DOWN the street away from the temple.

"No what?" I knew what, but I wanted him to spell it out. That way I could shut him down better.

"I know what you're thinking and the answer is no. You're not pulling that stunt."

"It's not up to you."

He spun around. "Roland did it during full magic. He passed out. The magic is weak, and you're not him. What the hell do you think it will do to you?"

"I thought about that. I'd need a power boost. My own mini-flare."

"Aha."

"The device contains concentrated magic. When you open it—"

"When you open it, it fucking explodes, Kate. It would be like standing in the middle of an atomic blast."

"She's dying."

Curran treated me to a full-blown alpha stare. His eyes glowed with primal power. Like looking into the eyes of a hungry beast emerging from the darkness. My muscles locked. I held his gaze.

"No," he said, pronouncing the word slowly.

"You can't tell me what to do."

Curran roared. The blast of noise erupting from his mouth was like thunder. I clenched up, fighting the urge to step back.

"Yes I can," he snarled. "Listen: this is me telling you what you will *not* do."

I raised the cookbook and tapped him on the nose. Bad cat.

He jerked the book out of my hands, ripped it in half, flipped the two halves, ripped them again, and raised his hand. The pieces of the cookbook fluttered to the ground. "No."

Fine. I turned and walked away, to the ruined houses. Behind me Curran's foot scraped over the ground. He leaped over me and landed in my path. He looked completely feral.

I halted. "Move."

"No."

I kicked him in the head. The pressure of the past forty-eight hours rampaged inside me like a storm, and I'd sunk all of it into the kick. The impact hit his jaw at an angle. Curran staggered back. I spun and snapped another kick. He dodged. Another. Curran moved forward and right. My kick missed by a hair. He grabbed my shin with his left hand, clamping it between his arm and his side, and swept my other leg from under me. Nice. A kung fu takedown.

I fell back. The pavement slapped my back. I rolled back up and hammered an uppercut to his chin. Hitting him in the body was useless. Might as well pummel a tank. The head was my only chance.

Curran snarled. Blood dripped from a cut on his cheek. I'd opened a gash with my kick.

I threw a left hook. He knocked my arm out of the way and shoved me back. I twisted out of the way on pure instinct—damn it, he was fast—dropped into a crouch, and swiped his legs from under him. He jumped up, avoiding the kick, and I took a knee to the head.

Ow.

The world shattered into tiny painful sparks. I tasted blood—my nose was dripping. I rolled back, coming to my feet, blocked his punch, and jammed my knuckles into his throat, interrupting his growl in midnote. *Felt that, did you, baby?*

Curran charged. His hand locked on my shoulders. He swept me off my feet and slammed me into the wall, back to the bricks, pinning me. His teeth snapped a hair from my cheek. I kneed him. He blocked and clamped me in place.

"Done?" he breathed out. "Hmm?"

"Are *you* done?"

"Baby, I haven't even started."

"Oh good. Go ahead so I can finish it." And how exactly was I going to do that?

Curran pushed me harder, grinding me into the wall. "I'm waiting. Show me what you've got."

"Let go and I will."

"Yeah?"

"Yeah."

"Promise me you won't do this thing and I'll let go."

I just stared at him.

Curran spun away, took two steps, and punched the wall. "Damn it."

The wall disintegrated in an explosion of bricks. I pulled a piece of gauze from my pocket and wiped the blood from my nose. There wasn't much. Occupational hazard of picking a fight with a man who killed gods for a living.

Curran let out a ragged snarl and punched the other wall. It burst and the entire wreck of the house came down in a fountain of dust. He shook his hand, his knuckles bloody.

"Bricks are hard," I told him patiently, as if to a child. "Don't hit bricks. No, no."

Curran picked up a brick and snapped it in half.

Idiot. "Oh, you're so strong, Your Majesty."

Curran hurled the chunks of the brick. They cleared the ruins and vanished into the Unicorn.

"If Derek were in trouble, you'd risk your life in a heartbeat."

He turned to me. "Risk, yes. I wouldn't slit my own throat for him. I like Julie. She is a great kid. But I love you. I forbid you to do this."

"That's not the way this mating works. You don't get to order me to do things, and I don't get to tell you what to do. That's the only way we can survive, Curran."

He swallowed. "Fine. Then I will ask. Please, don't do this. Please. That's as much as I can bend, Kate."

"Do you remember when I told you that you couldn't fight Erra, that it was stupid and reckless, because she would drive you insane?"

Curran's face snapped into his flat Beast Lord mask.

"I begged you not to go. Begged." I closed the distance between us. "You told me that you don't get to cherry-pick your battles and you came anyway."

"And we won."

"And you were in a coma for two weeks. Give me another brick so I can beat you over the head with it. I told you! I told you her magic would screw you up. Did you listen? No. Would you do it again?"

"Of course I would," he snarled. "She kicked your ass twice. I wasn't going to let you walk in there alone. She was a challenge and it was my job."

"And my job is to keep Julie safe. Opening the device alone won't be enough. I'll need someone to channel the magic into me. I'm going to ask the witches for help. I promise you that if Evdokia says no, I will let it go."

Curran stared at me, his eyes furious molten gold.

"I'm not going to run off, lop the top off the device, and slice Julie's throat. I might as well just murder her in that case. I'll have to speak with Doolittle about my blood. I'll have to arrange things with the witches. I'll have to talk to Kamen and see if the device can even be opened without triggering a giant explosion. I give you my word that if things look hopeless at any point, I will stop. Meet me halfway. That's all I'm asking."

His face was grim.

"You have to let me at least try. I can't just sit on my hands and do nothing."

"If I keep you from doing this, you will leave me," he said.

"I didn't say that." Giving an ultimatum to Curran was like waving a red cloak in front of a mad bull.

"You will. Maybe not right this second. But eventually you'll walk away." Curran took a long deep breath. "I sit in on every meeting."

I had won.

"As long as you're honest with me about your chances, I'll support you. Kate, if you lie, it's over."

I crossed my arms. "You expect me to lie."

"I don't. I'm just getting it out there so there are no surprises."

We stared at each other.

"Are we cool?" he asked.

"I don't know, you tell . . ."

He pulled me over to him and kissed me. It was a hell of a kiss.

We broke apart.

"You talk too much," he said.

"Whatever, Your Fluffiness." I slid close to him, so his arm was around my shoulder. I felt better. He did, too—his posture lost some of the tension.

We walked to the car and kept walking. "Where are we going?"

"To the Temple," Curran said. "I owe you another cookbook."

IN THE THREE HOURS WE'D BEEN GONE, THE STEAK house had been transformed into the Pack's field headquarters. Groups of shapeshifters patrolled the road and guarded the building. Knowing Jim, sentries lay in wait, hidden and watching for an enemy's approach. People were crawling on the roof, installing a ballista and machine guns.

The parking lot lay empty, but the field behind the building was filled with cars spaced about ten feet apart. If the Keepers launched a rocket into our parking lot, not every vehicle would go up in flames. I hoped they tried something. My hands itched for my sword.

Curran parked in the front. Jackson, one of the guards, ran out and Curran tossed him the keys.

Jim met us at the door. Behind him Derek emerged. He looked like death: pale, his eyes bleak.

Shit.

I stopped. Curran's hand brushed mine, and then he went off with Jim.

Derek came to a stop in front of me.

"Is she dead?" I asked.

"No. She's sleeping."

I exhaled. "You almost gave me a heart attack."

"If I hadn't—"

"Please, don't flatter yourself. We both know the kid needed about five years of hard training before he could've taken her on. Your little beating made absolutely no difference."

"She's . . . there is no change."

"That's good news," I told him. "Any change now will be for the worse. I need to have her stable, until I can get my ducks in a row."

He glanced at me. "Kate, you can't help her."

"I can try. Are you going to help me or will you just stand there and mope?"

His head snapped up. Much better.

"Are the witches here?"

"Yes. The Russians are here too, and they're pissed."

Oh good. "Where are they?"

"In the back of the main room."

"Find Barabas, tell him I need him to attend. And when Curran is done with Jim, tell him that I'm holding the meeting until he can join us." I wouldn't want His Arrogance to miss anything. "And fetch the staff, please."

Derek took off. I strode inside the steak house.

GRIGORII WAS TALL AND THIN. HIS PLAIN BLACK robe hung on his shoulders like wet laundry on a coat hanger. Chernobog's volhv's long black hair, shot through with gray, framed a severe face with hazel eyes under thick eyebrows and a hooked nose that made him look like a bird of prey. You half expected him to clench his talons, let out an eagle shriek, and tear you to pieces. A black raven perched on Grigorii's shoulder. Behind Grigorii's chair, Roman waited, looking about as happy as the groom at a shotgun wedding.

The man in the chair next to Grigorii was even older. He wore a plain white robe that came to his knees. Pale blue embroidery, faded to almost gray, ran in a three-inch strip straight down the front of the robe. Belobog's volhv. Had to be. Belobog was Chernobog's brother; they were diametrically opposed, benevolent god to malevolent one.

A furry creature lay at the white volhv's feet. It looked like a medium-sized dog with gray fur. A pair of large feathery wings lay folded along its back, stretching on the floor behind it. A celestial wolf. Holy crap.

Across the table Evdokia smiled serenely, knitting something blue. Her duck-bunny-kitten rolled around on the floor, playing with the yarn. The celestial wolf watched it with a slightly hungry look on its face.

Behind Evdokia two witches waited, both young, pretty, and looking like they wouldn't back down from a fight. Same dark hair, same small neat mouths, same large eyes. Probably sisters. The witch on the left wore a long hooded robe of gray fabric. Her friend chose jeans and a sweater instead. She'd pulled her sweater sleeves up to the elbow, exposing bright turquoise tattoos of mystic symbols sheathing her arms.

I came to the table, pulled up a chair, and sat. "Everyone brought a pet. I feel left out."

An enthusiastic howl broke the silence, and Grendel bounded through the doorway. He galloped through the steak house, skidded on the floor, smashed into my chair, and dropped a dead rat on my lap.

Awesome.

The volhvs stared.

"Thank you." I put the rat on the floor and petted Grendel's throat. "We will begin shortly."

"What is that?" Grigorii stared at the dog.

"A shaved poodle." Technically he was now a closely cropped poodle, but who cared about semantics.

"This is ridiculous." Grigorii leaned back. His voice was clipped and had no accent.

"Have you looked through the window?" I asked him.

The steak house was set on the apex of a low hill. Beyond it Palmetto lay, flooded with cops and people in paramedic scrubs. They methodically bagged the corpses and loaded them into trucks, one atop the other, like cords of wood.

"That is a horrible thing," Belobog's volhv said.

"I do not like this waiting," Grigorii said. "What are we waiting for?"

"For me," Curran said.

The volhvs startled. Curran pulled up the chair and sat next

to me. Barabas materialized behind him. "Grigorii Semionov-
ich, Vasiliy Evgenievich, Evdokia Ivanovna, welcome. May I
get you anything? Coffee, tea?"

"Hot tea with lemon," Evdokia said.

Barabas waved. Jezebel brought a platter with a teapot and
several cups on it, set it on the table, and took up position at the
nearby booth.

Jim pulled up a chair and sat on Curran's right. Andrea sat
on my left. Barabas and Derek remained standing behind our
chairs.

"This thing is none of our concern," Grigorii said. "You do
not rule us."

"We will leave when we decide," Vasiliy said.

"Did you bring Kamen?" Curran asked.

Grigorii leaned back and crossed his arms. "And if we did,
then what?"

Curran leaned forward. "You are sheltering a man whose
machine caused hundreds of deaths. Because of this device, my
ward, a fourteen-year-old girl, is dying. One of my people is
dead; two are critically injured. Your volhv attacked my mate.
Before we go any further, we require a show of good faith. You
will give us access to Kamen now."

Vasiliy's white eyebrows rose. "Or?"

"Or this meeting is over. We will consider your actions to be
a declaration of war."

The two volhvs looked at each other.

"We will abide by the agreements of peaceful assembly,"
Curran said. "You're free to leave. Go home, kiss your wives,
hug your children, and put your affairs in order, because tomorrow I will burn your neighborhood to the ground. We will kill
you, your families, your neighbors, your pets, and anyone who
will stand in our path. An attack on my family will not go
unpunished."

That was the best smackdown I'd ever seen.

"No," Vasiliy said. "No war."

The raven on Grigorii's shoulder cawed. The black volhv
grimaced. "Roman."

Roman bent down.

"Tashi yego suda."

Roman took off at a run.

I leaned to Curran. "They're bringing him."

"Good tea," Evdokia said.

A long minute passed and Roman entered, leading a man by his shoulder. The man wore wrinkled khakis and a sweater over a dress shirt that had seen its better days—grime stained the bend of the collar where it touched the neck. Some effort had been made to comb his light brown hair out of his bloodshot eyes, but it stuck out on the back of his head in untidy clumps. He gazed about him, looking lost, as if he weren't sure where he was or why.

Adam Kamen. The source of the entire mess.

Roman pulled a chair out and pushed Kamen into it. As Roman straightened, his gaze snagged on something to my right. His eyes widened. He caught himself and stepped back, behind Grigorii's chair. I glanced to my right and saw Andrea flipping through her notes. Oh boy.

Jezebel pushed off her seat. "Can I kill him? Can I kill him now, please?"

I shook my head. She dropped back into the booth, exhaling. It took all of my will not to pummel Kamen's face into a bloody pulp. I barely had enough restraint for myself, let alone for her.

Curran pointed at the window. "Look."

Down in Palmetto, a truck was backing up. Another slid into its place. The paramedics paused while it maneuvered toward them and resumed loading the bodies.

"I saw," Adam said. "I was watching through the car window. Many people are dead."

"Because of you," I said. "You built it. Why?"

"For my wife," he said. "I just wanted the hospital machines to work, that's all."

"The first one was for your wife," Evdokia said. "Why did you build the second one?"

Adam shrugged. "Because that's what I do. If you make a small one, you have to make one bigger. Just to see. Can't build anything anymore." He raised his hands. The bases of both thumbs were red and swollen. Kamen curled his hands into fists. His thumbs didn't move. They'd severed the ulnar collateral ligament.

"You maimed him?" I asked Vasiliy.

The white volhv sighed. "We warned him. He didn't listen. *Durnoi chelovek.*"

Foolish man. That's putting it lightly.

"The head is bright," Vasiliy continued, "but no wisdom. His father was very respected in the community. Did a lot of good for a lot of people."

"It was that or kill him," Grigorii said. "Can't trust him. He'll build something else and kill us all."

"Can't build anything now," Adam said. "Can't hold a screwdriver. Can't hold a wrench. Or a brush. Finished. *Zakonchen.* My life's over."

I surged to my feet, grabbed him by the hair, and twisted his head to the window. "Their lives are over. My kid is dying because of you, you damn asshole, and you are whining about your hands? Look at me. Look me in the eye. I want to skin you alive, do you understand?"

"I never meant for this," he said, his arms limp. "I meant it for good."

"There were armed men guarding you. Why the hell do you think that was? You tested it. You saw things die in the forest. Why didn't you destroy it?"

"I couldn't do that. That's what my purpose is, to build things. It was special. I gave it life. It was important."

"More important than dead children?"

Adam's mouth went slack. I glimpsed the answer in his eyes. Yes, his gadget was more important than dead children. Nothing I could say would reach him.

I shoved him back into his chair.

"I told you," Vasiliy said. "Not right in the head. Defective."

"There is a sect of anti-magic fanatics," Curran said. "The Lighthouse Keepers. They have the blueprints for the device. They've built their own version."

Grigorii paled.

"How big?" Vasiliy asked.

"Five-mile range."

Grigorii swore. Vasiliy leaned back, dragging his hand over his mouth. "Five miles?"

Curran nodded and looked at Adam. Kamen cringed.

"How long does it take to activate?"

Kamen blinked. "The smaller model took forty-two minutes. For the larger, I never tested . . ."

"Three hours, twelve minutes," Jim said.

"There is a coefficient . . . Ten hours, fifty-nine minutes, and four seconds," Kamen said.

"That's our time frame," Jim said. "Ten hours and fifty-nine minutes from the start of the magic wave. Magic hits, we start the countdown."

"Can it be turned off once activation starts?" Curran asked.

"Yes," Adam said. "There is a switch to power it down. I will show your people."

"What about the machine that has been used?" I asked. "What happens if you open it?"

"Do you have it?" Kamen's eyes sparked.

Grigorii leaned over and slapped him on the back of the head. Kamen rocked forward and glanced at Grigorii like a kicked dog. "No need to hurt. I know, I know. Do you have a beer?"

Barabas stepped away for a moment and set a beer in front of Kamen.

"There is a valve at the top." Kamen shook the beer. "The device is of limited capacity. There had to be a way to empty it so it could be refilled."

He'd built the equivalent of an atomic bomb, and he'd made it reusable. Words failed me.

"So they can go from town to town murdering us," Evdokia murmured.

Kamen set the beer down. "You push the switches and poof." He grasped the beer again, tried to twist the cap, and stared helplessly at it. No working thumbs. Barabas leaned over him and twisted the cap off with a snap of his fingers. Liquid shot out. Foam spilled over the sides of the bottle.

"Have to be careful to push the switches correctly or it goes sideways," Kamen said. "Boom and the cylinder breaks. Everyone's dead."

Great. I made a heroic effort to ignore Curran's stare. "If you open it correctly, does most of the magic shoot straight up?"

Kamen nodded. "Yes. Some goes down, but most straight up. Like a laser."

"The magic that washes down, is it potent?"

"Very."

"Like a small flare?"

"Yes." Kamen nodded several times. "Just like that."

I looked at Evdokia. "Can this magic be harnessed by a coven and focused on one person?"

"Possibly," Evdokia said.

Grigorii snorted. "That much magic, your witches would break. And your focus would overload. You'd need an anchor for it, an object, to take the brunt of it, then draw power from it."

The duck-bunny-kitten stopped its rolling and hissed at Grigorii.

"Was she asking you?" Evdokia raised her chin.

"I'm just saying. There is a proper way to do things."

"Mind your own business."

Vasiliy gazed at me. "Why do you need the power?"

"Blood magic."

The table went so quiet you could hear a pin drop.

"What for?" Vasiliy asked softly.

"To purge Lyc-V from a little girl."

Grigorii pointed a long finger at me. "That is an unnatural thing."

"Some would say wolves with wings and wooden staves that bite you are unnatural things," I said. "Some would say that sacrificing a man and turning his innards into ants are unnatural also." *If you live in a glass house, don't fire any shotguns.*

"We will do this for you," Evdokia said. "My coven will do it. I'll bind them to silence. Nobody will talk about it."

Aha. "What's the price?"

"You will sign a writ of kinship. A document that acknowledges your mother and her ancestry. It will be kept sealed, so do not worry. We just want a paper. In case things do not go as expected."

What was the catch? There had to be a catch in there somewhere.

Grigorii came to life like a shark sensing a drop of blood in the water. "Why? What is so special about her?"

Evdokia slapped the table. "I've told you to mind your own business, old goat! This has nothing to do with you. Go kill something and revel in its blood."

Grigorii's eyes bulged out of his head. "You will keep a civil tongue in your head!"

Evdokia leaned forward. "Or what?"

"Or I will teach you some manners, woman!"

The tattooed witch behind Evdokia glared in outrage. "Dad! You will not speak to Mother this way!"

"I will speak to her in whatever way I please!"

The witch in the robe heaved a sigh. "Oy. Papa, really, there is no need."

I backed away from the table in case somebody started throwing things. Andrea backpedaled right behind me. Curran stayed, his chin resting on his hands clenched into a double fist, probably trying to decide if he should get in the middle of this.

"Yes, go right ahead." Evdokia pointed at Grigorii. "Live up to your reputation. Civil like a rabid badger."

The duck-bunny hissed and growled. Grigorii's raven cawed, beating its wings. Grendel lost it and broke down in a cacophony of excited barks.

Vasiliy put his hand over his eyes.

Grigorii slipped into Russian. *"Crazy old hag!"*

"A hag?" Evdokia rolled up her sleeves. *"Let me show you how haggish I can be."*

"Roman!" The tattooed witch pointed at the younger volhv. "Do something! You're the oldest."

Roman startled. "They've been at this since before we were born. Don't bring me into this."

So that was how he knew I would be at Evdokia's. His mommy told him. Of course. They even looked alike. I should've seen it before. Was there anyone in here who wasn't related?

The tattooed witch turned to Vasiliy. "Uncle?"

Nope. They were all one big happy family.

"You be quiet, child!" Vasiliy snapped. "Adults are talking."

"Uncle, I'm twenty-six!"

"That's the problem with bringing children into the magic," Vasiliy said. "The lot of you get a taste of power and grow up mouthy."

Grigorii spared a single glance in his brother's direction. If looks were daggers, that one would've sliced straight through the volhv's heart. "Here it comes. 'My oldest son . . .'"

"Is a doctor," Evdokia finished in a singsong voice. "And my daughter is an attorney."

Vasiliy raised his chin. "Jealousy is bad for you. Poisons the heart."

"Aha!" Evdokia slapped the table. "How about your youngest, the musician? How is he doing?"

"Yes, what is Vyacheslav doing lately?" Grigorii asked. "Didn't I see him with a black eye yesterday? Did he whistle a tree onto himself?"

Oh boy.

Curran opened his mouth. Next to him Jim shook his head. His expression looked suspiciously like fear.

"He is young," Vasiliy said.

"He is spoiled rotten," Evdokia barked. "He spends all his time trying to kill my cat. One child is a doctor, the other is an attorney, the third is a serial killer in training."

Vasiliy stared at her, shocked.

"We're taking a short recess!" Curran roared and took off. We staged a strategic advance to the entrance of the steak house, right past Barabas, bent over double and making high-pitched strangled noises.

Outside, Curran exhaled and turned to me. "Did you know they were crazy?"

"I didn't even know they were married."

"They aren't," Roman said next to me. Somehow he'd gotten outside. "They love each other, they just can't live together. When I was younger, it was always drama: they are together, they are apart, they are seeing other people." He shrugged. "Mom never could stand all the blood, and Dad has no patience for the witchery. We're lucky the magic isn't up. At the last New Year's they set the house on fire. There was alcohol involved. Did you bring my staff?"

I looked around for the boy wonder. "Derek?"

Derek popped up by my side and thrust a stick with a trash bag on top of it at the volhv. Roman ripped the black plastic off. "What's with the bag?"

Derek bared his teeth. "It tried to bite me."

Roman petted the staff. "He was just scared, that's all." He took a step toward me and lowered his voice. "Can I ask you a question?"

"Sure."

We walked away a few feet, like it would make a difference with a bunch of shapeshifters. Roman leaned to me. "The gorgeous blonde, does she work with you?"

I glanced to where Andrea stood by the doors. "Andrea? Yes."

"Oh, that's a pretty name," Roman said.

"Bad idea," I told him.

"Why? Married?"

"No. An ex-boyfriend. A very dangerous, very jealous ex-boyfriend."

Roman grinned. "Married is a problem. Dangerous, no problem."

Over Roman's shoulder I could see Curran. He stood absolutely still, his gaze fixed on the back of Roman's neck.

Houston, we have a problem.

"Step away from me," I said quietly.

"Sorry?" Roman leaned closer.

Jim was saying something. Curran started toward us in that unhurried lion gait that usually signaled he was a hair from exploding into violence.

"Step away."

Roman took two steps back, just in time to move out of Curran's path. The Beast Lord passed by him and deliberately stepped between the volhv and me. I touched his cheek, running my fingers over the stubble. He took my hand into his. A quiet growl reverberated in his throat. Roman decided he had someplace to be and he really needed to get there as soon as possible.

"Too much excitement, Your Majesty?" I asked.

"He was standing too close."

"He was asking about Andrea."

"Too close. I didn't like it." Curran wrapped his arm around my shoulders and started walking, steering me away from the group, His Possessive Majesty in all of his glory. "This writ of kinship, what the hell is that? Does it make you allied with them?"

And he changed the subject, too. "No. I've only run across it a couple of times before. It's a document that states that I acknowledge that my mother is my mother and that my mother was born to such-and-such family. The witches are big on family record keeping."

"Will she take it to Roland?" Curran asked.

"It's not in her best interests. She hates him."

"So what's the point of it?"

"Your guess is as good as mine."

"I don't like it," he said.

"You've been saying that a lot lately."

He dipped his head, his gray eyes looking into mine. "Are you going to take them up on it?"

"Yes. Nothing has changed. Julie is still dying."

"Then do it soon," Curran said.

"Why?"

He pointed at the road. A caravan of black SUVs slithered its way up the highway. Thin emaciated shapes dashed along the shoulder of the road, their gait odd and jerky.

"The People are here," Curran said.

CHAPTER 21

———✦———

AN HOUR LATER THE INSIDE OF THE STEAK HOUSE had been cleared, every table in the house set into a square. The People had brought four out of their seven Masters of the Dead, headed by Ghastek. Nataraja must've declined to make an appearance. Because the meeting was held in the Pack's territory, the People had their choice of seats and positioned themselves with their backs to the window, so they could observe the front and back doors.

The four Masters of the Dead—Ghastek, Rowena, Mulradin, and Filipa—took their places at the table. Behind them a gaggle of journeymen sat in their chairs flush against the window, their faces carefully blank. Between the journeymen, vampires crouched like monstrous gargoyles: hairless, corded with a tight network of steel-hard muscle, and smeared in lime-green and purple sunblock. Bubble-gum-tinted nightmares.

I had to fight the urge to keep glancing at Rowena. Short, only about five two or so, Rowena was a teenage boy's wet dream. Perfect figure, sensual face, emerald-green eyes, and fiery red hair falling in a cascade of glossy waves all the way past her waist. An elegant business suit molded to her curves like a glove. When she smiled, male heads turned. If she said something, people nodded in agreement. There was something about her that made you want to earn her approval. She could make you feel like a hero for passing her the salt.

This was what my mother must've been like. I might've had her DNA, but not a drop of her magic had made it through.

To the left of the People sat the representatives of the Mercenary Guild. I recognized three veteran mercs and Mark, nominally the Guild's admin and in reality the Guild's overseer now that Solomon Red, the Guild's founder, lay six feet under. At least some of him did. After my aunt was done with him, there hadn't been much left.

Next to the Guild sat representatives of the Natives. I recognized shamans from the Cherokee, Apalachee, and Muskogee Creek tribes, but the other two I'd never seen before.

Norse Heritage took up the next three seats. The Norse Heritage Foundation claimed that their goal was to preserve Scandinavian cultural traditions. In reality, they took the idea of Vikings and ran with it as far from any cultural or historical accuracy as they could go. Norse Heritage took everyone in. As long as you were willing to drink beer, get rowdy, and proclaim yourself a Viking, you had a place at their table. Ragnvald, their jarl, a huge bear of a man, came easily enough, but Jim's people had the devil of a time getting his escort to surrender their axes and horned helmets. There was a lot of roaring and cursing and promises of doing indelicate things and screams of "Make me!" and "Over your dead body!" until Curran came out, looked at them for a while, and went back inside. Ragnvald read the writing on the wall, and his crew decided to disarm voluntarily.

The College of Mages provided three representatives, followed by us, and then by the witches, volhvs, druids, and half a dozen other smaller factions. Getting everyone to take a seat and be quiet was like trying to roll Sisyphus's boulder up the mountain. By the time we were done, I wanted to stab myself in the eye. Nobody seemed ready to make trouble, but I kept Slayer on my lap under the table just in case.

We put Kamen in the middle of the square in his own special chair. Just in case he decided to wander off and invent a black hole generator out of a box of matches and paper clips while we weren't looking. Rene and the Red Guard brass sat at the table directly behind Kamen. Rene looked a bit green in the face.

Tea, coffee, and water were served, and then Jim rose and gave a succinct summary of Kamen's invention and the aftermath of its usage. The Red Guardsmen were presented as being heroic; the volhvs' involvement was tactfully omitted. When he moved on to explain the third device, silence claimed the steak house. Five miles. Absolute destruction. If you had a drop of magic, you would not survive.

People paled. The jolt was so strong, even Ghastek looked disturbed.

Next Andrea stood up and profiled the Keepers. Most of it I already knew, and I watched the faces while she spoke.

"The Keepers are very well connected and financed. During the attack on Cutting Edge, the Keepers deployed exploding boltheads," Andrea continued. "Analysis and an m-scan of the residue provided a profile consistent with Galahad Five warheads. These warheads are manufactured exclusively by the Welsh to combat giants. They're prohibitively expensive and their export into the United States is limited and only semilegal. I had obtained a small number of said warheads for the Atlanta chapter of the Order during my tenure there, and I had to call in several favors just to get them through customs. Either the Keepers have a unique connection or the Order's armory has been compromised."

"Or the Order has been infiltrated," Rowena said.

"It is a distinct possibility," Andrea agreed. "I can guarantee that no boltheads had left the Order's armory prior to November, because the inventory and security of the armory had been my responsibility up to that point."

"Is that why there are no representatives of the Order at this Conclave?" one of the druids asked.

"The Order has never been a part of the Conclave," Curran said.

Ghastek permitted himself a narrow smile. "Considering the success the Keepers had with infiltrating the Pack, if we were to exclude all the organizations whose screening and security measures couldn't stand up to close scrutiny, this assembly couldn't take place. Banning the Pack alone would halve our numbers."

Even now, with threat of complete destruction, Ghastek couldn't pass up the opportunity to poke at Curran.

Jim bared the edge of his teeth.

"They recruit damaged children," Andrea said. "Victims of abuse and tragedy, who have reason to hate themselves and their own magic. They find teenagers who are most vulnerable and indoctrinate them, and then these children go on to have careers and lives until they are called to duty by the Keepers. Nobody is immune. Not the Pack, not the People."

"Where is the device now?" Ragnvald asked.

"Hidden," Curran answered. "It will be destroyed shortly in a secure location where it will cause minimal damage to the environment."

"How can we be sure that you will follow through with it?" Mark said.

Ghastek condescended to stare for half a second in Mark's direction. "I was led to believe that you possessed at least moderate intelligence. That assessment was obviously in error."

"What?" Mark recoiled.

"How do I know that if I hand you a loaded gun, you won't thrust it into your mouth and pull the trigger? Of course he isn't going to keep it, you idiot. None of us would keep it. Using it would be tantamount to suicide."

Jim nodded and Derek and Barabas circled the table, handing out paper. "This is a list of the chemicals with quantities required to build the device. Some of these are rare. Purchasing them would leave a paper trail."

"We have ten hours and fifty-nine minutes from the beginning of the next magic wave," Curran said. "Either we find the device or we . . ."

Barabas leaned over to him and whispered something in an urgent tone.

Curran's eyes flared with gold. "Bring it here."

Barabas nodded. A female shapeshifter set a phone in front of Curran. He pushed the speaker key. "Yes?"

"Who am I speaking with?" a clipped male voice asked.

"You're speaking with the Beast Lord." Curran's face could've been carved from ice.

"Ah. You're a difficult man to reach. Of course, I'm using the term 'man' loosely."

"What do you want?" Curran asked.

"As I told your staff, I represent the Lighthouse Keepers.

These are our terms: Return the device you've taken and cease all efforts to find us. In return, you have my personal guarantee that the Keep will not be targeted."

Aha. And that seaside property in Kansas he was selling was a steal.

Curran graduated to a full alpha glow. "Is that so?"

"To be honest, destroying you isn't on our short-term agenda. It's simple logistics: the location of the Keep makes it impossible to target you and the city center at the same time. We prefer to deploy within the city limits. Returning Atlanta to its natural state and making it suitable for habitation by an unpolluted population is our primary goal. However, if you refuse our terms, we will classify you as an imminent threat. Evacuating will accomplish nothing. We will simply follow your people to their destination and destroy you at the evacuation point. Cease your endeavors to apprehend us."

Andrea's eyes widened.

I'd heard those words before. Shane had used them in a letter he'd sent to Andrea about her guns. Shane. Holy shit.

To the left, one of the Vikings whispered, "What did he say?"

Ragnvald glared at him.

"Will you acquiesce to our terms?" the man asked. "Your answer?"

"No," Curran said. "Here are our terms: you line up in front of the Capitol, beg forgiveness for murdering hundreds of people, and blow your brains out. You can hang yourselves or fall on your swords. You can set yourselves on fire. I guarantee that any method of suicide you choose will be pleasant compared to what we will do to you. You have until the end of the tech."

The disconnect signal sounded like the toll of a funeral bell.

Ghastek grimaced. " 'Cease your endeavors to apprehend us'? Really?"

"Clearly he reads a thesaurus before bed," a Cherokee shaman opined.

Bob, one of the Guild's mercs, grimaced. "He sounds like a rent-a-cop who read too many police procedure manuals."

"Or an MSDU officer," someone from the other end of the table offered.

No. No, he was a knight of the Order. Ted had to know. We would never prove it, but Ted had to know.

"As I was saying, we have ten hours and fifty-nine minutes from the beginning of the next magic wave," Curran said.
"That's how long the device will take to charge. Either it's in
position already or they are moving it into position now. If we
find it with time to spare, Adam here will disarm it."

A vampire at the far left tensed, gathering its muscles. It was
a minute movement, barely noticeable. I squeezed Slayer's hilt,
feeling the familiar texture under my fingers.

"If there is no time, whoever finds it may have to disarm it
themselves," Curran said. "Now Adam will explain to us how
to do this . . ."

The vampire jumped, claws raised for the kill. It sailed
through the air toward Kamen, clearing the table in a single
powerful leap. I jumped onto the table and sliced left to right, in
a classic diagonal strike. Slayer's blade cleaved through undead
flesh like a sharp knife through a ripe pear.

The bloodsucker's body dropped at Kamen's feet.

The bald, fanged head flew and bounced off the table, spray-
ing the People with thick undead blood.

A dark-headed journeyman jumped to his feet so quickly
that his chair toppled backward. A gun flashed in his hand. I ran
to him. I was jumping over Rowena when he shoved the barrel
against his temple and pulled the trigger. The gun spat thunder.
The gory mess of blood and brains sprayed the window.

The steak house exploded with noise, Ghastek's voice
cutting through it, shaking with rage. "Find the person who
admitted him, find the people who did his background check,
find his Master. I want these people in front of me in half an
hour!"

I SAT IN THE GLOOM OF THE HOSPITAL ROOM. JULIE
lay unmoving on the white sheets, her exposed semihuman arm
caught in the web of tubes of the IV drip feeding sedative into
her body. Her face was twisted, her jaws too large and distorted,
with fangs cutting through her lips. Her eyes were closed. A
shock of pale blond hair was the only thing that remained of
my kid.

It felt unreal.

I'd come here straight after the furor at the steak house had died down. I'd been watching her, sitting here hoping against everything I knew that somehow her body would beat this, that she would flow and streamline and shift back into a human. Or a lynx. I would settle for a lynx at this point. Anything but the twisted thing she was.

The magic would hit tomorrow. If not, then the next day. I would have to perform the ritual. If the device worked as Kamen promised, if the witches managed to channel power into me, if if if . . . If everything went as expected, I still had no idea how exactly I would pull the blood from her body.

At the end of it either Julie, or I, or both us could end up dead. Of all the strange and rash things I'd done, this was the craziest. If someone had told me a week ago that I would be contemplating cutting Julie's throat, I would've knocked them out on the spot.

Doolittle said she couldn't even hear me. To keep the loupism at bay, he'd had to put her completely under. I wanted to tell her that I loved her, that I was sorry, so, so sorry. That I would do anything, give anything to fix it. But she wouldn't hear.

The door opened. A tall, lean woman slipped inside. Jennifer. Surprise, surprise.

She sat next to me. How did she even get here? The room was supposed to be restricted.

"Came to gloat?" I asked.

The wolf alpha startled. "Do you really think I would . . . ?"

"You tell me."

Jennifer said nothing. We sat side by side and looked at Julie. Her chest rose and fell in a steady, slow rhythm.

"Do you ever think about how fucked up life is?" Jennifer asked.

"Yes. That's why I have a punching bag."

"I think about it a lot lately."

We looked at Julie some more.

"I'm pregnant," Jennifer said. "Four months. Doolittle says it's a little girl."

"Congratulations," I told her. My voice came out monotone. "Does Daniel know?"

"Yes. My scent has changed," Jennifer looked at Julie. "Every time I see you, you remind me of the way Naomi died."

"I can't help that."

"I know," she said. "But every time I see you, you make me think of all the things that can go wrong. I hate you for that."

"Is that a challenge?" I asked, unable to keep fatigue from my voice.

"No." Jennifer looked at her hands.

We sat quietly for another long minute.

"I can't do it. I can't kill my own daughter, if she becomes a loup. That's all I think about. It would be my duty as a mother and an alpha, and I just can't."

"That's why there are two of you," I said.

"What if he can't do it? Things happen to alphas. Daniel could be challenged. He could fight a threat to the Pack and lose. If something happens to Daniel and later our daughter becomes a loup, I'll have to kill her. Then there will be nothing left." She looked at me. "Nothing."

If she was looking for wisdom, I had none to offer. "Look at it this way: if we don't find that device tomorrow, we will all die. Problem solved."

Jennifer shrugged her narrow shoulders, her eyes haunted. "I suppose so. I didn't ask to be born a shapeshifter. It just happened. Sometimes you want to stomp your feet and yell, 'It's not fair,' but it won't change anything."

I didn't ask to be born Roland's daughter. I just had to live with it. The world was screwed up. Fanatics tried to murder us, and sometimes we had to kill our own children.

"I'm so angry," Jennifer murmured. "If I could just get over my anger, I'd be all right."

What the hell did she want from me anyway? Was I supposed to hug her and tell her everything would be all right, with Julie lying there as far from fucking all right as she could get?

"Sometimes it helps to live through it," I told her. "Find a time when nobody will bother you, and imagine it. Imagine the worst-case scenario in as much detail as you can manage. Let yourself live through it; feel the fear, feel the pain. It's a terrible thing to put yourself through, but once it's done, the anxiety goes away. It never disappears completely, but it leaves you alone enough so you can function."

"Thanks," Jennifer said. "I might try that."

Doolittle walked into the room, quiet as a ghost, and patted my shoulder. Jennifer rose and slipped out of the door as silently as she'd arrived.

"It's time to take a break," Doolittle murmured. "Come. I'll fix you a nice glass of iced tea."

I rose and followed him out into a small room across the hall. It looked just like an ordinary kitchen: a stove, a fridge, a table with a bench and three chairs . . . Doolittle pointed at the padded bench. I sat. He got a pitcher of iced tea from the fridge and two tall glasses. Oh no.

The iced tea splashed into the glass. I picked it up and drank. Fifty percent honey. Maybe more.

"People think it's the beast that makes us lose our sanity." Doolittle sampled the tea in his glass and sat down with a sad smile. "They think the beast takes over and we become loup. Animals don't destroy each other for pure pleasure. They don't have serial killers. They kill, they don't murder. No, it's not the beast in us that makes us lose our balance. It's the man. Of all the animals, we're the most aggressive and the most predatory. We have to be, otherwise we would've never survived. You can see it in children, especially adolescents. Life is hard for them, so they attack it and fight for their own place in it. *Homo homini lupus.*"

"Man is a wolf to his fellow man?"

Doolittle nodded. "A wise Roman playwright once said that."

"Did he write tragedies?"

"No. Comedies. Good ones, too." Doolittle drank his tea. "I don't trust tragedies much. It's easy to make a person sad by showing him something tragic. We all recognize when sad things happen: someone dies, someone loses a loved one, young love is crushed. It's much harder to make a man laugh—what's funny to one person isn't funny to another."

I valiantly drank my tea. "That's what I don't understand about the Keepers. They're people. They laugh, they cry, and somehow they kill hundreds of their friends and neighbors with no remorse. There is no emotion involved in any of it."

"No, my dear. It's all emotion," Doolittle said. "It's rage."

"Against what?"

"Themselves, mostly. Rage is a powerful thing. People get upset over many things. Frustrating jobs, small paychecks, bad hours. People want things; people feel humiliated by others who have the things they want; people feel deprived and powerless. All this gives fuel to rage. The anger builds and builds and if there is no outlet for it, pretty soon it transforms the person. They walk around like a loaded gun, ready to go off if only they could find the right target. They want to hurt something. They need it."

He refilled his glass and topped mine off. "Humans tend to segregate the world: enemies on one side, friends on the other. Friends are people we know. Enemies are the Other. You can do just about anything to the Other. It doesn't matter if this Other is actually guilty of any crimes, because it's a matter of emotion, not logic. You see, angry people aren't interested in justice. They just want an excuse to vent their rage."

Doolittle sighed. "And once you become their Other, you're no longer a person. You're just an idea, an abstraction of everything that's wrong with their world. Give them the slightest excuse, and they will tear you down. And the easiest way for them to target you as this Other is to find something that's different about you. Color of your skin. The way you speak. The place you're from. Magic. It comes and goes in cycles, Kate. Each new generation picks their own Other. For the Keepers, it's people with magic. And for us, well, it's the Keepers. We will murder them all. No matter if some of them are confused, or easily led, or feebleminded. Or if they have families. They will die. It makes me despair sometimes."

There was such profound sadness in his voice that it made me want to hug myself.

"And then there are lost souls like Leslie, so full of self-hatred that they trample the world in a rush to blame someone for their pain." He shook his head. "Well, look at me, getting all melancholy in my old age. I don't know what came over me."

I knew. It was looking at Julie's tortured body for the last twenty-four hours. He looked on her and felt terrible sorrow. I looked at her and I felt rage.

"When Erra died, did you get hold of any tissue samples?" I asked. "Blood, hair, that type of thing?"

Doolittle looked at me from above the rim of his glass. "Why don't you just tell me straight what it is you're hunting for."

"There is a ritual that may be able to save Julie. To do it, I need to be able to do what Erra did. I need to know if there are any differences between my blood and hers so I can figure out if it's possible to compensate for them."

"That will take time," Doolittle said.

"Can you keep her asleep long enough?"

Doolittle nodded and stood up. "Follow me."

We walked down the hallways, deeper and deeper into the medical ward. "This ritual, how certain are you that it will work?"

" 'Certain' might be too strong a word."

"And if it fails?" Doolittle asked.

"Then I will finally be out of your hair and you won't have to patch me up anymore."

Doolittle stopped and looked at me. For a moment he looked stricken, and then he crossed his arms. "There will be none of that, now. You are my finest work. If I ever go to one of those medmage conferences they keep inviting me to, I will take you with me. Look!" He held his hands out toward me. "Bone dragons, sea demons, rakshasas, and worst of all, our own people, and these magic hands kept her alive through it all. Look at her walk! You can't even see the limp anymore. As long as you don't open your mouth, you will appear as a perfect example of a healthy adult female. With your history, they'll be calling me a miracle worker."

I snickered. "I promise to keep my mouth shut."

Doolittle shook his head in mock sorrow. "It's bad luck to promise impossible things. How is the knee? Honest now."

"Hurts."

"I'll take another look at it when the magic wave hits." Doolittle stopped before a door. "Ready?"

For what? "I was born ready."

Doolittle thrust a key into the lock and unlocked it with a quiet click. The door swung open, revealing a small chamber with a metal barrel in its center. Two feet wide, three feet tall, sealed with a flat lid. Doolittle approached it, twisted the metal clasp, and swung the lid aside. Cold assaulted my face. Inside, bags of red ice sat in neat rows.

"Erra's blood," Doolittle said. "After you and our lord fought her, Jim brought me her body. Before we buried her, I drained it dry."

CHAPTER 22

———◆———

I MADE MY WAY UPSTAIRS AND WASHED OFF ALL OF
my grime. Doolittle said he'd need at least twenty-four hours
to review my blood and Erra's. Normally by now Voron would
be screaming warnings at me from the depths of my memory,
but he kept quiet. Perhaps it was because I trusted Doolittle, or
maybe because Voron's ghost no longer had an iron grip on me.

I stood under the hot water, letting it run over my skin. Julie
would have to wait, and not just for Doolittle. First, we had
to find the Keepers, because if they managed to activate the
device within the range of the Keep, nothing would matter.
Curran had already warned the guards to notify us the moment
any important news came or the magic wave hit. I didn't know
how much time we had, but whatever it was I wanted to spend it
well. For all we knew, we'd all kick the bucket tomorrow.

When I slid the shower door open, the smell of seared meat
curled around me. A garment bag hung on the towel hook. With
my luck, it would contain a French maid outfit.

I toweled off my hair and unzipped the bag. A silvery fabric
caught the light and shimmered with a gentle light, as if someone had captured a crystal-clear mountain stream and somehow bound it into the creamy white silk. I ran my fingers over

it, feeling the slickness. So beautiful. I'd seen this dress in the window shortly after Christmas. The strapless gown actually made me stop. There was something magic about the dress, something ethereal and otherworldly. No matter how much I looked at it in that store window, I couldn't picture myself in it. Curran told me I should get it. I told him that I had no place to wear it and besides, where would I put my sword?

He'd remembered.

A tiny voice nagged me that we should be out there, searching for the threat, but then the entire magic population of Atlanta was already searching for it. Andrea and Jim had joined forces, trying to pin down Shane's hiding place. The Order was under constant surveillance. A domineering werelion and a loud-mouthed merc wouldn't make that much of a difference. I found the blow-dryer. A dress like that deserved dry hair. If I had been by myself, I would've turned in by now to conserve energy before the fight. But then things could go really wrong tomorrow. I had to make the most of tonight.

Twenty minutes later, hair brushed, eye shadow on, and mascara on my eyelashes, I slipped the dress on. It hugged my body, curving over my breasts, clasped between them with a small crystal flower, and slid over the curve of my hips all the way down. A long slit went from the floor to my upper thigh.

I opened the door. A pair of transparent shoes sat on the floor. I slid my feet into them. Perfect fit.

I stepped out into the kitchen. Curran stood at the table. He wore gray tailored pants and a white button-down shirt. The shirt was semitransparent, and it molded to his muscled torso like a glove. He'd shaved, and the light from the candles on the table played on his face, throwing faint highlights over his masculine jaw. He looked almost unbearably handsome.

I stopped.

He was looking at me with a kind of need that somehow managed to be raw and tender at the same time. He took my breath away.

We looked at each other, a little awkward.

Finally I raised my hand. "Hi."

"Hi," he said. "I made dinner. At least I made the steaks. The rest came from the kitchen . . . Would you like to sit down?"

"Yes, I would."

He held out my chair and I sat. He sat across from me. There was some kind of food on the table and a bottle of something, probably wine.

"You're wearing a formal shirt," I said. "I had no idea you owned one." The way he looked at me short-circuited the link between my mouth and my brain. *Formal shirt?* What the hell was I going on about?

"I figured I'd match the dress," he said. He seemed slightly shocked.

"Do you like it?"

"It looks great. You look great. Beautiful."

We looked at each other.

"We should eat," I said.

"Yeah." He was looking at me.

Silence hung between us. I had to know why he was with me. I thought it didn't matter, but it did.

I met his gaze. "My mother had a power that made men do whatever she wanted. She brainwashed Voron. She cooked him like a steak, until he left Roland for her. She needed him to take care of me. Except she overdid it. Voron was so hurt by her death, he never cared for me. He just wanted to watch me and Roland go at it. He said that if he watched my father kill me, it would be enough for him."

"Where is this coming from?"

"The witch," I told him. "Evdokia. She and I are very distantly related. She's telling the truth."

Curran's expression turned guarded. "That's fucked up."

"Before you and I mated, did you and Jim have a conversation about what it would mean for the Pack?" It would be something Jim would do. He'd suspected what I was, if he hadn't figured it out already.

"Yes," Curran said. His face was still flat.

"What did Jim say?"

"He advised against it. He had bullet points of why this was not a good idea."

My heart skipped a bit.

"He also said that since I was going to do it anyway, despite whatever he said, I should get on with it, because it took too much manpower to track me all over the city. He always sent guards to shadow me, and I usually dumped them before getting to your apartment. He said his life would be a lot easier if I just moved you into the Keep."

"Is that why you wanted me here?"

Curran leaned forward. The mask that was his face vanished. "I wanted you here because I wanted to be with you. For better or worse, Kate. You didn't brainwash me the way your mother did. You don't have her powers. You have the complete opposite, if anything."

All or nothing. "Did you know that Roland was my father before I told you?"

"Yes."

Suddenly I was ice cold.

"How?"

"Breaking Roland's sword was a big clue," he said. "Jim obtained some pictures of Roland. You resemble him. And there is a story floating around about a child Roland supposedly killed. I put two and two together."

I had agonized about telling him who I was. It took every shred of will to admit it, and he had it all figured out already. "And you let me sit there and tell you all about it, when you already knew?"

"It was important," Curran said. "You had to do it, so I listened."

"Did you take who I was into consideration before you offered me the mating?"

Curran leaned forward. A faint glow touched his eyes and vanished. "Of course I did."

And here it was. At least he hadn't lied. Deep down I had known it. Curran was too used to calculating the odds. Like Evdokia said, it wasn't his first time at the love rodeo. It's not like he would have fallen head over heels into it, the way I did.

"I have a string of safe houses set up all across the country," he said.

I must've misheard. "What?"

"I have a safe house in almost every state. I have more than enough money to keep us comfortable for the rest of our lives, if it comes to it. I've moved most of my funds to places outside the Pack."

"What are you talking about?"

"I know he is coming and you are afraid. If you don't want to fight him, you and I can disappear."

I stared at him.

"The mass transit is gone. No planes, no reliable roads. The world is big again, Kate. He will never find us."

"What about the Pack?"

His upper lip trembled, betraying the edge of his teeth. "Fuck the Pack. I gave them fifteen years of my life. I fought for them, bled for them, and the moment my back was turned, they attacked my wife. I owe them nothing."

Curran reached over and covered my fingers with his hand. "I'm serious. Say the word right now and we're gone. We can take Julie with us, if you want."

"Jim would find us."

"No. I covered my tracks. If Jim does find us, he'll wish he hadn't. Besides, Jim is a friend. He would understand and he wouldn't look for us very hard."

It wasn't a bluff; I heard it in his voice. He would do it. He would walk away. "You would leave all these people, all the bowing, and the . . ."

His gray eyes looked into mine. "If I fought for them and was crippled, they would all say nice things, and then they would replace me and forget I was ever there. You would stay with me. You would take care of me, because you love me. I love you too, Kate. If you ever became hurt, I would not leave you. I'll be there. Wherever you want 'there' to be."

I felt like crying. Great, he'd turned me into a weeping weakling.

"Would you like to leave?" he asked.

I swallowed. "Not unless you want to."

"Then we will stay. For now."

"Yes."

"Okay," he said.

I was lucky. Somehow, maybe because of all the messed-up shit the Universe had thrown my way, I'd gotten him. He was mine, completely mine. He loved me.

I kept making barriers between us and then heroically knocking them down. Whether it was because of fear or mistrust, or for whatever other reason, I had to stop doing it.

I glanced down. The food was cold, our plates sat empty. "Do you think it will keep?"

He stood up. "Hell yes."

THE CANDLES DIDN'T KEEP. BY THE TIME WE MADE IT back to the kitchen, the candles had dripped wax over the candelabra. I poked my steak—lukewarm. The baked potatoes were cold. Corn on the cob was barely warm. I didn't care.

"I'm starving."

"Got to keep your strength up." Curran grinned. "So you can keep up."

I clasped my hand to my throat and made some strangled noises. "Help me, I can't breathe, your ego is pushing all the air out of the room."

He laughed.

"This menu looks really familiar," I said, loading my plate. I'd switched to a sweatshirt and sweatpants. My dress had been discarded anyway and besides, we had agreed to take our plates back to the couch, and I didn't want to get food on it.

"Mm-hm," Curran said, spearing a chunk of meat. "Apple pie is in the fridge."

He'd recreated the menu he requested for the naked dinner. Ha!

"How did you even know my shoe size?"

"I've seen your foot up close." Curran pointed to his chest. "I've seen it here." He moved his hand to his jaw. "Here." He touched the place over his cheek where my kick had cut him. "And here."

Aha. "Would you like to watch a movie while we eat?"

"Sure. What sort of movie?"

"It has everything: action, drama, comedy, beautiful soundtrack. Hot male lead."

His thick eyebrows crept up half an inch. "That last one isn't exactly a plus."

"Jealous of the actors now, are we?"

"What, of some fancy boy on the screen? Inconceivable."

Oh, this was going to be good.

We took our plates to the coffee table by the couch, and I slid Saiman's disk into the player. The warehouse full of cars solidified on the screen. Curran's face went blank.

When the first notes of the song sounded through the living room, he looked at me. "He set it to music?"

"His exact words were, 'It begged for a soundtrack.' "

A Ferrari flew across the screen and crashed into the wall. Curran looked impassive.

I chewed a piece of my steak. It had to be the best steak I'd ever had. "I seem to recall a certain man boasting about his 'superhuman' restraint."

"I did show remarkable self-control."

"You destroyed five million dollars' worth of luxury cars."

"Yes, but none of them are wearing human heads as hood ornaments."

I dropped back onto the pillow. "So you want credit for not repainting the place with blood?"

"The guards walked away. Saiman walked away. Tell me that's not superhuman." Curran pulled me close to him and kissed my neck where it joined my shoulder. Mmm.

"Where did you get this?" His voice was entirely too casual for comfort.

"That source Jim keeps referring to is Saiman. He is knee-deep in this whole thing. He left some evidence at Kamen's place, and I tracked him down."

"Did you go to see him?" Curran asked.

Warning: danger ahead. Rocks fall, everyone dies.

"Yes."

"At his apartment?"

"Yes."

"Where is Saiman now?"

"I'm not sure. Under the bed? Maybe you should try the closet."

"Kate!"

I laughed. "You should see your face. Don't you trust me?"

"I trust you," he said. "I just need to talk to him."

Aha. Talk. His Majesty, Master of Negotiation. "I took Derek with me when I went to see him. Saiman is so scared of you, he didn't even want to let us in. And the Keepers sent a team into the place to finish all of us off. How can you be jealous of him? It's like me being jealous of Myong." Not that his latest ex-girlfriend didn't inspire jealousy. She was a stunning woman, elegant, beautiful in an exotic way. She was also fragile like a delicate glass ornament.

"Nothing ever happened between me and Myong," he said.

I rolled my eyes. "Right."

"I'm serious. Not that I didn't want to at the time, but I tried to kiss her once, and she got a deer-in-the-headlights look. I got a feeling that if I went any further, she'd shut her eyes and pray for it to be over, so I backed off."

"Maybe I should check the closet to see if the beautiful Myong is hiding in there, since you are so hot for her . . ."

He blinked. *How does that foot taste?*

"Blah-blah-blah."

"You're so eloquent, Your Majesty. So kind and generous to your subjects. So full of snappy comebacks."

"Don't forget brutally honest. To my own detriment even."

"Oh, yes. Honest to a fault."

"You never told me where Saiman's hiding."

I took my plate into the kitchen.

He followed me. "You like to screw with me, is that it? Saiman, that Russian mage, that merc . . ."

"What merc?"

"Bob."

I racked my brain. I'd barely said two words to Bob. "He stopped by our table to ask me which way I'd vote in the Guild elections. They still haven't figured out who is in charge, and I'm technically on the roster."

"Yeah. Did he have to lean over you while he was talking?"

"He was trying to let Mark think that he and I were buddies."

"And you are not."

I threw a bread roll at him. Curran snapped it out of the air.

"Would you like me to carry a foot-long stick? I can just poke people with it when they get too close."

"That's a good idea." He held his arm out. "If you can extend your arm and touch them with the stick, they are too close."

"You're insane."

"If I'm insane, what does it make you?"

"A terrible judge of character."

I went back to the couch. I could've fallen for someone steady. Dependable. Well grounded. But nooo, I had to lose my head over this idiot.

Curran pounced. It was an excellent pounce, executed with

preternatural speed. He pinned me to the couch. "Tell me where Saiman is."

"Or what?"

"Or I will be displeased."

I rolled my eyes. "He's worried himself into paranoia, Curran. When Jim and I were dealing with the rakshasas during the Midnight Games, Saiman went into the Pit to plant a tracker into a rakshasa opponent. He was so terrified, he could barely move. The rakshasa cut him, and Saiman snapped. He bashed the rakshasa to death and kept beating his body for about five minutes. When he finally calmed down, there was only mush left. I know you can take him. I can take him, too. The question is why. Why make an enemy of him? You have to either kill him now or stop screwing with him, and if you're going to kill him, I really *am* a terrible judge of character."

Curran growled and moved to sit next to me.

"He wants the pressure to go away. He's prepared to soothe your ego. He gave us everything he knew about Kamen and the device for this precise reason, and he fully expects you to ask for more."

"My ego doesn't need soothing," Curran said. "I don't want him soothing anything of mine, including you."

"Jim has him stashed away at one of the safe houses. Do as you will."

I stared at him.

"What?" he growled.

"Waiting to see if you're going to run out on me on the night before the Apocalypse to go beat his ass."

Curran reached for me. "He'll keep. There is no rush."

"Keep your hands to yourself. You said you didn't need any more soothing."

"I changed my mind. Besides, I'm the hot male lead. Actors get all the chicks." He kissed me. "You're still going through with this?"

"Yes," I told him honestly.

"Don't," he said.

I slumped forward. "I have to at least try. Are you going to try to stop me?"

"No. You made a decision, and you're following through with it. I don't like it, but I'll help you with it, because you're my mate and I would expect the same from you." Curran grimaced. "It would be worse if you sat on your hands and moaned about not knowing what to do. I couldn't deal with that."

The Beast Lord way: often wrong but never in doubt.

"As long as we're on the subject," Curran said. "'The man thrust it back into the wound and spoke the words that bound the wolf to obey him forever.' If you do this, Julie will never be able to disobey a direct order from you. You will be making a slave."

I glanced at him. "I thought about that. I don't know if it's even necessary for the ritual, but I can't take that chance. I'll have to do it exactly the way Roland did."

"She can never know," Curran said. "Look, I've been in charge of people for a long time. Trust me on this, you can't take Julie's free will away from her. If you do this, that's your secret and you have to live with that. You have to be strong enough to keep that from her, and that means you'll have to think twice before any instructions to her come out of your mouth."

I rubbed my face. He was right. If Julie got as much as a hint that she had no choice about obeying me, I'd lose her. The most natural things like, "No, you can't go out to the woods with Maddie in the middle of the night" now would have to become, "I would strongly prefer that you stayed home." I had a hard enough time steering her as it was.

"I'll deal with it," I said. "As long as she's alive. Everything else we'll figure out along the way."

The magic rolled over us like a suffocating blanket.

The countdown had begun. We had ten hours and fifty-nine minutes.

Someone knocked. Curran went to the door. From where I lay, I could see his face in profile. His mouth curved. He came back, chuckling to himself.

"Yes?"

"The witches have sent you a gift."

MY PRESENT SAT BEHIND THE TABLE IN THE SMALLER conference room. It hid in the folds of a dark cloak. Only the hand was visible, a small feminine hand with manicured nails that gripped a spoon, stirring the tea in a blue cup. Jezebel leaned against the opposite wall, glaring at the cloaked woman as if she were a fire-spitting dragon. Barabas waited by the door. He saw me and smiled. It was a sharp, nasty smile, like a cat that had finally caught the mouse and was about to torture it to death.

What now?

I pulled my hair up into a bun and headed for the door. Barabas handed me a note in Evdokia's curvy Russian script. It read:

A gift for you, Katenka. Thank me later.

Beware of gifts from Baba Yaga—they came with strings attached, and sometimes if you took them, you ended up in the oven as dinner.

"Did she come alone?"

"No, Evdokia's daughters brought her." Barabas's grin got wider. "I checked into it and she and Grigorii have five children. They're their own private Russian mafia."

I stepped through the door and took a seat at the table. The woman pulled her hood back, exposing a wealth of glossy red hair. Rowena.

If she had pulled off her hood and turned out to be Medusa with her head full of vipers, I would've been less surprised.

We looked at each other. A red feverish flush colored her cheeks. Bloodshot eyes, puffy nose. Slightly smeared eyeliner. Rowena had been crying. That was a first. Rowena kept her composure no matter what. The roof could cave in and she'd smile against the backdrop of falling rocks and ask you to do her the favor of moving toward the exit.

"Okay," I said. "I want an explanation. Now. What are you doing here?"

Rowena swallowed. "Bozydar, the journeyman who killed himself today, was my nephew. I'm banned from navigation pending an investigation. I will be cleared of all charges and they will reinstate me."

"You seem very sure of that."

Rowena sniffed. "Ghastek is ambitious. Nataraja won't last much longer; something happened, and he mostly hides in his quarters now. Ghastek and Mulradin are running things, and each one of them wants to be at the top. They are scrambling to form alliances. I'm ranked third in finesse and fourth in power, and I support Ghastek. He can't afford to lose me."

"So why are you here?"

"Bozydar had a girl," Rowena said, her voice barely above a whisper. "Her name is Christine. She would do anything for him. She loved him so much. I spoke to her. She said that my nephew had been recruited by the Keepers years ago, when my brother and his wife died. They were on Route 90 crossing over the Mississippi, when the bridges collapsed due to magic erosion. They drowned. Bozydar was pulled out of the river comatose. By the time I found him, they'd shipped him to an orphanage." Rowena clenched her hands. "He suffered a lot of abuse. They'd done things to him. I've given him a chance at revenge, but I didn't realize it wasn't enough."

She fell silent. I waited for the rest.

"He was doing things for the Keepers, and Christine helped him," Rowena said. "She was in it knee-deep. She covered for him, she fed him classified information he needed; whatever he asked for, she did it."

"Is she a member of the Keepers?"

"No." Rowena shook her head. "She is just a foolish girl who was in love with a broken boy. When Palmetto was hit, she was horrified."

I bet.

She gripped her slender fingers so hard, her manicured nails left red indents in her skin. "We have been publicly embarrassed, and Ghastek is looking for a scapegoat. If he finds out what Christine has done, he will purge her. Purged journeymen don't go home, Kate. They disappear. One day she won't be there for her shift and then the new schedule will be posted and everyone will know what happened to her. He'll kill her, Kate, to demonstrate that he's capable of making problems vanish."

I was still waiting for the punch line.

"Christine is five months pregnant," Rowena said.

Ah. Here we go.

"People in my family have a difficult time with fertility. I've been trying to have a child for years. So far, I've failed. Bozydar was the only relative I had. Now he's dead and his baby is my only family. Do you have any family, Kate?"

Now there was a loaded question. "No."

She leaned forward, her eyes wide and desperate. "This unborn baby is everything to me. I can't protect Christine. Even if I give her money and send her away, Ghastek will find her. He can be so single-minded, it's terrifying."

I finally put two and two together. "So you went to the witches."

"Yes," Rowena murmured. "Yes, I did. My family has roots in that world. So I went and offered the covens anything they wanted to hide Christine."

She must've been truly desperate. "What's the price?"

Rowena looked up at me. "Three years of service. To you."

"Excuse me?"

"They bound me to you for three years. I swore a blood oath. I will do whatever you require, and I am sworn to never speak of it." She raised her hand. A fresh scar cleaved her palm. "I don't understand any of it, and if Ghastek finds out that I helped Christine or that I came here, I am dead. So." Rowena leaned on the table. "What service can I perform for you?"

I rested my elbow on the table, leaned against my hand, and exhaled. To have access to a qualified necromancer was akin to finding a case of ammo in the middle of a gunfight. Here was my chance to learn and train. I needed her desperately. Unfortunately, I trusted her about as far as I could throw her. I was strong and she was small, but it still wasn't very far.

"The problem is, I don't trust you," I said.

"I don't trust you either," she said. "But if I don't do as they say, Christine's life is forfeit."

"They actually made you swear to it."

She nodded. "She was right there. She stood right there when I swore. She heard every word. If they kill her, she will know it's because I failed."

Note to self: avoid being in debt to the witches like the plague.

"Whatever it is you want, Kate, I will do it. No matter how foul. Even if it means debasing and humiliating myself . . ."

Fantastic. Who did she think I was, exactly? "I guess we will start with humiliation, move onto debasing, and perhaps do some torture for a spiffy finish." I glanced at Jezebel. "Is our Torturer in residence?"

Rowena opened her mouth, looking as if she were about to say something sharp, and must've thought better of it, because she clamped it shut.

"How accomplished are you in necromancy?"

She gathered herself. "I'm rated as Master of the Dead of the Third Caliber, Level Two, which means I can simultaneously hold three vampires and effectively pilot two at the time. I've passed all the prerequisite examinations. I rank third in finesse and fourth in power in Atlanta and seventy-first overall among the People. That rank is misleading, as when you're that high up, the differences between the ranks are minute. For example, the range of the person above me is only twenty inches longer than mine. I hold the shield of the Silver Legion. The Gold Legion is—"

"Roland's top fifty," I finished. "You had to climb the Ladder, correct?" The Ladder was Roland's way of promoting education among the People. Each step of the ladder consisted of a work on magic, necromancy, or philosophy. Some steps were books, some scrolls. Once you mastered a step, you took a test to prove your knowledge. The more steps, the higher the pay.

Rowena's eyes narrowed. "Yes, the Ladder of Knowledge. You have to complete ten to be rated as a Second Caliber Journeyman, and twenty-five to obtain the title of Master. How do you know this?"

"How many steps did you complete?"

"Eighty-nine," she said.

"And Ghastek?"

"One hundred and sixty-five." She grimaced. "The man is a machine. As I've said, Ghastek can be extremely single-minded. If you are considering using me against him, I will obey, of course, but you should understand that though I can injure him, he'll win this fight."

"When Roland made Arez, he used a ritual to purge him of loupism. The technique involves withdrawing a person's blood and purifying it. Are you familiar with it? Rowena?"

Rowena decided it would be a good time to close her mouth. "Yes."

"Tell me about it?"

"It's the same process he uses to create his Chosen," she said. "You receive a gift of his blood and power, but in return you're bound to him forever. He doesn't use it often."

"Is Hugh d'Ambray bound to him?"

"Yes."

I'd thought as much. Since both Arez and Hugh had been preceptors of the Order of Iron Dogs and were bound to Roland, Voron must've been bound, too. That was why my mother had stayed behind to fight Roland. Voron couldn't disobey a direct order from Roland. If my father had ordered him to hand me over, Voron would've done it; he'd have had no choice.

"Have you ever seen it done?"

She shook her head. "Only what I have read."

"Is the use of the obedience power word necessary?"

"Yes. That's what gives him control over the blood once it's removed from the body."

I leaned back. There was no way around it. If she survived, Julie would be bound to me forever.

"Kate, it's a very difficult ritual. Other people, high-ranking members of the Gold Legion, have tried and failed. You can't just do something like that. Roland's blood and power are unique."

Yes, yes.

Rowena kept going. "I've met him, when I was initiated into the Silver Legion. The magic radiating through his blood is unlike anything I've ever felt."

To the right, Jezebel rolled her eyes.

"It's like meeting a god in person. It's . . . I can't even describe it."

I wondered what she would do if I cut my forearm, dipped my fingers into the red, and touched her hand with it. *Was it something like this?*

I bet she would jump.

I folded my arms on my chest instead. "Just tell me about the ritual, Rowena. That's all I need for now."

She was looking past me. I glanced behind me and saw Curran looking through the glass doors, radiating menace. He opened the door. "The Keepers were sighted at Nameless Square. I need you."

I looked at Jezebel. "Get our guest some paper. Once she writes everything down, make sure she leaves safely."

CHAPTER 23

———✦———

I CROUCHED ON THE HUGE CONCRETE BOULDER jutting from the pavement like the stern of a sinking ship. To the left, an abandoned building rose from the street, its stucco and concrete long turned to dust. Only a rusty cage of the framework remained, thrusting brown grates to the sunlit morning sky. Down below, the wreckage of Downtown unrolled: once-solid buildings reduced to heaps of rubble and abandoned ruins, crisscrossed by roads, once busy, now mostly atrophied, and stubby blocky structures born of the new age. To the right, the golden dome of the Georgia State Capitol building caught the light, the copper statue of Miss Liberty on its top thrusting her torch upward. To the left, in the distance, Unicorn Lane boiled with wild magic. The air shimmered there as a dark mist rose between the fallen high-rises marked with garish stains of magic-mutated vegetation.

I scanned the horizon. Nothing.

The sighting at Nameless Square turned out to be a bust. Someone had caught a glimpse of a large metal cylinder and sounded the alarm too early. The metal cylinder turned out to be a massive charged-air converter being installed at the Capitol as a backup system, in case the main charged-air lines went down. Since then we'd been to a half dozen spots within the city, as the magic users scouring the city for the Keepers raised the alarm here and there. Every lead sounded promising, and every lead turned out to be a miss. We were playing Whack-A-Mole and we were almost out of time.

I squinted at the sun. Around ten. Four hours left? Less? Atlanta was a huge sprawling beast. Every ruin doubled as a potential hiding place.

I hadn't seen Jim or Andrea or Derek since yesterday. It worried me.

Below me, Curran gathered himself, jumped ten feet in the air, bounced off the concrete into another jump, then another, and landed next to me.

"Me Kate. You Tarzan?"

"No." Curran bared his teeth at me. "In the first book, he grabs a lion by the tail and pulls it. Never gonna happen. First, an adult male lion weighs five hundred pounds. Second, you grab my tail, I'll turn around and take your face off." He surveyed the city.

"Nothing," I told him.

Curran stroked my back. "If the countdown is down to an hour and we still don't know where it is, I want you to leave."

I turned to him.

"The children are out of the Keep," Curran said. "They were shipped out overnight into the Wood." The Wood, otherwise known as Chattahoochee National Forest, served as the hunting grounds for the Pack. Curran had bought a hundred-year lease, and once a month each shapeshifter made a pilgrimage there to run among the trees without his or her human skin. "They have orders to scatter. Julie is in Augusta under heavy sedation. Barabas and two of our guards are with her."

"I'm staying," I told him.

"No." His eyes were clear, his voice calm. "You owe me for agreeing to the ritual. If the countdown reaches one hour and we still have no leads, you will leave. The Pack must have an alpha. You will take over. The betas from each clan have evacuated; they are spread out all over the state. They will be your new Council."

Fear grabbed my throat and squeezed, crushing. In a blink I could lose him. "I can't run the Pack, Curran. You're kidding yourself."

He looked at me. He wasn't giving me a hard stare; he just looked at me. "I need you to tell me that you will do this. No arguments, no bullshit heroics. Just do this for me."

"Why?"

"Because I want you to be safe. I want you to survive and if I'm not there to protect you, the Pack will be the next best thing. Promise me," he said.

"Okay," I told him. "But if we find them, I'm staying to the end."

A bright burst of green blossomed to the right. South. A new lead. What was south of the Capitol . . . "The airport?"

Curran swore.

BEFORE THE SHIFT, THE HARTSFIELD-JACKSON AIRport had served as the primary hub for all flights to the Southern United States. Almost three miles wide and flanked by highways on all sides, the airport ate a huge chunk of the city's Southside. The damn place was so big, there was a train going through it. If you died in the South, you had to stop in Atlanta for a layover before getting to the other side. The Shift fixed that right up. The commercial aviation industry took a century to grow and only five minutes to die, as the first magic wave dropped five thousand planes out of the sky. Overnight, the airport was dead.

The structure didn't sit abandoned for too long. When the MSDU officially came into being, christened in the blood of the Three-Month Riots, the local Unit took over the airport, turning it into a fortified base and the HQ of military operations for the Southeast. Over the decades that followed, the MSDU's forces had continued steadily increasing the airport's defenses, turning it into a full-fledged fortress.

As I drove along a narrow access road, I could see the edge of the runways, the concourse, and beyond them the white and sea-foam spire of the control tower. The place looked impenetrable. The long gray building of the terminal bristled with siege engines and machine guns, aided by square boxes of concrete bunkers. A hundred yards out, the second row of bunkers guarded the concourse. Between the bunkers and us lay half a mile of clear ground. Nothing but the old pavement of the runways and brownish grass, mowed down to mere fuzz. No cover, no safe approach, nothing.

Three wards shimmered in the air. The first sheathed the tower in a bluish translucent cocoon. The second rose just past the bunkers. Glowing threads of pale magic wound through it, swirling like colors on a soap bubble. The third and final ward, a translucent wall tinted with red, extended the length of the field.

Why were all three wards up? MSDU usually didn't bother with activating the defensive spells unless they had to contain something nasty, and even then, only the perimeter and the killing field ward went active. I could see the killing field to the left—no ward shielded it. What the hell was going on?

"Could the Keepers have taken the MSDU?" I murmured.

Curran stirred in the passenger seat. "If they have, the device is in the tower."

I'd stick the device in some sort of storage room in some forgotten concourse, but if the Keepers somehow claimed the base, they would choose the tower. They knew we were coming. The tower was an excellent place for their last stand. Stick enough sharpshooters with crossbows at the top and we'd all look like hedgehogs by the time we got to it. Assuming we'd manage to breach all the other defenses first.

"The red ward is a bouncer," I said. "It's not too hard to break. With all of our magic juice, we can breach it in fifteen, twenty minutes. We go through it, and it will bounce shut right back behind us. We'll be pinned between that ward and whatever is in those front bunkers."

"How can you tell?"

"The red is more opaque near the ground, which means magic is concentrated there. That's usually a mark of a bouncer. Regular wards have uniform thickness, like the ones I used to have on my apartment. They can be opened or closed, but once they break, they take several magic waves to regenerate. This one will surge right back up."

"Your wards are transparent, too," Curran said.

"I could make them in color. Transparent wards take more effort. In this case they are warding an area about three miles in diameter. They went for the most bang for their buck—the strongest ward with the least effort. And to people who don't know about wards, giant red domes look impressive."

The access road spat us out into the field. It was half full—search parties trickled in via the other two roads. A vampire completely covered in purple sunblock rose at our approach and waved his claws.

I parked. The moment I stepped outside, Andrea was there. "The Keepers took over the MSDU."

"How?"

"Remember that buddy of mine I called to check out de Harven?" Andrea said. "He has three kids. All of them chock full of magic. So I called him." She held up her hands. "I know, I know. I wasn't going to say anything. I just wanted to suggest to him that he take his family on a trip to the coast or something. He wasn't at his number. So I called the reception in his building. Some guy I never spoke to answered and said that my friend was on bereavement leave. I was right there, so I dropped by his house. His wife says he didn't come home last night. She called the base, and MSDU told her they were holding him overnight due to an emergency. She didn't think anything of it. So I came by here. Look!" She thrust a pair of binoculars at me. "Third bunker from the left."

I looked through the binoculars. First, second, third . . . A leg in urban fatigues and an Army-issue steel-toed boot stuck out from behind the bunker. I waited a couple of seconds. It didn't move. Either he was suffering from a sudden bout of severe narcolepsy or we had a dead soldier. A body like that wouldn't be left lying about if the base were still under military control. The Keepers must've taken the base.

I passed the binoculars to Curran. He looked through them.

Jim came striding up, his cloak flaring behind him. "The gate's shut down. The ward's blocking the approach."

"Did you try the emergency channel?" Curran asked.

"Twice. No response. The People tried it on their end as well, and nothing. The base is shut down. Phones are working, but they aren't taking any phone calls."

"All right," Curran said. "Send up the flares. Get everyone here."

Jim turned and raised his hand. A young shapeshifter ran from group to group. At the far end of the field, mages raised their staves. Magic popped, like a large firecracker, and seven green bursts exploded in the sky.

• • •

THE SHAPESHIFTERS LINED UP ALONG THE WARD'S perimeter. Some I knew, some I didn't. I sat on top of the Jeep. I'd need the energy for the fight.

Next to me Ghastek stood, leaning on the Jeep's hood, looking slightly absurd in a formal black suit and a gun-gray shirt. Two vampires sat at his feet like bald, mutated cats, both coated in bright lime-green sunblock. Ghastek had enough range to navigate vampires from the other end of the city. Unlike us, he didn't have to be here in person.

"Why are you here? Shouldn't you be off hiding in some armored bus miles away?"

Ghastek glanced at me. "Derision, Kate? How unlike you. I'm here because when this unfortunate affair is over, people will remember who was here and who wasn't."

"I take it Mulradin chose to evacuate."

Ghastek bent his lips a little. It was almost a smile. "It's an unfortunate fact of life that some people value discretion above valor. As the saying goes, fortune favors the brave."

Or the foolish. "And of course, the fact that if we survive this, you'll come out looking like a hero has nothing to do with your decision."

He widened his eyes. "Why, Kate, you might be right. If only I had thought of that."

Maybe one of the Keepers would shoot him.

Below us Kamen stared at the ward. Two younger volhvs watched him. He said that about twenty minutes before the activation, the device would send out a "plume" of magic. Whatever the hell that meant. When the shit was about to hit the fan, we'd get a short warning.

Kamen also said that raising the device off the ground extended its range by about a mile. We thought the Keepers were aiming for the city center. We were wrong. They were aiming for the densely populated neighborhoods just outside. The MSDU provided protection in case of emergency. Real estate next to the Unit was highly priced, and the Pack owned a quarter of it. That was where the shapeshifters who worked in the city built their homes.

All the Keeper claims of "we regret casualties" had been

complete bullshit. They aimed for casualties. Wiping out these neighborhoods would snap the backbone of the city. Atlanta's citizens would panic and flee, and the Keepers could purge the entire city at their leisure.

A long forlorn cry rolled through the sky. I raised my hand to my eyes, shielding them from the sunlight. A huge dark bird circled the dome once, enormous wings stretched wide, and landed in the far field. A man slid off its back and jogged over. Amadahy, one of the Cherokee shamans.

Amadahy came to a stop near Curran. His voice carried to us. "The bunkers have no roof. There is a catapult in each one and a small cheiroballista. There are guns, too."

"Are there people in the bunkers?" Curran asked.

Amadahy nodded. "They were priming the catapults as I flew over."

The catapult would lob something nasty our way, and the cheiroballista would shoot us with bolts while we ran around trying to avoid it. Great.

Thomas and Robert Lonesco came along the line of the shapeshifters. Thomas was tall, well over six feet. Robert, his spouse, leaned toward dark and delicate, with large brown eyes and a narrow face. They spoke to Curran.

"Just out of curiosity, does your paramour have an actual plan to breach this ward, or is he just making it up as he goes along?"

"Ghastek, do you want to lead this attack alone?"

"No thanks. I'm after the benefits, not the responsibility."

"Then shut up."

Robert Lonesco stepped forward to the ward and raised his hand. Behind him members of Clan Rat formed into five columns, four people wide, three people deep. Robert closed his hand into a fist. The columns split into an upside-down V formation, with Robert at the head of the center V.

Robert stripped off his sweats. For a second he stood nude, and then his skin burst. Muscle whipped and stretched like elastic cords, and a wererat crouched in his place, one enormous clawed paw leaning on the ground. A green glow washed over Robert's eyes. Behind him the rats shed their humanity. Robert raised his muzzle to the sky. A deep ragged voice broke free of his mouth. "Foooooorrrrrrwaaaard."

The rats crouched down as one and dug into the ground. Dirt flew.

"Interesting tactic," Ghastek murmured.

We wouldn't need to break the ward. We would simply tunnel under it. Nice.

Andrea ran up to the Jeep and climbed up next to me. "Hey."

"Hey."

Teams of four shapeshifters began dragging wooden beams and laying them down behind the rats to reinforce the tunnel.

I glanced at Ghastek. "Aren't you going to help them dig?"

Ghastek shrugged. "A vampire is a precision instrument, not a bulldozer."

The front lines of the rats had vanished into the ground. They only had to go about fifty feet or so. The ward itself was narrow, but to get under it would take some effort.

Twenty minutes later the ground on the other side of the ward shifted. The first of the wererats emerged from the dirt.

Something sparked with orange in the slit of the bunker's narrow window. Probably the catapult inside. Sound rolled, and a bright orange ball shot from the roofless bunker. It whistled through the air and crashed right at the middle column, exploding into orange liquid. The liquid splattered in a wide arc. Two other bunkers followed suit, adding more orange goo to the mess. Yellow lightning danced on its surface. The fluid caught fire.

Hoarse screams, half growls, half yelps followed. The tunnels on our side of the ward vomited the wererats in a dark flood. The front ranks of the diggers bore blisters where their fur had been burned clean. Robert was the last to emerge. His left arm was a mess of scalded muscle, the skin charred, almost black. He snarled and walked over to Thomas. The rat alpha clasped his mate's hand into his and pointed at Doolittle and his medics, set up in the field behind us.

The fire raged beyond the ward. The shapeshifters continued to carry wooden beams into the tunnels, reinforcing them.

I petted my sword. Every second counted.

"Does Curran not involve you in his strategic sessions?" Ghastek asked.

"Nope, I'm just here to look pretty." Curran didn't need me. I wasn't a general; I was a weapon in need of a target. Arranging large groups of people into an attack force wasn't my thing.

Finally the flames subsided. A group of volhvs stepped forward, led by Grigorii. The druids formed up next to them behind Cadeyrn, their leader. The two groups split among the five tunnels and went in.

Silence claimed the field. The three bunkers closest to the tunnel blazed with orange, ready and primed to throw more burning crap on our heads.

Above the tunnel exits, beyond the ward, the air shimmered like heat rising from the pavement on a scorching summer day.

"What is that?" Ghastek squinted.

"Insects."

The shimmers condensed into dark clouds. For a long second the five swarms hung above the ground, and then they streaked across the field to the bunkers. The swarms sank into the fortifications as if sucked in. Sharp screams followed. A man dashed from the right bunker, chased by a dark insect cloud, ran ten feet, and fell. The cloud peeled off. He didn't move.

The volhvs and druids emerged from the tunnels and into the open.

Ghastek took a box from his pocket and checked it. "One hour and three minutes until activation."

I rose. First ward down. Two to go.

THE SECOND WARD OF TRANSLUCENT PALE BLUE wasn't a bouncer. Less than two miles in diameter, it covered the concourses and the inner buildings of the airport. It also looked thick and hard to break. Solid concrete stretched for twenty-five yards on either side of the ward. Digging under it would take forever, and we were short on time.

Beyond the ward, a barbed-wire fence rose. The ground directly behind it looked freshly plowed. Odd.

To the left, a gate opened in the bottom of the concourse. Bodies poured out, about six feet tall at the shoulder, dark, with sharp bristles rising in a crest along their necks and humps on their backs. The animals galloped along the inner perimeter, flooding the space between the strip of the plowed ground and the tower.

"Are those buffalo?" someone asked behind me.

The leading beast braked directly in front of us and dipped

its head. The colossal maw gaped open, displaying twin pairs of yellow tusks; the larger set looked bigger than my arm. A deep grunting roar burst from its mouth and broke into pissed-off snorts. It wasn't a buffalo.

"Boars," a druid next to me said. "Calydonian boars."

I'd fought a Calydonian boar before. They were strong and aggressive as hell, and pain only pissed them off. Their bristles cut like razor blades. It took four mercs to bring one female down, and two of us had automatic weapons. There were at least three dozen pigs out there, and all of them were male. Each pig was six and a half feet at the shoulder. Two and a half tons of pure stupid rage. Curran might kill one in single combat. Mahon could as well. Aside from that, a regular-sized shapeshifter didn't stand a chance. Not even in a half-form. The pigs would bulldoze over them.

Curran came up to me. A group of alphas followed: Mahon and his wife, Martha; Daniel and Jennifer; Thomas Lonesco; Aunt B; Jim . . .

Curran nodded at the tower. "Can you break that ward?"

I glanced at the tower. Six hundred yards away. About two thousand feet of distance, full of boars. "If you can get me to it."

My blood would break almost anything, with enough magic. The question was, did I have enough power in me? I guessed we'd find out.

Curran grinned, looking slightly evil. "Get ready to run."

Daniel and Jennifer stepped in front of me. I looked at Jennifer. *Should you really be here?*

Her upper lip trembled in a precursor to a snarl. Right. She would do her job, and I had to do mine.

Derek took a spot to my left, Jezebel to my right. Aunt B and Thomas brought up the rear. Behind them six shapeshifters formed into two rows, three people in a line. The renders.

Bob from the Mercenary Guild shouldered his way into the group and heaved his sword.

Eduardo emerged from the tunnel, dragging a huge sack. Over six feet tall, the werebuffalo was slabbed with thick muscle even in his human form. Behind him three members of Clan Heavy pulled identical sacks.

Eduardo dropped his burden on the ground. The canvas fell

open. Inside, thick tangles of leather belts and chains connected a mess of spiked armor plates and chain mail. "Get your glass slippers and fairy wings, ladies."

Members of Clan Heavy began pulling the tangles apart. Mahon gripped a mess of belts, arranged it on the ground, and stripped. He took a deep breath, and a giant Kodiak bear boiled forth, filling out the belts with his shaggy body. The harness caught him, stretching and sliding into place. A row of armored plates sheathed the bear's back and hindquarters, flaring down on the sides to guard the vulnerable flanks. Mahon stretched his front limbs and rose up, testing the armor, and dropped back down. On all fours, he was at least a foot taller than me.

All around us werebears, some gray, some brown, and one white, rose up. A wereboar snorted next to a huge moose.

The beasts of Clan Heavy formed an armored line around us, with Mahon in the lead. Eduardo stomped over to his right, a colossal buffalo, almost eight feet tall at the shoulder.

Curran kissed me. "See you there, baby."

"Try to keep up," I told him.

His body twisted, sprouting fur. The gray lion shook his mane, winked at me, and took his spot on Mahon's right.

To the left, the mercs finished hammering long wooden platforms, brought together board by board through the tunnels. They'd had the same idea I did—touching that strip of plowed ground wasn't a good idea. It just didn't look right. There was no reason for it to encircle the base, unless something nasty hid in it.

The mages formed into a semicircle near the ward, right between the two closest bunkers. Behind them the witches formed their own line, and then the druids and the volhvs. Three vampires crouched on the ground across each bunker, hugging the dirt.

The mages raised their hands.

"On three," one of them called. "Remember, low spectrum. And three. Two. Go."

Power burst from the ten mages, flowing into a single bright current, threaded with flashes of green and yellow. The current smashed into the ward, dancing on its surface.

The druids and the volhvs raised theirs staves. Between the two lines the witches snapped into a rigid pose, their arms outstretched. Magic poured from the volhvs into the witches and out into the mages. So much magic. The current shook, sliding back and forth against the ward, like caged lightning.

On the left one of the druids went down. Then another. A volhv fell.

Hairline cracks formed in the ward.

The witch on the left screamed.

With the sound of a collapsing building, the ward fractured and broke. Chunks of it floated to the ground, like weightless shards of foot-thick ice, melting into nothing as they fell.

The vampires charged, clearing the fence with laughable ease.

The three lines of magic users collapsed onto the ground.

The bloodsuckers swarmed the bunkers.

Before the first mage rolled to his feet, the vamps emerged, their claws bloody.

On the left a shapeshifter tossed a rock at the strip of plowed ground. A green fiery glow shot from the ground, licking the stone. The rock sparked with white. The glow vanished, leaving the stone, smoking on the ground. Trapped. That was what I thought.

Behind us, the shamans conferred and began to chant in unison, their voices like a beat of a human heart, rhythmic but overlapping. Magic flowed from the shamans and condensed directly in front of us. The mercs heaved the platforms forward. The boards slid over the plowed ground and froze, suspended three inches above the dirt by the shamans' magic.

The wereboar on my left roared, snorting and pawing the ground.

The four boars in our view raised their heads at the challenge.

The wereboar lowered his massive head and charged across the makeshift bridge with a fierce screech, hurtling like a cannon ball.

For a split second the Calydonian boars stared in shock, and then as one they gave chase. The group galloped behind the buildings, out of sight.

Mahon started forward. We followed. The bear picked up speed, at first moving slowly, then faster and faster, until I was running full speed in the middle of a stampede.

A boar shot out from behind the concourse. The bear on the left peeled off to intercept. Another boar came from the right, a grizzled scarred male. Eduardo sped into a charge and rammed him head on. The boar and buffalo went down in a tangle of tusks and hooves.

I could barely see. The huge furry backs blocked my view. A snort, and another shapeshifter went down. Again. Again. And again. Mahon and Curran made a sharp left and suddenly I saw the tower, a hundred yards in front of us, and three giant pigs rocketing toward us like shots from a sling.

"Get her to the tower," Curran roared, and charged toward the pigs. Mahon followed. Our armored barrier was gone. It was just me, Bob, the alphas, and a handful of renders.

We ran. The air turned to fire in my lungs. Blood pounded through my temples.

Eighty yards.

Sixty.

Forty. I pulled Slayer from its sheath.

Above us, within the ward, magic streamed from the tower, unfolding in iridescent feathery smudges. The plume. We had twenty minutes before the device went active.

To the left, a squat building flew by, and out of the corner of my eye I saw a huge boar rushing at us, mouth open, tusks ready to gore. He looked as big as a house. Vicious eyes glared at me.

I sprinted, squeezing every last drop out of my muscles.

The boar loomed, closer and closer.

Twenty-five yards. The boar was on top of us. We wouldn't make it.

Jennifer spun toward the pig, baring her teeth. Daniel's clawed hand closed on her shoulder. He shoved her aside and flung himself at the boar. The werewolf's claws raked across the pig's head, gouging the left eye. The boar squealed in mad fury. His tusk caught Daniel in the stomach. The boar shot forward, half-blind, and smashed into the ward. Daniel's blond head hit the pale glow. The back of his skull exploded, his face still intact, his blue eyes staring straight at us, and then both the werewolf and the boar disintegrated in a flash of blinding white.

Ten yards.

Jennifer screamed a single hoarse howl of pain, ripped straight from her heart.

I sliced Slayer across my forearm, coating the blade with my blood, and rammed the ward, sinking all of my magic into the power word. *"Hesaad."* Mine.

Agony ripped through me in a fiery cascade.

The ward shuddered. Veins of pure, intense red shot through the magic barrier. It shattered and the shapeshifters burst through it, smashing into the tower.

I stumbled forward, trying to hold on to reality. *Don't pass out, don't pass out . . .*

Derek ripped the tower's door off its hinges. A man raised a crossbow, blocking our way. Jennifer lunged at him. The bolt took her in the thigh. She ripped the man's head off, pulled the bolt out, and bounded inside, where more shooters waited on the stairway.

We climbed the tower, step by step. For the first couple of minutes Jennifer was in front venting her fury, and then she took off into the side corridor raging, and someone else took point. We killed and killed and climbed, and the stairs behind us ran red with blood.

A door loomed ahead. The shapeshifters crashed through it, drunk on blood fumes and anger. People spun to us, a familiar face among them. Shane. I lunged and disemboweled him with one precise strike. He clutched at his stomach, trying to hold the slippery ribbons of his intestines inside. I sliced across his chest and neck and kicked him to the ground. He crashed at my feet, bleeding to death.

The device loomed in front of me, a cylinder of gleaming metal, encrusted with gems and inlaid with glyphs and patterns, spinning magic from its top in feathery glowing strands. A control console rose next to it, bristling with levers. Three gauges, long narrow rectangles half-filled with pale light, glowed above the console.

Around the cylinder, the shapeshifters tore into the Keepers like sharks into baby seals. I pulled Kamen's instructions from the pocket of my jeans and unfolded them, careful to keep my bloody fingerprints off the text. According to Kamen, shutting down the machine required pushing the levers in a precise sequence. He said it would take anywhere from three to ten minutes. I had no idea how many minutes I had left.

Don't think about it; just do it.

I pushed the first lever. The gauge on the left turned blue. If it turned bright green, the device would become unstable and we'd all vanish in an explosion of magic. I jerked my hand back.

The gauge glowed with blue, slowly growing lighter and lighter.

Seconds ticked by. *Come on.* If I ever commissioned a world-destroying device, it would have a two-second shutoff: turn the key and that's it.

Come on.

The gauge turned white. I pushed the second lever. The third gauge shot into blue-green. I held my breath.

The light shone, holding at the almost-green mark.

Turn white. Turn white, damn you.

Behind me someone snarled.

White. Turn white.

The gauge paled, sliding into pale gray. Good enough.

I pulled the first lever again. All three gauges remained steadily pale.

Third lever.

Second lever.

Third lever again. When this was over, I would screw Kamen's head off his shoulders like a cap off a beer bottle. First lever.

All three gauges turned green.

Fuck.

The top of the device slid open, magic curving around it like veils of white smoke, nipping at my skin.

Don't blow up. Just don't blow up.

The gauges slid into blue. Wait for it.

My hands shook. I clenched them into fists.

Wait for it.

Wait.

Wait.

The gauges turned white. I pushed the final lever.

Nothing.

What the hell?

I had done it right, I'd memorized the instructions, they were in my hand . . . Maybe Kamen had lied. Maybe he wanted the device to activate . . .

Something clanged within the machine. The gauges drained, the glow vanishing. The veils of magic dissipated, dissolving into nothing. The last sparks of power melted from the device and it sat inert, just a hunk of metal, dull and harmless.

I slumped on the floor. Around me shapeshifters moved. Someone threw a body out the window.

We'd won. Somehow we'd won.

My gaze snagged on Shane, sprawled on the floor in the mess of his innards. He stared at me, his eyes wild.

"We won," I told him.

He glared at me with eyes full of hate.

Behind him Curran loomed in the doorway. He was human and smeared with blood. He stepped over Shane and crouched by me. I put my arms around his neck and we kissed, both covered in gore and neither one caring. We kissed while around us, the soldiers of the Pack tossed the bodies out the windows, stepping over Shane as he lay dying slowly, bleeding his life out, watching his intestines contract and shiver on the floor in front of him.

EPILOGUE

———◆———

THE KEEPERS WERE DEAD. THE MAGIC ELITE OF Atlanta celebrated, right outside the fallen MSDU headquarters. Food appeared as if out of thin air, bonfires flared here and there, and a couple of Calydonian boars had been carved into chunks for a barbecue. Mages, the People, witches, and shapeshifters reveled in the simple glory of being alive. We all knew that the next morning the alliance would fracture and old rivalries would rear their heads, but for one evening, we celebrated and watched the cops and the MSDU from neighboring cities try to sort out the wreckage. The law enforcement agencies were none too happy with our impromptu cookout, but given that we had just cracked their best fortress like a walnut, they didn't make any waves.

The Keepers had brought as many of their members as they could muster. The MSDU lost forty people; the rest had been herded into an underground bunker—the Keepers didn't want to waste the ammunition. The rats found them and let them out. Andrea's friend didn't make it.

I wandered past the tables. Smiling faces, lots of food, the hum of excited conversation. Ghastek came walking toward me, carrying a plate. "Humans are fickle creatures," he said.

"Three days ago I bet none of these people would have found a cause to throw a party. Here we are celebrating, when all we've done is return things to normal."

"Nothing like a great tragedy to make you appreciate life," I told him.

"Indeed. You aren't celebrating, Kate."

Hard to celebrate when visions of your kid in a hospital bed keep floating through your head. "I don't know what you're talking about. I'm thrilled."

"Rowena came to visit you this morning," Ghastek said. "Why?"

Ha! "Remember how I asked you to get the information from that navigator who fainted and you blew me off? Go screw yourself."

I walked away.

A lone figure sat away from the bonfires, hugging her knees. I came closer and saw pale hair. Jennifer. I came to sit by her. She stared straight ahead. I wasn't sure she even knew I was there.

We sat for a long time, looking out at the base swarming with cops.

"I don't even have a body to bury," she said.

"You'll have his child," I said.

She rested her hand on her stomach. Her voice was bitter. "And if I am very lucky, I won't have to kill her."

"Jennifer!" A woman came up to us. She had Jennifer's lean, long body and pale hair. One of her sisters. "Here you are. Come with me. We have a table set up."

Jennifer didn't move.

"You need to eat," the woman said. "You're eating for two, remember?"

Jennifer rose slowly.

"That's it," her sister murmured. "Come on. Let's take care of that baby."

She led Jennifer away. I sat alone.

Curran dropped next to me. "Hey."

It's hard to jump while sitting down. I still managed. "Why do you sneak up on me like that?"

"It's funny."

"It's not." I leaned into him and he put his arm around me.

"It's hilarious. It's almost as funny as your snoring."

"I don't snore."

He nodded with a wide grin. "It's a quiet peaceful kind of snoring. Like a small cuddly Tasmanian devil. Kind of cute when sleeping, all claws and teeth when awake."

"You snore worse. At least I don't turn into a lion in my sleep."

"I only did it once."

"Once was weird enough, thank you."

He looked at me. "You're still going through with the Julie thing?"

"Yes. Why do you keep asking me?"

"I keep hoping you'll change your mind."

"I won't."

He sighed and pulled me closer to him.

"YOUR BLOOD AND ERRA'S BLOOD ARE BASICALLY the same," Doolittle told me.

I rubbed my eyes. I hadn't slept much the night before, and I had spent all morning trying to get a sample of shapeshifter blood to respond to my magic. I'd accomplished exactly nothing. The blood sat inert in the small plastic dish. It didn't help that Curran had insisted on watching me and spent the past three hours sitting in the corner, looking pissed off. There was the aftermath of the Keepers chaos to deal with and shapeshifters returning to the Keep, but no, he put it all on hold so he could sit here and watch me fail.

"The only difference between you and her is the concentration of magic," Doolittle continued.

She'd had thousands of years to accumulate hers, while I'd barely had a quarter of a century.

"I believe this is getting us nowhere," Doolittle said. "And don't be giving me dirty looks, my lady. I didn't say we should give up."

"I think we should," Curran said.

"What we need is an anchor. Something in Julie's blood that would respond to your magic," Doolittle took a syringe from the table and let a single drop from the syringe fall into the blood. Foul magic tugged on me.

"Vampire blood." I felt it, felt the undeath shoot through the blood in the dish.

Doolittle nodded. "Try it now."

I concentrated and pulled.

I could do this. I should be able to do this.

Sweat broke on my hairline.

The blood rose from the dish about an inch, curling into a globe of red. I held it there and stretched it into a disk. It flowed, obedient and pliant.

"How did you know?" Curran asked.

"Erra has traces of vampirism in her blood sample," Doolittle said. "Not in a virulent form. It's a very odd thing, almost like a dormant precursor to the virus itself. Our lady does too, in smaller concentration."

I let the blood drain into the dish.

"I would venture a guess that most navigators of the dead also possess the same, probably in much, much smaller quantities. When I have some spare time, I want to look at your blood in greater detail." Doolittle frowned.

"What, we have it, too?" Curran pushed up from the floor.

"It reacts to magic," Doolittle said. "Perhaps it's an evolutionary adaption to the world where magic was a constant presence. I would have to run more tests, but for now we must deal with the problem at hand. We need the vampiric vector."

"Are you telling me I have to infect Julie with vampirism?" This was crazy. Vampirism was irreversible. But then so was Lycos-V.

"I wouldn't presume to tell you anything," Doolittle said. "This whole scheme is an exercise in insanity. However, if you persist in this harebrained, ill-advised endeavor, this is the only way for you to mold her blood."

"How about we just don't do it," Curran said.

I took a deep breath. "Can you tell me with absolute certainty that Julie will go loup the moment she wakes up?"

They both answered in unison. "Yes."

"Then I have to do it," I told them. "I have no choice."

THREE DAYS LATER I TRAVELED TO PERFORM THE Arez ritual deep in Sibley Forest. The witches were there, and somehow Grigorii and his brother were there, too. I had never quite gotten to the bottom of how they'd solved their differences, but I decided not to look a gift volhv in the mouth.

We chose a spot on top of a lone quartz boulder, thrusting from the forest floor like a miniature version of Stone Mountain. Kamen operated the device we'd taken at Palmetto. The witches stood around me in a circle, while Julie lay in front of me on a stretcher. Her sedation was wearing off, and muscles and bone bulged and moved under her skin as if they had a mind of their own. Derek and Jezebel stood on both sides of the stretcher, waiting.

Kamen opened the device. Magic spilled from it in a dense cascade of pale glow. The witches strained and then a flood of power hit me, so cold it felt like my muscles froze. It spread through me, flowing from cell to cell, saturating my blood, setting my nerves on fire.

The witches kept feeding me power, more and more and more. The ice turned into agony, shaving at me from the inside, scraping layer after layer from my core.

In the haze of magic Doolittle took a step toward Julie. The syringe in his hand rose. The needle touched her skin and the Immortuus pathogen entered her body.

In a normal victim, it took seven hours for full colonization of the body. Seven hours from the infection to full-blown vampirism. The process was irreversible. We didn't need seven hours. We just needed one minute for the vampiric blood to fully circulate through Julie's body.

More magic came. My hands and feet dissolved into pain. Every instinct screamed for me to stop. *End it. Just end it and the pain will stop.*

Julie's body began to glow. It beckoned me, like a swamp light, drawing me closer and closer. She kicked and convulsed on her stretcher, muscles and fur bulging.

I was almost there. A little more magic. A little more pain.

A searing blast of magic smashed into me, pushing me over the edge.

Julie snarled. Her restraints snapped and she shot up, her flesh boiling. Grotesque jaws thrust from her face, She stood hunched over, half human, half lynx, but whereas a shape shifter's warrior form was streamlined, Julie's body was a mess of mismatched parts. Her left arm was huge, her right leg had a knee that bent backward. Fur sheathed her stomach, while human skin stained her back in pale patches.

She stared, mesmerized.

I felt the blood sliding through her veins, flowing in a current of tiny particles of magic.

Julie opened her mouth, her monstrous face uncertain.

Derek clamped her in a bear hug and Jezebel sliced her neck, severing the jugular. Blood shot in a pressurized spray and I grabbed it with my power, gathering each precious tiny drop, condensing, turning, spinning it into a globe of brilliant magic.

All sound faded, except the beating of my heart.

I kept pulling it, drawing it out of the container of flesh, until I had taken all of it.

The creature who had owned the blood before me toppled to the ground.

I beckoned the sphere and it floated toward me, settling in the palms of my open hands, so alive, so bursting with magic.

Something was wrong with it. It was corrupted, tainted somehow. But it was so breathtakingly beautiful.

A distant presence tugged on me, coming from impossibly far, stretching toward me across distance or time, I couldn't tell. It peered inside me, permeating my magic, examining the blood in my hands.

I was supposed to do something with this blood, wasn't I? Or maybe not. It sat in my palms, so warm and throbbing with power.

The presence watched me. I watched it back.

A thought formed in my head and it wasn't my own, yet somehow it also was. *"Well done."*

At the creature's body another creature was screaming at me, her face contorted. A third creature stared at me, an expression of pure horror stamped on his face.

Odd, this blood. All wrong. I had to do something with it, but I wasn't sure what.

I held the blood out to the presence. *"It's dirty."*

"Then you should clean it," the presence suggested gently.

I had to clean it. Yes, that was it.

"Let your blood flow," the presence murmured.

I sweated blood. It poured from my pores, bleeding magic.

"Now bind them together," the presence suggested.

I molded my blood, stretching it in thin filaments to the glowing core of the creature's blood in my hand, wrapping my magic around it, piercing it, cleansing.

"That's it. That's it," the presence told me. *"Excellent. Now return it."*

"It's mine!"

"You must give it back or the child won't survive."

"But it's mine!"

"No. You only borrowed it. If you keep it, you'll kill its vessel."

The creatures were screaming.

I didn't want to kill anyone.

I held the sphere for another long moment, savoring it, and thrust it back into the creature's body. It flowed into her, rushing through, filling her collapsed veins and arteries.

The creature didn't stir.

"You must will her to live," the presence told me gently. *"She needs your help."*

"Mine," I told the blood. *"Obey me. Live. Survive. Obey, obey, obey . . ."*

The creature drew a hoarse breath, jerking. The wound on her neck bled. Her body whipped, gripped by spasms. The others lunged to her.

The world careened on its side, went dark, and all was still.

I OPENED MY EYES. CURRAN SAT NEXT TO ME, HIS gray eyes watching me.

Julie . . .

"She survived," he said. His quiet voice gained a rough growl. "If you think that I will ever let you pull that fucked-up shit again, then this thing between you and me is done. We are fucking done."

We made it. We made it through in one piece. He didn't die, Julie didn't die, I didn't die . . . It was some kind of bloody miracle.

"I thought you loved me and would never leave me."

"That was not you. That was fucked up."

I put my arms around him and kissed him. Curran clenched me to him. My bones groaned. "Never again."

"Never again," I promised. "I give you my word. Never again."

"I'm so glad you woke up."

"Aha! The shoe is on the other foot."

"Shut up." He kissed me, and I pulled my personal psycho into bed with me.

TWENTY MINUTES LATER I WAS EATING CHICKEN soup. It was the best soup I ever tasted. "How long was I out?"

"Three days."

"That's nothing. You were out eleven."

Curran shrugged. "Three was enough."

"How's Julie?"

"Freaked out and under house arrest, but okay."

"Why under house arrest?"

Curran shook his head. " 'Oh no, I killed Kate. Kate is dead because of me. If she dies, I'll kill myself.' And other stupidity along those lines. I ordered her locked up so she doesn't do something idiotic. Doolittle says she's healing well. No trace of Lyc-V. No vampirism." Curran focused on me. "I thought I lost you both back there."

"I think you might have. I was really confused at some point. I think I hallucinated. I can almost swear I heard somebody."

"Who?"

"I don't know. I promise, never again. I don't think I can survive another one like that."

Curran sighed. "I suppose you'll want to see the kid now."

"Yes."

Curran roared. "Barabas!"

The door opened and my nanny stuck his spiky head inside. He saw me and his face split in a sharp grin. "My lord, my lady, may I say that I am delighted that my favorite alpha is feeling better. Why, you'll be running recklessly into danger against overwhelming odds anytime now."

Curran growled. "Shut up. Bring Julie."

Three minutes later Julie stepped into the room. She stopped at the entrance, a pale, skinny wraith. I waited, but she didn't come any closer.

"Hey," I said.

"Hey," she answered.

"Are you okay?"

"I don't know." Julie swallowed.

Oh boy. "What's the problem?"

"You did something to me." Julie hesitated. "My magic looks like yours."

I glanced at Curran. "You didn't tell her?"

"Oh no, that's your mess. You can have that job. You go right ahead."

I sat up straighter. "When Leslie bit you, she infected you with Lyc-V. I used an old ritual and cleaned your blood with mine to save you."

Julie blinked a few times. "So what does it mean?"

"It means that you are now immune to Lyc-V and vampirism. You might develop some new powers. It might be strange for a while, but I will help you through it."

Julie swallowed. "So I am like really your niece now?"

"Something like that. I almost died saving you. Am I going to get some sort of hug or what?"

She took a step, broke into a run, and hugged me.

Curran shook his head.

I stuck my tongue out at him. Whatever. She was alive. I would deal with everything else as it came.

"You can never tell anyone," Curran said. "What Kate has done for you can't be done to anyone else, do you understand? The Pack is full of desperate parents whose kids might go loup. You can't go around telling people that Kate cured you of it. If anybody asks, you pulled through on your own. Your magic was so strong, your body rejected Lyc-V. Julie, answer me."

"Yes, sir," Julie said in my arms. "I pulled through on my own."

A knock sounded and Barabas stepped back into the room, carrying a narrow blue vase filled with flowers. "Happy reunion. Also, these came for you, Kate. I put them in a vase. Not quite sure what these flowers are, but they smell divine."

The vase held a dozen small flowers, their petals pristine white, like small stars solid black at the center. I froze with Julie still hugging me.

Morgan's Bells. I knew these flowers; I had made them. They'd sprouted during the flare on the spot where I'd cried my eyes out, holding Bran's lifeless body.

Next to me Curran was very still.

I willed my mouth to move. "Is there a card?"

Barabas nodded and passed me a small white rectangle folded in half. I flipped it open.

Congratulations on your victory, Your Highness.
  Looking forward to our next meeting.

                                                                Hugh

FATE'S EDGE

BY ILONA ANDREWS

The Edge lies between worlds, on the border between the Broken, where magic is a fairy tale, and the Weird, where the strength of your magic can change your destiny.

Audrey Callahan may come from a family of thieves and con men, but she left that life in the Edge behind and has gone straight with a legitimate—and thoroughly unmagical—job in the Broken. Then her brother gets in trouble, and her father cajoles her into helping out on one last heist.

But Audrey is about to meet her match in Kaldar Mar, an Edger who has been on the wrong side of the law himself. Kaldar, a sometimes gambler, lawyer, thief, and spy with some unusual talents of his own, is assigned to track down a stolen item . . . and the trail leads him to Audrey.

Forced to work together, Kaldar and Audrey discover that the missing item has made its way into the hands of a dangerous criminal organization—one they will have to outsmart if they want to live . . .

ABOUT THE AUTHOR

Ilona Andrews is the pseudonym for a husband-and-wife writing team. Ilona is a native-born Russian, and Andrew is a former communications sergeant in the U.S. Army. Contrary to popular belief, Andrew was never an intelligence officer with a license to kill, and Ilona was never the mysterious Russian spy who seduced him. They met in college, in English Composition 101, where Ilona got a better grade. (Andrew is still sore about that.) Together, Andrew and Ilona are the coauthors of the *New York Times* bestselling Kate Daniels urban fantasy series and the romantic urban fantasy novels of the Edge. They currently reside in Portland, Oregon, with their two children and numerous pets. For sample chapters, news, and more, visit www.ilona-andrews.com.